The Millennial Series: Book One

EPHRAIM'S SEED

~~~~~~~~~~~~~~~~~~~~~~

Pam Blackwell

Seed: Mysterious potentiality
the presence of which
sometimes unsuspected
is the justification for hope
Cirlot's Dictionary of Symbols

To Cliff--editor, husband, friend

ISBN #: 0-9653327-6-4 (previously published by Onyx Press, ISBN #1-57636-018-0)
Library of Congress #: 96-68894

Cover Design: Brett Peplinski

Foreword

Essentially man is not a slave either of himself
Or of the world; but he is a lover.
His freedom and fulfillment is in love,
Which is another name for perfect comprehension.
                    Sadhana, Rabindranath Tagore

A convert in my early 20's, I found in tracing my father's ancestry that I come from pioneer stock who were in Nauvoo, at Haun's Mill, and who arrived in one of the earliest parties into the Salt Lake Valley. Like these forebears, I have been a traveler. My own spiritual odyssey has taken me to many parts of the world. However satisfying those adventures were, it was not until I married a man with a theologian's thirst for truth, fresh from the baptismal waters, and watched his progression in the Church and priesthood, that I truly became aware of what Mormonism is: a theology that is both unique and absolutely mind-stretching. And, perhaps most importantly, it can satisfy the most spiritually gifted seeker.

All of my life I have been caught up with millennial stories. This book represents my attempt to make fictional sense of those stories, apocalyptic scripture and Joseph Smith's writings. I do not pretend to have prophetic powers or to be on any doctrinal fast-track. What I have tried to do is create characters who resemble Latter-day Saints I have known, but only in an archetypal sense. These characters spring from my travels, my years spent counseling individuals and couples, and my inveterate need to people-watch. I also have a novelist's itch to create plots lines that slightly terrorize me. In that vein, there is nothing that excites my imagination more than the epic return of the Lord.

The spiritual experiences, dreams, and apparent miracles in the book are all based on true experiences related to me firsthand by individuals in different parts of the world—most were Latter-day Saints. Since they represent just a small portion of the experiences that have been related to me, it is my plan to weave more faith-promoting stories into the next books in the Millennial Series.

I am indebted the very most to my husband who, from our first meeting, had faith in me as a writer. To my father who demanded that I think, and to my mother for her great curiosity about psychology, I give much thanks. To my daughter, Dana, who has been my sidekick on many treks, I am grateful for her great creative gifts and love which have sustained me over many rough and lonely years.

My thanks for help goes to: Karen Horman and Donna Nielsen, great friends and literary critics; Orson Scott Card for his encouragement; the Olander family—Sharlene, Fran and Matt; Margaret L. Low; Brook Horman; Roger and Eileen Horton; Amanda and Kris Matthews; Dawn Ann and Robert Bullough; Col. Robert Averett and Captain Loren Ramos; Dr. Lynn Lyon; Dr. Todd Eberhard; Ken Southam; Lynn Pugh; Robert Angus; Mark Eubank; the Catos; Fred and Chris Graham; Lisa Williams; Mary Goring; Brian Carter; Joshie and Lizzie; B. Donald Pedersen; Colin Forbes; and the many Latter-day Saints who were willing to share their spiritual experiences as I travelled around the globe in search of God's hand in individuals' lives.

May *Ephraim's Seed* stimulate your imagination about the exhilarating days that lie ahead and nurture a longing for the Lord's return.

Prologue

To me every hour of the light and dark is a miracle.
Every cubic inch of space is a miracle.
Walt Whitman

The story takes place right before everything fell apart. Just a few years into the 21st century, at a most perilous point in world history, various international trade agreements finally came together into one global network, the UWEN (the United World Economic Network), which was a union of the European Common Market, the Pan American Trade Alliance and the Asian Co-Prosperity Union.

The leaders of the UWEN, however, soon saw there were significant gaps in the structure they had built. So they turned their attention to consolidating their power by drawing certain sectors more tightly into the new socioeconomic net. Although, at the beginning, religious communities in general were being targeted, the UWEN focus turned on Latter-day Saints and Jews as time passed. They were the two big holdouts. The UWEN would have ignored them were they not both so wealthy, and in the case of the Latter-day Saints, so unified. Viewed as powerful homogeneous trading blocs, they needed to be brought into line. The government wanted what they had. Simple as that.

A black market sprang up along Utah's Wasatch Front in reaction to the high fixed prices. A quiet and efficient network of ranchers and farmers gave what was required to the government, then sold the rest to church members at a discount. This gradually led to underground financing where members could get loans outside UWEN supervision.

When the UWEN wasn't able to break the Mormon back by economic tactics, they resorted to more direct political means. After a year-long television campaign slurring Mormons as polygamists, unpatriotic, rich and greedy, the UWEN bombed the church administration building on South Temple. Eight people were killed, including an apostle. The UWEN-run media blamed it on a splinter group of Mormon dissidents, thus giving them the excuse they needed to send the international police (Interpol) to "stabilize" the area. Then after several more staged bombings of the Capitol building, two shopping malls and the sports arena, the government decreed the Church was a menace and had to be abolished. Protesting did no good. Mormons were once again on the run, persecuted for their beliefs and feared for unyielding unity.

Joseph Smith who prophesied about the last days, particularly about the American continent, was both optimistic and pessimistic. He described a safe haven, Zion, where good people worldwide could flee to be spared from the ravages of war, pestilence, and other natural disasters; he also said those days would be no picnic—and they weren't.

(For non-Mormon readers unfamiliar with Joseph Smith's prophecies, see the Afterword.)

Chapter One

Turning and turning in the widening gyre
The falcon cannot hear the falconer;
Things fall apart; the centre cannot hold;
Mere anarchy is loosed upon the world,
The blood-dimmed tide is loosed.
Surely some revelation is at hand;
Surely the Second Coming is at hand.
*   "The Second Coming," William Butler Yeats*

The thunder of military planes woke Ben out of a dead sleep. It was 3:00 a.m. He had been dreaming he was on the Salt Flats in an old-fashioned, red and white roadster, wind in his face–free–flying along at 60 mph. The roar of the engine was deafening; the steering wheel began to shimmy and.... He was out of bed before the image faded. Ben dreaded waking up at this hour, but these days he never knew when he might get a call to be downstairs and out in front of student housing at precisely 3:15. Now he didn't need a phone call; the planes said it all.

There had been threats of a UWEN crackdown in Utah, especially in Salt Lake City–threats in response to the continued resistance to the international government's strict new economic policies. The planes meant they had upped the ante.

Ben groped in the dark for two matching shoes. Peg took long deep breaths in her sleep. She lay on her stomach in her white-and-blue flowered flannel nightgown. She was a heavy sleeper, but he still didn't want to turn on the light, lest he wake her. *Let her have a few more hours*, he thought.

Ben was a slight, balding, brown-haired doctoral student with a kind face and clear blue eyes. Their intensity was diluted behind brown tortoise shell glasses, which habitually slipped down his nose. After he grabbed his black down coat, baseball cap, and long red muffler, he adjusted his glasses and opened the door to the dimly-lighted hallway. He half expected to find it filled with soldiers, although that wasn't yet possible–the planes hadn't been on the ground that long. No one came between him and the elevator door. Still Ben couldn't be certain, so he ran down the six flights. *I don't want to be a sitting duck in an elevator if the student housing unit is taken over*, he thought. On the bottom floor, Ben paused before opening the fire exit door. He didn't hear anything unusual, except the wild thudding of his heart, so he eased out into the lobby and through the glass doors.

The cold of the February morning caused him to catch his breath. He didn't look like a guerrilla, yet on given nights, he would leave his warm bed to stand in a darkened dumpster area at the agreed-upon time. He was part of the organization which helped members of the Mormon church get financing outside of the strictly controlled international banking system.

Ben wasn't sure they would risk it tonight. He looked at his watch, 3:16. "Come on, come on," he muttered and stamped his feet to keep warm. A car slowed down, flashed its lights. He stepped out of the shadows and the car slowed to a halt. The driver reached across and opened the door. It was Steve Lewis, his friend and former elders' quorum president of the Bryan Ward, when the church organization was in place.

Ben felt his stomach muscles relax and release the built-up acid. He put his hand over it for comfort. Steve, Ben and other men in his ward had been meeting for months in the bishop's warehouse office on the northwest side of town. "We're not going to make it from the University clear across town," Steve said tersely. "We're meeting at the bishop's house."

Ben sucked in his breath and said, "It must be really bad for him to risk it."

"It is."

They said nothing during the fifteen-minute drive. Under the occasional street light, Ben watched brick home after brick home appear and disappear on the drive down 13th East. Peg's not going to get her little *casita*, he thought dejectedly. She's been so good about waiting until I finished this graduate work. Now it looks pretty bleak. Ben stared out the passenger side window, involuntarily watching for police vehicles coming up from town. He realized he'd been holding his breath and let it out audibly. Steve looked over at him but couldn't read Ben's expression in the dark.

Ben began to conjure up scriptures to help quell his rising anxiety, but the first one that emerged from his unconscious was in the 24th verse of Matthew: "But pray ye that your flight be not in the winter. For then shall be great tribulation, such as was not since the beginning of the world to this time, no, nor ever shall be." It did not do much to comfort him. *I'm forty-four years old*, he moaned to himself, *and I'll never get a chance to lead a normal life*.

His thoughts went to his two young children, living in California. Oh, how he longed to make it right for them. Not this, Lord. Let them know a normal childhood, please. He doubted the Lord could answer that prayer if He wanted to—not in these times, not with the rapid deterioration of economic systems, not with wars in every nation, and not with the moral bankruptcy in every institution. It just can't go on like this, he sighed and shook his head.

When they arrived at the modest home in Sugar House, Steve led the way around back. He had been told to go into the basement apartment of the bishop's daughter and her husband. He knocked lightly and the door opened immediately.

Ben had never seen such strain on the face of the normally good-natured bishop. The bishop, Robert Olson, shook both men's hands. They tried some light banter, but fell silent as they walked into the living room. The fact that the bishop seemed upset worsened Ben's mood. For the past five years since his conversion, Ben had depended on Olson as he would a father. The bishop, sensing Ben's tremendous intellectual prowess, coupled with his theological bent, had spent many extra hours with him away from regular Church activities, discussing fine scriptural points of doctrine and helping him make the transition from Jew to Christian to Latter-day Saint.

Fifteen men sat around the small room—on the floor, arms of chairs, squashed together on the couch—all men Ben cared for—men he'd come to know through the many elders' quorum activities they'd shared in the past few years. Now they were fifteen fellow soldiers in a skirmish that had just turned ugly.

"Brethren, I've called you here tonight to tell you that we've failed—our organization has been infiltrated by the international government. They have each of our names...."

I never thought this would really happen, Ben thought fiercely. *Not here. Not in Salt Lake. I really can't believe it. Somehow we're supposed to be protected; aren't we God's priesthood army?*

"Ben, how about you?" asked the bishop. "Are you armed?"

Ben struggled to refocus on the conversation. The bishop repeated himself, "We're trying to determine who has a weapon and needs one. You own a gun, don't you, Ben?"

"A .22 and 150 rounds. I took a pistol-shooting class a couple of years ago and I handled a rifle in ROTC a hundred years ago."

Rather than laughing, which he did easily, the bishop just made note of what Ben said and tersely continued going around the group. After an international ban on new gun sales, handguns had become rare and expensive, and Bishop Olson wanted everyone who had been in on the resistance movement to be able to defend themselves and their families, if it came to that.

"As you men know, the prophet has been warning for some time that each priesthood holder is going to have to rely on his own spiritual connection with the Lord. Well, I'm afraid that time has come," he said biting his lip.

Then more planes roared overhead and the windows shook in the darkened apartment. "Are we going to try to fight them?" someone finally asked. The bishop solemnly shook his head.

The second set of planes woke Peg up. She was so sure this was another earthquake, she began scolding Ben before she opened her eyes. "Okay, this is the last one I'm going to live through in this sixth floor apartment. I don't care if we only have one more quarter in school, I'm looking for another place in the morning."

Her curly hair flopping over one eye, Peg reached across the bed to wake him, but his side was cold, the sheets hastily shoved to the bottom of the bed. "Honey?" she called out into the darkened apartment. No answer. *He's gone to do his spy thing,* she thought. *I wonder how big that quake was. I never thought I'd live to see the day when Utahns would be as casual about earthquakes as the Japanese,* she mused. *Every week some newscaster tries to scare us about the big one cracking open the Wasatch Fault. It's disgusting.*

Suddenly Ben's disembodied voice cut through the night air. They had turned off the ringer on the phone but forgotten to turn down the volume on the answering machine. "Peg, pick up the phone. Honey, it's really important you wake up."

She surprised him by picking it up so quickly. "What?" she asked, heart pounding. "What, Ben, what is it?" No matter what his answer, she knew it wasn't going to be good. She knew the feeling all too well.

"This is it. It isn't a drill. I'll be there in fifteen minutes."

"Don't forget to get the $200 out of the bank machine," she reminded him.

"I won't."

How many times over her lifetime Peg had imagined this moment. She inventoried the small apartment in her mind. *Thank heavens for a mother who was a preparedness freak. Should I call her now?* she thought. *No, I'll find a phone in the morning.* She felt both numb and shaky as she began to dismantle their life. The first trip down the elevator to the car was devoted to boxes of genealogical research, Ben's papers, photo albums, pictures, Rachel's artwork.

Rachel, I'm glad right now you're in Heavenly Father's care, Peg thought. *I might be joining you soon.* Peg's daughter from her first marriage was killed in a crosswalk on her way to school six years ago. After her first husband drank himself into alcoholism and left the church and his family, it had just been the two of them. When Rachel died, Peg thought her life was over. She struggled through depression, therapy and two years of teaching English in a Salt Lake junior high school...she loved kids, but hated the early teenage behavior problems.

And she thought she was doomed to a life of failed relationships. Then Ben moved into her ward, and she was hired on as an English teacher at the Brentwood School, a new private high school. *Now we're four years into a second marriage that has all the elements of a spiritual bestseller*, she thought, as she repeatedly pushed the elevator button. *I've been given the literary magazine to supervise and Ben's one quarter away from graduating. Why now, Lord? Just when things are getting good.*

Like Ben, Peg expected the doors to open to either armed men or a mob scene, but it was quiet except for a baby crying down the corridor. She tried not to run to the car, but didn't succeed. She drove it crazily up to the same dumpster area Ben had waited in, threw open the Honda's hatchback and shoved the boxes inside.

Calm down, Peg, she scolded herself. *This is just adrenalin. It can be your friend. Breathe. Okay, next on to the storage area.*

Keys shaking, she flipped on the light and quickly unlocked the padlock. Two large cans full of gas. *Oh, how Ben argued against storing it*, Peg remembered, *but I knew it would come in handy some day.* She lugged the cans to the car. Back for bottled water. *How many?* She surveyed the dozens and dozens of plastic containers she had carefully cleaned out with bleach. She made two trips, got ten half gallons in the car then went back for the sleeping bags.

Peg returned quickly to the lobby. She was a plump 39. Her broad face displayed a sweet intelligence. Not a stylish dresser, she preferred jeans and T-shirts, which she was wearing as she stood waiting for the elevator. When Ben appeared in the lobby looking scared, she felt a maternal rush to gather him in her arms, but didn't.

"Where are you in the process?" he asked anxiously.

"Going up for clothes and food. You need to do your books. Did you get the money?"

"Uh-huh. Where's your coat? You always go out without it."

She ignored the barb. "How'd you get back so fast?"

"We met at the bishop's house."

The doors opened and he pushed 6. The doors didn't close quickly enough for Ben. He whacked the button twice then smiled wryly and said, "6...66."

"What did he say?" Peg asked.

"Who he?" Ben sounded more irritated than he felt. She always talked in this indistinct way. He had even jokingly given it a formal linguistic name, "pronomial aphasia".

"The bishop, of course."

They were approaching the sixth floor, so instead of answering her, he put his finger to his lips. She nodded. Nothing stirred. *Incredible. Hadn't anybody heard the planes?* he thought. *Why would they care anyway? They haven't taken the risks we have,* he thought bitterly. He stuck the key in the lock before she could reach for hers in her yellow T-shirt pocket. "We've got to be out of here in a half an hour, tops," he said more tenderly and gave her a squeeze.

"Did you call Alex?"

Peg nodded. "He's expecting us."

"Are you going to call Jed?" Peg asked.

Ben went to the phone without responding to her. He paused, wondering if it were being monitored. He'd just have to chance it--have the faith this wasn't the moment of the month when U.S. Interfone tapped in. She watched him in profile as he waited for the Rivers' to answer. She thought her husband was such a curious blend of scholar, radical, and innocent. He was calling a good friend in Ukiah, California who agreed to bring Ben's children to him if there were a dire emergency.

"Jed, Ben here. Look, they've infiltrated our underground. Troops just arrived. I want you to get the kids today. At school. Why school? It's Tuesday, man."

Peg turned away to shove food into plastic bags and wondered if their plan would work. It involved Ben's two children from his former marriage, Danny, 10, and Miriam, 8, who now lived with their grandparents, since their mother had died of heart failure at a young 38. The plan was to take the children from their northern California home and bring them to Zion National Park where Alex, another long-time friend of Ben's, had built his home and his art studio on acres of remote desert land.

"The money you'll need has been wired under the name Thomas Jefferson," Ben said tersely. "Hey, I know I can count on you. Why? 'Cause the Lord loves you, dude...No, it's not really kidnapping. Think of it as an extended visit. Okay? Bye."

Ben turned quickly as he hung up the phone, so Peg would not see just how concerned he was. He walked over to the bulging bookcase where he moved from one precious book to another, weeding out a lifetime of learning to a pile of twenty or so tomes--T.S. Eliot's Complete Works, Shakespeare, the *I Ching*, the standard works, some of his favorite Nibley works, *Autobiography of a Yogi* and the *Tao Te Ching*.

Suddenly an ambulance's siren wailed. They froze. Five to six times a night ambulances from throughout the city sped up the hill to the University hospital.

"Normal, I think," he whispered. She blew him a kiss and returned to packing the bathroom essentials. He watched her with great admiration for a few seconds as she knelt down to clear out the lower shelf of the cabinet. She sure called this one.

He decided on the spur of the moment not to leave the computer and stereo in the storage unit, but to give them to a woman friend down the hall, who was struggling through the Ph.D. program along with raising her two teenage sons. She was surprised to be awakened at that hour, but took his explanation of a family emergency without question. She said she'd use them as he insisted and would care for them. He doubted he'd ever see her or the electronic hardware again.

He and Peg didn't have a television to give away. Both refused to watch what they felt was either garbage or propaganda. They weren't alone in their feelings. There had been a strident consumer group called, "Pull the Plug!" that blocked entrances to television studios, stalked TV moguls, filed lawsuits before the UWEN crackdown. Ben and Peg had contributed to their annual fund raising drive and then turned to entertaining themselves with piano and guitar duets.

When they were done undoing their life, Peg paused in the doorway and said, "Well, good-bye apartment. You've been wonderful, old piano. Good-bye furniture from the D.I. Good-bye plants who loved me."

Then they left 604, the "Aerie" she had insisted on calling it, laden with bags of all sizes and Ben's classical guitar. She couldn't bring herself to think about the friends they were leaving behind, much less her young English students.

"Twenty-two minutes," he said mournfully. "That's got to be some kind of record."

Now at 4:30 there were a few more sounds echoing down the halls: babies' cries, mothers' muffled voices. But they made it without detection to the two old cars. Peg had packed them carefully to look like they were just taking a casual trip. She unzipped Ben's big down coat, snuggled inside, wrapped her arms around him and held on tight. She kissed his neck and tried to remember his smell in case they never saw each other again. Maybe she was being melodramatic, but she hadn't done that the morning Rachel was killed.

"Which way are we going?" she asked as she looked up into his strained face.

"You're the seer. What do you think?" he said, holding her tightly to his chest and nestling into her soft roundness.

"Let's just take I-15 south. I can't imagine they're that organized yet."

"You were never one to back down from a fight, my love. Okay, let's make a run for it."

"I have to get gas," Peg said and felt for her money belt as she slid into the Honda wagon. In it was $885 she'd saved in nearly four years of student life. Each week she would lift the lid on the piano, carefully tuck the extra bills into a dog-eared envelope and mark the accumulated amount on the outside. Ben didn't even know how much she had managed to squirrel away. He had $200. So between them they had a grand total of $1,085. What an irony, she thought. Ben had left a small fortune for his ex-wife to raise the kids. With the stock market shut down and the stocks worthless, they were now the rich ones with *$1,085.*

They didn't want to drive separate cars, but decided that doing it had two distinct advantages–they might not be seen as a fleeing couple, and they knew it would be helpful to have two cars in Zion. Ben, in particular, hated driving. Peg did most of their driving; now he followed her in the eleven-year-old Toyota. There was a normal light flow of traffic. And since this was the driest February on record, they weren't facing a normal winter storm.

Ben's mind stayed focused on driving for the first twenty miles or so. As they approached the prison with its floodlights glaring on the right side of the road, he wondered if the government would follow the pattern used in other cities of releasing prisoners armed with guns and money in exchange for hitting certain homes and citizens. Probably.

Over the Point of the Mountain, he could feel himself relaxing somewhat, but he knew the net could drop at any time up to and past Spanish Fork. Beyond that point was mostly federal land leased to farmers. The international police only patrolled populated areas. Local police were more lax about their duties, since they weren't paid well and mostly composed of Mormon men who were resentful of the UWEN.

He now found he could keep Peg in his sight and let his thoughts wander back to his last moments with his friends. He remembered the bishop finishing with the gun questions and then pausing. "We've been infiltrated by who-knows-who, but the stake president has advised me that it's so." Ben had felt an instinctual rage fill up his belly. *We've only been trying to keep a fair market economy going here,* he thought fiercely. *It's not like we've tried to overthrow the government.*

When Ben tuned in again, the bishop was solemnly repeating to the silent men that the government had their names. They had to leave the area immediately. Bishop Olson distributed to the shocked men a list of individuals and families in outlying areas that would shelter them, if they didn't have anyone to take them in. *At least I won't have to pay off my student loans. What luck*, Ben said sourly to himself.

"I'll give each of you a blessing if you would like," the bishop said in his warm, fatherly voice which had comforted many over the years. He was a grey-haired, slender man in his late 60's, now bent with arthritis. Most of the men did want his blessing. He singled Ben out to be first. No one minded; after all he had been the ward's first counselor. Because of the congestion in the front room, they stepped into one of the bedrooms and moved a chair to the side of the bed. As Ben sat down, the bishop walked up behind him, leaned over to ask his full name, then placed his crippled hands on Ben's head.

"Benjamin Abraham Taylor...I lay my hands upon your head to give you a blessing...." Ben was surprised to find himself tearing up. *I may never see this good man again*, he thought.

"Ben, the Lord has been aware of you every day of your life. You had been lost to the gospel of Jesus Christ, but not to your Father in Heaven."

Ben was startled. *That is almost verbatim what my patriarchal blessing says. How could the bishop know? Did I ever share it with him?* He was completely mystified by the correlation as the bishop continued to recite his blessing point by point, and sometimes word for word.

"I bless you now with the health and strength to carry forth, to complete your mission here on earth. Your life will be extended in time. The Lord is very mindful of you. On your shoulders will be placed grave responsibilities which only you can fulfill for the Lord."

Ben looked out on the highway and realized that he'd lost contact with Peg's taillights. He panicked for a moment, because he had never been to southern Utah. *What had she said? Oh, yes.* "Make no turns, dear. This road will lead you straight to Zion." He laughed and relaxed. She understood him so well by now. Ben was dreadful about such things as following directions, repairing machines, "anything earthbound," she'd kid him. Once he drove to a friend's house, then left, walked to work, walked home and was completely puzzled by the fact that the car wasn't in the parking stall. Friends kindly compared Ben to the church scholar, Hugh Nibley, who had been the classic absent-minded professor.

As the light began to fill the very early morning sky, Peg turned on the radio. She listened to classical music for a while, then became curious what the news reports might say about the troops' arrival. She found KSL's 6:00 a.m. news disturbing. Not one word. Everything else about the fighting in Cleveland, the Chinese invasion of Afghanistan, typhoon devastating Gilbert Islands. (*Where were they?*) Local news about gangs, drugs, murders (*Same old same old*). She turned the knob and waited for other reports. (*Maybe it's too early*). Then a couple of disc jockeys on Talk Radio joked about the calls to 911 in the night. "People thought we had had another quake," one said mockingly. "Just transport planes refueling for the Pacific," the other laughed. "Hey, folks, how many times do you have to be told? Don't call 911 unless it's an emergency."

Peg snapped off the sound and sat in silence. She was tired and irritated. The fields south of Spanish Fork began to open up. With the early morning light filling out the landscape, she involuntarily let out a sigh. The sight of the open, empty winter fields lent her comfort. In her youth in Idaho Falls, she had the same reaction when the family rounded the bend to the family sugar beet farm and drove up the long driveway to their large brick home. There no one could get to them.

Why did Ben have to get involved in this spy thing? Peg returned to the present. *We were doing okay. But no-o-o...he always wanted to fight the war in Vietnam, but that was before his time...then he wanted to protest the President's radical shift in ecological policy, but the University policy stated that any student involved in the demonstrations would be expelled.*

Then another mean thought crossed her mind—*maybe these guys who have been playing the spy game are deluded. Maybe this whole thing isn't real. Maybe we just tore up our home for nothing.*

The sky now was tinged with pink. As Ben looked around, he realized they were out in open countryside. Involuntarily he looked in the rear view mirror for government troops. No one looked like they fit the description. Then ahead on the road he saw that Peg had pulled off the side of the road, the brown Honda's turn signals flashing. *She must be waiting for me to catch up,* he laughed. *My homing beacon—she is that. What would my life be without her?*

Ben looked back once more in the rear view mirror, and to his horror, he saw a motorcycle which had come out of nowhere was nearly riding on his bumper. In fact, it was so close, he could see the terrified eyes of the red-helmeted biker. He swerved around Ben at the last minute. Ben started to mouth a choice obscenity at the mad driver, when he heard the dreaded sound of an Interpol helicopter overhead.

Peg jerked around in her seat and craned to see the copter in the early morning sky. She was terrified. She involuntarily felt for the couple's .22 in her needlepoint bag. Then the red and black motorcycle roared by, easily going 80 mph. She strained to see Ben in their white Toyota. *I don't want to get caught in any Interpol dragnet, especially with this gun, extra cans of gas and food on board. It'll be a pretty dead giveaway!* "Ben, honey, hurry," she moaned.

She always drove ten miles over the speed limit. She told Ben it was a matter of principle—to be able to drive at any speed she liked. He kidded her that she needed to work on her authority hangups. But now she was frantic that, in his need to follow the posted speed limit, he'd bring them straight into the Interpol net.

"Finally!" she exclaimed as the little foreign car, lights still on, came up over the small hill.

Sweat ran down Ben's brow and over his upper lip. He clung to the steering wheel, not knowing what to do. If he tried pulling up behind Peg, the police might suspect they were one of the couples on the fugitive flight list. Yet if he continued on down the highway, he'd pass right by the arrest scene leaving Peg alone and unprotected.

Ben assumed they had nabbed their man by this time, but he couldn't tell for sure, because the bike and copter had disappeared around a bend in the road. He said a quick prayer, slowed down and gestured to Peg to turn out in front of him. *Act like nothing has happened,* he thought furiously, hoping she'd pick up on his wave length. He found he couldn't keep his knees from shaking.

The hated blue and white helicopter was hovering near the ground as the couple drove up. They could see the figure of a uniformed Interpol agent hanging out of the copter door, a shotgun of some type aimed at the head of the biker. As they passed, several car lengths apart and at the exact speed limit, they could hear, "... now lie down on the ground with your legs spread apart..." blaring from the bullhorn the other officer held as he guided the helicopter in its hovering position.

Ben was so terrified he could hear his inner ears pounding along with the wild beating of his heart. His ulcerated stomach felt like it was on fire. "Come on, come on, Peg. That's a girl. Okay, now look straight ahead," he murmured. "Don't look back at me. Just keep driving the speed limit."

Neither dared look back. They drove like statues for several miles. When they drove past the Mt. Nebo exit, Ben let go of his single-focused terror long enough to regret that he hadn't gone to the Tibetan monastery there while he had a chance. He wondered what it would be like to learn how to meditate from a real Tibetan teacher.

It wasn't until they passed Nephi a half hour later that both felt they were out of immediate danger. In fact, both were pleased to see an old familiar black and white highway patrol car with its red lights flashing–heading the other way. Ben let his mind wander back to Bishop Olson's blessing. "Grave responsibilities." "Life extended in time." *Now that certainly can be interpreted a couple of ways. The obvious one is the posse's on my tail and angels have to work over-time getting my butt out of a sling.* (Sometimes his inner city origins showed.) *Or, what would Peg speculate? She'd say that I am going to be translated so I won't have to die.* He had kidded so often about her theological musings. *I repent, Lord. Who knows? It'll probably be a woman like Peg who leads us to the promised land. After all, this is the 21st century.*

Ben's thoughts turned to school. *The only thing I've done for the past four years,* he thought bitterly, *is read for four hours a day and write another four. I really understand now why everyone I've known who's gone for a Ph.D. said if they had understood what it really takes to get a doctorate, they never would have done it. All I know how to do is read and write, and think about sociolinguistics and Neo-Marxist educational models. Which reminds me, the dissertation is sitting at the printer's. What should I do? Call them? Say what?*

Suddenly he felt very tired and depressed. *Weeks away from defending my dissertation. Why couldn't the Lord wait one more month?* He felt an old anger seep through his very tired body, and he draped his arms over the steeling wheel and let out a loud sigh.

Being really fatigued, the emotional pockets of the psyche are turned inside out. Out falls the change one doesn't want to sort through. The next couple of hours were true to that pattern. Ben's psyche was haunted by an archetypal Jewish intellectual, who looked like Ben's uncle, Stanley, and could convince Ben that God simply did not intervene in the lives of limited and unredeemable men.

He began his life with a Jewish mother who didn't practice her religion and a Catholic father who gave up on church-going for Sunday golf long before the children were born. It was in this religious void that Ben worshipped Beethoven as a child, but always there was the desperate hunger for an absolute morality to make sense out of his often pathetic and sometimes sordid home.

As a 15-year-old undergraduate at UCLA, he would find himself standing outside a Catholic Church near his dormitory, wondering what special knowledge or mystical ritual it took to get in. Later, in graduate school, he tried to turn the study of literature into a religion–almost a monastic vocation. But the English Department at University of Oregon was filled with socially-correct existential despair, so that he began to believe there wasn't anything to worship, save his two babies.

While Linda worked on a teaching degree, he took over as primary caretaker to his children. One day in Eugene, with both children in a stroller, he made up his mind–Jew or no, angst or no, he was taking his children into a church. He walked around to the disabled entrance to St. Jude's. With jaw set, he pushed the stroller up the concrete ramp. *This is for their sake*, he said to himself.

Upon entering the foyer, Ben was immediately soothed by the dark, cool quiet, the rich smell of votive candles, and the gently colored light that streamed through the stained glass that Thursday afternoon in May (*May 8th*, he'd tell those of his friends and family who would listen).

No one stopped him in the entryway, so he pushed on one of the large wooden doors and held it open with one arm as he backed in the stroller with the two sleeping children. He walked timidly down a side aisle toward the altar but suddenly stopped–so overcome with the figure of the dying Christ that he couldn't walk any farther.

Ben stared up at the back lit sculpture for a moment. *So this is the Messiah*, he thought, then felt a strange energy in his solar plexus. On a warm beam of light, he felt himself being lifted up out of his body and drawn toward the altar. In his disorientation, he thought he was dying and began weeping for his children. But as he neared the crucified figure, he felt himself "explode" (that was the only word he could find to describe it) with love. He shattered into a million shards of light and merged with Christ. He and Christ, as one figure, then began a slow ascent up through the ceiling of the chapel into the rainy afternoon.

Ben was seized for a moment with worry about the children, but was swept by an assurance that they were being cared for. Higher and higher they went, until he felt a slight tap on the leg and looked down at a sleepy-eyed Miriam with droopy, wet diapers. She had climbed out of the stroller and was looking for her "banky". He tucked her back in and, uncharacteristically, she fell back to sleep. Ben tried to return to the ecstatic state, but couldn't, so he slid onto a wooden bench, knelt down on a kneeler and with great emotion said his first prayer, "Lord, I am yours. Show me the way."

He was a man on fire with Christ, as his new evangelical friends would say. For months afterward, he had vivid dreams of the Lord, night after night. But from the very beginning, his ardor was mixed with bitterness, for he soon found that Linda was frightened, even repelled, by his conversion. She would have nothing to do with any of it. "I don't know you any more! Your whole personality has changed," she cried. "What about me?"

Ben took the children with him to St. Jude's week after week, sure it would be just a matter of time before she converted. Instead, Linda became withdrawn and cynical. They drew farther and farther apart, until three years later, the distance and pain had become so great for both of them that Linda filed for divorce. He was too emotionally exhausted to protest.

Ben took a job at Cal State Ukiah to be near the children, when Linda returned there to live with her parents, Abe and Lydia Breyerson. Ben was used to being with his son and daughter, playing with them, tending to them hours each day. Now the court decree allowed him to have the children only every other weekend. He felt like an organ had been ripped out of his body. He couldn't eat (he was sure he had an ulcer), and his sleep became ragged and irregular. Even his mother, Esther, turned her back on him, convinced that the divorce was his fault—his conversion had been selfish and eccentric, not to mention a betrayal of his Jewishness and her unconscious desire for her son to be the yet-revealed Messiah, like many Jewish mothers did.

In that black depression, Ben believed Christ had abandoned him. He had always known it: he was a damned man, a son of perdition, and so began to think seriously of suicide–looking a little too closely at razor blades, eying the valve of his gas heater, taking the turns on country roads way too fast. In one desperate moment, he asked himself if he should take the children with him. *How can I? But how can I not?* He could not imagine their delicate psyches surviving the legacy of a father who had taken his own life. He stopped eating, started drinking and took up smoking again–putting away three packs of Camels a day. Sitting on the back lawn of his apartment at night, he would often burn the back of his hand with the end of the cigarette that glowed in the dark.

It was at this time that an LDS office mate in the English Department gave him a *Book of Mormon* and suggested he might at least look into it as biblical literature, if nothing else. The book sat on his dining room table for weeks. Ben had been warned by his Christian friends to stay well away from the Mormons. They were a demonic cult and a powerful one at that. One Protestant minister had even proclaimed from the pulpit that it was Mormons Paul was prophesying about when he wrote in Galatians, "But though we, or an angel from heaven, preach any other gospel unto you..., let him be accursed."

But God hadn't abandoned Ben, for a day after he had composed his suicide notes and decided to make his death an automobile accident, two sister missionaries knocked on his door. It was a Saturday morning. He peeked through the curtains and seeing it was women and thinking they might have a flat tire, he answered the door and invited them in.

Clearly visible from the front room were dishes in the kitchen piled high on the counter, spilling over into the sink; mounds of unemptied garbage; and newspapers stacked in clumps by the back door. Ben was so despondent, it was difficult to prepare meals for himself, much less clean house. Besides, he was past caring what people thought of him. "What can I do for you?"

he asked, unshaven and weary as he stood with them in the hallway.

"It's what we can do for you," Sister Paulsen said cheerfully. "We've come with a message from the Lord."

Ben knew they were telling the truth in that instant. In fact, he was baptized the next Saturday. He was so hungry for the "whole truth and nothing but the truth," that a year later he even applied to the University of Utah to do work on his Ph.D., so he could be in Salt Lake City, at the "epicenter of Mormonism," as he called it, flying back to Ukiah to be with his kids every month until the UWEN halted his travels.

The very first day in his new ward he spotted Peg. He followed her to the Sunday School class, sat in back of her and fell in love with her naturally curly hair and the way she talked about the Lord. On their first date, they went on a picnic in the mountains. Kneeling by a stream, Ben cupped some cold river water in his hand, and letting it run through his fingers and splash back into the glittering current, he recited a couple of lines of poetry,

> *The world is charged with the grandeur of God;*
> *It will flame out like shining from shook foil...*

Peg was swept off her feet--a man who loved words! After a very short courtship, they married in the temple. Now, four years later, he was to have it all, as soon as he had his doctorate and a teaching position. Then he would go to court to get the kids from their grandparents, bring them to Utah. He'd buy Peg her house, they'd adopt a baby (his vasectomy prevented them from having their own children) and live happily ever after. "That plan is blown all to hell," he swore in a voice that sounded quite like his uncle's. In this state of mind, he had no faith that God cared one whit about the whole human race. He doubted Jed would succeed in getting the kids, let alone make it past the electronic guard system that had been set up along state borders. One had to have a pressing reason to move from one state to the next. Not impossible, but most people were unsuccessful.

"It's a go...goshdanged fascist country." Ben slapped his hand down hard on the steering wheel. "It can't go on." (He had promised the Lord he would clean up his language.) When he was tired and hungry and displaced from his bed, he wanted to escape the world in his accustomed, introverted fashion–into books and classical music. So, at that precise moment, when Beethoven's 9th began to play on the radio station out of BYU (which was no longer a church-run school) and the sun peered over the top of the Wasatch Range, he had to admit he did feel a great deal better. *If Peg was here she'd insist it was synchronistic,* he thought.

Peg watched the sun play tag behind big, dark clouds that had begun to roll up from the southwest. She was daydreaming about Rachel, her dead daughter–something she rarely let herself do these days. When Ben began honking, she was miles away in fantasy. After several sharp beeps, she came back to reality. Thinking Interpol after her, she veered into the left lane, nearly sideswiping a passing pickup truck. Frightened, she quickly corrected the path of the Honda, pulled off the shoulder of the road, and sat teary and hollow-eyed–on the verge of irrationality. Ben screeched up behind her and walked briskly to the driver's side of the car. He poked his head in and said, "Hey, sweetie, are you okay?"

"Frankly no. You scared me nearly to death." She stared straight ahead.

Ben opened the door and pulled her out into his arms. "I love you, you incredibly wonderful woman," he said as he brushed back curls from her freckled face. She relaxed against his body. "Come on. Let's take care of some of the basics. Okay?"

He gently took her hand, led her around to the passenger side of the car and asked, "Remember me? You're the one with the iron bladder. I've got to avail myself of the facilities. And I'm starved. What have you got?" He didn't wait for an answer but disappeared down a deep arroyo.

Peg smiled, shook her head and struggled to remember what

highway sign she'd seen last. The hours of sleep deprivation were taking their toll on both her tired body and psyche. *Are we close to Cedar City?* she asked herself. She'd only driven the route a couple of times.

Ben reappeared as suddenly as he had disappeared. She rustled around a picnic basket she had packed, pulled out a couple of items and said, "Okay, hunk-of-mine, here's some ulcer food—a cheese sandwich and carrot sticks. By the way, I think we're only a half hour out of Enoch."

Ben couldn't help laughing out loud. "Where but in Utah would you find biblical and *Book of Mormon* town names?" he asked rhetorically. "And who but Joseph Smith, for that matter, would dare suggest that a group of Jewish Indians colonized a part of the Western world?" That brought a smile to Peg's face. He then took her hand, kneeled down in the gravel, blessed the food and prayed gravely, "Please Lord, protect us on this perilous journey."

Back on the road, Ben's mind returned to his last minutes with the bishop. He had saved thinking about the end of their conversation until now. He knew it had happened, but simply couldn't assimilate it. When the bishop finished the blessing, he walked around Ben's chair and sat down on the unmade bed. "Ben, I've got a message from the Brethren."

Ben stared at him, "You're joking."

"You know me well enough to know that I'm not. They have been aware of you for awhile, particularly the articles you've written for church publications."

"But they are in hiding. How...?"

The bishop smiled, bent closer to Ben and said, "Do you believe that Jesus Christ is the head of this church?"

"Yes."

"Do you believe he communicates with His chosen servants?"

Ben steadied himself, then said, "I think so, Bishop. I haven't been in this church that long, as you know. And a lot of the higher happenings seem both wonderful and fairy tales at the same time."

"Well, Ben, although it may be hard for you to understand, the Holy Spirit is able to communicate on behalf of the Lord, so the Twelve are able to continue His work. The Lord also uses the priesthood to do his handiwork."

Ben felt a familiar irritation with what he called "Mormonese." *Talk to me straight, Bishop,* he thought.

"They want to encourage you in your spiritual progression. There are a number of obstacles yet to be overcome. Your relationship with your dear wife must be secured. But if you are able to withstand what testing the Lord provides for all His servants who wish to be called saints of God, you will find that you will be bound up for eternal life and have fulfilled the dearest desires of your heart."

Boy, if anything, that was less clear than the first statement, Ben thought. Being a linguist had its problems. He was so sensitive to verbal nuances. "I'm a bit slow here. I'm to continue working out my salvation in fear and trembling. And I'm to love my wife. Then if I endure the slings and arrows of outrageous fortune...." Ben looked up into the older man's kind face..."Other than having my children with me, the only desire of my heart is to be with my Savior."

The bishop nodded slowly.

Ben searched his face, "But I haven't been in the church that long."

"I don't know a more zealous lover of Christ, Ben. You are an exceptional man, and the Brethren want to encourage you to continue in your efforts. They are mindful of you."

Ben shook his head in disbelief.

"Yes, Ben, really. Now go with God's blessings, and be careful. I'll miss you."

They embraced. "I'll see you around, Bishop." Ben hung on a little longer than he intended. He hadn't had a father since his died when he was seventeen. It was hard even at this age to let go of such a caring paternal figure.

Ben looked up just as the road sign for Enoch passed by. Peg's turn signals were flashing. She's probably had them on for five miles, knowing me, he thought. They turned down the off-ramp and pulled up to a small country store. "So this is the City of Enoch," Ben joked in his best sardonic voice as she opened the door to the Honda.

"Take a good look. We won't be here long," Peg smiled, then said seriously, "Alex told me we should call from here. We need to split up. You call and get directions. I know where I'm to go."

"How do you know?"

"I called Alex before you got home, remember?"

"Oh, yeah. Where's the phone?" He could see it on the wall outside the store, but he habitually asked her help with physical things. *Funny habit, but endearing,* she thought, pointing to the phones. He ambled over to the small, wooden building stretching out his arms one at a time and then shaking each leg to get the kinks out.

"I'm going to see if they have Tums," he said over his shoulder. He wasn't really serious. There was such a shortage of items that were commonplace just a few years earlier, he thought he wouldn't find any, but he'd try for old times' sake. No Tums. Too bad, because he needed them with that phone call as he took down the directions from Alex. It was the tone of Alex's voice--his curt instructions on where to meet to avoid having someone tail them. Ben felt frightened and a bit disoriented. He hadn't understood that he and Peg were going to split up.

Peg could hear him trying to repeat back the directions Alex was giving him. *Lord, you've got to translate this guy quick. He'll be a wandering Jew out here without a bus schedule. Bus. Bus!* "O my gosh, I forgot to call for a substitute," Peg cried out.

Ben hung up and moved immediately to her side. "What's the matter, honey?"

Peg burst out laughing. "I forgot to call for a substitute. School has started. I can just see my first period class trying to cover up the fact that they don't have an English teacher. I wonder how long into the day they can pull it off. Second, maybe third period?"

They were both laughing hard now. Peg never could laugh out loud. She would double over breathless, holding her stomach, while tears rolled down her cheeks. Now it felt good to find something to laugh about in the middle of this madness.

"Okay now, Ben. We've got to get serious. Should I call or not?"

Ben sobered up, frowned and said, "Don't. We can't make calls for a while. Interpol might find us."

"Well, I'm calling my mother, and I don't care what happens."

Ben knew that tone of voice very well. Normally he made the final decisions about major things in their life, with her input. But not when she put her hand on her right hip and jutted out her chin. "Call from here." Ben sighed. "Do it now. And don't stay on the line very long."

Peg hunched over the phone and watched as a newer model car pulled into the parking lot. The phone rang and rang. Her heart sunk. No answer. It infuriated Peg that her mom refused to use an answering machine. I'll keep calling until I reach her, she vowed. *I don't care what he or anyone says. She's my mom!* she thought fiercely.

"No luck?" Ben asked, leaning on the Honda.

Peg shook her head and turned her face toward the store, so Ben wouldn't see the tears, or the determination, for that matter.

"We'll find a way for you to call, sweetheart. I know how much she means to you."

Smiling, Peg walked to him, pulled open his coat and snuggled inside. "Thank you, husband," she said and kissed his neck.

After the other car pulled back onto the highway, Ben straightened up and said very soberly, "Let's say a prayer, Peg." They didn't embrace before they drove off; they felt quite paranoid, sure someone might see them together. Giddy, exhilarated at having escaped, they also sensed this might be the beginning of an outlaw's life.

A light snow began to fall. "I thought this was the dry February. Great," said Ben, "just great. All I need now is to maneuver in snow." He stuck his head in the window of the Honda and gave her a peck on her freckled cheek. She headed out of Enoch back the way they came. Alex had given her an alternate route to the house. Ben turned east onto the highway, looking for the first Zion National Park exit. This was to be the first meeting in ten years with one of his most remarkable friends, Alex Dubik.

Chapter Two

I am no prophet -- and here's no great matter;
I have seen the moment of my greatness flicker,
And I have seen the eternal Footman hold my coat, and
*   snicker,*
And in short, I was afraid.
*   "The Love Song of J. Alfred Prufrock," T.S. Eliot*

Ben worried about the flashing red lights on a hill to his right as he drove out of Cedar City. They seemed like part of a radio tower, but these days he couldn't be sure. He started the drive down the canyon past the town when a blinding snowstorm came out of nowhere. "We had a lot of freaky weather in L.A...but nothing like this."

It was mesmerizing–the gritty snow blew directly at his windshield–a kaleidoscopic pattern that splayed out from the center and drew Ben into its hypnotic dance. He tried looking down at the midsection of the road, but that didn't work. Slowly he pulled off to the side of the road and sat shaking. *How long is this going to last?* Ben had trouble focusing on passing images in a car as it was. *But this...*the only thing he could do was lock the cars doors and pray. He slid the seat back and released the lever that kept the seat upright. He was asleep in moments.

An hour later a large semitrailer truck swept so close past the little Toyota that the rumbling brought Ben back to consciousness. The snow had stopped as suddenly as it had come. Relieved but scared because he had done very little winter driving, he waited until he could see no traffic coming for quite a distance, then eased the car back onto the now snow-packed road. White-knuckled, he clung to the steering wheel and drove as slowly as traffic would allow to the Toquerville/ Hurricane exit.

"Alex told me to get off and drive to the first gravel area on the right side," he reminded himself. "I wonder how long he's waited." He sat for about ten minutes, then said aloud, "And what sort of turns in the road has my friend taken?" He laughed at the pun. "No, what I really mean is how will we manage to get along. A few phone calls don't really tell me where he's at. It's one thing to marry an LDS woman like he's done; it's quite another to become a Mormon. One of my last memories is of him struggling to get up the courage to tell his Czech Catholic parents that he didn't believe in God. I hope he doesn't think I've gone completely off the deep end."

Two cars got off at the exit, but no one came from the direction of town. Then a light-blue Jeep Wagoneer slowed down, and the driver waved as he drove by. *Can't be sure,* he thought. *It's been so long I don't know if Alex has gone grey. Maybe he thinks I'm someone else.* Ben's stomach and eyes hurt, his back and, if possible, his brain hurt. *Where's Peg?* he worried. *Did she get caught in the storm?* Suddenly there was a toot on the horn from the same Jeep Wagoneer, which now drove up behind him. It was Alex, who signaled to Ben to follow him.

Ben drove faster than he was comfortable with, but at least he was following someone who knew the way. His self-esteem had dropped to a new low. He berated himself with, "Great, I'm this dauntless freedom fighter who faints at the sight of snow."

A few miles down the winding road and through a couple of small towns they came to the Virgin River. Right after the river a faded sign indicated they had arrived at Pah Tempe Hot Springs. They turned off down a broad, paved road flanked on either side with bare-limbed trees. These would come to life in another month in southern Utah's mild climate, but now they served as powerful images that sucked Ben back into a series of childhood nightmares. Almost always the same, they would begin with him driving down a long driveway at night–a driveway guarded by trees that looked like skeletons. He shivered and tried to swallow the acidic fear snaking up into his throat.

At the bottom of the hill the sign on the gate warned people, "This is now private property. Trespassers will be prosecuted or shot, whichever is more convenient." In spite of himself, Ben smiled. Definitely Alex's sense of humor.

When they pulled up to a large adobe house that stood a hundred yards past the gate, Alex jumped out of the Jeep Wagoneer followed by a golden retriever. In a second Alex was at Ben's car. He helped Ben out of the driver's seat and the two embraced, pulled back and looked at each other, then embraced again. Still a handsome man at fifty-six with chiseled features and a flair for dressing theatrically, Alex wore a calf-length sheepskin coat and Stetson with a turquoise hat band.

"It is so great to see you, Ben, you young whippersnapper."

Ben grinned, "And you, you old geezer."

They patted each other on the back.

They were on the grounds of Pah Tempe, Paiute Indian healing grounds. The air was tainted with sulfur. A wonderful geologic mistake had sent sulfur springs bubbling up to provide healing waters for both Indians and tourists. But when the big earthquake hit the San Andreas fault, the effects were felt as far away as Utah. The dam broke upstream, and the water pressure to pump the sulfur water into concrete baths disappeared. The large swimming pool which had been the main attraction had cracked in so many places it wasn't worth saving; so when Alex bought the property a couple of years back, it wasn't fit for the tourist trade. Locals still climbed over the fence on the far side of the river and waded upstream to sit in the warm pools that pocketed a portion of the river near Alex and Moira's studio and house. But Alex had dogs and guns, if necessary, to run off whomever he pleased. But he usually didn't. He just looked the other way, and he was such a charming man, many people in town felt like they just didn't want to bother him.

"Peg's fine," Alex responded to Ben's worried countenance. "She beat you here. What did you do? Go to sleep on the side of the road?"

Ben nodded and headed for the fire he could see blazing in the front room fireplace. It wasn't the fire, but the figure of his wife standing near it that was the magnet. *Peg probably drove the canyon at eighty miles an hour, knowing her,* he thought.

"This building used to be a bed and breakfast place," Alex volunteered. "Lots of bedrooms and a kitchen. About right for you two, for now. Our house and the studio are across the river and up a ways."

Moira stood in the small kitchen smiling, clearly relieved to see the two men come through the door. An elegant Maori woman–high cheekbones, tawny skin, dark hair half-braided down her back–she wore a beige woolen caftan and wielded a large wooden spoon. Although she was five months pregnant with her first child, a boy, she did not show it. "Where has he been?" she asked in a marked New Zealand accent.

"Just as we thought, sleeping by the side of the road."

Peg rushed into Ben's arms and hung on silently. After a moment he pulled her away. "I'm fine, honey–really–just starved."

Ben ate four enormous whole wheat waffles and all the while played with Peg's feet under the table. When left alone, they said nothing. They walked into the room with the fireplace, which had two large beds, snuggled into one and fell asleep almost immediately. They looked like they might have been sculpted out of one piece of Michelangelo's marble, they lay so still together.

They awoke hungry just as the sun was setting. "Are we dead?" Ben asked jokingly as he tried to stretch out and untangle from Peg and the bed sheets.

"I hope so," Peg's answer was said only half in jest. "Have I told you in the last half day how mad I am about you?" she asked. She reached over and tried to pull Ben back into bed.

"No."

He succeeded in reaching the fireplace.

"I couldn't live without you. I realized that driving down here. I'd just waste away."

"Peggy, sweetheart, I love you too. You worry too much. We've made it this far, and I'm sure the Lord has something greater in mind than an ignoble death squashed on the highway somewhere." He sounded more convinced than he felt. He smoothed her cheek and pulled her to close to him. Peg's warmth comforted him. Ben began to think about climbing back in bed with her when a knock on the door startled them. "Hey, you all, chow line." Alex sounded pleased to have company.

"See, honey, someone's looking after us. You don't even have to cook," Ben said soothingly.

Peg turned so Ben couldn't see her tear-filled eyes. She really did believe she'd waste away if she lost one more person. She knew she was too much sometimes and worried he would tire of her need for reassurance that he wasn't going to die or leave her. Most of time she tried not to let it show, but this was an extraordinary situation. "Okay, cowboy, give me a moment to get beautiful," Peg tried to sound cheery. She took her cosmetic bag into the communal bathroom. A shower lifted her spirits.

It seemed so natural to sit around the table with Alex and Moira, it was like visiting family. Ben and Peg found very few couples they both liked, but this was more than like. This was a familiarity and peace that transcended friendship. Even though Peg and Moira had never met, they had talked a number of times on the phone and fell into an easy conversation over dinner. By the time they washed dishes, they were sharing autobiographical detail saved for close friends.

Alex and Ben excused themselves to go down to the river. Alex suggested that they try the sulfur baths. "These waters have been relaxing and healing people for centuries. Wanna try it, Ben? You look pretty stressed." Ben didn't want to seem ungrateful for the offer, so he went, but he would have preferred to stay with Peg.

Night had come calling. Even with the flashlight, Ben felt suddenly terrified as they walked across a bridge and up a muddy track toward the large house and studio. Now nightmare images from his youth returned: the light flashing back and forth on the ground, a man walking ahead in a large hat. Although there were stars, there was no moon. Ben shivered partly from the cold and partly from fear. He had not spent much time in nature and now he was surrounded by unfamiliar smells, sounds, things just out of sight. He hated not to be in control. *Pull yourself together, buddy*, he chastised himself. *Are you a man or a marmot?* The smell of sulfur grew stronger. A couple of times Ben whirled around, sure someone was following them. He could not remember if this was the part of the dream when the gunshots erupted. He would always wake up screaming when the deafening noises from the exchange of gunfire began.

Alex walked calmly, silently in elegant cowboy boots, Levis, a gray cable-knit sweater. "Down here," he said and pointed to the stairs that led to the river.

"You first." Ben didn't want Alex to know how unnerved he was.

Alex disrobed, laid his clothes and small backpack over a low tree, put down a cellular phone near the water's edge and slid into the pond that skirted the river. Ben followed, but really did not want to get in. When he did, he was surprised to find it quite warm and very relaxing. "What's in here that makes it so restful?" *Dumb question*, Ben thought. What he really wanted to say was, I'm really freaked out and I hope I survive my nightmare. Instead he led them into talking about the days when they had met at UCLA, a graduate art history class. Ben was sixteen, the child prodigy, and Alex, a graduate art student. They took to each other immediately–a sort of brotherly bonding–Ben was brighter, Alex more artistically talented and protective.

"I never could get you stoned, you know," Alex laughed.

"I was already tripping, trying to keep up with life. I didn't need any more disruption."

"From acid, I went to Buddhism," Alex said.

"Yeah, you really are a lot different now than you were in those days. You always seemed uptight in spite of the mellow exterior. Meditation agrees with you."

Alex reached for a bottle of water in his backpack and passed it to Ben. Ben took a long drink, passed it back to Alex and began talking about his family, whom Alex had met once.

"Lakewood was a lot smaller then. Mostly lower-middle class, chain link fences, trucks and boats. Ours was a California adobe with two palm trees out front and a backyard filled with those trees with the terrible-tasting oranges. You know the ones?" Ben's tense frame began to relax in the warm sulfur water.

Alex laughed and said, "They were in my yard too. Why anyone would deliberately plant them was always a mystery to me."

Ben snorted, then continued, "When my dad had drunk his fill of booze and begun his nightly harangue at my mom, I'd take a ladder to the roof and wait for Beethoven to appear to take me away."

"Beethoven? Really?"

Ben nodded soberly.

"You were always a weird, mystical kid."

"I still am."

They laughed and fell silent. After a few minutes, Ben said, "I've missed you."

"I've missed you too," Alex said with a great deal of kindness in his voice. "I'm so sorry to see you in this mess. I told you becoming a Mormon was going to get you in trouble."

They both chuckled. Alex went on, "Of my many friends, Ben, I can't think of anyone I admire or value more. You are one of a kind, you know."

Ben began to cry. He hadn't meant to. It just happened, rolling from his belly up into his shoulders. Alex reached out and laid his hand on Ben's shoulder to comfort him, but Ben moved away. He leaned on one arm against the side of the muddy pool and dropped his head to his chest. His cries joined those of a coyote a long way off.

This was humiliating, crying in front of a friend he hadn't seen in ten years. But his body ruled and he cried and cried—some tears that hadn't been shed at his dad's funeral when he was seventeen, some at the loss of his children when the divorce took him away from his daily duties, and some for the young Ben who was always a little frightened of life and never fit in. He compensated by being the brightest and nicest student. He was tired of trying. Finally the sobbing slowed down. Alex remained silent and attentive. When Ben dropped down into the steamy water, Alex said soothingly, "That's got to feel good."

"It doesn't. I feel rotten," Ben said honestly, which also surprised him. "I feel rotten about my whole life. And now, it's all messed up. What in the Sam Hill is going to happen now? I'm a criminal–on the run. Didn't even finish my degree." He took another sip of the water Alex offered him.

Alex sat silent for a while, then said, "Want to learn how to get past the pain?"

"Drugs? Suicide?" Ben said half-jokingly.

"Breath and silence."

"I'll try anything once."

"Got to be more committed than that," Alex laughed.

"Okay, I'll try two breaths with three silences in between," Ben teased.

Alex laughed, and Ben felt better in spite of himself. "Breathe in and out naturally. Be aware of your breath. Clear your mind and watch what comes to the surface." Alex sounded very fatherly.

"At least this isn't laced with acid." Ben relaxed and let his breath go. Occasionally a feeling would start out in his body somewhere and form into a thought that would take him away from his concentration, but he was fairly good at this game. The crying had emptied him.

Time passed, maybe a half hour. Ben let his awareness expand into the night's sounds, the stars, the glow just over the mountain which was the moon trying to rise above the narrow canyon cliffs.

"I really feel different," Ben had to admit. "Will you teach me more?"

"Sure, no problem. Then I can say I finally got you high." Both men laughed, then Ben gave a start. He thought he saw a shadow moving up river on the other side. Alex instinctively reached for the phone. "What do you see?"

Ben pointed. "There. Right there. Can't you see someone?"

Alex squinted, then relaxed. "Nah, you're hallucinating."

Ben continued to stare. There was a man moving from shadow to shadow; he could see the figure clearly. His heart began to beat faster. The man now moved toward him, across the water. "Al, this guy is coming at us!" his voice rose. *This didn't happen in my dream*, he thought, nearly hysterical.

Alex stared out at the quiet night, "No, man. I told you, it's nothing."

Heart pounding, Ben continued to stare at what appeared to be a familiar figure. As the man grew closer, Ben strained to see his face. "It's Beethoven!" he blurted out before he realized what he was saying. A youthful, scowling Beethoven walked the rest of the way across the water to the side of the sulfur pool. When he got within a yard of Ben, he did something uncharacteristic. He smiled.

"What are you doing here?" Ben asked, trying to control the fear.

The figure only continued to smile.

"What do you want from me?" Ben shifted from afraid to decidedly embarrassed. He glanced over at Alex, who sat very still and straight-backed. And when he looked back, the figure melted into the steam rising from the pool.

"Alex, are you sure you didn't see anyone?" Alex shook his head. "Boy, I really need help." Unnerved, Ben decided to stop the breathing routine and just enjoy the effect the sulfur water was having on his very tired body. *I'm just tired, that's all*, he reassured himself. *Just very, very tired.*

"You know?" Alex interrupted Ben's reverie. "I know someone I want you to meet."

"Who? Mozart?"

"My meditation teacher, Sangay Tulku. He's a Tibetan rinpoche. I think you'd really appreciate what he knows about these higher states."

The cellular phone's high ring cut through the conversation. "There's someone at the gate." Alex looked into the screen to see Moira's tense face.

He had wired the front gate with a speaker so they could be in their home or office and hear the sounds of people at the gate. They were not expecting more company. Could just be town folk, but then again neither Alex or Ben knew how badly the government wanted him.

"Can you tell who it might be?" Alex asked calmly.

"No, honey, or I wouldn't have bothered you."

"Where are you?"

"Still down with Peg."

"Where's the nearest gun?"

"I've got it."

"Good. I'll be down there shortly. Keep me posted."

Alex stepped into his clothes without drying himself. "You stay here for the moment, Ben. You'll only get in the way. I'll whistle if there's any trouble." He demonstrated his whistling, and a chocolate-colored Doberman Ben hadn't seen emerged from the shadows of the art studio and sat down obediently by Alex's side. "Good girl, Angelina." He patted her.

"Hey, you take it easy getting out, Ben. Do you hear me?" Alex said over his shoulder as he left.

Ben couldn't have risen to the rescue if his life depended on it. He was spent. His limbs felt like limp rigatoni. He dragged himself up onto a rock. The night seemed surreally clean. It couldn't be real trouble, he thought, or surely Alex would have sensed it. Then Ben heard male voices echo up the canyon. They sounded friendly, so he relaxed into a heap up against a rock and struggled to get into his clothes. He stopped to pray. "Please, Father, make this right for all of us." Fresh tears fell onto his reddened cheeks. He felt a warm reassurance, so warm in fact that he was beginning to believe it was possible his Heavenly Father actually resided on a planet near Kolob and cared enough to intervene in his life. Ben remembered a recent mind-stretcher Peg had told him at Christmas time. "Noah," she had said in an even voice, "was the archangel Gabriel, who visited Mary." *Good gravy! These Mormons. What one has to believe!*

Alex stealthily walked the eighth of a mile to the entrance. Angelina kept pace on his right heel. Two vehicles idled at the gate. No one was outside either of them. He wished he were armed. Have to make do with the phone, he thought, then said, "Honey, what have you heard?"

"Where are you?" she replied tersely.

"Near the gate. I've got Angelina with me."

"I'm not sure, but I think there are two cars."

"There are. What else?"

"I thought I heard a child."

"Walk up to the gate slowly like you're responding to the sounds. Bring your gun. I'll cut across the back and join you."

Moira left an ashen-faced Peg and walked out into the night. She wasn't frightened, in fact she relished a fight. Since she had married Alex, she had been a bit bored in the isolation of this small community. Ancient Maori warrior instincts surfaced, and she broke into a grin as she shifted the Browning .22 semi-automatic pistol from her left to right hand.

Once across the bridge, Alex ducked behind a trailer and waited for Moira. The full moon floated above the scene quite suddenly. Now he could count at least seven figures in the two vehicles. *We're badly outmanned here if this is the law,* he thought. Moira cut a tall, stately figure as she strode down the gravelly road to the gate. Alex felt a flush of desire for his woman. Combat did bring the best out in her.

The driver of the first car got out and walked to the gate as he saw Moira walking toward them. She just kept coming–didn't miss a stride. "Can I help you?" she asked rather gaily, keeping the gun down at her side.

"Yes, I hope so. My name is Robert Olson. I'm a friend of Ben Taylor's. When I last met with him in Salt Lake, he mentioned he was coming here and said you and your husband had a large ranch. I know this is a surprise, but there are several of us who had to flee quite unexpectedly and hoped you might help us find shelter." He seemed particularly frail as he placed his crippled hand on the gate.

"Just a moment, please." Moira signaled Alex to join her and backed away from the gate. When he reached her, she quietly explained the situation. "What do you think, honey?" she asked.

They stood there, momentarily silent. "I can't imagine anyone making up such a story, and I can't ask Ben. He's out of it at the moment. Talking to Beethoven."

"Excuse me?" Moira asked.

Alex waved his hand to dismiss the remark. "I'll tell you later. Let them in. What the hay!" *Noah's ark*, he thought as he walked up to the gate, opened it and gestured to the cars to move forward. *Moira told me this would happen when we bought the place.* He shook his head. A friend once said Moira was his talisman. *More like a tiger that I've got by the tail,* Alex laughed to himself. *Who was it used to sing that song? Buck Owens?* He couldn't remember. What the song did bring up was a memory of the San Fernando pool hall his father used to take him to–the acrid smell of beer and smoke, his father's eyes, mean, demanding that he not blow this shot in doubles–he had twenty bucks riding on it. Alex could see the other men's faces too. Cold. They were unsympathetic to the slight, sensitive ten-year-old boy who just wanted time with his father.

Ben staggered back across the bridge in time to hear the bishop's voice. He thought he was having another hallucination, but that fatherly face in the crowd of people who were unloading their suitcases into cabins and trailers was unmistakable. Ben slowly wobbled down the path to the bed and breakfast. He was enormously pleased to shake the bishop's hand once more, crippled as it was. To do so reminded him that this saintly man probably was in constant pain–and, amazingly, Ben had never heard him complain.

The kitchen opened for a second time that night for the nine people, six adults and three children, who sat dazed and tired. This time it was Peg and Moira who cooked and served. It was good for Peg to be on the helping side.

"We'll just stay the night," the bishop promised. "We have other southern Utah contacts."

"Why did you leave so suddenly?" Ben asked, but then felt a

little silly. *We left suddenly from Salt Lake ourselves,* he thought.

"It wasn't more than ten minutes after everyone left that I got an anonymous phone call. It was chilling. A male voice said, 'You'd better leave now or you're a dead man.' I rounded up my family and we left with just the clothes on our backs. Simply terrifying."

Ben fell silent as he sipped a cup of hot chocolate. *Another Mormon mystery,* he thought. *Why can't I drink coffee when I can rot my teeth with cocoa?* Peg had patiently explained it was the spirit of the law. He winked at her as she leaned over to refill cups. She couldn't wink very well, so she mouthed I love you.

The bishop was now talking with Alex, who asked what he thought would happen now that the government had moved more troops into the Salt Lake area. Ben rejoined the conversation. The three talked for some time and speculated on what resistance might be mounted in Salt Lake against complete economic control. They finally agreed there probably would not be much, given the history of what had happened in other parts of the country.

"What's to become of us?" Peg cut in. Her large brown eyes searched Olson's face.

"The Lord will provide, dear," he said in a tired but firm voice. "He always has and He will this time."

Peg felt a familiar irritation with what she experienced as a patronizing dismissal from the bishop. She tightened her jaw and returned to the kitchen to wash dishes with Moira.

Ben excused himself, saying he couldn't hold his head up any longer. He shut the door to their bedroom, didn't reach for the light and stumbled to the fireplace. He pulled out of a decorative container a large wooden match, struck it against the mantle piece, rolled up a nearby newspaper, lit it and held the burning torch to some twigs he laid in the fireplace with his other hand. These cracked and sparked and hissed. He watched the dance of the flames for a moment then added kindling. This primitive fire building ritual was all he had left in him. He felt like every cell in his body was on fire. He couldn't get one more thought to pass from dendrite to axon terminal. *Log jam, mental log jam.* He poked at the dancing fire, groaned as he picked up a large log and deposited it into the growing fire. He intended to read the *Book of Mormon*, which was his nightly ritual, but he didn't have the energy to move from chair to bed.

Shortly afterward Peg came in. She kissed him on the forehead and climbed into bed. "Are you coming to bed soon, honey?" she said opening her deep-red Triple Combination to the *Doctrine and Covenants*.

"No, I'm trying to think." In his state that stock phrase, which he used to distance himself from Peg when she was too insistent, took on new meaning. He was trying to think, only nothing came. Ben sat there well into the night after Peg had fallen asleep. When he finally climbed into bed, he took the scriptures from Peg's side, quietly turned off the reading lamp and placed the book on the night stand beside him. He found her devotion to the *D&C* endearing and somewhat mystifying.

"Anyone can claim they are getting some message from God about selling a parcel of land next to a dry goods store," he muttered as he snuggled over to the warm side of the bed. *The Book of Mormon is something no one could fake. Its internal evidence and structural complexity are so overwhelming, it couldn't be fabricated*, he thought fiercely.

Can't let these lessons with Al get out of control was his last thought before drifting off. Then Beethoven was back, smiling an enigmatic smile, this time behind his closed eyelids, but Ben was too tired to respond. *I'll think about it in the morning*, he said to himself and pulled the navy-blue coverlet up over his ears. In his exhausted dreaming, he went from the long drive down to the hot springs with its frightening skeleton-like trees to Beethoven walking the waters. Although he tried to get out of the nightmare, he couldn't bring himself to consciousness.

Chapter Three

The love of God, unutterable and perfect,
Flows into a pure soul the way that light
Rushes into a transparent object.
The more love that it finds, the more it gives
Itself; so that, as we grow clear and open,
The more complete the joy of heaven is.
And the more souls who resonate together,
The greater the intensity of their love,
End, mirror-like, each soul affects the other.
                    Purgatorio, xv: ll.67-75, Dante

The next morning, Ben decided to explore the property to see if it continued to match the hideout of his childhood nightmares. He crossed the bridge and headed up the hill toward the canyon. He felt empty, calm. The university life he had just left seemed something he had dreamed years ago. *Why haven't I felt this good for ages?* he asked himself. *I should have come down here to visit Alex on a regular basis. It takes a national disaster to get me out in nature, for crying out loud.* He felt like he had just brushed past the furs and stumbled out the back door of the wardrobe into Narnia.

Past the Dubiks' house and studio, he found a greenhouse and garden with high fence, topped with barbed wire and strung intermittently with cow bells. Alex, in bib overalls and blue denim shirt, worked vigorously in the garden hoeing and weeding. Because the giant supermarket was a thing of the past (stores carried only a few brands of necessary items and local produce), most people with any kind of land planted gardens to supplement their diets. Now in February, the local grocer would only have a couple of baskets of mushy apples and pears and the few precious, expensive oranges and lemons from southern California.

Ah, California, Ben thought as he neared the garden. *Between earthquakes, insects and fires--it's a candidate for outer Gomorrah.* He laughed then sighed. *It's really a shame. I thought*

it was bad growing up there, with the smog, the gangs, economic
depression. But now. Whew!

"Hi, there, Farmer Brown," Ben called out. "How does your garden grow?" Alex looked up and grinned. Ben did not recognize the plants being weeded, except the cabbage and lettuce. The heartland of America, "bread basket to the world," scarcely supported Midwesterners any more, much less the entire country. The UWEN, with its global distribution network, kept the shelves stocked with just the basics.

"Not bad, except for the fact that some desperate critters are trying to get through the fence. It's hard enough eking out food for us, without feeding the entire feral population of the valley," Alex said and sighed.

Ben didn't ask what critters. But his mind went to something he had read recently by World Animal Watch that said almost every week now several species were being eliminated by starvation. He tried not to let his imagination flare up. If he did, he would probably see Big Foot, complete with large fangs, leaping over the eight-foot-high fence in a single bound.

The two men patted each other on the back. "You've got a little Shangrila here, Al—beautiful spread, wife, baby on the way," Ben said seriously. "I've been meaning to ask you a serious question...why take us in? Why get involved in a cause that's not really yours?"

Alex shaded his eyes with a dirty gloved hand and said without hesitation, "Because we're really not safe. No one is these days. It's time to take sides," he said rather tersely and returned to hoeing.

Ben stood for a moment looking at his friend, admiring the fact he had stayed in great shape, then asked, "Can I borrow your dog here?"

Alex looked up. "Sure. *Mi perro es tu perro.*" They both laughed. They used to practice their fractured Spanish on each other at UCLA so they could pick up Latino girls. Ben was not very successful because he was so young, but Alex always had a "chocolate" beauty on his arm. His first wife, Lisa, was Mexican, Indian and African-American. A knock-out. And a tragic drug addict as years went on. In Los Angeles, she overdosed in a grocery store parking lot in her new red Maserati.

Ben walked around the garden's perimeter and began the easy climb up the canyon. His senses were mirror clean; he felt at one with the smell of the desert plants, the warm sun on his head and shoulders, the sound of the water swooshing around a boulder at a bend in the river. Ordinarily his thin, southern California blood would have him shivering in the fifty degree weather, but he didn't feel cold in his lightweight jacket, even though it was the end of February. Alex's golden retriever padded along.

"I don't think this is the same place," he said aloud. He stopped, shivered and let out a long sigh. *I wish that dream would just leave me alone,* he thought fiercely.

The retriever slowed and looked back. Ben threw a stick for the dog to fetch and remembered a neighborhood dog, a Basset Hound. When he was young, he'd go next door and ask to play with Buster. They'd race around his backyard, Buster woofing his baritone glee. Ben didn't feel so lonely with him. His brother, David, six years younger and a toddler, was no fun for an eight-year-old. Although there were other kids in the neighborhood, he preferred Buster's company.

That summer he began to read his way through the set of World Book encyclopedias his mother purchased for him. Even at that age, he had a marvelous ability to retain details of things he'd read. Whenever there were assembled guests, his father insisted that he tell them about whatever new section of the encyclopedia he was reading. Ben somberly related the dates of the French Revolution, the pounds per square inch of gravity exerted on the human body, how a bill became a law.

After his performance his mother always said, "My little rabbi! Isn't he wonderful?" And his father, who by then had drunk his first six pack of beer, routinely retorted, "He's only half Jew, and he's not going to be no rabbi, not if I can help it!"

At that point Ben retreated to his bedroom and carefully placed a piece of classical music, usually Beethoven's *Violin Concerto*, on his stereo. Earphones covered the descent of his parents' squabble into a full-blown argument, which led to shouting and finally icy silence. Later he'd go to the roof and wait for Ludwig.

"What's your name? Huh?" Ben leaned down to the retriever who had shoved her muzzle into Ben's hand. "You're a girl, I see," he said looking down to see how she was equipped."What is it? Harriet? Honey Bun?" When she didn't answer, he heaved another small stick high up the path and watched with pleasure as the frenzied dog bounded up the hill and chomped on the stick.

I can't ever remember my dad saying he loved me. I don't think he ever cared, Ben brooded. *David became his favorite, my extroverted athletic brother. I was left to my crazy mother.*

Ordinarily he'd now withdraw into a book or his music to escape the pain of that reality, but today, because of last night's experience, he decided he'd try Alex's Zen approach. He took in a deep breath and let it out. Then another...The dog came back, dropped the stick expectantly. He filled his lungs, stretched out, then let his arms fall to his sides and exhaled slowly.

Ben began to feel a little heady, but in control. He started walking quickly up the path; the dog bounced beside him, occasionally knocking him off balance. He laughed when that happened, surprised at how good he felt. He let himself imagine there were no police looking for him. He and Peg would settle into the bed and breakfast; he'd find odd jobs tutoring in the community; the children would grow up straight and tall in a healthy environment. Life would be Rousseauesque.

He kept climbing–his legs, which normally gave out after seven or eight flights of stairs, carried him uncomplainingly farther and farther up the canyon. He focused on his breath, concentrated just on his sensory awareness and felt exhilarated. *This stuff really works!* he thought. He felt like he did with Buster in the backyard. Free–free to laugh, free to move and breathe and feel high without the fear of the fall into a crushing blackness that always followed. Oh, how he had prayed to escape the handicapping depression that had haunted him since he was nine or ten. Now he dared to hope.

Nothing about the canyon landscape he was passing brought up the same intense feelings he had had the night before when he had driven down the driveway. *Nope. Maybe it was just a coincidence,* he thought.

Then, a good quarter mile away from Pah Tempe, a fresh pile of unusually large turd stopped him mid-step. *Not a dog or deer,* he thought, trying to fight back the terror, *and too big for rabbit. Could be a mountain lion or bear. That's what is probably tearing down Alex's fence.*

His heart rate rose dramatically. A quick scene flashed before his eyes. In it he saw his mauled and mangled body discovered by Alex and Peg. They were overcome with grief at the loss of their loved one to the powerful jaws of a hundred and eighty-pound cougar. "I can't help myself," he said aloud. "I'm melodramatic; I'm Jewish."

Fear made jelly of those piston legs. He whistled sharply at the retriever. She came back and jumped up on him. "Guard me, sweetheart, till we get back. Okay?" he asked as he held her paws and looked into her face. She barked sharply, jumped down and headed back down the path.

Both angry and scared, Ben shouted, "Heel!" The dog quickly returned and sat down at his right heel. "Good girl," he said patting her on the head. "Now stay here!" She obeyed and they hustled down the gravelly path. "Okay, enough of this Eastern power breathing. I'm falling back on the known. How about a joke to while away the terror? Is that okay with you, Honey Bun?"

The retriever barked happily.

"Okay, have you heard the one about the Martian? He lands at Abraham's Deli, lower Manhattan. Now this is the best Jewish deli in the city. Are you following me so far, Honey Bun?"

The retriever looked up expectantly.

"Good. So Abe says, 'So you're a Martian?' and the Martian says, 'That's right.'" Ben strained to see if the buildings and safety were in sight, but nothing came into view, so he continued, "'You all have green skin?' The Martian says, 'That's right.' So Abe says, 'You all have googly green eyes?' The Martian says, 'That's right.'"

Suddenly the dog left Ben's side, her interest shifted to smelling something farther down the path. Ben ran to catch up with her, reached down and grabbed her fur at the neck. "Look, dog," he shouted, "you can smell this path any time you want. Right now I don't want to die from bear bites. You got that?" He pulled her back to the center of path and commanded, "Heel!"

She looked down guiltily, like she knew she had left her post. Ben then exhaled and said warmly, "It's okay. Just don't abandon me in my hour of need. That's all I ask." He took a deep breath and continued, "Okay, so let's see, we had googly green eyes, right? Okay. Then Abe says, 'You all have little antennae on top of your heads?' The Martian says, 'That's right.'" Pah Tempe came into view and Ben whooped and said exuberantly, "Here's the punch line, Honey Bun, are you ready?" The retriever barked happily.

"So Abe says, 'You all wear those funny little caps on top of your head?' The Martian says, 'No, only the orthodox.'"

"So what do you think?" he asked the retriever. "You're not laughing. You don't like Jewish humor?" The dog barked again, cocked her head to one side and looked up quizzically.

"Oh, go on. You deserve it." He waved his arm in the direction of the house, signaling that she was free to go. She bounded off to Alex's studio, sensing her duty was done. "And thanks," he called after her.

Suddenly the narrow valley shook with the vibrations of low-flying aircraft. Ben looked up to see the white bellies of two cargo planes, flying so low he could make out the UWEN insignia on the tail of each.

"Planes!" he yelled out. "UWEN planes!" He ran, arms circling the air like pinwheels the rest of way to the bed and breakfast. "UWEN!" he called out breathlessly when he reached the door of the dining room.

"In here!" Alex called out from the adjacent office.

Ben darted through the kitchen door, ran across the entryway and jerked open the office door. Alex and Bishop Olson, who had been sitting at a small table near the windows, abruptly pushed back their chairs and stood to face Ben as he rushed through the doorway. "What did you see exactly, Ben?" Robert Olson asked in a curt, administrator's voice.

"Definitely UWEN planes. Two of them. I could see the tail insignia, they were flying so damn low."

Alex grabbed an old desk-type phone, then walked to the other end of the room, dragging the telephone cord behind him like a trail of corded gray powder leading to a dynamite charge. Ben could hear "...all cordless phones–take out the batteries, don't just turn them off–and computers–unplug them from the wall. Get the ammunition from...." Robert Olson cut in, "Ben, I don't want you to worry about the children."

Ben's stomach felt like it was spewing out hot lava. He tried to answer calmly,"What do you mean, Bishop?"

"Because if the troops are true to form, it will be about 48 hours before they completely seal off all the state borders," Olsen replied. Then the two men stopped talking as the valley reverberated from the noise of more planes. Ben tried to think back to the Interpol invasion of Colorado, but he had so much adrenalin coursing through his body, he could hardly put two thoughts together, much less converse calmly, so he slid out of the leather-backed chair he'd fallen into and began to pace back and forth. He became aware of the smell of oil paint and clay which permeated the tastefully decorated place which served as office and storeroom for Alex's art supplies.

Ben walked to the large desk shoved up against a far wall. It overflowed with papers. Alex's stock excuse for the constant mess was that he was an artist, not an accountant.

Old nightmare images took Ben away. *This is the place! Is this where the men in masks rush in to break down the door? Or where the men lunge forward and are riddled with bullets?* Fear pounded in his ears.

Maybe it was the adrenalin or maybe it was getting back in touch with his feelings, but whatever it was, in that fearful split second, it seemed to Ben that some internal gear shifted into drive—permanent drive—and he suddenly felt in control like a man who had conquered the world. Later he'd tell Peg, "I felt like some demon who had gnawed at my innards since I was a kid, had suddenly died of a coronary and was taken home to be laid in state, complete with all kinds of medals for meritorious deviltry. He was gone; I stood there unafraid. I can't tell you what a high that was!"

Then the thundering stopped, and the bishop finished saying, "...probably like they did in Colorado. One thing—the military isn't known for its originality. If we get the standard package, it'll go Army Rangers securing airfields throughout the state, probably tonight, after dark." Ben nodded in assent.

More air traffic and once again the men broke off their conversation. Ben walked over to the windows. A light snow had begun to fall. He got a lump in his throat. *Where are those kids? Please, Lord, please,* he prayed silently, *they're your children, too. Bring them here safely.* No sooner had he finished the prayer, when a strange calm, like a liquid tranquilizer, poured gently throughout his system.

Then Alex returned, put the black phone back down on the table, and joined the conversation. Ben turned to hear him say, "Next the Delta Force will slip through the streets to the homes and offices of every important politician, religious leader...."

The men looked out at big slow snowflakes that had begun to drift past the floor-to-ceiling plate glass windows which overlooked the river. Then the bishop picked up the thread of the familiar tale. "We'll probably see hundreds of Marines leaping from helicopters to seize command of the television stations, government offices—any communication points."

To all three men who still could not fully register this sudden and wild jumble of events, this invasion seemed like something they had seen in a horror movie. It was hard to focus the searing reality that Utah was being invaded and overrun by international forces, and that they, their wives, their children–all of them were potentially standing at ground zero.

Alex looked to his elegant, two-story house across the river several times, then finally said, "Gentlemen, I'd like to suggest that we not tell our wives right now. For one thing, we don't know just how affected we'll be here. Moira is pregnant and Elizabeth, well, she's not even here yet, but when the ambulance arrives from Salt Lake, I'm sure you'll want to give her some time to settle into the Barlow place, right?"

The bishop nodded.

Ben struggled to grasp what they were talking about, *Elizabeth...oh, the bishop's wife.* Then he remembered the bishop's wife had become an invalid and had to be placed in a residential nursing facility. Evidently Robert Olson was going to try to bring her down to southern Utah from Salt Lake. Ben wanted to hug Peg right then, grateful she was so healthy. *That would be really hard to take,* Ben thought. *I don't know if I could handle having a wife who was an invalid.*

"What about it, Ben?" Alex asked. "You agree?"

Ben returned to the conversation with, "Sure, Al, I think it's a good idea to keep things quiet for now. So, Bishop, Alex has found you a place to stay?"

"Thankfully, yes," he replied. "Alex, you are such a good man to stick your neck out in this situation. You're a better Mormon than a lot I know."

Alex waved his hand, skillfully deflecting what he interpreted as a missionary probe by turning to Ben who paced back in his direction and said, "Are there more friends out there, besides the ones with your kids?"

Ben began to compute the refugee influx. "Ah, let's see. Jed and Jody and the kids, five. And Jed mentioned on the phone he was bringing another, ah...thirteen, I think. So about eighteen, nineteen. Not to stay here, of course."

Alex smiled and shook his head. "What are you? Moses?"

"Feels more like Father Lehi." Ben sighed.

When Alex raised an eyebrow, Ben continued, "I forgot you haven't read it. *Book of Mormon* story. Really fascinating."

"Right," Alex said a bit sarcastically, ignoring Ben's missionary probe. "I sure hope they make it. I've known people who set out to cross borders who get blown right out of the sky."

"So have I," the bishop said sadly.

Alex chewed his lip and looked out over the men, then said, "I thought that you and the kids, Ben, could have the bed and breakfast. That's four bedrooms, bath and kitchen area. I've got the two cabins and the two trailers. If the rest of the crowd only stays a night or so, it won't draw much attention to the place."

Ben fought back tears and wished he knew for sure if Jed and Jody had been successful at getting the kids. He worried less about the border crossing; Jed was resourceful, if nothing else. "I can't promise they all won't land on your doorstep at the same time," Ben said, "You know, Murphy's Law."

"I'll do what I can to help. It's actually pretty exciting," Alex tried to sound jaunty, "getting in on the Mormon underground."

The three fell silent as another wave of planes thundered overhead. The enormity of the situation hovered over them like a some great bird of prey. The bishop leaned back, looked up at the ceiling and shook his head. Alex gazed through the light snowfall across the river to his home and studio. Ben sat down and looked at his hands.

It was the bishop who finally spoke up. "I think we should have a sacrament service as soon as possible." Since LDS church members had been officially banned from practicing their religion, they met in families of ten at times other than Sunday morning. They still had a bishop and stake president. They just met in secret.

"Hey, you guys, plan on meeting here," Alex joined in. "Just don't make me come, okay?"

Ben and the bishop smiled. "Agreed," they said in unison.

It lifted their spirits to think they could take some positive action that could counteract the evil that had just descended from the sky and landed at St. George International Airport.

Chapter Four

Glorious things of thee are spoken,
Zion, city of our God!
On the Rock of Ages founded,
With salvation's wall surrounded,
Thou may'st smile on all thy foes.
"Glorious Things," John Newton

The 3:00 a.m. call from Ben in Salt Lake thrilled Jed and Jody Rivers. Jed hung up the phone with a thumbs-up signal, "It's a go!" he shouted. "Finally we are on our way to Zion!"

"Utah, not Missouri," Jody cut in, "but beggars can't be choosy right now."

Jed danced around the darkened bedroom in his striped pajamas, bumped into a work boot and kicked it high in the air. "Yahoo!" he shouted. "Yahoo!" The mobile home walls shook.

"Shhh!" Jody wrapped her arm around his neck and tried to cover his mouth to quiet him, but he would have none of it. With one arm he easily pushed her down on the water bed. "Glory to the Lord!" punctuated the early morning air.

Jed was a really unique man. He was both a professional nurse and a modern-day mountain man. He could tenderly care for the children in the critical care unit where he worked, and then disappear for a weekend with just a small backpack and canteen to return with small game, mushrooms, and herbs for the dinner table. Now thirty, he came into the church after a life at sea. That had been followed by a few years as a merchant growing and selling marijuana in the fields around Ukiah, California. Muscular, compact, like a scrunched-up spring, he could take down a man twice his size.

When he met his wife in a laundromat, she agreed to date him if he read the *Book of Mormon*. He put aside his *Bhagavad Gita*, pulled out a beer and began to read. Later that night, drunk, he called her and slurred out, "This book is bloody great!"

It was Ben, though, who taught him the gospel. Ben had only been in the church for several months, but his knowledge of LDS scripture, Buddhism and Taoism were just what Jed needed. When Jed came out of the baptismal waters, he said to Ben, "Hey, man, anything. I owe you my life and my wife! Anything you ask, I'll do it." He slapped Ben on the back and laughed his very raucous laugh. Now Ben had taken him up on that post-baptismal promise.

Picking up Ben's children at Oak Manor Elementary in Ukiah went smoothly. Earlier Ben had given Jody's name as an emergency contact, so there was no fuss when she informed the school secretary that she needed to take the children out of school. "It's their father. There's been an accident."

The high-heeled secretary scurried down the hall and in minutes returned with both children. "These poor children–first their mother, now their father. Tsk, tsk."

No one paid attention to the fact that neither Danny nor his sister, Miriam, knew Jody or that they were reluctant to leave with her. Jody breathed a sigh of relief when they were finally snapped into their seat belts and out over the last speed bump in the school parking lot.

"Is my dad going to die?" asked Danny soberly. He was a ten-year-old towhead who seemed older than his years. He took off his seat belt, moved over next to his sister and protectively put his arm around her.

"Oh, heavens, no," Jody replied guiltily. "He just needs you to come to him in Utah, sweetie. Where did you get that idea?"

"Mrs. Swensen, the school secretary."

"What did she say exactly?"

"She said, 'First your mother, and now your father.'" Danny began to tear up. His lower lip quivered.

Seeing this in the rear view mirror, Jody pulled over to the side of the road, pulled up hard on the hand brake and turned completely around in the seat. "Hey, you guys, your dad is just fine. Really, really. We're just going to go see him, okay?" She reached across the space that divided the seats and wiped a tear from Danny's cheek.

"Are you and my dad friends?" Miriam piped up. She squirmed in her seat and shoved Danny back in the direction he'd come. She was a perky, brown-haired eight-year-old with her dad's startling blue eyes.

"Yes, we're friends, but we're going to see my husband, Jed, who knows him even better," Jody answered. "In fact, your dad baptized him into the church." She noticed that didn't mean much to either child. "I've told your grandparents," she lied, "and they said they were going to send some of your things to Utah."

The children sat quietly in the back seat of the truck and exchanged worried glances. Danny finally broke the silence. "Are you a kidnapper?"

Jody laughed, "No, I'm Jesus' special helper, just like you guys are." Ben told her to use that phrase if she needed to assure the children he was involved. Each week when he called, he'd include talk of God and the church. He called the children Jesus' special helpers to try to keep up their interest in spiritual matters in the godless home they shared with their grandparents.

Both audibly exhaled and sat back against the worn seat amid long, blond dog hair. "That's good. You have a dog?" Miriam asked.

"Used to. He's staying with friends, while we go to Utah." Jody continued to chat with the children until they were actually laughing and telling her jokes by the time they reached the former Ukiah Third Ward parking lot.

Jody had a wonderfully expressive, broad face, which had never seen a touch of make-up. Even at twenty-one, she remained a tomboy, physically and in spirit, long after her friends had developed shapely feminine bodies. "Oh well, I can still play football with the guys and you can't," she told them.

She was ten years younger than Jed but nearly his height at 5'7". The oldest granddaughter of a former mission president, she had rebelled against the strictures of maintaining what she felt was the family religious dynasty. Let her brother be put in that straight-jacket, was her hue and cry in high school. She hung out across the street from the school with the smokers and "druggies," although she never indulged.

Her parents insisted she go to BYU. She failed classes her freshman year, hitchhiked to Texas to see an old boyfriend, and was finally dragged home to spend a summer's penance babysitting younger members of her large family. It was at this juncture that she met Jed, this crazy guy, who had stripped off his khaki work shirt and stained T-shirt and stood half-naked in the middle of the Coin-Op in Ukiah, California, while he washed his clothes, drank a Dr. Pepper and read the Family Circle magazine. They married, he converted, and she found a renewed interest in the faith from her husband's expanded perspective.

They knew they were going to get the call from Ben. No one told them; they just knew it. They were spooky that way. He had quit his job; they had their business dealings all tied up, furniture sold, money converted into black market gold coins. They hoped that this trip to Utah was the first step in a journey that would take them to Jackson County.

Like many young people of their age, both Jed and Jody felt certain they would be involved in the building of Zion, if they were faithful. And like many of their peers, their patriarchal blessings spoke of this promised time. Jody's was very specific: "You will be called upon to help build the temple in Independence, Missouri." Jed's blessing promised him he would raise his children in the millennium. So, unlike the generation that preceded them, they felt hope, not that the world could be fixed by an ecological movement or a dazzling new political leader, but that the whole world would be revolutionized by Latter-day Saints and other outstanding people under the direction of the Lord Himself.

Jody pulled into the largely unused church parking lot; clumps of grass and weeds poked out through cracked pavement in the part of the lot that was still used. The other half, the part that had been chained off, had been completely overrun by ground cover. It made her sad to see the church empty, even though she resisted going in earlier days. "You really don't know what you have until it isn't there any more," she said softly to herself. She looked over the ragtag refugee caravan that had gathered on that grey, drizzling day and wondered if they really could make it past the radar guarding the borders.

Among those waiting for Jody's return was the family of Nate and Laurie Winder. He was a former financial planner with the Bank of America and grandson of a revered general authority who had been a major force in shaping Church policy in his time. Nate carried his dead grandfather's name, only he went by Nate, not Nathan Winder, to avoid the temptation to capitalize on his grandfather's fame. He wanted to make it in church circles on his own merits. He and his wife, Laurie (nee´ Whitmer, an apostle's daughter) were parents to nine children. After the World Bank regulated the U.S. economic scene, Nate found himself out of work. The couple struggled to get by for a while with two low-paying jobs. But nine children made more economic demands than their meager resources would allow, so they decided to go back to Utah and their families, where they could get some financial help. But when they petitioned the government for permission to return to Utah, they were denied access. A copy of their thirty-page request was returned with "insufficient need" stamped brazenly across the front. They were now desperate enough to risk going along with Jed and Jody.

Bobby Whitmer, Laurie's nephew, paced back and forth, impatient for Jody's return. He was a small, thin and handsome young man, who, six months ago, had been sent home from his mission in England. He wasn't alone. When the UWEN outlawed the Church, every missionary was called home, worldwide. He finished out his "tour of duty" with stake missionaries who preached the gospel surreptitiously in Ukiah. When he was released, he too had petitioned to go home, but was denied permission. Now he couldn't wait to get going. He ran and slid barefooted across the wet and slippery parking lot. Bored, he returned to one of the Whitmer cars where he began to tease and harass his younger cousins.

Jody smiled when she saw Peter Butler, a 30-year-old mechanical engineering professor at Cal State Ukiah. She was really fond of him. He was a windsurfing, motorcycle-riding Aussie who had joined the Church during a world-class wind-surfing competition in Hawaii ten years earlier. She had become his friend when he and Jed had worked long hours at their house designing a bogus satellite transmitter for each car in the caravan. It was necessary to have one mounted on any car that crossed a state line. Satellites helped border officials keep track of unauthorized cars. Cars that attempted to breach the borders were blown up by high-flying aircraft.

It didn't take a genius to replicate the device, although Peter definitely fit in that category. He had patented a better solar engine for cars and was "awarded" a substantial sum by the Big Four auto-makers not to market it. He only taught college classes to stay in the country; he didn't need the money. With Jed as an able assistant, these two young sea dogs were now launching into enemy waters with their own version of the DAI (Driver's Authorization Instrument).

Jed rushed up to the driver's side window when Jody and the kids pulled into the parking lot. He was dressed in a black and turquoise-striped shirt, tail out (which made him look like the referee for this occasion), "holy" jeans, and the old-style tennis shoes that one could pump up for cushioning. These had been taped and retaped so many times, no one could tell if he was just wearing taped feet or shoes. "You got the cops on your tail?" he asked.

Jody laughed at the kids, then frowned at him to keep it down. "Boy, are you a kidder, Jed. Honey, this is Danny. Take a bow, Danny. And pretty Miriam. Can you curtsy sitting down?" She laughed along with the kids. Frowning at Jed, she said in a low voice, "I've got them in a good mood. Let's keep it that way. No problems at the school."

"Do you know my dad?" asked Danny earnestly.

"Do I? He baptized me!" Jed replied enthusiastically.

Once again, that answer seemed to make little difference to either child. "Are you going with us to Utah?" Danny continued.

"Am I? I'm leading the band," Jed guffawed. "You guys are going to have a fun time, I promise." He reached into the back seat and tickled Miriam. She squealed. Then he said, "Excuse me, guys, I've got to get this wagon train on the trail," and loped off across the parking lot to the waiting cars.

After some last minute discussion and a group prayer, the Winders, Bobby and Peter turned left out of the parking lot in two older model station wagons and headed for Highway 5 to the Oregon border. They would drive through southern Oregon, down to Winnemucca and Battle Mountain and then take the rarely driven back roads to Utah. Their fervent prayer was for continued dry weather.

Jed drove a maroon-colored mini van with his baby, Craig, in his car seat in the front, followed by Jody in the banged-up Ford truck with the "precious cargo." They headed south to Lake Tahoe. They had planned to cross the border near Topaz, but when they got close, both felt a real uneasiness and decided to keep going south. Outside of Yosemite Park, near Mono Lake, they headed east, crossed the Nevada border without setting off any alarms and crisscrossed their way through the western Nevada desert until both were so tired, and the kids so cranky, that they camped outside of Mina.

They spent the next morning trying to replace a flat tire. (Like many other basic items, tires were scarce and expensive.) Mid-afternoon, they pulled into a campground site near Tonopah, where Jed pulled out his ham radio. In Cedar City, another ham radio operator picked up his message for the Kiwi (Alex's code name) which read: "Cargo loaded, in transit. ETA 2100. Ephraim's seed headed for the promised land."

The Rivers wound their way over bumpy, winding roads down to the interstate highway. Near Hancock Summit, Miriam threw up, quite unexpectedly. Jody did her best to clean up the pasty-faced girl, but the truck reeked. They rolled down the windows, dust poured in. So by the time they reached Ash Springs, thirty minutes later, every one in the van was as sour as the air they were forced to breathe. Danny, in particular, did nothing but complain and when they found the Washing Room, a laundromat in the middle of town, he insisted that his clothes be washed with Miriam's and refused to go in with the others, but sat in the van and sulked, dressed in one of Jed's T-shirts.

Watching the clothes turn around and around in the dryer, Jed and Jody fell into a kind of meditative trance. They sat hand in hand in metal folding chairs pulled next to each other. Slack-jawed, Jed moved his head in a clockwise motion in sync with the dyer. Then Craig bumped his head against the corner of the folding counter and began to cry. After Jody had calmed him with a graham cracker, she checked on Danny in the van. "That boy's driving me crazy," she complained to her husband on her return.

"Oh, he's a good kid," Jed said as he laid new, wet paper towels over Miriam's forehead. She was lying on a bench near the window, grateful for the lack of motion. "This is his way of handling fear. Yeah, I've known kids like that," Jed mused, and before his mind's eye, he saw beds and beds of sick children he had nursed in the last seven years. "Super clean, has to have everything in order. That's all. He's a good little guy!" Jody looked at Jed lovingly. He's such a good dad to Craig, she thought, then quickly caught their 16-month, 32-pound giant baby by the shirttail as he headed out the front door.

No one believed he was less than three years old. The first time the Aussie, Peter Butler, set eyes on him, he exclaimed, "Biggest baby on the planet. What'd you do, cross him with a rhino?" Jody laughed to herself when she remembered the moment.

"Can we please switch cars for a little while?" she pleaded. "The stench alone is making me sick, much less the level of conversation."

Jed swung his son over his shoulder and hung him by his ankles down his back. "Sure. Craig could use some of your tender motherly care. Couldn't you, Tiger?" he asked, reaching back with one hand to tickle Craig, who began to squeal and kick with delight.

After the car had been hosed out, and they had dressed in freshly cleaned clothes, Danny settled down when they had eaten soup and grilled cheese sandwiches in an air-conditioned restaurant nearby. Later, when the sun lay low in the western sky, pink and mauve clouds floated across the horizon like giant popcorn balls, and sheep grazed in speckled white streams, the two cars neared the major Interstate 15.

The highway would take them up through lower Nevada, across the Arizona border for about twenty-five miles, then on into St. George, Utah and Pah Tempe. But the closer they got to the Arizona border, the more uneasy Jed became, and when Jed got antsy, it was always an ominous sign, a sure bet that danger was just around the bend. At least, that's what his UWEN buddies who served with him on the SS *Reagan* would say. They called him "Radar" because he could sense the approach of enemy fighters before the electronic equipment registered an attack forming on the horizon.

"If old Radar starts getting quiet and serious, it's time to put down the cards, rake in the chips and start thinking about battle stations," they used to say.

The couple tried not to keep secrets from each other, so when they made a pit stop in Mesquite, Nevada, just miles from the Arizona border, Jed shared his worry with Jody. "Let's just keep our eyes peeled," he said as he slid under the car to check the DAI.

Still, all seemed normal in that late dusk time when color goes out of everything, like the chiaroscuro in a Rembrandt painting, and when people can't decide whether or not to turn on their headlights. Traffic moved along normally, in both the north and south lanes. But Jed's nerves got tighter and tighter. He chewed his bubble gum so intently that he kept biting into his cheeks.

Then he saw it. An Interpol helicopter headed out across the open countryside, north to St. George. "Something fishy's going on!" Jed exclaimed. "These boys almost never fly out this far into the desert. They're not trained for it." He shook his head and gnawed on the already raw interior of his cheek. "They usually leave that kind of stuff to special chopper units—normally Army," he said. "And when they do get out this far, they just fly the highway, swooping down whenever they feel like it, to stop a car because it's speeding or just plain looks suspicious. Just like fat, greasy hawks." He glanced back at the children who now stared out the side windows with worried looks on their faces. "But this is different, real different," he muttered under his breath. "Something is cooking, and it's happening just down the road!"

With that thought, he abruptly slowed down and pulled off at a dirt road barred by a metal gate. Jody followed suit. Jumping out, he ran around the back of the van, ripped off the wire tied around the gate, waved to Jody to follow him, then sped down the road. Halfway down and around a bend, he stopped. Pulling out his ham radio, he quickly contacted Clinton Rasmussen of the Zion Amateur Radio Club in Cedar City, who had sent the first message to Alex.

Rasmussen was a white-haired, 60-year-old ex-Army officer, who wore a short-cropped beard and perpetually tinted glasses. He'd been housebound now for a couple of years with a bad heart, so he spent a lot of time at his radio, helping when he could. The message he received read, "Yipees partying too close to the edge. Suggest new repair stop for cargo."

Clinton scratched his beard. He knew "the edge" must refer to the state border. That was a pretty good guess. "Yipees," on the other hand, was a little hard for him to decipher. He chewed on a pencil and puzzled over the phrase until after a few moments, he suddenly realized that yipees probably referred to Interpol—I.P.'s to yipees. That was it! Interpol was setting up along the border.

"Now what in the blazes are they doing that for?" Clinton asked aloud. "Them Feds leave border patroling to the National

Guard. Unless...unless...something a dang sight bigger is goin' on, Prince," he confided to an old springer spaniel who was curled up in the corner and lifted an eyebrow at his master's rumbling tones. "I'll be hog-tied if them UWEN boys out there ain't mobilizin' for some blasted reason, right when Alex's friends are tryin' to cross the border."

He slapped his leg and stood up. Prince struggled to his feet and headed to the door, hoping it was time to go out. But just as abruptly as he stood up, Clinton sat down again. Immediately he phoned Alex's cellular phone number. It was dead. He hurriedly looked up the emergency private line; it rang and rang. He was just about to hang up when Peg finally wandered into the office and picked up the phone, more to shut it up than anything.

"Hello?" she asked.

"Is Alex there?" the tense voice asked.

"I don't know. Let me check."

What an uptight guy, Peg thought, walking out onto the deck. She could see Alex in the garden across the river and hollered to him that he had a phone call in the office. He was out the garden gate, down the slope, wading through the thigh-high river and up the other side before she could return to the kitchen.

"Thank you, Peg," he called after her, nearly breathless.

"You're welcome, I think," she said in some dismay as he disappeared into the office, leaving big, sloshy footprints in his wake.

"Hello?" Alex grabbed the receiver off the desk. He sounded curt, trying to catch his breath.

"Hey, boss, Clint here. Cargo having trouble edging into Deseret. Suggest alternative freight route."

Alex thought for a moment, then said, "Barlow trucking in Colorado City does good repairs. Tell them to see Todd at Red Hills Service Station."

After thanking Clint, Alex hung up, leaned over and put his hands on his aching sides. He remained in that position for a few moments, then straightened up, stretched and winced. His years had begun to slow him down, even though he loathed to admit it.

He walked to the windows to watch the gray February day come to a dismal end–a low cloud cover shrouded the sun's demise. Pulling a leather thong from his ponytail, he ran a hand through his thick, silver, shoulder-length mane. "God," he addressed Him reverently, "I sure hope you're watching over your Mormons. Ben's kids don't deserve to die out there."

His mother-in-law, Grace, came to the door of his house, shook out a white tablecloth and disappeared back inside. "She looks pretty good," he continued his conversation with the Lord. "Thanks to you, Sir." Alex turned and walked to the desk, "I was afraid she'd brought the plague with her from New Zealand, but it looks like you've spared us."

Pulmonary Distress Syndrome, PDS, or the "plague" as it was dubbed by international newscasters, was sweeping the globe with alarming and deadly speed. This pandemic was carried by mice who prospered in the lush coastal areas warmed by the waters of the diminishing polar caps. Since she was recovering well, Grace was not likely to be a victim, since death from the killer disease usually occurred within twelve hours.

"I just hope our luck holds out with the kids," Alex said, shutting the office door. He walked in the back door of the bed and breakfast where he protectively checked on Moira who was cooking dinner. He'd find Ben when he could face him, but first he had to think of a way to contact Todd and alert him to the pilgrims' arrival without raising suspicions.

Jed paced back and forth on the dirt road. He was creating a dust canal from scuffing so many times up and down in his tennis shoes. Dirt began to creep higher and higher up his jeans. "Come on, come on, you guys. Quit messing around and give us a call."

"N8JMX, this is N7RKW," cut through the stillpoint.

Jed grabbed the instrument in a death grip, "N7RKW, this is N8JMX, go ahead."

"Kiwi suggests Todd Barlow, Red Hills Service, in Colorado City. He does your kind of repairs."

"Tell the boss the cargo's in good shape. We'll get the sucker repaired and wait for further orders. N7RKW, this is N8JMX. Over and out." (Jed didn't have to say, 'Over and out'–he just liked saying it. It sounded like World War II lingo, and he loved the intrigue.)

Alex called Todd and found him at the motel. "Todd, Alex Dubik, here. How's the hunting?"

"Deer and grouse this time of year, Alex. You comin' down soon?"

"I am, and I'm meeting a very special party who'll probably beat me there, since they're coming from another part of Arizona. The Rivers."

"Don't know 'em, do I?"

"No, but I want you to take care of them and put it on my tab, okay?"

Alex gave him the rest of the details and hung up frustrated he couldn't work in a caution or a message to Todd, but since Todd wasn't picking up on his hints, he didn't want to risk being blunt. U.S. Interfone (the federal telephone system) randomly tapped all conversations. No one knew when it was his turn, but it was well known that at least one conversation a month, sometimes one a week, would be recorded and analyzed by the USI, particularly in areas seized by the UWEN.

After calling Todd, Alex found Ben rearranging border rocks in the driveway that he'd backed over the previous night. *I've got to talk to him about some meaningful work*, Alex chuckled. Walking down the gravel road, his mind flowed back to the day he spent meditating as he sat cross-legged before the famous Zen rock garden in the Ryoanji temple in Kyoto. His meditating skills were good enough by that time that he could tune out the constant stream of tourists (mostly Japanese) and the relentless recorded message that violated the sacred place. Instead, he fixed his consciousness on the mystic beauty of how the monks had so arranged the rocks that their pattern kept shifting before his steady gaze into forms that reflected the landscape of his own soul. *But, looking for satori in the placement of rocks*, he thought, *would never do for this outlaw Mormon-Jewish buddy here, who saw Beethoven in sulfury steam. Nope, I've definitely got to find something else for him to do.*

Ben knew there was trouble the minute he looked up into Alex's face. His stomach clamped into a vise grip."The kids? Is it the kids?" he asked without letting Alex answer the question.

Alex nodded, but quickly said, "It's not that bad. They're having trouble getting into Utah, past the blockade, I guess. I've diverted them to Colorado City to a friend of mine who runs the motel in town. They'll be safe, I promise."

Ben relaxed a bit. It wasn't what Alex said so much as his presence–calm, he radiated a confidence that this situation, or most situations for that matter, could be conquered without due anguish. This was nothing Ben ever experienced as a child. His mother was in and out of mental institutions after his dad's death, and before that, his dad's way of handling pressure was to drink and blame the nearest scapegoat, usually Ben.

Alex affectionately poked Ben in the arm, Ben punched back, then remembered something about Colorado City. "Isn't that a polygamist town? How did you get to know a polygamist, Al? You sure get around the Mormon scene for an old Czech agnostic."

"Used to eat at the restaurant in town there. One day Todd Barlow–nearly everyone there is named Barlow–and I struck up a conversation, and before you knew it we were both talking about grouse hunting, something not many people take as a serious sport," Alex chuckled. "We've been friends since. I go down there hiking and hunting quite a bit."

"They aren't really Mormons, you know," Ben said seriously.

"Oh, yeah? That's funny. He told me the same thing about you guys."

Ben winced.

"Oh, well," Alex went on, "maybe you two can kiss and make up now that your church has been outlawed too."

"Pretty unlikely. Particularly the polygamy part." One man looked at the other and they both laughed. Then Ben said with a gleam in his eye, "Kind of appealing, though, isn't it?"

Alex nodded, then said seriously, "Todd's motel is forty yards from the Utah border. We'll find a way to get them across, don't you worry."

"And Peg? What shall I tell her?"

Both men fell silent.

"The truth," Ben said, answering his own question. "The truth. At least in this case I can tell her what I know."

Chapter Five

Be of good courage now,
Since I have put inside your chest
The strength of your father untremulous;
I have taken away the mist from your eyes,
That before now was there, so that you may
Well recognize the god and the mortal
The Iliad, (5. 124-128)

Jed walked back to the rusted, dust-covered van, opened the glove compartment and began rummaging through it for a map.

"What are you doing, sweetheart?" Jody asked.

"Looking for the western states map. Have you seen it?"

"Unfortunately, I have. I had it out when Miriam threw up. I used it to clean up the mess."

"Great," Jed said in exasperation, throwing down his grey baseball cap on the seat.

"Why?"

"Do you know where Colorado City is?" he said sarcastically.

"No. Don't get snappy with me, honey. We can always get another one at the next rest stop. This is I-15, not a dinky side road."

Jed looked off in the direction of St. George. "I don't want to do that." He turned around, shaded his eyes against the bright red of the setting sun and stared at the old, weather-beaten house 200 yards down the road. "Get in the truck, honey. I'm going to ask the owners of that lovely establishment down there what they know."

They hustled the kids into the van. The two Taylor children who had been playing quietly with pebbles in the road put up no protest; they were very tired. The two vehicles left a train of dust that billowed, then hung motionless in the steely air, as they headed down the long drive. A gnarled, old man sitting on the top step of the worn porch with a shotgun in his lap watched as

Jed jumped out of the van grinning, his hands away from his sides. "We're lost," he said in his best sailor's voice.

"I've been watchin' ya. Whatja need, son?"

"Colorado City. Where in the Sam Hill is Colorado City?"

The old man guffawed. "Boy, you aren't anywhere near there."

"Well, can you tell me how to get there?" Jed asked a bit irritated.

"Have to ask the missus. She got a cousin lives near there," he said as he slowly pushed himself off the step to a standing position, tucked the gun under his arm, and let the screen door slam as he shuffled out of hearing range.

"Can he help us?" Jody leaned out of the truck.

Jed waved at her to put her head back in. "I don't know yet," he half-shouted. His apprehensions about the border were rapidly growing, and he was anxious to get as far away as he could. "Come on, come on, old man," he said under his breath.

A couple of minutes passed. Then the old man slowly made his way to the door, opened the screen and said, "It's too far tonight. Indian country, back roads. The missus says you all better stay here. You can start in the morning."

"Well, I'm not sure. Have to talk to my wife," Jed said as he started down the stairs to the truck, "And thank you, Brother... ah, Mr...I'm sorry. I don't know your name."

The old man's face lit up. "Did you say Brother?"

Jed nodded slowly. He didn't know if that was bad or good.

"You wouldn't happen to be Mormons, would ya?"

Jed stood up taller and said, "Yes, sir, we are."

"Well, so are we. So are we. Welcome," the hump-backed old man said extending his hand, "I'm Nephi Bingham, stake patriarch of the Mesquite Nevada Stake."

Jed felt some of the same shocked delight that the two disciples on the road to Emmaus must have experienced when they learned that the man walking next to them was the Lord. "It's an honor to meet you, Brother Bingham," Jed said motioning to Jody and the kids to get out of the truck.

Jody signaled that she was confused about what was happening, but with Jed's insistent gesturing, she climbed out of the truck, unfastened Craig from his car seat, took him and the now cranky Taylor children up the old worn stairs.

On the porch were two double swings, facing each other on either side of the doorway. The scuff marks on the wood indicated that a lot of swinging had been done over the years. Jody yearned to settle in, rock Craig, and gaze out at the mountains in the distance—snow at the peak—reddening in the last rays of the day. But Jed pulled her and the kids into the house.

"Honey," he said, "This is Brother Bingham. He's the patriarch around here. He and his wife have invited us to stay with them for the night. It turns out Colorado City is too far to reach in a couple of hours."

Jody looked around the room. The maroon wallpaper was dressed with large flowers like she'd seen in old movies in the 1930's and 40's. The arms of the overstuffed furniture were draped with faded, white doilies. A large round rag rug hugged the floor. Two men, dressed in dirty bib overalls and work boots sat on the fireplace lip, near a fire that was just beginning to blaze up.

"Brother and Sister Rivers," Nephi said, "these here are two of my sons, LeGrande and Dee. They work the ranch with me. We just finished for the day, and my wife was sending some cookies home to the grandkids."

Jed nodded to the two men who nodded back. Then he plunged ahead with the conversation, asking Brother Bingham, "If we stay, we want to help out with the chores in the morning. Okay?"

That was fine with Nephi. Jody smiled pleasantly but felt shy about staying with strangers. Just then Sister Bingham emerged from the kitchen with two plates of cookies, each covered with a white cloth napkin. She was plump and wore a cotton print dress with a white collar and a beige full-length apron that was spotted with flour and stains of an unknown origin. She smiled when she saw the knot of pilgrims in the hallway. "Come in. Come in!" she said in a loud welcoming boom. She gestured for Jed and Jody to sit down in the living room with the men. Then she headed for Danny and Miriam with a big smile. "You young ones look like you could use some cookies."

"What kind?" Danny asked suspiciously.

"I don't care, Danny," Miriam whispered in a high irritated voice. "Whatever you have is just fine. Thank you, ma'am," she said looking at Danny with narrowed eyes.

"Oh, yes, thank you, ma'am," Danny hurriedly replied.

The two children followed Ruth Snow Bingham into an old-fashioned kitchen with wooden cabinets, no dishwasher, no garbage disposal, flour and sugar tins gracing the counter. The linoleum floor, green with black specks, had grooves worn in the places where the traffic came and went. The wide-eyed kids peered into the pantry which was stocked with home-canned peaches, beets, carrots, jams and honey. Floor to ceiling, it was crammed with hanging dried herbs, meat jerky, beans, rice, sugar, flour in cans and bottles. Along the top of the kitchen cabinets there was an old tinted bottle collection and twenty or so blue glass insulators used on telephone poles. A bulging recipe box sat in one corner near the sink. The spattered and yellowed 4x6 cards were neatly written in blue in a woman's handwriting.

Ruth pulled out two wooden chairs, padded with rag-rope seats, and placed a plate of oatmeal raisin cookies near Danny and Miriam. She shook the bottle of milk she took from the refrigerator and poured out two glasses for the wide-eyed children. "Do you think this is what a real grandma is like?" Miriam whispered to Danny. "Probably," was his only response as he began making his way through the cookies. "Not like ours."

After a few minutes of small talk, Nephi's sons excused themselves and disappeared out the front door into the twilight. The children finished off the whole plate of cookies and emerged looking very contented. So the stake patriarch pointed up the stairs and said to the couple, "There's plenty of room up there. Take your pick. We raised seven boys in this house, so I'm sure you'll find a bed to lay your head." He looked to Jed. "We go to bed by nine and we're up by five. Does that suit you?"

"Sure," Jed said and thought, *The last time I went to bed at nine was when I was in the Navy.* He carried Craig as they climbed the stairs and found three well-used bedrooms with furniture just as old as that in the living room. They put the three children in a room right across the hall from them, the one with a crib for Craig, leaving the hall light on and promising they'd be right there if needed.

Danny sniffled and complained to Miriam after the light had been turned off. "I heard them say we're going to be in Arizona tomorrow. Let's try to escape and call Grandpa and Grandma. I hate these people. They're probably kidnappers, you know."

That got Miriam going and she cried softly for a while, but Jed wouldn't let Jody go in to comfort them. "Let them be. This is a scary situation and they need to get their feelings out." Bone-tired, the whole crew was asleep in less than ten minutes. It was five o'clock before they knew what had happened.

Walking out to a chicken coop at 5:15 a.m in the Nevada desert on a February morning gave Jed a new appreciation of the words "cold" and "dark." He couldn't believe anyone did this on a regular basis, but after throwing grain to the chickens, searching for eggs in straw boxes and holding the milk bucket for Nephi while he squeezed warm streams of milk from one of the two Bingham milk cows, Jed felt himself come alive. A grey light started to glow over the eastern mountains and Mercury followed the nearly full moon down to China. They finished with the second cow. Jed tried his hand at milking her, but the cow was nervous. It seemed Jed was too jumpy for her, so he turned the chore back over to the patriarch. Neither man had said a word. Nephi finally broke the silence, "Son, it's clear to me that you've found yourself in some trouble." Jed was an easy read.

"Yes, sir, that's true." He was bursting to tell the old man all. "Why don't we take a stroll around the property before breakfast? But first I reckon I'd better take these buckets and eggs to the breakfast chef. She and I have been married fifty-five years next month. The twentieth. She had to wait for me to go on a mission to Hawaii before we could get hitched up. High school sweethearts," Nephi volunteered hoping that Jed would take the personal information as a sign it was safe to open up. They dropped off the warm milk, steam rising from the buckets, and eggs in a wire basket on the kitchen table and began a slow walk around the fenced perimeter of the Bingham property. "Do you own land?" Nephi asked after a few minutes of silence.

"Did. We sold it for the trip out here."

"Did you care for it? I mean care about every rock and blade of grass?"

"Can't say that I did," Jed replied wistfully.

"Well, that's how I feel about this place. It's been mine since my daddy died in the big world war–1942. Yep, he died and left us. Guess I love this place because I miss him. Miss him every day still."

Jed's eyes misted over. He had no such bond with either his father or the land. "I'm sorry," was all he could think to say.

The old man stumbled and Jed reached out to steady him as they climbed a small rise nearly on the other side of the property. "Do sheep always lie down to sleep?" Jed asked a question he'd wanted to know for a long time.

"Only if they want." Nephi chuckled.

The two sat on a couple of large rocks. They could hear the sheep, even the voices from the house as lights went on and people began to rustle around. Suddenly Nephi Bingham, a man most acquainted with scriptures, said, "You know what Elisha said when his servant came running to him to report that the city was surrounded by enemy horses and chariots?"

Jed couldn't remember.

"Second Kings, 6 and 16, 'Fear not: for they that be with us are more than they that be with them.'" Nephi pursed his lips and looked searchingly into Jed's eyes.

Jed felt confused. He didn't know what to say. *What is he getting at?* he asked himself. *I wonder if the old man is a little senile.*

Nephi continued, "'And Elisha prayed to the Lord and asked, 'Lord, I pray thee, open his eyes, that he may see.'"

"Oh, I think this is coming back to me," Jed piped up, like a schoolboy happy that an answer was forming in his mind.

"That's good, son," Nephi said encouragingly. "And what did the young man see?"

Jed was halfway through,"...a mountain full of spirit horses and chariots of fire," when it hit him—what the old man was trying to say. "Oh, I see! You're trying to tell me that me, my wife and the kids—that we're not alone out there in this desert. That the Lord has sent angels to guide and protect us!" And now a line of scripture burst into Jed's consciousness, and he said joyfully, "'And Elisha saw it, and he cried, My father, my father, the chariots of Israel, and the horsemen thereof.'" Jed grabbed the gnarly old man, picked him up and hugged him. "I see what you mean. Oh, that's beautiful, really beautiful." His eyes misted over as he gently set Nephi back down on his rock.

"The translation of Elijah. Second Kings 2:12. Very good, my boy. I take it you believe in help from the other side," Nephi said straightening out his faded overalls, gently amused at Jed's passionate antics.

"I believe that God can do anything He pleases. He's saved my life more times than I care to remember. I've always believed that Bible stories are real."

"Then let me tell you some things about what the Lord has let me see," Nephi said very kindly, patting Jed's broad shoulder. Looking up at the sky gradually changing from dark turquoise to azure blue, the 82-year-old grandfather of 27 grew quiet. "I seen a small band of Latter-day Saints making a semi-circular journey from Salt Lake City to Jackson County, Missouri. It seems they are the first group, the lead group, with apostles—to dedicate the land for the return of the Saints. Not an easy journey, but not the kind our pioneer forefathers imagined either. It'll be done in motor vehicles," Nephi said pointedly. He looked to Jed, who gazed longingly out over the large herd of sheep.

"Behind them," Nephi continued his vision, "come a few men

I understand to be Church record-keepers, carrying the Church's most important accounts, histories, genealogies, the like. They'll be followin' the same route the first group took, and then come the flood of refugees, some on foot and in buses, cars, motorcycles, what have you—not necessarily following that particular route, but flowing in from wherever they can."

A flock of birds pitched and swirled around the open field in front of them, lighting on stubbled ground to feed. Giant sprinklers came to life in an adjacent field. "I have seen the everlastin' hills of Zion, son, I have," Nephi's voice waxed richer and deeper, "and they're as real as them mountains over there. As real as the Rocky Mountains."

Transfixed, Jed was sure that the Spirit was resting on Nephi, whose wrinkled and weathered face seemed on the point of dissolving into light. "The Lord, in His mercy, has let me see the temple there," he said turning to Jed. Nephi now literally glowed in the early morning sun. "It is most glorious. And I have seen the Lord walkin' in the hallways, greetin' Saints in their temple clothes." He paused and looked off to the mountains that bordered his reality.

Caught up in the old man's vision, Jed could imagine walking down the carpeted hall of the beautiful stone structure to the chapel. He'd walk in and sit down with Jody; they'd hold hands, scarcely breathing they would be so excited. Then the Lord would enter, walk over to them, hug first one then the other, then lead them into the depths of the temple.

Nephi's voice floated into Jed's vision. "The city, oh, what a city—big, wide streets, stretched out for miles on the floor of a magnificent valley—homes and trees and land for each man to farm, if he chooses. Everybody busy. Not many white folks though, lots of Mexicans, South Americans, Injuns, even Orientals."

"My blessing says I'll raise my children there," Jed almost whispered. "And my wife's—it says she'll help build the temple."

"My, my, what promises, son. You should be most grateful for those sacred opportunities."

"I am. I really am. In fact I'm on the first leg of that journey right now. I just have to get to Colorado City."

"Even that can be a dangerous trip these days," Nephi said somberly.

"Yes, sir, I know. We were going to cross over into Arizona then Utah on I-15 yesterday, but I had a really bad feeling about it. That's how we ended up on your road."

Nephi sighed, leaned back on both arms and stared up at the sky. Jed looked at him quizzically. Neither man spoke for a time. Then the patriarch said, "You're very wise, young man, to listen to the Spirit. And now listen again, for I saw in a dream last night that you're to take a little-known route across the Arizona border," he said sitting back up. "I'll have LeGrande take you there. From that point on, you'll be able to find your way." He leaned forward and gazed into Jed's eyes, "May I caution you not to try to communicate with anyone until you reach there?"

Jed wouldn't have touched that ham radio now even if it were chocolate ice cream covered with whipped cream, walnuts and a maraschino cherry. No way.

"Have I helped you understand that the Lord is watching over you, Brother Rivers?" the patriarch asked tenderly.

"More than I could ever say. I hope to see you in Zion one day in the very near future."

"Well, it will have to be in the spirit, if we do meet," Nephi said in an even voice."The Lord's let me know I'm to go home to Him real soon."

Jed felt a sob start to rise from his solar plexus. He didn't want to lose this great man almost as soon as he'd found him. He'd known too much of that in battle. Nephi read his thoughts. "I'm sure we'll meet again. You were not directed to me for nothing, you know." He winked, then rocked forward and stood up slowly on the dewy ground. "Let's see what the breakfast chef has scrambled up for us. Whadya say?"

Chapter Six

Everything is miraculous. It is a miracle
That one does not melt in one's bath.
Pablo Picasso

Brigadier General Hazrat Patel, Pakistani commander of the southern Utah invasion force, paced back and forth with a swagger stick under his left arm; his head was wrapped in the red turban of a Moslem sikh. He looked out wearily over the heavily armed troops; he was tired, jet lagged, cranky. He had been pulled out of the Chinese-Afghanistan border conflict to oversee UWEN operations in southern Utah, which he considered to be much beneath him. In fact, he had questioned his orders, something he rarely did. "Why is this so important?" "Economic reasons, Haz," was the reply. He wanted this done quickly so he could get back to a more important front, one where he could count on advancing his career. He did find satisfaction, however, knowing he would be striking a blow for Allah against these filthy infidels, these Mormons who claimed that it was not Mohammed, but some blasphemer named Joseph Smith who was the true prophet of God. "What sacrilege!" he had exclaimed and spat on the ground when he got off the jet and stepped on Utah's soil.

The outlying airport hangar at the St. George International Airport was filled to overflow capacity with rows and rows of soldiers in blue and white uniforms (over 15,000 in all) of every nationality. The UWEN strike force. "Men, we've done this before," he said with just a slight Punjabi accent. "You know the drill." Surveying the gathered strike force, he walked to his left, down the front row of the men, all of whom had been pulled out of hot spots in different parts of the world as he had. "I've heard some of you think that this state isn't like the other ones we've secured. 'The people haven't tried to revolt in Utah,' I've heard.

Well, let me tell you, men," he had reached the end of the row and was returning the other way, "these people in this state, particularly the Mormons, are enemies to our government!"

General Patel stopped again in the middle, turned sharply to his left to face his men and raised his voice even louder, ignoring the young corporal who was desperately trying to keep the roving microphone next to his face. "Why are these people enemies to us? Because they are sneaky and conniving." He paused for effect. "They don't kill our soldiers or blow up our supply warehouses. No-o-o, that's too obvious. They steal our money. Just like the Jews. Do you understand?" he shouted.

"Yes, sir!" came the roar back from the troops.

He started to pace again, swagger stick under his left arm. "We've received reports that Salt Lake City has been secured. There was light resistance at the airport, and again downtown at some kind of a Mormon cathedral, but it didn't last long."

Patel adjusted his red turban at the back of his neck. "We've occupied all radio and television stations. All communications are secured. Everything is going like clockwork. If we can accomplish our objectives here in the next few days, then we can relax our numbers and they'll know we can come back any time we please. Then most of you men can be back fighting a real war."

And I can be getting that second star on my shoulder, he thought.

Patel began his stroll, this time to the right. "We're placing most of you men along the border with the usual infrared equipment and aerial support. We've targeted a triangular traffic corridor between the Arizona and Utah borders to use as an example for these southern insurgents. Any cars with illegal DAI's slipping through the electronic net will not happen."

He paused for effect. "We also know there will be a lot of Mormons trying to get back to their 'promised land' in...where the hell is it, Captain?" He turned and whispered to a young British aide standing nearby.

"I believe it's somewhere in the state of Missouri, sir. A place called Johnson County, if I'm not mistaken," he replied, his eye quickly searching through the briefing notes that he had taken that morning. "...Ah, sorry, sir. Make that 'Jackson County.'"

Patel turned to his troops, "Their promised land in Jackson County, Missouri." He paced back down the tarmac. "Random road-blocks will be posted. Cars with illegal DAI's will be blown up with the occupants inside. No questions asked. Word will spread quickly, I assure you." He grinned again, displaying his gold-capped front teeth. Then he pulled the stick from under his arm and pointed to the assembled men. "We want those illegal DAI's. And to sweeten the pot," Hazrat continued with an artificial gaiety, "$2,000 to any man who can claim such a kill! See your platoon sergeant for details."

"I also have a list here," he pulled several pages from the clipboard on the podium and waved the list high over his head,"which is posted in your barracks—a list of the Utah underground who are fugitives from justice. They are enemies of the UWEN. Consider them armed and dangerous. There is a $5,000 bounty on their heads. Some of you could be wealthier men before this little vacation is over."

Among the several hundred names on the list were Robert L. Olson, Benjamin A. Taylor and Margaret L. Taylor. But the names Alexander S. Dubik and Moira I. Dubik were not on the list, yet.

About eight in the morning, Nephi's son, LeGrande, drove up the long drive in his antiquated Ford pickup, leaving a trail of dust in his wake. Jed and Jody warmly thanked the Bingham's for their hospitality and the huge breakfast they had lingered over.

Nephi put his large, warm hand on each of the children's heads then took Jody's hand between his two and looked her straight in the eye, "You build that temple carefully, you hear?" She blushed and nodded several times. "Good girl," Nephi said. "Good girl."

While Jody put the two kids in the truck and strapped Craig in his car seat, Jed lingered on the porch with the white-haired patriarch and said, "I guess this is goodbye. It's possible we'll get back this way soon."

Nephi nodded and smiled.

"But if we don't get back before the Lord calls for you...,"Jed wiped fresh tears from his face with the back of his hand, "we'll see ya in Zion. Okay?"

"You can count on that, young man," Nephi said in an upbeat voice.

They shook hands vigorously, then Jed turned, bounded down the stairs in one leap and they were off, headed back out to the freeway. He needed to do something active to suppress the pain of separating from his new-found grandfather figure. When they reached the highway they turned left, instead of right, and headed the direction of Las Vegas, then turned off a few miles down the freeway at the exit marked Riverside. They felt "serene and clean," as Jed put it. Ruth Bingham had packed a large lunch and given Danny and Miriam each crayons and paper pads for the trip.

Nephi and LeGrande had decided that the best route was through a church member's ranch that straddled the border. With LeGrande in the lead, they wound down a dirt-packed road for half an hour to a cattle guard. He got out, opened the large metal gate, and then led the little caravan out over what looked like Jeep tracks for nearly five miles, occasionally dodging cattle along the way. The kids loudly complained the ride was too bumpy; they couldn't color.

Then suddenly LeGrande stopped, hopped out and walked back to the van. "See that road over there?" Jed leaned out the window and squinted. He could barely make out the outline of the road. "That's on the map I gave you. We're in Arizona."

Jed hollered to Jody who whooped and jumped out of the car. "How'd you get across without problems?" she asked innocently, as she ran up to the van.

"Just the way you did," LeGrande raised his eyebrows then winked. "Just the way you did."

Jody's jaw dropped. She couldn't imagine this taciturn sheep rancher with an illegal device of any kind, much less something as dangerous as a DAI. *Boy, am I a poor judge of character*, she thought as she climbed back up into the cab.

"What's happening?" Danny wanted to know.

"We're in Arizona."

Danny looked knowingly at Miriam who couldn't think what he was trying to convey. She had forgotten that in Danny's mind Arizona was where the kidnapper's hideout was. Besides, she was content to make this journey which she had been told would only last a few hours. Then she'd be with her daddy.

She felt safe with him—the weekly phone calls and visits from Utah all throughout her childhood, special summers at the beach. Although they had never been granted permission to visit Salt Lake City, these memories of her dad surrounded her, reminded her of his warm, predictable presence. Besides, Daddy could make her laugh more than anyone could—especially with his stories about Freddie the Fox, a fictitious character who lived in the wilds between Utah and California and whose lair Daddy visited each month on his way to Ukiah. Yes, with Daddy she always felt safe.

As they drove across the no-man's land of the northern Arizona desert—a land of flat, dry brush and mesas that looked like long banquet tables covered with flowing red tablecloths—Jed wondered what it was like to be in the cavalry riding down these valleys, knowing they were being watched by wary Indian warriors. It gave him the shivers. Jody felt like she could see into tomorrow, maybe into the millennium, there were so many uninterrupted open vistas. Everyone felt rested and filled, body and soul. Right before lunch they drove into Colorado City from the south. It was a small, simple town with broad streets, old trees—shades of an early 20th century ranching community. The Vermillion Cliffs behind the town hovered like giant red crystal guardians on the planet Krypton.

They were relieved to find Todd Barlow at the service station just as Alex had said. Joking with the children, he escorted the party to the motel, checked them in and said he understood Alex

Dubik was joining them for a little hunting. Jed looked at him quizzically, but said nothing. As he walked back to the service station, Todd wondered why they would bring children along on a hunting party. *Maybe to tire the grouse*, he laughed.

Later in the day a worried Alex risked calling Todd again, "Have my people arrived?"

"Yup. When are you comin' down?"

"Tonight, late." Pause. "Todd?"

"Yes?" Todd was a little distracted as he shuffled through paper work on the motel desk. He was trying to get a deposit to the bank before it closed.

"Todd, I need a favor."

"Shoot."

"Funny you should say that."

"Why?"

"That's what I'm trying to prevent from happening.

"Huh?" Todd put down the bank receipts he was looking through. *I thought Alex was coming here to shoot. What's he driving at?*

Alex lowered his voice and quickly said, "Todd, I'm going to try to talk to you about a situation that's a little touchy. Kind of thing that's a little tough to do on the phone. Savvy, Amigo?"

Todd's heart skipped a beat. This time he knew at once that Alex was "clipping"–a term that everyone used to refer to camouflaging sensitive information during a phone conversation that could be monitored. Some were better at clipping than others. Todd and Alex were masters. He connected what Alex was saying to a conversation he had just had with a cousin who told him about UWEN troops massing at the border. Some were seen in Hildale.

"You with me, Todd?"

"Uh, huh, sure. I'm onto the topic. Go ahead."

"My guests need your help."

"I understand."

Alex breathed a sigh of relief. *Finally, Todd's picked up on my clipping. Maybe we'll get this right.* "When I arrive there, I'd like a little diversion, say, ah, something smashing."

Todd thought for a moment. "I've got just the ticket. We're having a house warming down the street from the motel, probably about the time you arrive. Want to come?"

"Sounds fun. See you about eleven when I get off work. Let my party know, will you?"

Todd knew immediately that "a little diversion" meant something to draw the UWEN guards' attention away for a few minutes. His thoughts went to his cousin's old house down on Cedar. It was due for demolition next week. *I think we ought to speed up the process*, he thought and grinned broadly as he slipped out the side door and headed for the bank.

Moira's mother, Grace, was sitting in the living room sipping chamomile tea when Alex came back from the phone call with Todd. Just one lamp shone—the one she was using to sew a white-sheeted doll for a granddaughter in Rotorua. Alex flipped on the recessed ceiling lights, walked across the living room, and asked, "Where's Iwi, Grace?"

"Upstairs, I believe, son." Grace looked rested with more color in her cheeks. Her grey hair wound around her head in a bun, helping her look like the archetypal grandmother. She stood to stretch and rotate her head around on her neck. Her height always surprised Alex—she was nearly 5'8" with such long legs that her school chums had called her "Moa" (an ostrich-like New Zealand bird, now extinct). "Shall I look for her?" she asked.

"No, I will," Alex answered tenderly. His family had become more precious than ever in the last two days, since Ben's plight had begun.

Moira lay on their king-sized bed with her eyes closed. She looked pale with dark circles under her eyes. He sat down on the bed gently and stroked her cheek. She wasn't sleeping.

"Hi, you," she said lovingly. "Where have you been?"

"Making arrangements to pick up Ben's kids."

"Oh, why?" she struggled to sit up.

"Because they couldn't get across the border. I'm going down to Hildale later on to get them."

Moira frowned. "It's not going to be dangerous, is it?"

"Nope, Todd Barlow is helping out. Piece of cake."

Moira now had swung her legs over the side of the bed and slipped into a blue Japanese kimono, tying a red sash around her bulging waist.

"I want to ask Mother."

She was halfway down the hall before Alex could ask, "What are you going to ask your mother?"

"About the kids."

"She doesn't know anything about them, Iwi."

Moira was now down the stairs and headed for the couch.

"Okay," Alex said hesitantly. *This should be really good*, he thought.

Moira smiled and slid across the beige couch to give her mother a hug. Alex went to the fireplace to coax a brighter fire. He then sat down on a brown leather ottoman nearby.

"How are you doing, Mom?" Alex asked solicitously. "How's that flu?"

"Much, much better," she said smiling. "You're going for those babies, aren't you, son?"

Did she hear us? Alex wondered. "Yes, I am.

"It won't be as easy as you think, but everything will be okay. Just don't trust anyone. Rely on your own intuition," she said with a firm finality to her voice.

"Can you be a little bit more specific?" He tried to sound like he trusted what she was saying.

"When you arrive at the town, there will be soldiers that you didn't expect. Your friend will try to help you, but in the end you will have to use your own wits to get the children out. I see a big explosion and a fire and a flood."

Apocalyptic fantasy, Alex thought. *Runs in the family.*

"Will anyone get hurt?" Moira jumped in.

Grace sat back, closed her eyes for nearly twenty seconds, then said, "Yes, two soldiers—one will die of burns, the other will have a very bad broken leg."

Alex's jaw dropped. He didn't know what to say. After their marriage, he and Moira had spent only a few weeks in New Zealand before moving to the States—certainly not long enough for Alex to get to know his mother-in-law very well. He could always kid Moira about her hunches, but Grace's "seeing" was way beyond a hunch.

"Has she always been this way?" he half-whispered to Moira.

"Yes. And her mother before her. She told me I've wasted my talents by being in the cities so much."

"I'm astounded. Will it happen...I mean, just like she said?" Alex asked hesitatingly, almost afraid to get the answer he knew would follow.

"Virtually every time." Moira put her head on her mother's shoulder. *"What about Alex? Will he be okay?"* Moira asked in Maori.

"What was that?" Alex asked, eager to catch every bit of this strange conversation.

"Oh, sorry, sweetheart, I asked her about the children," Moira lied.

The two women exchanged knowing glances. Grace quickly nodded her head to indicate nothing would happen to Alex. Moira let out a sigh of relief.

Alex marveled that Moira could fall so easily into another language. She never displayed a hint of anything other than a strong New Zealand accent. But then she had been instrumental in a renaissance to restore the Maori language and customs to her people, he reminded himself. In fact, she was a great proponent of language nests where Maori children were immersed in the language all day, every day.

"That is really spooky, Grace," Alex said.

Grace smiled a knowing little grin.

"You think that's weird?" Moira retorted. "You know my brother, Tom, the one that lives in Rotorua?"

"Yeah."

"Well, Mom called him to her home one day and told him a

daughter was coming to him and his wife, Leslie."

"Do you remember that, Mom?"

Grace's face lit up.

"Well, Tom was delighted," Moira continued, "since they had been married ten years and were childless. Because both of their patriarchal blessings said they would be parents to many, they were sure that Leslie would get pregnant sooner or later."

Alex stood up and moved back to the fireplace. He was wearing a tan suede cowboy shirt complete with long tassels. With one arm resting on the mantle, his mouth slightly open and his brows furrowed, he looked like a young boy waiting for the monster to appear in a horror movie.

"A couple of days later, my sister called them and said she learned there was a baby available for adoption. Were they interested? Normally they would have said no, but since Mom had talked to Tom, they agreed to at least look at the baby girl."

Clearing his throat, Alex shifted his position and asked, "How long ago was this?"

"Ten years or so. Anyway they drove down to Auckland, sure they weren't interested. My sister had picked up the baby from the adoption agency and had her at her house. They're a lot more casual about the adoption process than we are," Moira explained. "While Leslie talked to my sister, Tom sauntered down the hall to a back bedroom. He opened the door, walked across the room to the bassinet where a tiny, two-month-old girl lay. She was part Maori, part *pakeha*."

"*Pakeha?*"

"Sorry–white. Anyway, when he leaned over to pick her up, she said, 'I'm glad you've come.'"

"What?" Alex blurted out. "What did you say? A two-month-old baby said what?"

"I'm glad you've come."

The hair stood up on Alex's arms. "Did you get her to talk, Mom?" Alex asked with quavering voice.

"Me? Oh, heavens, no," Grace laughed, her flashing eyes moving from Moira to Alex. "I assume the Holy Spirit did."

After a brief silence, Alex said, "You're absolutely sure? Tom wouldn't make up a story like that, would he?"

Moira moved over to Alex and hooked her arm through his."No way. Hey, that kind of thing happens a lot. I could tell you stories about animals talking."

"No-o-o, thanks." Alex gently removed her arm and stepped a couple of feet from her. "So did they decide to take her?" Alex asked, dumbfounded.

"Of course. That's Katy, their ten-year-old," Moira replied matter-of-factly. "You remember. You met her at the wedding. The cute one with great big brown eyes."

All Alex could do was shake his head, from side to side, and make a kind of "uh, uh, uh" in his throat. He looked out the west windows at a sky growing dark. The three grew quiet as the house filled with late afternoon shadows. Grace sat with her eyes closed, hands folded in her lap.

Moira moved back to her mother and laid her head down on Grace's shoulder, *"Ka pehea tera atu ropu? (What about the other party?)"* Grace fell quiet. Her eyes moved back and forth under her eyelids as if viewing an inner screen. Then she startled the couple by abruptly sitting up and saying, "Those other people from California, not the ones with Ben's children, but the other ones–they will be here soon." Her countenance shifted almost imperceptibly into a frown. "Only some of the people will decide not to come here, but to go to Salt Lake City."

"Really? Who, Mother?" Moira said, surprised.

"As I sat here, I saw, in my mind's eye, two cars out in the desert. People arguing, slamming doors. A woman is driving the car to Salt Lake City. She shouldn't–she'll put everyone in grave danger. An angry man, possibly her husband, is driving a car here with four others."

Alex reached out and took Grace's empty cup off the coffee table. He walked into the kitchen area and numbly laid the cup down on the brick-colored tile counter top. He found he was unconsciously hugging the kitchen cabinets with his body, trying to create a protective barrier between these women of his and himself. He'd experienced some interesting phenomena when meditating, but his mother-in-law was off the graph.

"Bye, ladies. Have fun," Alex said, threw up his hands and laughed. Excusing himself, he walked out into the chilly dusk. Behind him he could hear the women speaking intimately in Maori.

Back in the studio, his eye fell on two sculptures of crucified men he had been working on. He wondered what Ben would make of them. He lingered in the dusk-lit work space for a while, cleaning up a little, pushing and poking at one statue in process. Alex kept turning over in his mind what had happened in the last breathtaking 24-hour period. He needed some quiet to digest what his mother-in-law just told him. He couldn't quite get a fix on it all. *I'll just go with the flow a little farther,* he concluded as he wandered into a small meditation alcove off to the left of the work area. There he changed into black cotton pants and shirt, lit some patchouli incense, and pulled up his round black meditation pillow. He had three hours before leaving. He wanted to make sure his mind was razor sharp.

Chapter Seven

Be ashamed to die until
You have won some victory
For humanity.
                    Horace Mann

About 9:45 that night, after hours of kneeling on his black pillow and meditating, Alex sat back, moved his numb legs around to the front, and began to massage them. As the blood began to flow, he felt peaceful and clear. Dinner had long passed, but he didn't feel like eating. He had given a lot of thought about how to approach Ben and Peg about what he planned to do. For he had thrown down a gauntlet and was marshaling his inner forces to confront a faceless enemy who, in azure blue and white uniform, was even now patrolling an electronic border in this long, deep desert night.

After all's said and done, this is for the children, he thought. *It's about saving my son and my friend's children. I've got my dogs. I've got my guns. And I darn well know when to stay and when to fly. I could take care of Moira and me. But that's not enough anymore. There has to be a world for kids.* His heart swelled with emotion.

Alex slipped into his black jacket and shoved a black stocking cap into his pocket. Although he whistled for Angelina, both dogs came running out from under the studio. "No, Renoir, stay," he said firmly. She whined but disappeared back the way she came. The Doberman jumped into the Jeep Wagoneer through the driver's side and sat down obediently on the back seat. "Good girl. Stay," he said as he turned to the house to tell his wife goodbye.

Grace was reading under the lamp on the couch. She put her finger to her lips to say, "Moira's gone to sleep." She watched worry cross his face, even though she had said nothing about Moira's cramping and spotting. *His plate is full enough,* she thought. *I'll tell him later.*

He tiptoed up to their bedroom and slowly pushed open the door, letting the light from the hall fall across her sleeping face. *She looks like Athena asleep in the moonlight, or better yet a Polynesian Botticelli,* he thought. He wanted to wake her, take her in his arms and tell her how much he loved her, but her labored breathing restrained him.

When Alex came back downstairs with the worry lines still on his face, Grace insisted that they kneel and pray. She struggled a bit as she held on to the couch on her way down. "Trick knee," she mumbled. Then she began praying in her deep throaty way, and he felt embarrassment melt into gratitude, as she petitioned God for his safety. *Certainly something my tight and timid mother would never have done,* he thought.

"*Kia kaha,* son, stay strong," she said squeezing his arm as they stood in the doorway and he turned to leave.

"Don't worry, Mom. I will."

Ben looked up from the book he was reading to see car lights move down the road across the river and realized the time had come. As Alex made his way across the bridge, Ben put on his coat, slipped out Miriam's bedroom door and walked briskly down to the gate to meet the car. Peg, who was washing dishes from dinner, missed seeing the Jeep Wagoneer.

"I'm going by myself," Alex said firmly, when Ben walked up to the side of the car. "Don't argue with me about this, Ben. You'll only slow me down, old buddy--maybe put us all in danger. You're in no shape for this kind of operation."

Alex climbed out of the car and stood facing his long-time friend. Ben opened, then shut his mouth. "I know where they are and how to get them out." Alex said firmly. "Besides I already have a sidekick." He pointed to Angelina who sat proudly in the back seat.

Ben started to protest again. "Look, chubby," Alex said, patting Ben's stomach as he tried to defuse Ben's anxiety about his children, "that gut of yours is meant to polish library tables, but not bounce across borders!"

Realizing he was right, Ben looked down at the gravel for a long moment, wiped some suspicious moisture from the corner of his eye, then looked up at his friend and said, "What's the plan, Al?"

"It's an hour drive down to Hildale, which is this side of the Utah/Arizona border. It's a twin city of Colorado City. They share a post office, utilities, that kind of thing. From there I'll call and get the final instructions from my polygamist buddy, Todd." Ben nodded and bit his lip. He felt like he wanted to ask Alex another question, keep him there longer, but nothing would form in his mind.

"Hey, Ben," Alex said in that deep warm voice that Ben remembered from their college days, "It's me. Remember. Uncle Al. I'll take care of it, *compadre*." He squeezed Ben's shoulder, then turned, walked to the car. As he rolled up the window, he called out, "Trust Jesus," put the car in reverse and did a tight 180 degree turn. Finally he flashed Ben a peace sign before disappearing up the hill and into the night. Ben stood a long time in the driveway, in prayer. He waited until he felt peaceful enough to go back inside to tell Peg what was happening.

The full moon was just a glow below the eastern mountains; Alex wished it weren't. All he could hope for was cloud cover. A full moon could only make things worse. The trip took longer than he had anticipated. The highway was slippery from rains, turning to black ice in patches. By the time he pulled into Hildale it was 11:30. He was a half hour late. He found a pay phone in the parking lot of the local service station and called the Copper Cliffs Motel. The phone rang and rang. Finally someone answered with *"Hola. ¿Digame?"*

"Where's Todd?" Alex snapped.

"¿Como?"

"¿Donde esta´ Todd?" He remembered a little of his fractured Spanish.

"No esta´ aqui, señor."

"I *know* he's not there!" *Dammit,* Alex grumbled to himself then added, "Where has he gone?" he asked slowly, with exaggerated emphasis on each word in irritated English.

"¿Como?"

"Oh, great," he said in disgust. "Well, tell him Alex called." He hung up, mad at himself for being so late. As he walked back to the Jeep Wagoneer, a white van emblazoned with UWEN insignia drove slowly by. Alex froze, his hand on the door handle. "Great! Interpol," he muttered. "What else can go wrong?" He pretended to fumble with his keys. The van slowed to a crawl; the men inside appeared to try to match Alex's face with a photofile they had, then speeded up. Alex let out his breath slowly and struggled to stay centered. Then he tried calling the motel again. *Ring, ring, ring*–same story only when the man answered, this time Alex asked for Señor Rivers.

"Señor Rivers. No lo conozco."

"Don't tell me that," Alex said angrily. "He's staying there."

"No comprendo."

Alex tried to think in Spanish, but he was mad and scared, *"El señor es con niños en el motel,"* was the best he could do. Veins pulsed in his temples. He heard the man on the other end put down the receiver and walk off. Alex didn't know whether he should hang up or not. Tapping his finger on the coin box of the pay phone, he decided to count to one hundred, then hang up. He had reached 94, when he heard what he assumed to be Jed's voice on the line.

"Hey, what's up, dude? We've been waiting for you. The kids are really excited," Jed said trying to sound fairly calm, but Alex could hear the fear in his voice.

"I'll bet they are. Glad you guys got there okay. What's the plan?"

"Ah, Todd couldn't wait. He's gone down to his cousin's house. They're planning to raise the roof tonight."

"Sounds fun." In this clipped code, Alex let Jed know that he needed Jed and the family to be stationed at the back exit of the motel in fifteen minutes, sharp.

Alex returned to the Jeep Wagoneer for Angelina and walked, as casually as he could, the two blocks to Todd's cousin's house which was an unoccupied, dilapidated house that had sat empty for several years after a hundred years of use. It wouldn't be long now before it would be blown sky high.

"This should keep the UWEN boys hoppin' for a few minutes," Jed muttered as he reached the corner where the house stood. Jed and Todd talked briefly on the porch. Anyone watching would not have suspected the two men who appeared to be passing the time of day. The message Jed conveyed to Todd was that he and his family would be making a dash for the border in a few minutes.

As Jed walked back to the motel, he thought how he really enjoyed the rush, then the calm that flooded him in any kind of battle situation. The last time he had experienced this addictive mixture of fear and exhilaration ("sweet and sour pork," he called it) was when he was stationed on the UWEN battleship, *Reagan*, during an especially nasty tangle with the Chinese battleship, *Mao*, in the South China Sea. If it had not been for Jody and the kids, he might have given in to the charge he got out of danger. But it didn't seem right to do that now, not with a woman and babies relying on him.

Back in their motel room, he found Jody reading, the kids asleep. He put his finger to his lips and pulled her out into the hall. "Ten minutes. We've got to be at the back door, ready to run in ten minutes."

Jody nodded. She was scared but calm. "What about the cars?"

"I've left the keys with Todd. They'll be okay."

They waited five minutes, then woke the kids, sent them to the bathroom, told them there was to be a fire drill (Danny looked skeptical), slipped them into street clothes and shoes and headed down the hall to the exit door.

Alex parked the Jeep Wagoneer as near to the Utah border side as he dared–in a grocery store parking lot–and walked with Angelina at his heel down the street, trying to act as nonchalant as possible.

He couldn't see the patrol from where he was, so he decided to risk cutting through an alley to State Street. From there he could survey the main border checkpoint between the two towns. Two UWEN vans sat parked near the border guard building. He counted three men in riot gear with their backs to him, talking and laughing.

"If that is all there are, it doesn't look too bad," he whispered to the Dobie.

Just then a short, dark guard turned around and Alex's heart stopped. The soldier had infrared night goggles pulled back, resting on top of his head. *This is no ordinary patrol--these guys are serious.*

Alex forced himself to stop breathing to see if he could tune into what the men were saying, but they were too far away. *And where are the rest of the men?* Alex asked himself. *If there are two vans, ten men to a truck, that probably means at least fifteen men moving up and down the border right now.*

"It doesn't look good," he said to Angelina, who whined back. Alex also knew the soldiers would have aerial backup. Besides the moon had become a factor. It had risen above the mountains, washing the town in stark streaks.

Alex turned, started back down the alley and said aloud, "Forty yards, dammit. That's all we have to go. Not even a half of a football field!" He took several deep breaths and centered himself, then patted the shoulder holster where his .45 lay waiting. "Come on, gal. Let's see what we can see," he said to the tense Doberman.

When he returned to his car, he stood and stared at the back of the motel, trying to put together a plan. The motel door opened; Jed peered out, looked around and ducked back inside. Alex now paced back and forth, then he stopped. He saw something he hadn't noticed before. Moonlight bounced off some source of water in the field halfway to the motel. He walked closer to the border, peered out from some trees and saw the outline of an irrigation canal. It looked like a pretty deep one from where he stood.

Up about ten yards and to the right, Alex thought he could

see sluice gates, at least he could make out the head gate that regulated the water flow. He glanced down at his watch. It had been nearly fifteen minutes. *What is happening with Todd?*

No sooner had the thought run through his mind, when a thunderous blast shook both towns. An orange fireball rose above the trees and Alex dashed like a runner out of the blocks across the border–Angelina at his side–to that head gate. When he got there, he ducked down and turned (whirled, would be a better word) the "steering wheel." The gate dropped too slowly for Alex.

"Please, God, keep the luck going," he whispered, then jumped into the watery concrete ditch. The water was draining, but was still up to his thighs. Angelina paced back and forth on the bank trying to decide what to do. Then she barked, just once, but that was all it took to turn the attention of a couple of border guards to the field.

Alex grabbed her collar and pulled her in. He couldn't tell from his crouched position if anyone had heard her. The water was receding, so he made pretty good time back to the middle of the field in spite of the occasional slippery moss he waded through. He stopped, held his breath, then popped his head up to see where he was in relation to the motel door. He was well-lined up, but the door was closed. He looked back over his shoulder, but he couldn't see troops, only the orange glow from the blaze. He grabbed Angelina and put his face right next to hers, "Gal, see that door?" She looked in the direction he was pointing. "Go to that door." He shoved her up over the top. She leaped out of the six foot high ditch and streaked to the door.

Just then Jed opened the door and saw the dog charging across the field. Thinking it was a police dog, he quickly slammed the door, but when Angelina got there, she whined and scratched at the metallic door, so that Jed slowly opened it a crack. As he did, she sat down and extended a paw.

"It's okay," he hissed back over his shoulder, "must be Alex's dog. Let's go." Jody heaved Craig on her back, along with the ever-present diaper bag filled with cloth diapers (plastic ones were a thing of the past). He had been sleeping, but was now half-awake, trying to decide whether to cry. Jed took the hand of each of Ben's kids, who had been sitting in the hall, half asleep, and said,"We've got to run a short distance. Do you want to run or do you want me to carry you?" Danny said he'd run. Miriam wanted to be carried.

"On the count of three." Jed held up his right index finger. "One... two...three...." Out the red metal door, scrambling across the moon-streaked field, they looked like German Jews fleeing Nazi pursuers. They nearly made the ditch when shouts, then shots rang out.

Jed shoved Jody ahead of him the last three feet, and she jumped into the ditch along with Craig. Alex helped break her fall. Craig began to cry. Jody put her hand over his mouth. Angelina was next. Then Jed literally tossed Miriam to Alex and fell to the ground, just as a bullet whipped by his ear like some crazy, kamikaze mosquito. More shots were fired. He covered Danny with his right arm. Then more shots–these closer–and voices on the run. They could hear one soldier calling for aerial backup on a portable telephone. Jed and Danny crawled as fast as they could and dropped down into the dirty water. It was now only ankle deep.

The group began running and slipping down the ditch, when they heard behind them the voices of the soldiers, struggling to reopen the head gate to let back in the water. Jed and Alex exchanged a quick glance. They both knew that the canal could fill back up again in seconds. They would drown if they didn't act quickly. A few yards farther down the ditch, they came to the place where the canal branched off both left and right. They turned left. Up ahead lay another valve. Suddenly a possible plan popped into Alex's mind. He motioned to everyone to stop. He pointed to the gate which was in an up position, gesturing they should duck through it.

They quickly slid through the narrow opening. Alex had to force Angelina through. Then he and Jed jumped up, released the door and dropped down the other side. Alex whipped out his .45

and waved to the rest of the group indicating they should run. But suddenly he changed his mind, stood up and put out his hand to stop them. He signaled they should come closer.

"Take off some clothing. I want to make it look like we've drowned," he whispered loudly. He pulled Miriam to him. "Honey, could I have your shoes? They're real important."

"Okay," said the wide-eyed girl who took them off obediently.

Then he gestured to Danny to come to him. "Can I have that vest?"

"Why?" Danny asked nervously.

"Because I want the bad guys to see it and think we've drowned."

Danny quickly took it off and handed it proudly to Alex. Alex gathered a coat, shoes, diaper, vest, shirt and his black knitted cap, then gestured to them to run. He took off his own shirt, slipped back into his coat and tossed the clothes, one at a time, over the top of the canal and down into the swirling waters which were backing up on the other side of the metal gate. He then turned and ran, sloshing through the muddy, ankle-deep irrigation water. For a time he ran forward, then turned backward, .45 in hand, trying to see who might be in pursuit. Angelina stayed close beside her master. Suddenly he slipped on a mossy patch and fell. Pain shot through his left arm. He grabbed it and rubbed it as he fought to regain his footing. "Damn, I'm really getting too old for this," he said in a low voice to Angelina.

Up ahead a stand of trees hung over the water's edge. Jed and the group were no more than three yards from it when one of the soldiers cracked off a few rounds, rapid fire. Alex slowed down, trying to figure where the shots were coming from. He gestured to the rest to get out, run into the trees, and hide. Jed shoved everyone up the side of the ditch. Craig was last. When Jed took his hand off the baby's mouth, he started to cry. Jed handed him to Jody, pulled a handkerchief from his pocket and stuffed it carefully in Craig's mouth. Then he slipped the belt from around his blue jeans and strapped the baby's arms to his sides. Craig struggled and agonized, but the homemade straight jacket held. Jed then looked to Alex for instructions. Alex waved him on, so he jumped out, ran through the trees to where the group was hiding, flopped down on his belly and lay there panting.

Alex crouched down, the .45 nestled snugly up against the fatty flesh under his thumb, his ring finger just brushing the trigger guard. The soldiers came into view, clearly visible with their white metallic helmets glinting in the moonlight. All I need is a bull's eye painted on each of those shiny suckers, Alex thought wryly. It seemed the guards had been shooting at the clothing that had floated down and was nearing the intersection of the canal.

"Hey, I've got something," the one with a Japanese accent shouted. He fished out Alex's black tai chi shirt. "Here's a baby diaper...and a kid's shoe. Sure looks like we might have drowned them," the other, who sounded like a Swede, said. "If not, the choppers will find them." They paused to look up at the moonlight sky. "Hey, did you hear about Jones, the Welshman?" the Swede asked, "Heard he bought it in the explosion."

"No! How?"

"He was standing out in front when the place went. And that Peruvian, Suarez, he's been medivacked out. Got his leg pretty busted up in the blast."

Alex checked a gasp. *That's just what Grace said would happen!*

"Glad I was eating dinner. Hey, I've got to find those goggles, Toshi," the Swede said running his boot along the bank of the canal. "If I don't, I'm gonna get mega-coins docked from my pay. I know they didn't drop in the water."

The two fished out Danny's vest and the black cap, then turned and walked cautiously back down the canal, guns poised, while they looked for the goggles which had fallen off in the run across the field. "Not worth lookin' any further," Toshi murmured. "They're dead. Drowned." His voice faded as they headed back to town, disappearing and reappearing in the light and shadow show the moon provided.

Alex sat in a crouched position, trying not to breathe too hard. Angelina stood poised for combat. When the voices receded back down the field, Alex sighed in relief, turned, ran the rest of the way to the trees and rejoined the knot of pilgrims."We have only minutes before the choppers get here," he said. He and Jed conferred. They decided Alex and Angelina would go for the car. The rest would wait, then make a break for the parking lot several yards away.

The escapees waited in the shadows, shivering now, muddy, without all their clothes, while Alex sprinted to the Jeep Wagoneer. When he brought the car to an abrupt halt, they dashed across the open field, climbed in and quickly lay down on the back seats, concealing themselves with Indian blankets that Alex had pulled from behind the rear seat.

"Hey, that was fun!" Danny said, sounding braver than he felt.

"Shhhh, Danny," Jody said, "We're not quite done." Jed said and pulled the boy to him. He leaned down and whispered, "You did a good job, pro." Danny beamed.

Jody pointed to Craig, who still had the handkerchief in his mouth, looking bleary-eyed, but still awake from all the nervous tension in the car. With efficient nurse moves, Jed surgically removed the wadded-up cloth and belt. Craig watched him with a look that he would never forgive his father. Then the newly-released jailbird crawled into Jody's arms and was asleep in moments. She carefully laid him on the floor on a quilt. Then the couple snuggled up to each other; Jody shivered in Jed's arms from a combination of fear and cold.

Angelina sat in a queenly posture in the front seat next to Alex. He patted her on the head and said, "Good girl," then headed the Jeep Wagoneer north out of town at exactly the correct speed, which required much restraint on his part.

Five miles up the road, the choppers suddenly appeared over the horizon. Jody gasped and clung tighter to Jed. Alex managed to maintain the speed he was traveling. Swinging back and forth down the road, the helicopters turned on their brilliant white spotlights and sweeping the area in wide arcs. First hovering over buildings and barns, they then descended on the highway. When they came up on a car on the road, they hovered a couple of hundred feet above, close enough for a passenger to look up and see a UWEN soldier peering at him through a telescopic lens.

Angelina looked up and barked at the light which flooded the van, but Alex continued focusing straight ahead at the broken white dividing line on the highway that kept emerging from the blackness and slipping under the car.

After twenty seconds, the choppers suddenly jerked back, and the leering face suddenly recoiled into the darkness, like a bungee jumper on his way back up to the bridge. As the choppers peeled away and headed for another car, Alex smiled, loosened his sweaty grip on the steering wheel, gently grabbed Angelina's neck in the crook of his right arm, and gave her a kiss. "We did it, girl!" he exulted. Her tail joyously whacked against the front seat upholstery.

"Okay, you guys, you can get up," Alex crowed. "They didn't find us very interesting. Personally, I'm a little insulted," he joked.

Jed and Jody popped up laughing, but the kids, dead tired, had fallen asleep. The adults laughed and congratulated each other, and Jed must have crowed, "Praise the Lord" at least twenty times until he got hoarse. Finally he woke up Danny, who wanted to go over the scene again and again on the way back to Pah Tempe. Finally the boy laid down and dozed off. Then the Rivers grew quiet and Jed began to snore. Finally it was just Alex, following the moon, full of gratitude for what he could only count as a miracle.

The hours of waiting were agonizing for Ben and Peg. Ben had made Alex promise he would call as soon as they were safe inside Utah's border. In all the confusion, he forgot. The couple thought they'd hear by 11:30 at the latest, but they couldn't know what difficulties Alex found when he got there. By the time midnight came, the couple was so tense, they were having trouble being civil to each other.

Peg stabbed a needle into the design she was sewing into a pillow and thought about what an emotional seesaw being a stepmother had been in the four years that she and Ben had been married. She regularly found herself torn between wanting to flat-out love her stepchildren and needing to keep a psychological distance so as not to get hurt. When Ben's wife was alive, Peg didn't try to win the children's hearts, because she felt that it wouldn't be fair, and Peg was determined never to endanger the that sacred connection between the children and their mother—although Linda often dropped dark hints about Peg's "designs" on her babies. But since Linda's death, Peg had been counting the months until Ben would be finished with his Ph.D. when they could go to court to get the kids. Just to have the chance to mother again. She wanted that more than anything.

After a celebration out in the driveway where she learned the children were really on their way, she had returned to their quarters and wandered from each empty bedroom to bedroom, straightening what didn't needed to be straightened, imagining each child angelically asleep under fresh clean sheets and homemade quilts. She had hummed as she moved about, content with the prospect.

Ben had felt an unaccustomed pang of jealousy as her attention started to crystallize around the children. He often felt crowded emotionally by her, but now...well, he might, well, lose center stage, just like when his brother, David, was born. *Oh, grow up, Benjamin. What is this? The Oedipus Complex revisited?*

Now neither Ben nor Peg had eaten much supper. Their stomachs rumbled, and Ben went for the baking soda. They walked down to the gate two or three times. "I'm sorry to keep asking, but when did they say they might be here?" Peg asked.

Ben tried to keep the annoyance out of his voice, "Any time from now to midnight, depending on whatever complications come up."

"Oh, really great," Peg said weakly and turned to walk back

to the bed and breakfast. She didn't want to deal with his irritation. It was enough to be facing motherhood in the form of a taciturn ten-year-old and an eight-year-old fireball.

It was well after midnight. They sat in the dining area. Ben's stomach was bothering him so much, that third glass of milk had only soured on the way down. He had picked up an old paperback of "Il Paradiso" from Dante's *Divine Comedy* to get his mind off the clock. At random, the pages opened to Canto XXIII. "Hey, honey, I just opened to my favorite canto," he said.

"Oh, that's great," Peg said in a somewhat flat voice. She was still annoyed at him for his irritation with her at the gate.

Ignoring her, he read aloud,

> *Fixing my gaze upon the Eternal Light*
> *I saw within its depths*
> *Bound up with love together in one volume,*
> *The scattered leaves of all the universe...*

He lifted his head and let the imagery soak in. It pleased him to remember the sulfur and smoke that first night in the pools. *I did feel like the universe was gathering inside my body*, he thought fiercely.

Then came the sound of tires crunching on gravel. Peg looked up from her needlepoint rendering of a garden cottage. It sounded like one or possibly two cars coming down the long driveway. She smiled broadly at Ben, tossing her handiwork into the nearby sewing basket. They both jumped up, grabbed a flashlight and cautiously made their way down the gravel driveway, trying not to make too much noise.

Jed bounded out of the van and jumped the gate without waiting for formalities. He reminded Ben of Tigger from Pooh Corner, all bounce and right-in-your-face. Ben and he were in each other's arms at once, hugging and laughing. Alex stood for a few moments at the bridge, watching the scene then turned to head back to his house, when Ben ran to catch up with him. He grabbed Alex's sleeve. "Hey, you're not getting away that easily, man."

Alex managed a weary smile. "So now I'm a hero, and you're

gonna pin a medal on me?"

"No," Ben said in a low tender voice, "I want to thank you for saving my family, you jerk. I can't thank you enough," he said and gripped Alex on both arms.

Alex reached out and gave Ben a quick hug. "Ah, shucks, weren't nothin'." They laughed warmly, then Alex turned and trudged up the road with Angelina right at his heel.

Peg swung open the squeaky gate as Jody climbed wearily out of the Jeep Wagoneer. "They were sleeping," she said, pointing to the kids. She hugged Peg, even though the two women had never met. Ben's children slowly untangled themselves and tumbled out. Peg wanted to rush to them and take them into her arms, but she held back. She wrapped her aching arms around her spacious bodice and watched the scene unfold.

"Where's Daddy?" Danny asked sleepily. "I want to see my dad."

"I'm right here, Buddy," Ben replied as he rushed up to him and scooped him in his arms. He brushed Danny's hair back from his eyes and curled it back around his ear, then he kissed him on both cheeks.

"Where are you hurt?" Danny pulled back and asked soberly.

"Oh, I'm not hurt, son. I just needed you to come here because it was going to be very dangerous to stay in Ukiah. How about you? Are you okay?"

Danny began to cry. He had held in the terror and the homesickness until now. "I want to go home," he whined.

"You are home, for now anyway," Ben said trying to comfort him, but Danny turned a sour face away over Ben's shoulder, looking for his sister. Miriam hung back with Jody, waiting her turn. Her pants were twisted at the waist and her purple blouse wrinkled. "Where are your shoes, honey?" Ben asked.

Jody piped up, "It's a long story, Ben. Don't ask right now." So Ben who had picked up Danny in one arm reached out for her hand. She turned away coyly.

"Why don't you come with me, Miriam?" Peg asked, extending her arms.

"No, Daddy has to carry me, too," she pouted.

"Whew, I'll try, sweetheart. You guys are getting so big." Ben shifted Danny into his other arm. "Come here, darling." Miriam jumped up, circled her legs around his waist, and laid her head on his chest.

Ben staggered a bit with the load, but he lovingly gathered his "babies" close to his chest. As he walked, he nestled his face into first one, then the other's hair. He couldn't get enough of their smell. Peg walked behind with Jody. Jed had taken one of the flashlights and half-ran ahead to see what the facilities looked like.

"What about our baby?" Jody asked annoyed, when he returned from exploring.

"He's fine," Jed replied testily. He, like the others, was on the verge of exhaustion. "I'll go check on him," he said as he plodded back to the van. "But let him sleep until we've got things settled." Jody nodded wearily.

Alex left instructions for the newly-arrived cars to be parked farther down the road, so they couldn't be spotted from the gate, just as a precaution. When this was done, Jed and Jody settled quickly into the small, beige adobe cabin next to the bed and breakfast. Peg hung back and let Ben put the children to bed. Danny was given the room decorated with Mexican pottery and a red and green sarape, farthest from Ben and Peg's. And Ben put Miriam next to them in the smaller bedroom, the one with a white-scalloped curtains and French provincial furniture. "Night, Mimi," Ben whispered as he shut her door. He couldn't call her Mimi to her face, because she was adamant that she was Miriam, not some dumb poodle dog name.

Ben spent a long time looking at each dear face. It was like the night Danny was born. He stopped by his crib, just to make sure the newborn was breathing. Two hours later, Ben was still there, transfixed, caught up in waves of love, staring at his sleeping son. Peg stood in the doorway and wondered how long it would take for them to want her to tuck them in. *Anytime is too long, now that they were here,* she thought.

Moira, who had been awakened by the shouting at the gate, stood in the doorway of their home and enfolded her brave husband in her arms as he returned. "Are you okay?" she asked softly.

"All parts working and accounted for, ma'am. I just need a stiff drink." They walked into the darkened house arm in arm. "Is Grace asleep?" Alex asked. Moira put her finger to her lips.

"Is she always right about her predictions?" he asked in a stage whisper.

"I told you. But no-o-o-o," she laughed, "you didn't believe me."

"I'm really grateful for the warning," he said suddenly weary. He took off his muddy coat, soggy work boots and even soggier socks.

"Where's your shirt? Just where have you been, young man?" she asked in a mock disgusted, motherly voice.

"Out running in an irrigation ditch. I'll tell you the whole thing later." He pulled her to him and hung on for a long time. "You are so precious to me, Iwi."

"And, of course, I don't care one whit for you," she teased and brushed back a stray grey lock of his hair.

"Never mind the drink. Let's go up to bed," he said, "but don't get any fancy ideas about what's to happen when we get there. I'm past tired, past exhausted, somewhere into *rigor mortis*, I think."

They slowly climbed the stairs. Moira held her stomach, but because it was dark, Alex didn't notice. She didn't want to worry him, but she had definitely begun cramping and spotting. When she called Dr. Hunter, he said she was to report any changes; he'd see her tomorrow no matter what. Alex pulled off his undershirt with a groan. "Aren't you supposed to be leaving for Missouri soon?" he asked.

"And are you coming with me?"

This was an old story line they had played out almost since the time they met. She told him she'd marry him if he understood her beliefs about the second coming of Christ. He said he'd come along if he could meditate and sculpt along the way.

"I wonder about the other people who are still out there," Alex said changing the subject. "It's really dangerous to drive cross country any more."

"Let's make sure we pray for them tonight," Moira added.

They knelt by their bed and gave thanks to God. Even Alex had to admit the luck held.

Chapter Eight

Batter my heart, three-personed God; for You
As yet but knock, breathe, shine, and seek to mend;
That I may rise and stand, o'erthrow me, and bend
Your force, to break, blow, burn, and make me new.
"Holy Sonnet 14," John Donne

Eight women from town and Peg and Moira sat in a circle of chairs and couches in the Dubiks' spacious home–an open, two-storied structure done in a southwestern motif. Peg looked up at the darkened beams which crisscrossed the ceiling. She noted that bedrooms led off from the second-story balcony which completely circled the upstairs. Old Navajo rugs hung over the side of the balcony at artful intervals. In between, plants cascaded down from earthen pots. *This is beyond my dream house, this seems like something out of* Arizona Highways *meets* House Beautiful, she noted wryly.

*How strange this all seems; not long ago, I was living another life.*Faces of dear, long-time friends she'd left behind formed in her mind's eye, and she began to tear up. The view from the couch, where Peg sat facing the river, was dominated by a large rock formation which looked like a coyote with its head back, mouth open, ready to howl. *Boy, do I know how you feel!* she thought.

On the opposite wall hung painting after alluring painting, all originals; none were Alex's. He stayed with sculpting, but he had a cultivated eye for what he wanted to collect. His work, however, was prominently displayed on tables and stands throughout the downstairs area. A large red patterned Oriental rug dominated the living area, along with a gigantic fireplace. Copper-colored pots hung in deliberate patterns in the open kitchen area. Peg felt small and unsophisticated.

They called themselves the Garden Club, these women who came weekly to do group therapy with Moira, who had been a practicing psychotherapist in New Zealand. They called it the

Garden Club because it raised fewer eyebrows than to say one was going to do therapy, especially in a small, southern Utah town. One of the techniques Moira used in helping them was dreamwork, and Peg had been invited because of the dream she had related at the breakfast table that morning.

"I had a really strange dream last night," Peg volunteered when just she and Ben were left sitting across from Moira and Alex in the dining area. The children had gone to explore the baths and the river with Jed and Jody. "I dreamt that the sun had experienced some catastrophe and gave out only a third of its light. I heard an astronomer say the situation was really bad." Peg paused to see if they were listening. They were, so she continued somewhat timidly.

"Then I saw a gypsy woman, dark and 50ish, come into an area where I was camping out with a bunch of people, I can't remember who. Ben wasn't there. She said to me, 'I'm going to Paris to die—under my favorite tree.' I was both shocked and attracted to her." Peg took the last bite of waffle soaked in maple syrup off Ben's plate. He grunted in protest.

"In the dream, the country had fallen completely apart, and I couldn't imagine her making it to Paris. On the other hand, I thought that she was so irrational that maybe she, of all people, could. Then we were back in our apartment in Salt Lake again and Ben was there, but he was very busy and uptight. He wanted everything clean and tidy, and quiet. It was good to feel the order of the place, but I wanted to go on with the gypsy. I was fascinated with seeing just how she might pull off this journey."

Moira looked out the window, and her mind wandered to the arrival of all the new people. *I imagined this would happen—that we'd have a latter-day sanctuary—but now that it is coming true, I'm afraid Alex and I are going to lose touch.* She was quite interested in Peg's dream, but she felt crowded. *I don't want to play therapist twenty-four hours a day,* she firmly told herself. She tried to ignore the contractions which were getting harder and closer together. She'd see Dr. Hunter soon enough.

"That is a really interesting dream, honey," Ben said warmly.

"What you make of it?"

"I'm not sure. I hope it isn't prophetic."

"Me too," Alex said.

Moira spoke up. "Why don't you come to a group I run this afternoon? It might take your mind off what you've been through these past few days. Besides you'll meet some interesting women," she said kindly, "and I'll see that you get a chance to work on that dream, if you'd like."

Peg looked at Ben. She wasn't sure what the parameters were now that they were suddenly parents. He smiled and shrugged, "Go, if you like. I'll take care of the kids."

There were a number of intelligent, refined faces among the crowd. Peg sensed these women had shared a lot together. Two of them hugged and talked with their faces very close together; the others formed tight circles of three, smiling and talking in low, intimate tones. She felt she was a stranger and she didn't want to be.

"These are all good LDS women," Moira said to Peg, "so you don't have to worry about losing your testimony. We ask that you not repeat what happens here, except in general terms to your husband. We want to feel free to unburden ourselves without the entire community knowing about it. Is that okay with you, Peg?"

"Oh, it's fine. I've done some group therapy. Right after my daughter died."

"Good. We usually go around the group and have people share what's happened during the week and see who wants to work."

Moira called the meeting to order. She formally introduced Peg, who warmed to the smiles and half listened to the women reporting what had had happened during the week. Two women stood out in Peg's mind: a lawyer's wife named Patricia who had been a concert violinist until arthritis ended her career prematurely, and a doctor's wife whose name Peg didn't catch, who was bright and sad and searching. Both, it turned out, were not local, but from Salt Lake. Peg wondered if it was worth opening up to them. She had no idea how long she and Ben were going to be there. That thought took her away into a blue funk for a time.

She was brought back to the conversation when Patricia began to relate a dream she'd had. After she'd finished, Moira asked, "Do you want to do some Gestalt with it?" Patricia nodded, so Moira brought a straw-backed chair to sit opposite the one Patricia was sitting in.

What in the world is she doing? Peg puzzled. *This isn't the way they ran my group therapy.* She became thoroughly engrossed in the therapeutic process, watching as Patricia gave a name to and description of a frightening male character who had tried to break into their house in last night's dream. The stark description of a rapist transfixed Peg. *Now what is Moira going to make her do? It's bad enough having to look at that man.*

"Tell him how you feel about him as you see him sitting over there," were Moira's instructions.

No way I would talk to the creep, Peg thought, but Patricia did. And when Patricia got up and sat down in the other chair and "became" the intruder, Peg instinctively put her hands over her ears. She turned away and looked out the window, not wanting to watch the misery, waiting for the emotional outburst. It didn't come. To her surprise, Patricia returned to her chair after conversing with "Wayne" in the first chair and said how relieved she felt and how much better it was confronting him and seeing he represented her repressed anger.

I am not going to do this chair-changing thing, Peg thought fiercely. The meeting continued and there was no more Gestalt, so Peg relaxed. Then Moira turned to her and asked, "Now that you've been with us for this past hour, Peg, are you feeling comfortable enough to work on the dream you related this morning? I think it's quite interesting and might be useful for some of us here."

Peg was happy for the attention and opportunity to get out of herself. She was an extrovert; this was a natural arena for her. At Moira's request, she recounted the dream to the group. She expected the group to ask questions and give their opinions as had been happening in the group, but Moira walked across the room and returned with the straw-backed chair which she placed in front of Peg. Peg, feeling dumpy and out of place, watched as Moira seemed to glide across the room, elegantly dressed in a simple white silk shirt, bloused over jeans. Her hair was piled up on her head and she wore turquoise earrings she had beaded.

But Moira felt terrible; she was still spotting and the cramping continued intermittently. She glanced at her watch. *Hunter will be here in two hours,* she thought. *Not much chance a five-month fetus can survive out of the womb.* She shook her head. I don't want to know what it all means. "Would you like to work on the dream, Peg?" she asked, wincing.

"I guess so—if you have time," Peg said a little testily. She felt cornered. I don't want them to think I'm a bad sport, she worried. *What if we continue to live here? What if these women turn out to be the circle of people I have to choose from as friends?* Peg squirmed in her chair. Moira patiently watched the range of emotions pass across Peg's face. Finally Peg said, "Sure, why not? Can't hurt, right?" She looked around the group, hoping for a laugh, but they too sat patiently waiting for her to begin.

Peg sighed and nodded to Moira signaling she was ready.

"Okay, then, let's pretend that the gypsy is sitting on the chair across the way here."

Peg recoiled.

"Is she too close for you?" Moira asked gently.

"Yes, could you move her back a couple of hundred yards?"

"Why don't you move her back where you're comfortable, but still within spitting distance?" Moira tried to lighten the tension. It wearied her even further having to work with someone new, who was clearly resistant.

Peg shoved the chair back with her foot until she couldn't touch it and was surprised at the fear this generated, a fear which moved up into her arms and throat. She didn't like the feeling of being on the spot and out of control. On the spot was actually okay, if she could be in charge of the improvisation. This, though, was way out of her comfort zone.

"The way this works," Moira said, "is that I will direct traffic, as it were. First you'll talk to the gypsy, then you'll move to the other chair and become her. Okay?"

Peg nodded slowly.

"We assume here for the sake of argument that the gypsy is an aspect of yourself that you need to integrate." Moira suddenly sounded to Peg like she had become clinical, distant. Peg felt abandoned, but desperately wanted to keep the appearance that she was a good sport, so she jumped in with, "So what am I supposed to do?"

Moira leaned forward and said softly to Peg, "What's going on in your body right now?"

"I'm fine. I think she's pretty ugly, though." Peg waited for a laugh. None came. She looked around at the faces of the women to see what they thought of her. She couldn't get a fix on what they felt. That made her more anxious. She was sure they were judging her performance.

Moira brought Peg's attention back to the immediate situation with, "Let me ask you to focus on the physical sensations in your body. What are you feeling?"

"My neck is really tight. My arms are tense. My legs feel really heavy, and I'm not breathing normally, but I'm sure it's just because I don't know any of you."

"Good." Moira ignored the last part of the statement. "Now I'd like you to address the gypsy. Tell her how you feel about her as you see her sitting over there."

Peg felt silly. Surely no one else had gypsies sitting in the opposite chair. She said so. Moira assured her they all had had strange people in chairs. So Peg tried to do what was asked.

Moira pulled her chair forward and sat very close to her. Peg could smell the slight scent of Moira's perfume. Reassured by her presence, Peg began with a lump in her throat. "I'm scared of you," she began talking to the empty chair and the imaginary gypsy. "You're irrational and dark and powerful, and I don't think I can trust you."

"What's going on in your body now?" Moira asked gently.

"I want to punch her...I want her to hold me...I don't know which I want." Peg could feel anxiety rising in her throat and arms. She pushed away a curl that had fallen over her eye.

"Talk to her. Tell her what you want." Moira nodded at the chair.

"I want to punch you," Peg said in a louder tone. She gripped the arms of the chair. "You are so much trouble. Why can't you fit in? Why do you make such irrational demands of me?" Peg became completely unaware of her surroundings. She had heard these very words flung at her by her father many times in her teenage years. She felt angry tears sting her cheeks.

"What about holding you? What about that?" Moira reminded her. She leaned back and let out a low moan. *That was another contraction*, she worriedly noted to herself. *Number ten since we started. Oh, God, please don't let anything be wrong with my baby.* Peg glanced over at her, but Moira gestured she wanted her to go on.

"I want you to hold me," Peg continued, "but you look dirty and maybe smelly." She could feel another old feeling rise up, one she tried to hold down when dealing with her mother. Her mother was the one person who could provoke Peg into screaming at her by the third day of a visit. When asked why, Peg could only answer, "She is so irrational."

"Okay, now go over and be the gypsy."

"Whew, boy, you sure ask a lot, you know, Moira." Peg looked to her for mercy, but was met with a kind but insistent smile.

She got up and changed chairs, expecting to have to act out the part of a gypsy. To her astonishment, she felt different. She sagged. She felt heavier. As she looked at the circle of women who sat silently attentive, she felt layers of wisdom and life experience burrow into her flesh. Even her voice deepened.

"Talk to us about Peg, Madame Gypsy. From your perspective, what should we know about her?" Moira asked.

"Ah, little Peggy. She's such a child. She wants to remain a child. She bothers me, and I don't want to have anything to do with her." Peg looked at the empty chair she had vacated and really felt disgust for Peggy.

"How can I feel so different when I'm over there?" Peg asked.

Moira told her again about the split that one experiences within oneself and the need for integration of different characters. *Come on, Peg, hang in there*, Moira thought. *I know if we both work at this, you can experience a profound shift in understanding.* Moira undid the clasp on her barrette and let her hair down.

"Is this because my mother didn't work out her stuff about her mother?" Peg kept trying to engage the crowd. She hadn't realized how much she played the stand-up comedian until she didn't have her high school students to play to. This was a hard crowd to please. She said so. "I don't know what other people think of what I'm doing. That makes me really uncomfortable. They don't laugh at my jokes."

Moira then indicated that Peg should return to her original chair and asked her an unexpected question, "How have you used your skill as an entertainer to avoid feeling pain, authentic pain?"

"I don't know. I honestly don't think that question applies to me."

"I see. So you don't see the connection between the need to entertain and clown around with the avoidance of pain?"

"Sure, but not in my case," Peg shot back in a surly tone.

"I don't know anyone who actively seeks pain. It's when we run away from it that we react in a childish way. Wouldn't you agree?" Moira asked evenly.

"Of course."

"Then I'd like you to just try this one on for size. Go around to each group member and say, 'I don't want to grow up. It's too painful.'"

Peg's face registered a flash of rage. She felt like she had been outmaneuvered. Moira ignored her response, knowing she was moving Peg to a critical intersection. Most clients hated her at this point in the process. She took it in stride.

Peg stood up and moved to Patricia, the violinist, who was on her left. She stood in front of her and said, "I don't want to grow up. It's too painful." She flushed with embarrassment. Patricia stood up and hugged her. Moira signaled her to move on. Peg tightened her jaw and moved somewhat mechanically to the next woman.

She actually handled the request pretty well until she came to the doctor's wife whose face reflected Peg's search for meaning in tragedy. Then she fell apart. She found herself, standing, encircled by the group, getting the hugs she'd hoped for. And she cried, as Ben had done that first night in the baths, wrenching sobs that seemed to come from a well deep in her stomach.

Moira waited until Peg could hear her, then said, "It seems to me there are three questions that each person has to ask herself, 'Do I love well? Do I live fully? Have I learned to let go?' In the little time I've spent with you, Peg, I've seen you love and take in life, but I'm not sure you've learned to let go of things and just live in the moment. And this gypsy woman seems to want to lead you to experience death gracefully. By death I mean transformation. It's like you learn to both inhale and exhale and enjoy both processes. Am I being obscure?"

Peg sat silent. *In group therapy when I cried like this, no one expected me to do more work. This woman is a taskmaster! Does Moira expect me to continue with this stupid drama in my condition?*

"Peg, until you face and finish this encounter, you'll be at the mercy of what she represents–always afraid of death. Not that all of us aren't, but the fear doesn't have to dominate our interior life," Moira said pointedly.

"I don't think it's fair to say that death dominates my inner life," Peg said defensively. "It's only when I'm not sure where I'm going to live or even I *am* going to live. How would you feel if you were just chased out of your house by troops who were after your husband?" Peg now was half-shouting. "You're not going through what I am right now, so it would be hard for you to understand." She tried to tone it down and gripped the arms of the chair.

Moira signaled the group members to take their seats. "Peg, you're very bright, and I can see that you can get sympathy when you need it. If you don't want to finish this work right now, I can certainly understand how you feel." She leaned back a bit wearily and waited for Peg to respond.

"I don't want to. I feel much better and I thank you all for your hugs. They helped tremendously," she said a little testily. "Now I'm sure I've taken too much time. Please let someone else work on a dream." She folded her arms around herself and leaned back in the couch. *I'm not going to be railroaded by you or anyone.* That thought surprised her. *When did I get into a power struggle with Moira? I thought she was my friend.*

Alex awakened late in the morning to the sound of muffled voices coming from the kitchen. He strained to hear if it was Moira and her mother, but it did not sound like their usual Maori chatter. He eased himself out of the bed, trying not to moan as his wrenched back muscles reached up and grabbed him. He wrapped himself in the blue kimono and padded barefoot down the hall. As he reached the top of the stairs, he recognized Sangay's voice as one of the two voices; the other was Grace's. With the night's high drama, he had completely forgotten that Sangay was coming.

Sangay and Grace seemed to be enjoying each other's company. Laughter peppered high-spirited conversation. Alex was warmed by the exchange. For a moment he thought he was young again and had a mother and father in the kitchen. When he stuck his head around the corner, Sangay, who had not lost his accent despite his twenty years in the U.S., greeted him with, "Hey, sleepy head. I understand you were out last night, working on your Ninja moves."

"Something like that," Alex mumbled. He flashed an embarrassed smile and reached for the cup of cocoa Grace offered him. Although Sangay was not much older than he, Alex always felt a little awkward and adolescent around his wiser meditation teacher.

"Mrs. Ihimaera and I were just sharing war stories." Sangay grinned at Alex's disorientation. "Spiritual war stories, that is. She is quite a warrior, you know."

"I do know." Alex leaned over and kissed Grace's cheek."You really helped me through that last night, Mom. That was a real nightmare at the border. I couldn't have done it without you."

She patted him lovingly on the arm in reply.

"Where's Iwi?" he asked.

"With the Garden Club."

Their exchange was cut short by a call from Ben. Could Alex please take some time to talk to him? He needed sage advice.

"Sure, Ben. Let me call you back when I'm fully awake and we'll plan something."

"Was that Ben Taylor?" Sangay asked.

"Yes. How do you know him? He was the guy I wanted you to meet." Sangay just grinned and, showing the gap between his teeth, looked a lot more like an imp than a *rinpoche* (abbot) and *geshe* (doctor of philosophy).

Alex stood up and faced the smaller man. "No, I'm serious," he said pressing the point. "How do you know him, Sangay?"

"That is for me to know and you to find out, Ninja," he said. Sangay was a whole head shorter than Alex, dressed in a pale orange robe over a red undergarment. His black-strapped Rolex watch seemed a funny contrast to the strand of wooden beads he wore around his neck. There was lightness about Sangay Tulku. Not only did he have no worldly goods, but one got the sense that he could make himself dematerialize (if it caught his fancy to do so)–that he wasn't even really attached to having a body. He obviously liked to laugh, as the smile lines around his face, especially the ones near his gentle brown eyes showed.

"Son, we were just talking about celebrating the Tibetan New Year 2135 with Mr. Tulku as chef and party master," Grace said enthusiastically.

"Great. When will it be?" Alex asked.

"In two days' time. After much will have happened here."

Sangay again waxed obscure.

Alex just shook his head and reached for the French toast and syrup on the bar separating the kitchen from the living room. "What happens then, Sangay?" he said with half-filled mouth.

"First morning prayers offered for all sentient beings, and, of course, for the long life of His Holiness, the Dalai Lama. Burning incense, we'll call for the triumph of good over evil."

"Great! I'm all for that," Alex said, then filled his mouth. He couldn't remember being so hungry.

"Then we'll feast on *la phuk gor zoe, dho thuk, tsampa,* and for dessert *khapsay* and buttered tea." Sangay grinned.

"Sounds delicious." Alex returned the grin. "Just get me my chopsticks and Tibetan dictionary, and I'll be all ready to chow down!"

"Alex! Mind your manners," Grace teased.

"And we have all these ingredients? The yak milk and donkey ears and such?" Alex asked with good-natured sarcasm.

Yet another phone call interrupted Sangay's answer. It was for Grace. She walked around the corner with the phone and talked in a hushed voice with Dr. Hunter about Moira's condition. She sighed as she hung up. Sangay's presence had momentarily taken her away from her grave concern for Moira.

How to get Alex out of the way so he won't know the extent of the bleeding problem until we know for sure what is going to happen, Grace worried.

That was solved when Alex arranged with Ben to hike in Zion Park. Alex hadn't mentioned Sangay on the phone. Ben had been somewhat ambivalent about meeting him, and Alex didn't want to complicate Ben's life with his eccentric rinpoche. Ben walked up the sodden path, stepping gingerly over mud holes, and stuck his head into the studio. "Want to take a quick peek," Alex said meeting him at the doorway along with the dogs. "Just a quick one, though. None of your long-winded tirades, okay?" Both men laughed.

Ben was overwhelmed by the scene that lay before him as he walked into the studio—sculpture after brilliant sculpture, those figures whose features radiated dignity in the midst of grief. He walked over to a three-piece rendering that depicted an Adonis crowned by light and flanked on one side by a male figure in rapture and on the other side a man sinking down in despair. "Oh, Al, this is so great. I've told you from the beginning that you were major. I'm in awe."

"You always were a big support, Ben. Why are you drawn to that piece?"

Ben took a minute to gather his thoughts. He walked over to a stool a few feet away from the piece, sat down and began, "Taken together, these three panels embody for me basic energies at play in a male psyche. No, let me say, my psyche. It's like some primitive acid has burned these images into stone–dark and radical–and they unmask the viewer." He shifted his position on the stool. "That's what art should do. It should make us more real."

Alex beamed gratefully.

Ben continued, "I've always felt your art does just that. Even in your earlier work, you were able to touch the archetypal."

"Ever the art critic," Alex laughed. "You should write for the arts section of the local paper here. The man from the paper who came to see my work called it, ah, let's see how he put it–oh, yeah, I remember–a group of nude men, who are as twisted psychologically as they are physically."

"Well, he's a jerk," Ben responded vehemently as he walked over to another group. The sun rode the clouds and then streamed in through the high westerly windows, suddenly illuminating a series of crucified men, surrounded by different figures of modern man–the businessman, farmer, laborer. "It looks like you're working your way through your eastern European Christianity."

"Possibly. Consciously, though, what I've been trying to do is reveal what is insipid in modern Christianity."

"How has this series been received?"

"Not very well. In general, passion is okay for the audience, but not passion connected with a Christ figure. The crucifixion theme also doesn't go down very well here in Utah. Maybe you could explain that one to me some day, Ben."

"Explain what?" Ben replied a little coyly, trying not to get noticeably excited at this rare proselyting opportunity with his stubbornly agnostic friend.

But Alex registered Ben's interest, so he deflected it with a quick, dismissing wave of the hand, and said simply, "Why Mormons seem to shy away from the cross and all that it symbolizes. Anyway," Alex went on, picking up where he had left off, "I don't really mind. I'm set financially, so I can work on my soul without worrying about sales or being socially correct."

"Well, I knew you were a major artistic talent when we first met. I said so. It's great to see the fruition of my prophecy." Ben smiled and patted Alex on the back.

"See? Mormons really can prophesy," Ben said half in jest, half as an attempt to open that little window of missionary possibility.

Alex ignored that comment. "Hey, thanks for believing in me. Even though you haven't been around, you've been in my head."

Ben hung his head modestly. "I have?" he asked surprised.

"Yes, you have," Alex said firmly, then perceiving Ben's discomfort, offered, "Let's do the rest of this later." *Intellectuals!* he thought. *Can't live with them and can't live without them. They're the ones who sense the passion, sure, but they never want to get too close to it on a personal level. Might get their fingers burned.*

At that moment, Sangay emerged from the meditation area off to the left and bowed slightly to Ben. Ben felt a tingle run up his spine.

"Ben, this is my meditation teacher, Sangay Tulku. I mentioned he was coming." Alex looked to each man.

"I'm really pleased to finally meet you." Ben was all charm, but underneath was nagged by the feeling that he knew this man from somewhere.

"You want to talk, amigo, and we want to go hiking," Alex said. "Would it be okay if Sangay tags along?"

"Well, ah...I guess so. I hope I won't bore you with my domestic problems," Ben said.

With a quick smile, Sangay put Ben at ease. "Not at all," he said, "not at all."

Alex pulled on his coat, pulled a brightly-colored South American hat on his head and gathered up his woolen gloves. "Let's do it while the snow is still just threatening. Zion is a jewel in the winter."

High-pitched squeals floated down the canyon as the men made their way to the Jeep Wagoneer. The kids were in the river's hot pools. Ben hadn't realized how much he had missed the sounds of children. He tightened his jaw and thought, *I'm not giving them up this time. I don't care what happens.*

As soon as Alex opened the door of the car, the retriever jumped in and bounded over the back seat. "Hey, Al, this couldn't be Picasso, could it?" Ben asked.

"No, she died about seven years ago. This is Renoir."

Renoir barked and tried to jump over the seat to get to Ben. She and he were old friends, after all. Ben thought about telling Alex of the large turd affair, but thought better of it. The men laughed at the dog's antics, and Alex put his foot to the accelerator. He was a maniac at the wheel. They burned rubber going out the upper roadway, turned out of Pah Tempe and sped through LaVerkin up into the entrance to Zion. Alex showed his pass to the guard and now drove much more slowly as they wound their way toward looming reddened cliffs. Dusted with snow, the cliffs looked like raw roast beef, powdered with flour and ready for the oven.

Ben was grateful the hike to upper Emerald Pool was an easy paved walk. The three walked in silence at a leisurely pace. His hands folded behind his back and his head down, Sangay walked along with a quiet air of one in great rapport with nature. The path was slippery in parts. "Should come here in the middle of a snowstorm," Alex said in husky, reverential tones. The echo of Refrigerator Canyon ice falls reached them. They paused to take in the tinkling melody. As they continued on up the path, they saw on one side of the trail tufts of green, sheltered by a sandstone overhang. Yet, when they turned to the sound of the falls, winter white covered the scene.

"Zion usually gets about fifteen inches of snow in a season," Alex offered. "But this year we've had almost none. That's not good. Maybe we'll get more now."

They reached Emerald Pool. Ben was overcome by the sight of sheer canyon walls soaring a good eight hundred feet or more in the air. A thin finger of water dropped from an indentation in the rock above. Around the pool everything was covered with snow, but there was no ice on the water—most unusual for February. The three pilgrims could hear little now except for the dropping of the spray.

Alex pointed to an overhang that wasn't snow-covered and pulled out of his pack a light-weight ground cover. The trio sat down facing the pool.

"Hey, Al, I hate to break the mood," Ben started out, "but I've got to talk through some issues and you've always been a great problem-solver." He turned to Alex, but both Alex and Sangay had retreated into a meditative silence. Alex opened one eye and said warmly, "Let's take a moment to get centered."

Ben felt embarrassed. He sat for a time, waiting for Alex to speak. He didn't, so Ben asked teasingly, "You are going to talk to me, aren't you?"

Alex nodded. "Give me another minute here, Ben. Try some of that deep breathing we did that night at the baths."

Ben crossed his legs, rolled his head around a few times, straightened his spine and took several deep breaths. A few minutes passed, but Ben was not very successful at calming his racing thoughts. Finally Alex and Sangay stirred and emerged from their meditation like bears waking up after a long winter sleep. They stretched and turned their attention to Ben.

"Okay, Ben, what's up? Talk to me, Bro," Alex offered kindly.

"I really need some advice. I've got to do something about the kids," Ben said soberly. "Their grandparents don't know where they've gone or if they're alive, for that matter. I can't do that to them, even though they screwed me in court."

"If I knew what happened...I've forgotten," said Alex, puzzled.

"Well, you know, money speaks volumes these days, in court, and Mr. Breyerson knew the judge–I'm sure he greased his palm–and that corrupt court granted temporary custody to the grandparents until I finished my degree."

"That's really terrible."

"Yeah, it's pretty crummy. It certainly has done a job on me and my poor stomach, fighting off ulcers. I've had to deal with that along with everything else. Peg was devastated. She had really counted on them being with us. Four years of traveling to California and back, just for weekends, whenever I could get a government pass, has grown very old, needless to say."

"I'm sorry, Ben. I hadn't realized how bad it was," Alex said and patted Ben's leg.

Sangay smiled and looked sympathetic. Ben felt like the man was probing him; he didn't know why. Ben couldn't express the pain inside. He was an honorable man, and now, by taking the children the way he had, he felt that he had done something that was hard to square with his rigorous moral code. But he needed to have his family more than to obey the laws of a rapidly disintegrating world. Besides, he had already done some ethical gymnastics involving himself in the black market financial community. He felt that the times mirrored the Vietnam years. Back then, people like Alex (after he returned from active duty in Vietnam), protesting the war for all they were worth, had had to put it all on the line for a higher principle: justice. Now, it was his turn, and this time the higher principle was kinship.

"Obviously, I don't want them to find us. I've thought of a couple of possibilities. Tell me what you think."

"What are your options?" Alex asked.

"One is not to contact the grandparents. The other is to tell the truth, but not tell them where we are. I don't think they can find us. The only way they might would be that my mother might remember you and put two and two together, although I doubt it."

"And what about the legal side of all this, Ben," Alex asked, slipping back into his big brother voice that had comforted Ben from college days.

"Abduction is a pretty serious crime. Kids go back to their grandparents. I don't hold out much hope of surviving a prison sentence. Not the way the government has been treating the resistance. Maybe it was a stupid thing to do. I just couldn't face life on the run without them."

"How are they handling it so far?"

"So far I think they're seeing it as a vacation with us, like we've done every year. In a few days, I expect they'll want to go home." Ben's stomach hurt.

They spent the next half hour hashing out the complexities of the situation. Finally they decided that Alex would ask his Cedar City ham radio contact, Clint Rasmussen, to phone the Ukiah newspaper with the information that the kids were safe with their father in hiding. He'd get off the line before the call could be traced.

"We can't stay here very long, though, Al," Ben continued. "You've got to get on with your life."

"This is my life. You've just enriched it. Look, we're kinda lonely down here. Moira has told me ever since we bought the property that it would serve as a sanctuary. Besides, we're set up for it. We want you here for as long as you want to stay. Really." Alex searched Ben's face. "Look, I married a wild Mormon beauty," Alex said and grinned broadly. "A high tolerance for apocalyptic scenarios comes with the territory."

Sangay, who had said very little, now laughed at Alex.

Ben looked to the lama who gave him a reassuring smile. Then he said, "Well, we don't have much money. About a thousand bucks."

Their attention was drawn to a high-flying hawk soaring overhead.

"Consider the lilies...Jesus himself said that, right?" Alex asked. "Hey, partner, we've got more money than we can ever spend. I had a trust left to me that was very generous, and I've learned a trick or two about playing the international market–securities, bonds, precious metals. Besides, I've made a lot selling sculptures. Let Moira and I decide what we can afford."

"I'm really uncomfortable living off you."

"Well, then, old pal, I'll just have to work your rear end off, okay? Will that make you feel better? There's a lot of work on the property you could help with."

"A Jewish ranch hand? Great! What do you want me to do–circumcise the horses?"

Alex laughed in his throaty, baritone way and Sangay guffawed. Ben waited for the laughter to subside then said seriously, "Well, then, maybe I can help with the books. That desk in the office looked a little lonely."

"Great," said Alex, relieved that they could work out something to preserve Ben's ego. Alex felt for his friend. *I'd hate to be in his shoes*, he mused.

The three men talked about the UWEN takeover of Utah and the worsening military situation in the United States as they walked back down the path to the car. There had been threats which sounded very genuine from the Chinese that they were planning on invading America. They were the one country the UWEN was having trouble containing.

"Sounds pretty far-fetched, but with the Chinese these days, anything is possible," Ben said.

"Some think their sterilization policy in the '80's and '90's when families only chose to have one boy–killing the girl babies–has to do with their aggressive and reckless behavior," Sangay said, sounding suddenly more like a sociologist than an imp. "Many millions of Tibetans have suffered from their barbarities since the 1950's, as you may know." Ben tried in vain to find even a trace of bitterness in the rinpoche's voice. His interest in Sangay was piqued. *A man of many faces*, Ben thought.

When they returned to the Jeep Wagoneer, Renoir barked, slobbered and turned around in circles in the cramped back seat looking like a rabid whirling dervish. Everyone had a hearty laugh at her expense. And Ben felt lighter and clear-headed on the return trip. Something Bishop Olson said in that darkened basement bedroom came back to him..."the Lord is going to use you, Ben, for his own purposes. Pray and ask him what it is. He'll let you know."

Chapter Nine

And what is the true nature of the miraculous?
Once the rationalist, vexed by paradox,
Surrenders to the vision in a dream
And receives an image of the double helix,
The diamond that vanishes perfectly in water
Reappears exactly when the thirsty man drinks.
"Sea-grape Tree and the Miraculous," Root

David Hunter, a tall, elegant man with a slight limp, walked very slowly over the bridge and up the long path to the Dubiks' house. He was searching for that tight, clear place he got into when he became just a physician and nothing else. He had to. After what he and Sandy had just been through, another miscarriage would have wrenched him. Smoke rose from the chimney and steam from the river as he plodded heavily to the door.

Grace led the thirty-year-old, blond-haired doctor up the wooden stairs. The fifth stair creaked. He reached for the banister, unconsciously afraid he'd fall. David didn't want to go into Moira's darkened bedroom—it would be like stepping into a gloomy chamber of his recent past. Nothing had been more difficult than standing by, helpless, while he lost his first baby. But by the time Grace had opened the drapes, he was Doctor Hunter again.

Abruption or previa, he wondered as he sat down next to the worried woman and skillfully pressed on the small 'melon' that served as home to the Dubiks' son-to-be. He was grateful for the numbing detachment that had settled over him like a mild anesthetic. The uterus was consistently hard. Not good. He placed a thermometer in her ear. When he pulled it out, he took in a deep breath—it read 104.5˚. The fetoscope's results weren't any better. They indicated that the baby's heartbeat was irregular and slow.

"How far along are you, Moira?" he asked kindly.

"A little over five months," she said.

"And the bleeding? How much blood would you say you were passing?"

"It depends. If I stay in bed, it's like the first day of my period, but if I get up and walk around, it's more." Moira looked to her mother who tried to smile reassuringly.

"And the pain?"

Moira turned her head away and said, "It's gotten pretty bad in just the last hour."

"I see," Hunter tried to register a bland, pleasant look. "How often are the contractions?"

"That's what scares me the most. They aren't really contractions. It's like one hard contraction, like one long constant pain."

The fever puzzled him. It wasn't consistent with abruption, which is what he had begun to suspect. *Damn!* he thought and shook his head. *I don't want another ambulance racing to Dixie Regional Medical Center. At least not one with the same outcome.*

"Moira, if you'll excuse us a moment," he said and signaled to Grace to step out of the bedroom.

"Oh, no," Moira protested. "Stay here and tell me. I can take it. I need to know," she nearly begged the doctor.

"I'm just going to ask your mother a few questions, then I promise to come back and be very candid, okay?" Hunter was firm.

She nodded and wiped tears away with the back of her hand.

David shut the bedroom door quietly, then turned to the brown, aging seeress. With her broad cheek bones and grey hair braided on top of her head, Grace reminded him of an old Indian warrior, one who had been in so many battles that she was immune to trauma. That made it easier for him to say, "I think we're dealing with abruption—a tear in the wall of the placenta." He was trying his best to stay emotionally even. Her placid presence helped considerably."With the amount of bleeding, pain and constant contraction, I'm guessing it's very serious."

Grace reached out, squeezed his arm, and said warmly, "Dr.

Hunter, please don't worry. Everything's going to be okay."

"No, it's not. That's what I'm telling you, Sister Ihimaera. You see, I can't do a vaginal; I don't know where my finger would go. It might go right into the placenta. Then that's really terminal. And even though I can't examine her vaginally, I feel certain we're going to lose the fetus."

What Hunter didn't say was that there was always the specter of DIC, the sudden loss of the body's ability to control coagulation, which could be fatal to the mother. "One of the things I don't understand is the high fever. Would you know anything about that?"

"I've been quite ill with a flu that I brought with me from New Zealand. But we're sure it's not PDS," she quickly added, "because I've obviously recovered. I'm sure that's where she got it--from me."

"Weakens her even further," the doctor said shaking his head. He looked out over the balcony at the elegantly appointed house. Even with the overcast sky, the house was filled with color and the inset lighting in the beamed ceilings made him feel like they had ascended to a realm of light.

This aesthetic elevation filled him with a sense of God's design in matters of the world and made it easier to say reluctantly, "I'm going to call for an ambulance, but I want you to know that we usually don't make heroic efforts to save the fetus until it's about 27 weeks along. So we'll probably have to suction her when we get there." Grace's composure was unnerving. *Did she really comprehend what I am saying?* David wondered. He managed to return her warm smile as they turned, opened the door and retreated back into Moira's bedroom.

Hunter walked over and sat down gingerly on the sick bed. Moira grasped his hand. "Please," she pleaded, "please tell me what's happening."

"There are a couple of possibilities, Moira. The uterus may be in tetany, and it's possible the placenta has detached. I can't tell without examining you. I'm calling for an ambulance. My concern right now is for you. We may lose the fetus." (That was easier to say than "We're going to have disrupt this much-wanted pregnancy and I can't promise you'll be able to have another child.")

The words swept over Moira, but didn't sink in. "No, Dr. Hunter, I don't want to go to the hospital. What can we do here?"

What can we do at all? David thought sadly, but said, "You must go to the hospital. We have equipment and help that I can't provide here."

He looked to Grace for help, but she was gazing out the window. The Jeep Wagoneer was crossing the Pah Tempe bridge. The men were returning from Zion. Grace looked back and caught his eye.

"I agree with Dr. Hunter, Iwi, but first I want to ask Dr. Hunter and Ben Taylor to give you a blessing," she said firmly.

Hunter looked to Moira, who had turned her face away and begun crying softly. "Do you want us to give you a blessing, Moira?"

"Oh, yes," she replied weakly, with a tone of desperation in her voice.

David Hunter went quickly to the phone to order an ambulance. Then he bounded down the stairs and reached the door just as the three hikers walked up. He pulled open the door, stepped outside, shut it and herded the men into the studio. Alex knew instantly it was about Moira.

"She needs to get to the hospital immediately. I've called for an ambulance. "

Alex went grey.

The doctor explained briefly where things stood, then said, "She's asked for a blessing before the ambulance arrives and has asked for you, Ben."

Ben immediately thought of at least twenty reasons he was unworthy to be asked to participate. *I've never really been in on an attempted healing. What if it's a sham? Or better yet, what if I'm one....*

"Now!" Hunter broke into Ben's reverie.

Sangay bowed slightly and walked quietly to his downstairs guest room, while Alex followed behind the two men as they climbed the stairs back up to the second-story bedroom. Moira lay propped up on several pillows, hollow-eyed, feverish, marooned in a sea of billowing sheets and blankets in the king-sized bed. Dominating the oak bedstead behind her was a large, delicately-detailed eagle with a serpent in its talon. Probably Alex's work, Ben guessed.

Ben felt great compassion for Moira; she reminded him of a noble horse who had broken a leg. She barely moved her head to follow the two men, who walked softly into the bedroom. Grace sat to the left on a leather chair. Dr. Hunter walked around to the right side of the gold-quilted bed. Alex, his face set, paced in and out of the open doorway. He occasionally bit his lip and looked through the gathered assembly out to the river. He didn't believe anything could come of the blessing–except, of course, to comfort Moira. Superstitious and silly, he said to himself. If he'd been completely honest with himself, he might also have said, "and profoundly archetypal."

"Moira, we've come as you've requested," Ben said in his best reassuring voice. "Is it possible for you to sit up in a chair?"

Moira nodded. Grace and Alex slowly guided her into the leather chair, which had been moved to the end of the bed. She sat in a multi-colored robe with a beige shawl over her shoulders. "Do you have someone you'd like to act as voice?" Hunter asked. She weakly pointed to Ben, then looked over at Alex as if to say she wished she could ask him. Ben caught the pain that passed across Alex's eyes before he looked away.

Dr. Hunter poured a few drops of consecrated olive oil from a vial on his key chain onto her head. "What is your full name?" he asked as he cleared away hair and placed his delicate hands firmly around the crown.

"Moira Iwignaro Dubik," she said and smiled weakly. "Quite a mouthful, isn't it?"

Hunter agreed it was and began with, "...we, your brothers, holding the Melchizedek Priesthood come here today to bless you

...." then turned to Ben for his pronouncement. Ben stammered at first with, "We come here today as the Lord's servants." (*O Lord, I hope I'm not impeding this process.*) Then, at the sound of a kind of an interior "crack", he felt as though he'd been split in two. The Ben he knew was somehow across the room watching an unfamiliar, new Ben reach out and bless his best friend's wife with "...and you will be made whole."

Why did I say that? the old Ben moaned within himself.

Alex turned and walked out down the hall, disgusted at the whole scene and angry at Ben's voodoo incantations promising Moira health, when the child would probably have to be aborted within the hour.

The new Ben began to speak again, this time in a slightly deeper voice. "I prophesy, in the name of our Savior, that your son will grow to be a great warrior in the Lord's kingdom, serving his Master faithfully and well." Moira's spirit soared as those words began to echo within her. Suddenly she let in a tremendous rush of warmth that pulsed first through each man's hands, then through her weakened body. Jolted by the sudden shock, Ben almost jerked his hands off her head when the rush surged through him. He looked to David Hunter, who looked back in amazement. The startled men felt her temperature drop instantly.

"Oh, I feel so strange," she said. Ben quickly reached out to grab Moira, thinking she was going to faint. But she was just stunned as much as anything. Alex returned to the doorway to listen.

"Please go on," she almost begged. Ben struggled to get back into the spiritual state he had been in, paused, then said, "Moira, the Lord is especially mindful of your desire to have your family under the Gospel's wings. Your prayers will be answered in His own time and in His own way. Rest now, for you are in the loving care of His Holy Spirit and His Holy Priesthood..."

Moira slumped at the end of the blessing. Spent, she was helped to the bed by Ben and David. Her mother quickly took over and shooed everyone out. No one understood the extent of what had just occurred, but Ben knew that he had never experienced anything like it—not even his conversion experience in that Catholic church.

As Ben and Dr. Hunter walked past Alex in the hallway to go down and wait for the ambulance, Ben patted Alex on the arm to reassure him. Alex stiffened. Ben searched his face for a response, but Alex just stared back at him.

"What an interesting name—Ee-wee-naro," Dr. Hunter said, sounding out the difficult name as he and Ben began their descent down the stairs. "I wonder what it means in Maori."

"Lost Tribe," Alex called after them. "It means Lost Tribe."

Ben and David Hunter stopped at the bottom of the stairs. Ben, who suddenly felt quite spent himself, slumped onto the nearest couch. "I'm sorry, Doc. I'm just a bit overcome by what just happened." He leaned back and closed his eyes. After a moment, he sat straight up and asked, "Just what did happen? I'm dumbfounded."

"I believe the Lord is healing Sister Dubik" was the doctor's subdued reply. Dr. Hunter fell into a nearby chair, loosened his blue-green tie and put his head back. "And to think that we were lucky enough to act as His hands," he said gratefully. For once in his life he could not think of one thing to say.

Both men sat in silent awe. More than a minute passed. Finally the pale physician spoke, "It's been my experience that when people become very discouraged, their body is finally affected."

Ben thought that Moira was the least likely candidate for discouragement he'd ever met.

"I believe that Sister Dubik has been weighed down by her inability to convert her husband. Of course, she's also worried about the health of her unborn child."

"And I promised her that both things would be worked out. What in the world was I saying? I've given a few blessings, but they have always seemed like it was just me talking. Not this time. I swear to you I would never say those things in my right mind." He looked over at the doctor worriedly.

Dr. Hunter laughed, reached over and patted Ben's knee. "Ben, don't worry about it. I've been in on a lot of bedside blessings. You didn't do anything out of the ordinary," he said and again leaned back against the rawhide-covered chair. The color was returning to his cheeks. "But I must say I've never experienced that kind of energy rush. Wasn't that something?" Ben nodded dumbly.

Just then Alex, who'd helped Grace pack a few things for Moira, came out of the room and leaned on the brown and white Mexican rug hanging on the balcony. What Ben was saying caught his attention. The men down below were unaware that he could hear them.

"The strangest part was when the Spirit prompted me that I could promise Moira that Alex would be converted. Boy, that wasn't me talking. That's for sure. Alex converted? Not very likely. Or so I would have thought. But now...Oh, I don't know. I'm pretty confused, to tell you the truth."

David then began to talk in low tones about Moira's condition. "I don't want to get your hopes up too high, Ben. She is seriously ill, and there very well may be complications with the fetus. However, if I could take off my conservative doctor's cap for a moment, I'd say the fact that her temperature dropped to normal is quite remarkable. In fact, it's astonishing!"

The two weren't aware of Alex's descent until he reached the bottom of the stairs. Ben turned and craned his neck to read Alex's face as he approached, but he couldn't decipher anything. *Bad sign*, he thought. *Very bad sign*.

Nevertheless, Ben stood up and extended a hand to Alex, but Alex would have nothing to do with it. He mumbled a thanks to Dr. Hunter and said he would be in the studio when it came time to go, then disappeared out the door. Ben and David looked at each other and shrugged. Hunter said, "Ben, don't take it too seriously. People say and do a lot of rude things under conditions like these."

Ben, in his black down jacket, stomped his feet and blew into his hands to keep warm while he waited at the front gate for the ambulance. The incredible scene was fading from his senses. A more sober reality began to replace it in the form of a white and blue ambulance with red running lights coming to take Moira Dubik to St. George. *There she would miscarry,* Ben thought, *be sewn up after surgery, and she and Alex could forget about their hopes for a child. This Mormon idea of divine intervention,* deux ex machina, *made life bearable for some, but it seems patently unfair. Why intervene in one woman's life and not another's?* And to believe that God had a reason for His seeming favoritism required even greater faith–faith that God knew what He was doing in this wretched world–than Ben could usually muster.

He heard the crunch of the tires before he saw the ambulance. The driver who had turned off the flashing lights drove down the tree-lined drive at an easy speed. He didn't stop, but turned and drove over the bridge at Ben's signal. Ben then walked slowly down to his house. Peg looked up and saw his flushed face. She quickly left the dining room table where she had been coloring with the kids and slipped into their bedroom. "What happened to you, sweetheart? You look like you've seen a ghost."

Ben filled her in on what had happened.

"I'm so proud of you," she said tenderly and hugged him tightly around the waist. "Let's pray for Moira right now," she whispered, pulling him to his knees beside the bed. *What faith,* Ben thought.

They stepped back out into the dining area in time to see the mercy mission flash by with Moira and Grace, her daughter's gray overnight bag slung over her shoulder, transported by the white-coated ambulance crew to St. George. Dr. Hunter was riding alongside the mother-to-be. Alex stood motionless in the road and watched the mercy mission disappear up the drive. There wasn't room for everyone in the ambulance, so he agreed to follow behind them. Dr. Hunter assured Alex there was nothing he could do at this point. It was now in the hands of medical personnel.

As he entered the studio to get his coat, Alex felt like he'd been duped. *What a sucker I am for getting my hopes up. What did I think would happen? That she'd get up and walk?* He stared across the half-finished sculptures into the chilly afternoon. He was embarrassed by the whole scene. But more than anything, he was very angry–angry at everyone involved. "What a spectacle," he said bitterly to Renoir, who came up and tried to put her head on his hand. He pushed her away.

"What in the hell was that man thinking? Ben, my supposed friend," he said bitterly. "Are all these Mormons totally out of touch?" He slammed his hand down on a work bench. "They make me sick." Alex walked over to the coat rack and put on his sheepskin coat. He couldn't find his black Stetson, so he grabbed a tan baseball cap and started out the studio door.

His two dogs jumped up and raced to the door. They sat down obediently and waited for his cue. He signaled they could come, so they bounded ahead to the Jeep Wagoneer and hovered expectantly near the passenger-side door. "Damn them for manipulating Iwi when she was at her weakest," he said to the Dobie as he opened the door for her and Renoir. "She and I have worked things out between us. Why do they have to throw in a religious monkey wrench?" Alex then gunned the car up the drive, heading into LaVerkin to the state liquor store.

As the Jeep went jolting and thudding over potholes in the road, Alex really began to boil over. *If these rotten people hadn't shown up,* he fumed (forgetting it was he who invited them), *Iwi wouldn't be in this shape. She wouldn't have worked herself to the bone, taking care of a damn bunch of lunatics!* He slammed the heel of his hand down hard on the steering column, and burning pain shot up and down his fingers. He ignored it and continued his tirade.

By the time he reached LaVerkin, he had decided to get really drunk. He bought a quart of Chivas Regal, started to leave, then went back for a package of cigarettes–something he hadn't done in years. He cracked open the seal on the bottle, which he had wedged between his legs. Unscrewing the cap, Alex took a long drink, then tossed the cap onto the seat, where Renoir sniffed it, then tentatively licked at it. He unzipped the cellophane from the UWEN generic brand, took out one cigarette and clenched it in his teeth. "Matches. Matches. Where are those stupid matches?"

As he turned onto I-15 headed south, he reached across, snapped open the glove compartment and pulled out an old book of matches from a 7-11 store, convenience stores long out of business. On the cover, Alex read the words, "Oh Thank Heaven" which had been part of the store's advertising jingle. He felt more cornered than he ever had in his life.

Sangay stood in the doorway and watched the ambulance disappear. When he turned back to go inside, he let a slight smile slip across his face. He sensed the miracle. The Dubiks' house, so quiet now, was still infused with a pungent spiritual aroma. "Like incense on a soft spring night," he said as he returned to his downstairs bedroom and placed on the dresser a picture of the aging Dalai Lama he always carried with him. To the rhythmic chirping of crickets, he fell into a delicious meditation. He was very pleased he had trusted his intuition about coming to visit Alex.

But Pah Tempe felt empty to Ben and Peg, who walked down to the baths after dinner. No lights on in the big house, no sounds of dogs, no smoke from the chimney.

Once in the ambulance, Moira struggled to tell the attendants she didn't need to lie down. But they had her strapped in, were monitoring her vital signs, and had poked a large bore needle in her arm to quickly infuse her with Lactated Ringers (a solution to bring up her fluid level). Everyone including Grace insisted she be quiet during the half-hour drive.

I'm fine! I'm really fine! she thought fiercely, knotting and unknotting her long fingers in frustration.

The ambulance sped up to the emergency entrance, and Moira was rushed into the emergency room behind a beige curtain. While they rapidly assessed her vital signs, Dr. Hunter filled in the ER physician on her condition. David was slightly embarrassed as each condition came up normal. Moira reported no new contractions since the blessing and upon checking, it appeared the bleeding had stopped.

"Hey, Big Dave," the ER doctor kidded Hunter. "You think you might have jumped the gun on this one?"

"No, she was abrupting, but if I told you she had been miraculously healed, would you believe me?"

The physician just raised an eyebrow and shook his head. "Let's send her down to labor and delivery overnight for observation, just in case this miracle doesn't hold."

Alex arrived at the emergency room at that moment, obviously drunk. He slurred out a demand to see his wife. Moira was shocked to see his reddened eyes and unsteady gait. "Alex, what are you doing?"

"Trying to numb myself, my love," he said morosely.

"Well, go sober up. You're a mess," she said as the orderly pushed her out of the room and into the elevator. "I'll be in 312 when you get presentable," she called out over her shoulder as the elevator door slid shut with a mechanical hum and three muted dings of a bell.

Once the orderly had left her tucked into her bed in the private room, Grace and Moira burst with joy. Grace sat down on the bed and pulled Moira to her. They hugged for a long moment. Then Moira leaned back, rubbed her hands around on her stomach and said with astonishment, "Can you believe it, Mom? Can you really believe it?"

"Yes, I can."

Moira half sang the words, "He healed me. The Lord healed me. I know it. I felt it. It was real..."

Finally Grace put her hands on Moira's shoulders and said, "Come on, you. Let's not press the Lord. You need to rest. Besides I have a little story I can tell you now that this has happened."

"What little story? You and your little stories, Mom."

Grace beamed and paused for effect.

"The Lord opened up all the doors for me to come," she began.

"You see, I had a dream."

"You and your dreams...."

"Will you stop interrupting? This is wonderful." Grace settled back into the orange plastic-covered chair.

Moira plumped up her pillows, leaned back and crossed her arms over her stomach. She looked drained but radiant. She loved being with her mother, whom she had "discovered" only after her father died.

"I saw your son, Iharaira (Israel) as a tall young man."

Moira gasped. "Oh, Mother, what did he look like?"

"A lot like your father, with some of Alex's soft face."

"Oh, how lovely! I'm so jealous. Why can't I have a dream like that?"

"You will. You will," Grace reassured her. "Now I understood in the dream that he is about to lead men into battle, but he is waiting for something. He's young–I'd say 17-18, no more."

"Leading men into battle?"

"Yes, and then I saw him walk up to the Lord and kneel before him for His blessing." Grace choked up at this point.

"Go on, what, Mother?"

"Nothing really. It's that I rarely see the Lord in dreams any more."

"Oh, I'm sorry."

"Anyway, the end of this story is that Iharaira said to me, 'Grandmother, I need you to help me come into this world. Will you do that so I can become a man you will be proud of?'" Grace then asked rhetorically, "What could I say? 'I have my friends, my house, my store?'" "No, I said to him, 'I will go and help.'"

Moira looked lovingly at her mother. "And how could Ben Taylor know to say such a thing about my son?"

"That was the Holy Spirit speaking through him, Iwi." Grace stood up, leaned over the bed, and softly stroked her forehead with her fingertips. "There is no other explanation."

Both women became quiet. Moira leaned back and closed her eyes. After a few moments, a shaft of soft yellow light suddenly streamed in from the door. A nurse, all in white, peeked in to check on her patient, but not wanting to upset the hushed scene, softly closed the door again. Grace pulled up the chair next to the bed, sat back down and propped up her feet on a small coffee table. She wrapped herself in the woolen, light-green shawl she was wearing, and Moira fell asleep. She just laid back against the mound of pillows, her hair flowing out on either side, sighed once or twice and was at peace, breathing at a long, slow pace.

Alex drank three cups of coffee in the hospital cafeteria, but they had little effect on his blood alcohol level. He put his head on his arms and let tears trickle over his suede sleeves and down onto the beige formica table. His hair had come out of its leather band and hung loosely over his shoulders. The heart-sick Czech sculptor found no comfort in the sterile hospital setting. He stayed in that position for nearly a half hour. Then a call over the hospital intercom brought him back.

Wiping his face with his wet sleeve, he sat up and tried to focus. He was alone except for the cafeteria workers mulling around behind the glass and steel food cases. He walked slowly over to them, bought eight hamburgers, stashed them in a bag, and tucked them under his arm. From there he went to the front desk and informed them he would be in the medical center parking lot in a blue Jeep Wagoneer, license name SCULPT, if there were any changes in his wife's condition. After using the men's room, he went out into the sodden dusk to feed his hungry dogs. When the dogs had swallowed the burgers whole, lapped up the last of the water and circled the grassy area several times, Alex climbed with them back into the Jeep Wagoneer and curled up—he to sleep it off. The last thing he remembered was the musky smell of the dogs, their meaty breath, and the occasional thump of a tail against his muddy boots.

In her first dream cycle, Moira saw her father as clearly as if he were standing in the room. Gordon Ihimaera loved and admired his first daughter. He had no sons and often told people that he was glad: he had found the perfect sidekick in his long-legged daughter. Together they fought for Maori rights, side-by-side, until his death in a freak accident five years earlier. Moira had needed no one, except her father. They braved politicians and poachers, ignorance and intolerance even among their own people. This father-daughter team was hugely successful, and powerful.

Now he came to her to say, "Carry on the work we started, Iwi. Carry on, but work for all Lamanites. Take what you've learned to liberate the slaves," then he disappeared.

She thought of Jesus at the synagogue in Nazareth, reading to a hostile congregation Isaiah's prophecy of him: "To liberate the captives, to set the prisoners free."

In the second REM cycle of the night (10-15 minute dream cycle when there is rapid eye movement behind closed eyes), she dreamed what had happened at the end of his life when the two of them were climbing up a small, grassy incline at the northern end of the North Island. They were planning the next step in a seven-year-long political struggle to assure that the Maori people were represented by seasoned Maori politicians who were making their presence known in the Parliament. As they climbed and talked, a large rock suddenly broke loose from an overhang above them and struck Gordon Ihimaera right between the eyes, killing him instantly. But this time, in her dream, he didn't die, but changed before her eyes into a vibrant young man.

Moira let out a loud sob while tears streamed out of her closed eyes. Grace jumped up and leaned protectively over her sleeping daughter. But she slept on.

On the early morning rounds, Dr. Hunter came to check on Moira. He found her dressed and looking out the window to the parking lot. "My, we're up early, aren't we?" he asked in a light voice.

Moira turned and smiled at the sound of his voice, "Yes, we are, and we are feeling marvelous!"

"Would that be you and your young son?"

"And my mother."

"Where is she, by the way?"

"Gone to fetch Alex. I want to go home."

"Sit down, Moira," Dr. Hunter said firmly and pointed to a nearby chair to check her vital signs. "I don't want you going anywhere until I'm sure it's safe." He pulled out a fetoscope and placed it on her stomach. "Honestly now. Any contractions? Bleeding?" he asked.

"Absolutely none. Not one," she said firmly. "I had the most peculiar sensation right after your blessing. I could feel my uterus readjust itself–pull back up and in. That was a medical miracle, wasn't it, Doctor?"

"By all accounts, I'd say it was," he said softly. "But let's not tell *The New England Journal of Medicine*. They might not be so inclined to believe it as, oh, say, your stake president." They both laughed. "Let's just keep you healthy now," Hunter said, returning to his serious doctor's expression, which to Moira seemed a little incongruous on his boyish face. "And let's just get Junior out of this thing alive, what do you say?"

She smiled and nodded.

He listened intently to the fetoscope, then exclaimed, "Hey, his heartbeat is sounding great!"

At that moment the door to Room 312 opened and in walked Grace, followed by a disheveled and rather grizzly-looking Alex. Moira stood up and rushed to him. She wanted to pull him to her and wash his dirty, creased face, then kiss it–his mouth, his eyes, his worried forehead.

"Oh, good, Doc, I'm glad you're here," Alex said, pulling his wife to his side. "You tell Moira she's not to go home. Grace tells me they're planning to leave."

David looked down to say a little prayer before confronting Alex with the news.

"Go on," Alex said impatiently. "I can take it. Just say it. We're losing our baby, right?"

"Wrong, Alex." Hunter looked up and grinned. "It seems that your wife was healed yesterday during our priesthood blessing," he said trying to keep an even, doctorly voice.

"No way!" Alex exclaimed and looked to the doctor then to Moira who both smiled and nodded. Alex felt a blow of surprise catch him in the midriff–like when, as a rookie on the college boxing team, a veteran would catch him with an upper cut, right to the gut. He sat down heavily on the hospital bed, ran his hand through his hair, then asked, "But how can this be? Just hours ago, you were telling me about scalpels, suctions and other horrible stuff." Alex shuddered as if trying to shake off the memory.

Moira watched her husband's face play out a range of emotions everywhere from shock to anger, disbelief to passionate love, finally to relief... and belief.

"So I was talking disaster. Before the blessing," Dr. Hunter explained. "But everything's changed now. Here, I'll show you." Dr. Hunter reached for the clipboard he was carrying. Alex waved him off.

"Moira, are you sure you were as sick as you said?" Alex said turning to his beaming wife. As the words escaped his lips, he realized just how stupid the question sounded, but he felt rational ground rapidly slipping from underneath him. "You didn't complain that much to me."

Moira sat down next to him and put her head on his shoulder. "Yes, I was very sick, and yes, I was healed," she said firmly. "These two things are very, very true."

For once, Alex could find no voice, no facile words, no way to wriggle out with a philosophical or politically correct formula. He just stared at her. Finally, he grinned a goofy grin, took off his baseball cap, walked across the room, picked up her night bag and ushered her out the door. He took her past Grace and the doctor and down the hall to the elevator. Several times he reached out with his free hand to touch her stomach. By all accounts, his mind was blown.

As they followed the couple, Grace, her brown eyes bright but soft, said to David Hunter, "How can we thank you? We shall never forget your blessing. You are truly a servant of the Lord."

"Well, thanks. Why not name your first grandchild Hunter?

That would do nicely," he kidded, a bit embarrassed by the compliment.

The news spread quickly around Pah Tempe and LaVerkin of Moira's healing. Some, like Jed, Jody and Peg believed it without question. Ben believed it when he could remember the electric rush that went through his hands as he blessed Moira. Otherwise he'd forget. When news reached Sandy Hunter, David's wife, she struggled with bitterness. But the person who had the most difficulty with the miracle was Alex.

At first he was delighted at Moira's recovery, which he attributed to "mind over matter." Then he'd remember how everyone in that room had been Mormons, and how angry he'd been at their manipulation of Moira. Then he'd distance himself from the whole lot of them–his wife included.

But he had started on a new piece of sculpture: It was of a young boy and a Collie. Its freshness stood out in stark contrast to the other tortured work that lay in various positions and degrees of polish on work tables throughout the studio.

Chapter Ten

One is faced with a danger that has to be overcome.
Weakness and impatience can do nothing.
It is only when we have the courage to face things
Exactly as they are, without any sort of self-deception
Or illusion, that a light will develop out of events,
By which the path to success may be recognized...
Then we will be able to cross the great water....
"Waiting (Nourishment)," the I Ching

The last vehicles in this circle of friends to try to reach southern Utah before UWEN troops sealed the borders were those belonging to Nate and Laurie Winder. The occupants of the old station wagons who were heading out north to Oregon were part of a tribe, of sorts. They had been drawn to each other in the Ukiah Third Ward as if they were part of an extended premortal family. Ben had taught Jed, who befriended Peter, who admired Nate. And so it went.

This "tribe" of Ukiahans decided to split up in Ukiah, so they wouldn't appear to be a fugitive caravan and automatically become UWEN suspects. Jed and Jody headed south, and the Winders, Bobby Whitmer and Peter Butler turned north toward the Oregon border where they would head east to Nevada and Utah.

As they neared the California/Oregon border, Nate thought back to good times he'd had in Ashland, a small town just across the Oregon border, when he went to see plays at the Shakespearean theater. Now it depressed him to think that the long arm of California developers had even reached Ashland, transforming the quaint town into a large metropolitan area that filled the valley and connected with the next large town, Medford. In fact, much of western Oregon was now a string of housing developments and shopping centers all the way up and down I-5. Like xerox copies of Anaheim and Long Beach, he thought bitterly as he drove into Ashland.

The border patrol, along with its sizable armada of small aircraft and helicopters, brought him abruptly back to the moment. Would the fake border-crossing device trip the alarm? The adults in the two cars tried to look relaxed; the children prayed to Heavenly Father and tried not to cry. Nothing happened as they drove through the checkpoint. They did not move as they drove the next five miles down the winding mountain pass into Ashland–they were like statues, scarcely breathing–afraid the patrol had been alerted. After they got off the interstate and made a series of turns onto side streets, they finally relaxed. No one appeared to be following them.

After a night's stay in Ashland, they traveled east through Klamath Falls and down to Winnemucca, Nevada. It was in this stretch of the drive, between Klamath and Denio, over winding canyon roads and barren desert floors, that the argument between Laurie and Nate began.

Actually it was an unresolved issue–where they were going to settle in Utah–that started the ball rolling. The daughter of an apostle, Laurie was determined to take the family to Salt Lake where her brother lived. (Her parents, along with other general authorities' families, were in hiding.) Nate wanted to put down roots near his parents, who had more to offer the kids in the way of a home in St. George, because they owned a lot of land in that semi-rural area where the Winders could build. This would be better than Salt Lake, which in the last decade had contracted all the social infections that now plagued all American cities, so that it was no longer seen by anyone as a clean and quiet refuge in the Rockies.

When the business district in Salt Lake closed down for the night, gangs roamed the streets, just blocks from Temple Square, armed with Chinese assault rifles and high on the new drug of choice--synetrope, an acid/speed blend. Interactive television allowed children to access and participate in graphic videos depicting terrorist tactics, rape, dismemberment, even cannibalism. By last count there seemed to be more virtual-reality arcades in Salt Lake than restaurants. *Living near their well-connected cousins will not be enough,* Nate thought, *to buffer these kids from the bestiality that literally lurks on Utah's capitol street corners. I want my kids in the country!*

Laurie was steely, determined to win the argument. She pressed the point again and again. He was hollow-eyed, run down by the endless arguments with her. Nate was a kind man, quiet, a really good administrator who was accustomed to arbitration in the business world. But with Laurie, he felt it was always a contest of wills—never a discussion for discussion's sake. Always a challenge to see who would emerge the champ.

Nate drove too fast. Their five younger children sat scared and quiet in the back of the station wagon. Given the mood of their parents, they knew they would be taken to task, especially by their mother, if they were at all noisy. Recently the little one had ventured to ask her, quite innocently, "When are you and Daddy getting a divorce?" The answer was a sharp slap across the face.

Laurie was furious that Nate was constantly caving in—to her, to creditors, to everyone. He never provided the kind of luxury that she had grown up with as the only daughter, along with two sons, to a financially successful corporate lawyer who became an apostle. Now, eighteen years into their marriage, Laurie was always trying to find ways to keep things together, kitchenware at the thrift shop, cheaper cuts of meat, last year's clothes redesigned as hand-me-downs for the girls. They hadn't had a real vacation for nearly five years.

So what began for Laurie several years ago as a few furtive images was now developing into elaborate daydreams, a daily ritual that occupied many waking moments, an inner soap opera, in which she was swept away from her present horror by a man, always blue-eyed, much more powerful than Nate—a man like her father. Her cup filled with contempt for her husband. And so, both to punish and awaken him, she went in after him, time after time, trying to rattle his cage, to make him more aggressive. The "perfect" Mormon couple's life (Nate, a high priest and first counselor in the bishopric, Laurie twice called as

Primary president) was unraveling. Nearly broke, marriage on the rocks–they still sat in a perfect line in Sacrament service, all the children combed, Sunday-best, so quiet and well-behaved. But people in their ward sensed the crisis.

Thursday morning in Winnemucca, two things happened which rubbed salt into the couple's already raw wounds. First, one of the station wagons' electric batteries would not hold a charge. Most cars were now run by large battery packs–quite expensive at $1200. They were designed to go three years. Theirs was less than a year old. This new battery which they had to buy would exhaust their savings. Laurie, alternately cynical and shrill, openly blamed Nate for the problem in front of the rest of the company.

Winnemucca parts stores didn't have a battery for the Winders' older model vehicle, so they had to wait for one to be shipped in from Reno. Peter and Bobby stood at the parts counter, while Nate went to the men's room. On the way back, he overheard Peter saying, "...and that's why I haven't got married–afraid I'd marry a witch like that."

Bobby replied, "Scares me, too."

"I'd put her in her place, right on her fanny, if I were Nate."

"She was nicer when I was young, but she's gotten pretty hard over the years."

Ashamed, Nate deliberately walked up to them, not wanting to hear more.

The second thing that compounded their misery was that Missy, their ten-year-old, got out of bed about 4:00 a.m., went into the bathroom and immediately began throwing up. She continued having dry heaves for most of the morning. When the three men returned with the battery so that Peter could install it (they couldn't risk having a mechanic find the DAI), Laurie took her daughter to the emergency room. She had to pay ninety-five dollars for the diagnosis of mild food poisoning and an anti-vomiting remedy. The hospital insisted on cash. Now the Winders were down to less than fifty dollars in hard currency.

Laurie blamed this on Nate, too. He was the one who insisted they eat at the truck stop in Denio. But it wasn't the food, it was the tension of trying to get past another border that made Missy ill. That, and her parents' constant bickering.

By the time they left Winnemucca, it was well into the afternoon. Cloudy, windy, it looked like it might snow. They had hoped to travel a while on I-80, before leaving it for smaller side roads, but Peter had overheard a couple of mechanics from the repair shop next to the parts store talking about being stopped on a roadblock right outside Battle Mountain. He struck up a conversation to get the details. "What about that roadblock?" he asked in his engaging Aussie manner.

The older of the two mechanics said, "Used to be we could go from one end of the state to the other without being stopped. Man, tourists used to tear through this state at a hundred miles an hour–and not that long ago. Now you can barely go from town to town without being stopped by Interpol."

"Why Interpol?" Peter tried to moderate the tone of his voice to sound interested, but not too interested.

"'Cause everybody knows there's folks who's got home-made DAI's. I had a guy just the other day, offered me five hundred bucks if I'd make him one."

"Why didn't ya?" asked the younger one with missing index finger.

"Who says I didn't!" the older one guffawed.

Peter laughed along with them, then excused himself to warn the "merry band." So the caravan headed directly south over what looked on the map like hard-packed dirt road for a hundred and ten miles. They would then follow a paved Highway 121 to 50.

Nate and Laurie drove with the five small children behind the other car driven by Peter. Peter, who had built and raced stock cars, drove fast, kicking up a dust cloud. The Winders soon found they were breathing the choking desert dust, so Nate slowed down at the complaints of his family. But they cried they were going to be lost, so he sped up again. Suddenly Peter slowed down to a crawl. "What is he doing now?" Laurie whined.

"I'm not sure. It looks like he's seen something," Nate said as they began to catch up with the first car.

What Peter and his carload had slowed down for was a burnt-out shell of a car that straddled the dirt road. It had been blown up by an Interpol missile. No one spoke as both cars negotiated around it into the brush then back onto the road. It sat as a silent monument to the long arm of the UWEN.

Peter then put his foot to the accelerator and sped off. The complaining from Nate's family began anew. Their howls brought Nate to a snapping point. Wiping sweat off his upper lip, he squeezed the steering wheel, leaned forward and pressed his foot down hard on the accelerator, flying down the hard-packed dirt road in pursuit of the other station wagon. Laurie gripped her seat belt and began to berate him, but he just kept going until he was nearly on Peter's bumper. They should have been traveling at 20 mph, but were going 40. Nate had to put on the wipers to see through the pebbles, shards of cactus and clumps of dirt that Peter's back tires kicked up on Nate's windshield.

Nevada roads are fairly well-maintained, even dirt ones, and this one was no exception. They made good time, slowing only where the path crossed rough arroyos. The late afternoon sky filled with clouds and the winds began to pick up. The children pointed to dust devils in the distance. The late afternoon sky filled with clouds. Laurie, who had been digging her red-lacquered fingernails into her palms, finally exploded. "Stop this car!" she shrieked. "Stop it immediately!"

Nate kept on at the same speed. He was enjoying that his wife's shiny emotional armor was finally cracking at the seams, although he was sorry that the kids had to see it. "I'm going to jump out if you don't stop!" she yelled. With a wry grin, Nate slowed down a bit, reached across the passenger side and opened the door. In one motion she slammed the door and slapped him so hard that his nose bled. The children burst into tears. Wiping away the flowing blood with the back of his hand, Nate began honking the horn to get Peter to stop, but Peter couldn't hear Nate over his blaring CD.

Nate and Laurie sat glaring at each other. "We're going to Salt Lake, I'm going to drive and you can do nothing about it," she said in a menacing whine. "Get out of this car!" The children cried even louder. Nate sat staring ahead, not sure what to do. Finally Peter noticed the loss of the brown station wagon and turned back to see what was wrong. He hopped out thinking the problem was with the battery again.

All four doors opened, and the Winders got out to stand in the cold windy desert. People were looking to Nate, but he was stunned. He just looked off at Job Peak in the distance. (Since he did not know the name of the mountain, the irony went unnoticed.) Confused, the passengers in the other car got out mumbling, "What's happening? What's wrong?"

At just that moment a low flying aircraft swooped down out of a cloud bank and buzzed the scene. Children screamed and tumbled back into the cars. The adults could only look to the sky and watch helplessly as the small plane set down on the paved highway. "What are we going to say?" came at Nate from several directions.

"We are going to say we had trouble with our battery, that we've been sightseeing and we're headed home to..." Nate quickly opened the glove compartment and pulled out a Nevada-Utah map, "...ah, Fallon. Let me do the talking. Laurie, you go quiet down those kids. Tell them this is just a nice guy who wants to help us."

The small band of adults stood quietly as a uniformed officer with the Nevada air patrol approached. Nate walked over to greet him. "What's the problem here?" he asked stiffly. Nate tried not to look down at the pistol the exceptionally tall man had strapped to his belt.

"Out sightseeing, officer. Trouble with the battery cable, it turns out." The officer stood silent. Nate couldn't see the man's eyes behind the one-way glasses.

"We've got it worked out."

Silence.

"We're headed home to Fallon. These darn battery-run cars–I wish we'd go back to gas."

The officer wrote down both California license plates, then said, "How long you lived in Fallon?"

"Just a few months. I'm a mining engineer sent out from Sacramento." Nate was grateful for his college improvisation training.

"You need to get new plates. They'll fine you."

"Thank you, officer, I will."

The man stood a moment more looking over the group, then turned and in long strides walked to the plane. No one moved until the engine had warmed up and the plane had begun its taxiing down the highway. At that point, Nate turned to Laurie and said, "Fine. Leave. I just want to ask Peter if he'll go along with you, for your safety." He headed over to the other car.

Laurie's mouth dropped. "You're not going?" she called after him.

"Whoever wants to go with me is going to St. George," Nate hollered back over his shoulder, ignoring Laurie's astonished posture. After much discussion, Peter agreed to go along with Laurie, but she would do all the driving. She wasn't about to be terrorized by another madman at the wheel, she insisted.

Nate called the children to gather around. Laurie's eyes flashed from Nate to the children and back to Nate. She knew he was the more popular of the two and if the kids had a choice they probably all would want to go with their father, so she quickly jumped in with, "No, you and I will decide. I don't want to leave such an important a decision as this to them."

Laurie chose the five youngest ones. The children weren't happy with the arrangement, but they climbed into the assigned cars, slamming doors in protest. As if to deepen her humiliation, Laurie had to borrow $100 from her nephew.

The two cars made it without incident to the paved Highway 121. Then Laurie took the northern route on 50 toward Salt Lake

City. She drove fast, grimly determined to rescue the rest of her family as soon as she had this half settled down in Salt Lake. She knew if Nate settled in too long with his doting parents, it would be a lot harder to reunite them. Nate, with Bobby and the older children, kept to a southerly route that took them to Tonopah. From there they followed the route Jed and Jody had taken. Nate felt nothing–except perhaps relief. He knew he couldn't think about those five little faces pressed to the car window as they separated at the junction.

Nate Winder wasn't really handsome–more rugged-looking than anything. His square jaw and curly black hair offset his small, dark eyes and large Roman nose. And his grandfather's pioneer body type had been passed down to Nate–tall, angular, but muscular–one could see how his ancestors were able to walk for days, survive one illness or accident after another and still live to be 80. Maybe this is what is meant by being the literal seed of Abraham.

Now Nate's dark eyes were narrowed, almost hooded, and his jaw fixed as he braced himself to face what seemed to have been the foreordained outcome of his marriage to Laurie Whitmer. Even her own father had taken Nate aside before the wedding and said, "Nate, I'm not sure you want to go through with this. I love Laurie and she's my daughter, but she can be willful to the point of obstinacy and has a biting tongue no amount of loving persuasion has been able to cure." Nate was sure she'd change when she was able to leave the competitive nest she'd been raised in.

That's the first of a lot of good counsel I ignored, he moaned to himself. He glanced in the rear view mirror at his four children, Nate III (Neddy), Cannon, Andrew and Cristina. The two older boys were stretched out in the far back of the station wagon and the other two curled up on the seat in front of them. He couldn't tell if they were sleeping or overcome by the enormity of the situation. Bobby Whitmer, his nephew, sat alongside him.

Bobby, who always loved a captive audience, now chattered on, with scarcely a question or grunt to keep him going. Nate was grateful for his company. He felt very old, very used up.

"So, Bobby," Nate interrupted the monologue,"we have not really had time to talk about the end of your mission in England. What was it really like in those last scary days?" *That should keep us going for thirty or forty miles,* Nate thought, somewhat amused at his nephew's theatrical delivery.

"Well, Uncle Nate, it was pretty scary. Once guns became plentiful in England, even Chinese-made AKA 47's (he paused for emphasis), it was an armed camp and we missionaries were targets, big time, but we didn't carry weapons. Being on God's errand, we had to rely on Him." As he said this, he tossed back the shock of curly mop that had flopped over one eye. His hair bore no signs of the military cut he had maintained on his mission.

The high beams of an oncoming car momentarily blinded the two. "Jeez, what are they trying to do?" Bobby asked.

"Highlight your story," Nate chuckled.

"But looking back now," Bobby plunged on, "I realize I probably would have been killed because it was such a temptation to rely on the arm of flesh instead of the Lord's. You know the old saying, don't you Uncle Nate, 'Trust in Allah, but tie up your camel?'"

Nate couldn't contain a snicker. "No, Bobby, I don't believe I do, but it sounds like good advice."

Bobby launched into a detailed account of the gang activity in Birmingham before he and his companion were shipped out in the middle of the night. "They were armed to the teeth and determined to hunt us down. It was really spooky." He hugged himself and shivered.

"I can't imagine the Church would leave you in such dangerous conditions, Bobby. Are you sure it was that wretched?"

"Well, close. The whole atmosphere felt that way."

As Bobby continued his melodramatic monologue, Nate felt himself spiral down into black bitterness. *How could the Lord let the world come to this?* he thought morosely. After several miles passed with Nate half-listening to Bobby's exaggerated version of political events in England, he tired of the anger that hung in the air, so he asked, "So how was it in Ukiah? How did the missionary work go there?"

"Really great!" Bobby exuded. "We weren't allowed to openly proselyte, but teaching members how to convert people was really great! We had a lot of success. People are scared these days. They want something they can hang on to. The Gospel gives them that...."

Having turned the conversation in a more positive direction, Nate let Bobby continue, grateful for his buoyancy and enthusiasm. Minutes into his Ukiah tale, Bobby suddenly changed the subject, "What about the invasion, Uncle Nate? Do you think the Chinese will really invade us?"

"You know, Bobby, I've been so caught up in my own affairs lately that I haven't paid that much attention to the rumors. What do you think?"

"I KNOW! We've only got weeks at the most, and it's war time, big time, right here on our soil." Bobby gestured broadly.

For a moment Nate thought it might be nice to be overrun by Chinese and shot dead in his bed, even the whole family. *Let us go home to Heavenly Father. Enough of this struggle.* Bobby was background to his brooding as he glanced out at the starry Nevada sky. *When will you come, Lord?* he asked. He let a few tears run down his cheeks. When he tuned back in, his nephew was in the middle of a laundry list of weapons. Weapons which Nate slowly came to realize were being transported in their station wagon--at that very moment!

"...a Winchester stainless steel shotgun, real good one back there. It's got plastic grips. A couple of boxes of slugs. Thought I'd get a laser scope for it but it's hard to get now and too expensive. A totally reliable 30/30–not as powerful as some, but a great all-around gun.

Nate felt a laugh well up in his belly and roll on up into his throat. "Ha, ha," he began. "Ha, Ha, Ha," he laughed harder. New tears formed in his eyes. "HAA, HAA!" He couldn't stop.

Belly laughs rolled up and out, one after the other.

The silent teenagers began laughing. Bobby, bewildered at first, joined in the outburst. Nate clung to the steering wheel, doing his best not to weave into the oncoming lane. Bobby tried several times to ask what it was he had said that was so funny, but Nate couldn't stop. He was breathless with the laughter.

Finally, paroxysms subsided and Nate managed to stammer, "You mean to tell me you've got weapons in the car? That's what you've been talking about, weapons?"

"That's what I was telling you, Uncle Nate. I've got enough for us to blast our way across any border crossing," Bobby crowed and pantomimed a shootout.

A couple of teenagers rose from the rear and leaned over the front seat, "Wow! Neat." But Nate cut them short with a sweep of his arm and they leaned back into the dark.

"Besides we're going to need it when the Chinese come pouring in from the north and Mexicans from the south," Bobby said smugly.

The kids in the far back began asking questions, but Nate again chopped the air with his arm, like a karate expert demonstrating a move. They fell quiet.

"Bobby, do you know what would have happened to us if we'd been stopped? Do you know what would have happened if that Interpol pilot had decided to search through our cars?"

"Yeah, I know exactly. I would have blown him away."

"No, Bobby, we would have been in boiling hot water, pal!"

A tense silence reigned. Then Nate broke it with, "So now that you've been released from your missionary duties, you're free to rely on the arm of the flesh, is that it?" He flashed a grin at Bobby.

"Got to." Bobby grinned back and breathed a sigh of relief. "It's only missionaries who lead charmed lives. Besides I'm going off to serve my country any day. May as well start practicing."

"So, okay, Bobby, we're dying to know. Fill us in on everything you've got. I'm not even going to ask where you accumulated this little arsenal." Nate glanced back at his kids who were wide-eyed at the turn the evening's conversation had taken.

"Let's see. I've got a .357 magnum revolver. I was going to get a .44 but it had too big a kick on it. It's a heavier gun and a slower gun, but when it hits, it's bad."

"Ahhh," came from the back of the car.

"A .38 baretta–holds a lot of ammo, a 9-round clip–doesn't kick too hard. Anyone can use it. Neddy could handle it."

"Yeah," from an eager Neddy.

"I've got to be honest, though, knives are my real passion. Guns are fun, but knives, they're cool. I've got a pretty good collection. You know that tool box back there? I've got 20 in there of varying sizes, a couple in my suitcase along with a 1909 Argentine saber bayonet with a 14" blade."

A chorus of "Ooh's" swelled from the rear.

"You're probably not going to believe this," Bobby whispered in a conspiratorial tone, "but I've got five knives on me right now."

"No way!" Cannon spoke up like a solo voice in the Greek chorus accompanying Bobby's litany of weapons.

Pumped up by the adoring audience, Bobby put back his head and laughed lustily. "One time, in Ukiah, I got dressed up in my old blue missionary suit, the one made of iron that my mother bought for me before I left for England, and I fit every single knife I own on me. And you know what?"

"What?" the children's voices rose expectantly in unison from the blackness of the car.

"Couldn't walk very well, but in all honesty, if I had taken about three of them out, I could have moved around normally. Hey, man, I had blades up to the teeth. "

Peals of appreciative laughter rose from the rear audience.

"It was really difficult on my mission because they wouldn't let us carry weapons. We had to rely on the Lord," Bobby spoke in a low serious tone. "Looking back now, I realized that if I had been armed, I would have been killed because I would have relied on weapons."

Heavy silence from the teenagers.

"Well, anyway. We're armed! I've got shoulder straps and holster for all the guns. All the knives have sheaths and we've all got pockets. So we can sure as shootin' take care of any Interpol patrol!"

"Yeah! Okay! Cool!" his audience enthused.

"I don't think so, pal," Nate said severely. "In fact, I've got half a mind to dump the whole stash."

Every child in the car froze. Bobby, mouth agape, stared at his uncle with a mixture of incredulity and outrage.

"Do you know what could still happen to us–if we got caught hauling around hardware like this?" Nate took his eyes off the road to glance meaningfully at his nephew.

"I'm not afraid of that," Bobby shot back, his voice growing suddenly husky. A slight twitch grabbed the corner of his mouth.

"Well, I am," Nate responded."They'd handcuff us around the neck, for crying out loud, and lock us up for a very long time, buddy. At best!"

Bobby turned his eyes to the glove compartment in front of him and started playing with the button.

"Still..." Nate's voice slid along the air, then trailed off.

All the energy in the car rushed to a sudden focus on him.

"Still and all, I can see where this stuff could come in mighty handy in the future."

A cheer began to rise in the throats of the huddled masses.

"In the future," Nate said in the voice of a drill sergeant with new recruits. "Not now. And not against the Interpol."

And not while I've a car full of kids, he thought.

"And since we're not planning on shooting anyone, we're going to keep all this hardware packed, nice and quiet, right where it lies. For the whole trip. Is that understood?"

"Ah...h...h," they whined, the wind taken out of their sails.

Bobby was grateful he and his weapons were not standing on the darkened highway, so he beamed broadly, changed the subject and said, "Hey, Uncle Nate, you know the old saying, don't you?"

"Another old saying?"

"You can't make a revolution with silk gloves."

Nate chuckled at his nephew. "No, Bobby, who said that?"

"Stalin."

"I see," he laughed. For reasons he couldn't articulate, Nate felt enormously invigorated by these last few minutes. It was as if that adolescent boy inside him, bound and gagged many years ago, had suddenly burst to the surface of his consciousness—Peter Pan flying into Neverland, crowing for the Lost Boys to rise up and prepare for pirates.

Nate eased the dust-caked ancient station wagon into a parking stall at a rest stop on I-15 just outside Glendale. He'd had a nagging suspicion during the last few miles he should call his parents in St. George before descending on them. The phone at their house rang and rang. Finally the answering machine clicked on. *Darn it*, Nate thought. *Where are they? It's the middle of the night.*

"Hi, this is the Winders. We're not home right now, nor will we be until Jericho falls to Joshua." Click.

Instantly Nate froze; terror seeped through his rigid joints like dry ice. This was the message his family had worked out in the event of an emergency that would be too risky to talk about over the phone. He stood there, phone in hand, trying hard not to let fantasies of dead parents flood through his mind. Then he walked slowly back to the car, mulling over what might be happening.

"Hey, Uncle Nate, why so glum?" Bobby bounded up.

"I can't reach my parents. Something's very wrong."

"How do you know?"

"The message on the answering machine. Whatever we do, we can't go on to St. George."

"Hey, maybe the U.S. has been invaded!" Bobby said excitedly.

"No, I think people around here would be acting differently," Nate replied noting the nonchalance with which a family of four got out of their car, stretched and chattered while the family dog relieved himself. "Where are the kids?" Nate asked worriedly.

"In the rest rooms."

"Go get them." Nate sounded sterner than he meant to.

While Bobby went to round up the kids, Nate remembered Jed had given him Pah Tempe's phone number. Normally Nate would not have risked calling there, but with Laurie gone, he felt a new forcefulness taking shape within him. He felt he could make a decision without having to steel his nervous system against the assault of her rage or cynicism. He pulled out the blue slip of paper, took a deep breath and dropped the requisite coins in the slots. His hand trembled as he dialed the number. The phone rang and rang but no one picked it up.

At that moment his children traipsed up to the station wagon. "What's happening, Dad?" Cristina asked.

"I don't know. I can't get ahold of Granddaddy and Grammy. We'll have to try again in the morning." He loaded his charges into the car and drove to the first motel that still had a vacancy sign in the window.

Later, when it was just he who lay awake, he wondered how his kids maintained hope in a world gone so bad. He decided they must know some things deep in their unconscious that he didn't--something about the millennium that allowed them the improbable luxury of being children in a world careening off into catastrophe.

The next morning at Pah Tempe, before seven, Jed walked down the path past the broken-up swimming pool and leaned on a boulder facing up river. He was feeling grey. He hadn't noticed the prominent rock formation across the river above the Dubiks' house, which looked like the head of an Indian warrior in war paint. Now he stared up at the native gargoyle. The overcast sky added to his mood, so he pulled out one of his harmonicas, a C major, and began to play a few lazy bars from "We Shall Overcome." Then he put it down, wiped it carefully and sang in a husky untrained voice,"...we shall overcome some day, oh yeah,

...deep in my heart, I do believe..." He was feeling a little homesick, but nothing he couldn't handle with an hour or so of courting the blues.

It helped him to remember one of his favorite heroes, Martin Luther King and the trials by fire that finally consumed him. He pulled out a copy of King's "Letter from Birmingham Jail" which he always kept in his *Book of Mormon*. He didn't open the well-worn paper, but fingered it for comfort.

Then he played and sang for some time before he became aware that the phone in the office was ringing. After another twenty or so rings, Jed finally got up and moseyed over to the office where he picked up the old black phone and said, "Hey there, who's calling at this hour of the morning?"

"Jed, is that you?" Nate asked.

"Yeah, who's this?"

"Nate!"

"Hey, Nate, where are you, man?"

"Ah, Glendale, Nevada's finest motel. A real dump."

Jed chuckled. "So, what's up?"

"Ah...ah...Jed, I've got a little trouble talking about this subject."

"Oh, no," Jed moaned. He felt his arms go leaden. No good at clipping, he never could think of nuances necessary to pull it off.

"Jed, are you there?"

"Yeah, go ahead. I understand," he said reluctantly.

"I'm having trouble reaching my parents. You wouldn't know what they'd be up to, in a larger sense, would you?"

Jed searched madly for an more exotic meaning to Nate's words, but nothing came, so he said, "Ah, ah, I don't know what they're doing, but I've got a great place you can stay until they come home."

Nate, relieved that Jed was reading him, asked, "A resort nearby?"

Jed then told him about Nephi Bingham and managed to clip fairly decent instructions to the ranch. "Thanks, Jed. You're a real lifesaver. Hey, just one last question. When do you think my folks might be home?"

"Can't say. Might be a week, ten days–hard to say. They usually return within a couple of weeks."

Nate was suddenly sure that Utah had been invaded, not by Chinese, but by the UWEN and that they were doing in Utah what they had done in other parts of the United States–sealing the borders. And when the UWEN had made it clear to the natives that they were calling the shots, they left only remnants of the invading army as a token occupation force and pulled out the rest to another hot spot, unsealing the borders.

With that information Nate was filled with the hope that his parents might be okay. "Thank you, Jed. We'll be in touch. Love to your family." And, for the second time in three days, a car with weary pilgrims drove up the long road to the Bingham sheep ranch, grateful for its sanctuary.

Chapter Eleven

Ah, love, let us be true
To one another! for the world, which seems
To lie before us like a land of dreams,
Hath really neither joy, nor love, nor light,
Nor certitude, nor peace, nor help for pain;
And we are here as on a darkling plain
Swept with confused alarms of struggle and flight,
Where ignorant armies clash by night.
   "Dover Beach," Matthew Arnold

Hazrat Patel, who was wrestling a cold, had his hand on the phone, ready to dial out. Inside a chilly, busy hangar at the St. George airport, he was in the process of telling his junior officer where to begin an electronic paper search for members of Utah's fugitive list, when the phone rang. Patel blew loudly into a handkerchief and answered tersely, "Patel here."

"Haz? This is Les." Lieutenant General Les Hackmann was calling from Central Command in Zurich.

Patel dismissed his aide with a wave of his hand. He waited until the door had closed completely to continue. "Afternoon, Sir," Haz responded.

"So how goes it down in Utah, General? Become a Mormon yet?" the three-star general joked. "Get you a few of those sweet little Mormon wives? I understand even a poor Mormon gets a minimum of five."

Patel snorted, then chuckled as he took a much-chewed Havana cigar out of his mouth and flicked stubby grey ash into an ashtray on his desk. "No, Sir, not yet. And how's life in Zurich? Do you still eat apple strudel with every meal?"

"Of course!" Hackmann boomed. "And I take my baths in *Kaffe mit Schlag.*"

"Say again?"

"Kaffe mit Schlag! Coffee with whipped cream. Remember? Haz, we gotta get you back to the world of civilization, boy. You're forgetting everything down there."

"You say the word, Les," Patel continued with the banter, "and I'll have the whole bloody brigade on transports in twenty-four hours."

"I'll just bet you would, old buddy. I'll just bet you would."

Both men laughed.

The obligatory repartee over, Patel leaned forward, put both elbows on the desk and waited expectantly during a brief silence—waiting for General Hackmann to come out with the real purpose of the call. It wasn't like him to call at all.

"Haz, we've got more on our hands than we thought with these damn Chinks. Scares the hell out of me, frankly. A billion of those slant-eyed gooks on the loose. Major trouble. Why, we've never been really able to get them to get with the UWEN program." Les cleared his throat. "Damn bunch of ideological fanatics! And now, with fresh intelligence reports in...well, like I said, scares the 'Be-jeebers' out of me."

"It is becoming extremely threatening," Patel agreed.

"You bet it is. They've even got themselves a Genghis Khan. What's his name?"

"Lu Han."

"Lu Hoo, whatever. Well, to cut to the chase, Haz, I'm sorry to end your vacation in Mormon-land, but we need to pull you out of there by Monday, 0800 hours. Have you enjoyed yourself?"

"Bored out of my mind."

"Hey, I said you should get ahold of some of those Mormon women, Haz. Can you mop up things by then?"

"No problem. Where to next?"

"Alaska. You'll be meeting up with four other divisions there. If our intelligence reports are correct, the crazy gooks are planning to invade Alaska by mid-week."

There was silence on the other end.

"Haz?"

"Yes, I'm here. I'm just a little surprised they'd do such a thing in the dead of winter. But then, I forgot there isn't much snow up there with this global-warming stuff. Still, it's gonna take some different moves than we used in Afghanistan."

"Well, I'll tell you, Haz. The big boys are getting real antsy and real worried about this one. I've heard lots of talk about the possibility of limited nuking. Anyway," Hackmann continued after a tense silence, "some boys from my staff will fly in there tomorrow to talk details with you."

When Hazrat got off the phone, he rose out of the swivel chair, ground the half-smoked cigar into bits and pieces and walked out into the hangar to find the young captain he'd just sent away.

"Mishec," he shouted over the noise of truck repair being done nearby. Mishec, a slender, worried man from Swaziland, jerked around. Patel gestured sharply for him to return to the office. Hazrat coughed into a handkerchief, turned and slammed the door to cut out the noise ricocheting off the metal hangar walls. The aide returned on the run.

"Shut the door quickly," he barked to Mishec who lingered in the doorway to say something to a fellow African, working on a nearby Jeep.

The harassed man quickly shut the door and saluted. Patel nodded, then barked, "It's more urgent than ever that we get into that fugitive list. We may have to leave soon," Patel said, not wanting to divulge any more information than was necessary to Mishec. He didn't trust Africans. "I don't want the time spent here to be for nothing. Only five illegal DAI's in as many days. That's nothing and no more than 50 illegals dead. It's pathetic."

Mishec looked down at his ill-fitting boots and waited for Patel to finish his tirade. Although they were fellow Muslims, he didn't respect Patel. He felt the Afghan's religious piety was affected. He was careful, though, not to let the thought cross his face. Patel could be very cruel.

"...and I want men pulled off that border patrol, out of the small border crossings. Leave the ones on I-15 and major towns, but the rest I want in here, NOW!"

"Yes, sir," Mishec snapped a crisp salute and nearly ran to the other end of the hangar to the communication center.

Patel paced back and forth in his office. *I want to really hurt these sneaky Mormon bastards before I leave,* he thought, rapping the desk smartly with the thick gold ring on his pinkie finger. *That old Thai, what's-his-name in northern Utah, at least he's had a few pitched battles, a couple of thousand killed. But here, only a couple of reported illegal border crossings. Definitely not much fun. And definitely no promotions. I want a second star before I go home!*

He decided right then and there they'd begin a house-to-house search for the top twenty-five on the fugitive list. At least he could terrify the residents of southern Utah before leaving for Alaska to join Operation Yellow River. "We're going to fill up the Yukon with a river of yellow Chink blood," Les had exuded. Patel smiled at the thought and lit up another cigar. He inhaled deeply and picked up the gold-framed picture of his family—wife, Sadia, and five daughters—from his neatly ordered desk.

Bobby Whitmer's intuition was right. The Chinese had decided the time was ripe for a long-planned invasion of the United States. The 90's and first years into the 21st century had been a time of heavy capital investment from both the Chinese themselves and from the West, leading to enormous technological and industrial strides within China—strides taken so far and so fast that the rest of the world looked on with both awe and a vague dread, especially as the Chinese began to make ominous rumbling against Russia, Japan and Southeast Asia. They amassed millions of troops on one or another of its fronts in what they called routine maneuvers. Then came the "Five-year Nightmare," as the Chinese themselves called it, which caused them again to press the borders in record numbers, but this time not as organized military troops. Their country was filled with roaming hordes of desperate and displaced people whose agricultural areas had been ravaged by floods, bugs, and calamitous weather. And probably Sangay's observation was right that the lopsided ratio of men to women was a contributor to a new aggressive energy. Whatever the combination of factors, one thing was for sure: the great sleeping giant, now modernized, had awakened–but only to a new nightmare–which was causing the confused goliath to thrash about for a new solution.

The United States had no national elections scheduled for November. The Chinese perceived, accurately, that the country had disintegrated into regional factions. That, along with the fact that America no longer had any real standing army of its own, left the country vulnerable to attack.

Like every other major industrialized nation, the U.S. had allowed its military to be absorbed into the UWEN, so the world would have "world peace through world government," as a popular UWEN slogan ran. Now the only Americans who wore U.S. military uniforms were a few National Guard troops in each state. Otherwise, every military base from Fort Huachuca to Fort Benning was filled with UWEN troops in their white and powder blue garb. Some were Americans, but most were not. And only the UWEN had the capacity to wage nuclear war. Supposedly.

This fact had deterred many nations from waging all-out war. There were those flash-fires here and there, which the UWEN quickly put out with its overwhelming military superiority. But, as a few astute Sinologists had pointed out, the Chinese had sheer numbers on their side. They could absorb any amount of nuclear hardware thrown at them. Having suffered losses of hundred of millions of people, they would still have many more trained and fanatically dedicated troops, poised to overflow and occupy any enemy the old-fashioned way.

Encouraged by the disintegration of American political institutions, Chinese general Lu Han told Chairman Zhu Hao that now was the time to strike. A week later, Zhu galvanized his people by declaring they must be reunited with the brave Chinese pioneers who had successfully colonized the West coast of the United States and take back the rich oil fields that had once been theirs.

Now, while Hazrat Patel and some of the UWEN forces worldwide were withdrawing from their present positions and heading to Alaska, the Chinese knew they had to take advantage of the time factor involved in bringing far-flung UWEN troops to the Arctic. They had amassed nearly one million men on the Siberian side of the international date line. Hazrat's 15,000 men would be in position in 48 hours. But his light infantry brigade and the four other divisions obviously would be no match for this swarm who waited for General Lu Han's signal to advance. The UWEN went into an emergency session to discuss limited nuclear "containment."

This Alaskan attack was to get the oil reserves, to be sure. And many of the defenders of the old Chinese policy argued that China should stop once she had the oil. Some even declared that China had a natural right to the Alaskan area and its resources. But the UWEN high command, very rudely awakened by this perilous turn of events, could not afford to trust that the Chinese would stop there. They suspected that Chinese troops were primed to invade all West Coast cities in the Northern Hemisphere—Nome to Panama City.

Two natural phenomena had occurred which gave the invaders access to Alaska that they did not have in the 20th century. First was the great Alaskan quake which filled in the land bridge across the Bering Strait. Second was the near-depletion of the Earth's ozone layer, causing a warming trend that left the Arctic above zero for long periods during the winter. As a result, the ice cap was melting and swamping coastlines worldwide, and the West Coast cities were no exception. Naturally, these floods caused many billions of dollars of damage. But what was even worse was that coastal cities from Seattle to San Diego were especially vulnerable to takeover, since utility workers, police and National Guard units were strained beyond their capacity in a frantic attempt to save homes, shelter flood victims, keep roadways open for food transports. In this frenzied coastal scramble to literally stay afloat, no one had time to think about guarding their airports against invading forces.

Patel's final act, the dragnet, accomplished what he intended. Although his crack troops found only one man who was wanted for political sabotage from the Most Wanted list, they succeeded in traumatizing the residents of St. George, Cedar City and surrounding towns. The people of Pah Tempe, whose nerves were already raw, were especially affected. When word reached Alex that troops were combing Hurricane and LaVerkin for wanted political criminals, he called everyone together at the big house.

Jody, Jed and baby Craig sat close together on one couch, while Peg and Ben sat on another, holding hands, with Danny and Miriam on the floor in front of them. Grace and Moira talked in low tones to Alex while he stoked the freshly-made fire. Sangay warmed himself in the occasional chair near the fireplace.

When everyone had found their seats, Ben announced, "Alex, we're going to leave here in the morning. I can't jeopardize your good wife any further. We feel guilty enough putting such strain on her." He looked over at Moira who had wrapped her arms protectively around her stomach. They exchanged warm glances.

"No, you aren't!" Alex was adamant. "There's no reason to believe those UWEN lackeys will come here. And, as far as my spies know, this is a one-time harassment before the troops pull out."

"Pull out?" Jody asked. "Thought you said they usually stay for a month or so."

"If my sources are accurate, they're headed for Alaska where there have been reports of a possible Chinese invasion," Alex said, shaking his head as if he could not believe what he had just said. After a few moments in which all the adults mulled over the bizarre news, Alex went on, "Let's ride this one out, before you guys do something so drastic. Okay, Ben?"

"What about the rest of you?" Ben looked around the room.

At the juncture Grace spoke up. "This is not the time for you to go. Everyone will be safe."

Couples looked to each other, a little in amazement, a little embarrassed.

"If Grace says so, I'm sure it's true," Alex said. "She was absolutely right about the Colorado City rescue. Weren't you, Mom?" Grace smiled and nodded. She looked both humble and regal at the same time.

After a few glances back and forth, everyone agreed to stay put. For now.

"Well, now that that's settled," Moira said turning to Grace, "Mom, why don't you tell us stories of your mother and the tribe to help us keep our minds off the present horrors? I bet Danny and Miriam would like to hear about animals talking to people."

The children nodded vigorously. Moira looked to Alex and grinned as if to say, "You see, we're going to hear about those animals talking, one way or another."

Grace plumped up a pillow, gathered her green shawl around her shoulders and began, "Well, first I want to tell you about how my people came to be Mormons. My grandmother was a remarkable woman–the village telegraph, she was called, and she had a dream."

Miriam snickered. Ben leaned down and whispered to her that she should be respectful. She leaned back against her father's legs content to listen to this grandmother with a strange accent, in the protective presence of her daddy, who also told wonderful stories.

The fire danced and threw shadows up and down the high walls. Everyone in the room, including Sangay, sat spellbound as Grace related a long story about her mother's dream: white men in stove-top hats carrying a new bible who came to their island and converted almost everyone.

"This dream, children, happened years before the first Mormon missionaries arrived from America," Grace said in a low, throaty manner and stared intently into Danny's, then Miriam's eyes.

Ben's gaze shifted back and forth from storyteller to children to see if they understood that Grace had just given them a living glimpse into the world of prophecy–a world which he knew (and which he desperately wanted his children to know) was accessible only through the Holy Spirit's promptings. His heart tightened and his eyes filled with warm, sudden tears as Danny returned Grace's wide-eyed gaze and whispered, "Neat!" under his breath. And touched by the spiritual energy in the room, Miriam rubbed her cheek against her father's hand.

Alex brought more wood from the porch and spoke firmly to the dogs that they were to stay at the door on guard. Craig fell asleep on the floor on the teddy-bear quilt Jody had made. And Grace continued, "Once when I was Danny's age, when we lived on Stephen's Island, my father sent me on an errand to my uncle's house which was about a mile away. I had very long legs in those days, too, and was a swift runner. When I was about halfway there, what do you think happened?"

"What?" Danny blurted out. People laughed kindly while he blushed and leaned back against the couch.

"A *tuatara* stopped me on the way."

"No!" Miriam's voice rose in alarm. "What's that?"

"That's a large lizard," she responded to questioning faces.

"How big was he?" Miriam asked with squinched face.

Grace held out her hands four feet apart."That big or maybe bigger. I can't really remember. He seemed huge to me. Now you may think that he was an ordinary lizard, but I knew right away it was my *taniwha*."

"What's a 'tanifa,' Grandma Grace?" Danny asked.

"It's a guardian animal and a guide."

"Oh, neat," Danny said and whistled softly.

"And it said to me, 'Return home. You are needed.'" Grace turned to Danny and asked kindly, "What would you do if that happened to you?"

"I'd be scared because I don't know what would happen to me if I disobeyed Granddad."

"That's just what I felt," she said dramatically. "Well, I stood in the middle of road not knowing what to do, when this same tuatara called me by name and said, 'Grace, go now. If you don't something bad will happen.' Well, this time, I knew that God must be using the lizard to talk to me, so I ran back."

Miriam cut in, "Did you get in trouble?"

"No, just the opposite. When I got home, my father had fallen and cut himself very badly, and my mother needed me to run for the doctor who lived about two miles in the other direction."

"Ohhh," both children breathed a sigh of relief. Ben looked to Peg and they both frowned, wondering what kind of discipline the kids might have received at the hands of their grandfather.

Then Grace surprised the gathering by turning to Sangay. "Mr. Tulku, you are a man full of stories. Will you grace us with a few of your own?"

Sangay bowed, stood up in front of the fireplace and began regaling the gathering with one story after another of miraculous encounters and adventures. One Danny especially liked was Sangay's story about the first time he tried the fire meditation technique he'd been taught, in sub-zero weather, outside his monastery in Lhasa. On a bitterly cold January day, when he was just sixteen, Sangay walked to a nearby hillside in a blinding blizzard with just a blanket for protection. The test: to see if he was able to produce enough body heat to keep warm. The rinpoche beamed as he recounted how he so warmed up the spot he was sitting on that the snow around him completely melted.

Delighted, the children asked for story after story, but finally they could not keep their eyes open and fell asleep on the floor. But the adults wanted Sangay to continue. They too wanted to be children, just this night. No one wanted to leave the safety of the island of couches. Sangay told a few more stories, then signaled he needed to stop, so they pulled out sleeping bags and couches, passed out guns and ammunition, and lay down together. All except Sangay, who sat up and meditated as the fire burned down low. Everyone had been affected by his tranquility in the face of potential danger and fell asleep easily. He looked over at a sleeping Ben, who cradled his daughter in one arm and son in the other. *This is a good, good man*, he thought.

Chapter Twelve

What has happened in the world?
The women are like little volcanoes
All more or less in eruption.
It is very unnerving, (and) rather agitating
Never knowing when you'll provoke an earthquake
"Volcanic Venus," D.H. Lawrence

While the Chinese assured the UWEN ambassador that the massive troop movement and build-up of military hardware in Siberia was simply a military exercise, Laurie Winder sat in a cheap motel room in Baker, Nevada, five miles from the Utah/Nevada line. Several days into her stay, she had decided to fill a tub with warm water and slit her wrists. As the water began to flow out of the tap, Laurie searched through her black cosmetic bag for a razor blade.

It's very thin, she lamented, as she pulled one from her razor. *It might not do the trick.* She glanced into the bathroom mirror, then stared at her sunken cheeks, eyes red-rimmed from days of crying, the straight, thin brown hair that had not had a professional cut for years.

What about the children? she asked herself again. *You know, Laurie. They're going to be happy with Nate. Everyone will be happier without you.* She ran the razor across her left index finger. It bled.

While she waited for the tub to fill, she gathered her robe tighter around her waist and walked to the window to take in one last look at the children. Peter Butler was horsing around with them in the gravel parking lot. Missy, her ten-year-old, was keeping a watchful eye on the four- and two-year-old. She nearly hissed when her eye fell on Peter. How dare he treat her like he did! "I hate him," she said vehemently and sat down hard on the lumpy bed. As she leaned back against the fake wood headboard, she could picture that long night when Nate had left, heading for St. George, and feel the tired ache that had run through her body.

After the split-up at the Highway 50 intersection, Laurie was at the wheel of the station wagon when they approached the border.

"Stop!" Peter suddenly yelled at her, "Stop!"

"Why?"

"Because I know there's problems up there at the border."

"How could you possibly know that?" Laurie asked in a mean, tired voice—one she regularly used with Nate.

"Look, woman, don't argue with me. Stop this car right now or we're dead." Peter's northern Australian accent thickened.

"I'll do no such thing. You can't just order me around," she retorted and pressed down on the gas to edge the car over 70 mph. The blue and yellow border patrol lights grew ever closer.

"If you don't stop this thing, I will!" Peter shouted.

"What are you doing to do? Slug me?" she snorted.

With that, Peter growled and grabbed the steering wheel from her, kicking her leg off the gas pedal. The kids screamed as Peter rode the station wagon to a stop on the side of the road.

"Shut those kids up!" he shouted as she panted in fear.

Laurie began to cry. "My leg! It's bruised," she whined, as she rubbed the red swollen area on her shin.

Peter threw open the car door, strode around the front of the car with a furious look on his face, then ripped open the driver's side door. "Move over," he commanded. Laurie sat stone-faced, with her arms folded. Grabbing her by the arm, he dragged her out of the car. She tried to slap him as she had Nate, but Peter was taller and stronger. He pinned her arms behind her back and forced her to walk around the car. She tried to wrestle out of his grip. He shoved her into the passenger side and decided Nate might savor the moment. *I'd never put up with this for a second,* he thought.

Peter, now in charge, looked back at the terrified, silent children, then cranked the steering wheel around 180° and headed the car back the way they came. Laurie glanced over at him. Although shaken, she was also aroused. *He's got the blue eyes. If you squint, he kinda looks like a Greek athlete on an ancient frieze with those close cropped curls and the aquiline nose. Weak chin though.* Then Missy coughed and she snapped out of her reverie and realized he'd taken command of her family, so she started in again, "Now what are you going to do? Kidnap us?"

"If your children were not in the car, madam.... This is what I'd do. I reckon I'd knock your block off. Bloody Hell....Shut UP!"

That stopped her cold. She fell silent, sullen, for a few minutes, while Peter tried to remember where the turn-off to Baker had been. "Couldn't have been more than five minutes," he murmured. Calling on his past experience as a race car driver, he floored the gas pedal, turned the car around, then sped off at speeds up to 90 mph. No one in the car made a sound.

Peter felt infuriated to have been trapped in this situation. It was clear that he was not particularly fond of kids to begin with, and he'd made his feelings known about Laurie, when they were in the Ukiah ward together. He thought that she was a spoiled brat that someone needed to take her down a notch or two. Only now it looked like that task had fallen into his lap.

"You're being hysterical, you know," Laurie resumed with a high whine as they turned off at the intersection marked 'Baker, five miles.'

Peter's mood turned murderous. "If you say one more word, I'll rip your bloody tongue out!" he shouted. Laurie and the children froze. She had never heard anyone talk that way. She sat very still until they reached the main street of Baker, if it could be called a main street. The whole town consisted of a motel, gasohol station, grocery store and ranger station.

They checked into two rooms of a clean but dingy motel. Peter took a room by himself, while Laurie arranged to have a pull-out bed brought in so all the kids would have a space to sleep. He paid for the rooms, but as they walked out into the brisk night air and across the gravel parking lot, he said icily, "You'd better come up with something real soon. I'm not about to be stuck with being head of your household."

Alone in his all-beige room—walls, rug, curtains, tile—these having not been replaced in thirty years or more—Peter pulled off his brown ski sweater, slipped out of his jeans, brushed his teeth carefully and began hatching plans how he could get out of this mess. He fell asleep before concocting a plan that wouldn't leave him looking like the bad guy for abandoning a woman and five children in the middle of nowhere. Especially since he had given his word to his friend, Nate.

After the children were more or less settled in, Laurie went to a pay phone at the gas station and called her older brother's private line. While waiting for an answer, she leaned down and rubbed her bruised leg. "I'll get him. I swear I will. No priesthood holder can do that to a woman. I'll tell my father. I'll see he has a church court," she swore.

"Hello," someone answered sleepily.

"Who is this?" Laurie demanded.

"Paul."

"Paul, go get your dad immediately."

"Who is this?"

"Your aunt, Laurie," she answered menacingly. "Hurry!"

She didn't have to wait long for her brother, Paul, Sr., to answer and clip that the borders were sealed. Troops were fighting at that moment with people in downtown Salt Lake.

"You'll have to stay put until we can find a way to get you over. It's too dangerous to try it with a homemade DAI."

"I don't care. You do something, Paul."

Her brother was firm with her. "I'll let Dad know you called," he said trying to be kind, but she had always tried his patience.

She called her brother the next day, even though he told her not to. "You're jeopardizing my family, Laurie!" he nearly exploded when she called the second time. "*Don't call!* This conversation may be monitored by Interphone!" She assured him she wouldn't call again, and he assured her that her father did know where she was, but being an apostle did not give him any magical powers to rescue her. They were doing everything they could.

It was on the third call the following day, when Paul slammed down the receiver as soon as he heard her voice, that she began to unravel. She sat in her room and wept uncontrollably for several hours. And not quietly. She howled and cried and moaned. Luckily there were no other occupants in the motel. Peter had to assure the owner that she wasn't being beaten.

And on that third night, after he'd turned out the lights and was kneeling by his bed in prayer, Peter heard a tap on his door. "Peter? It's Laurie. Can I come in and talk?" She'd tried every other man in her life. Peter was her last hope for a savior.

He wasn't particularly excited to talk to her, so he slowly ambled to the door, opened it a crack and looked out to see a carefully made-up Laurie Winder, dressed in a soft white sweater, and black stretch pants. "You do have blue eyes, don't you?" she asked seductively as she swung open the door.

Peter burst out laughing. She pushed past him, sat down on the freshly-turned sheets and crossed her legs. The moonlight spilling through the open door gave her a ghoulish appearance. "You get up and get your butt out of here right this minute," Peter said, still a bit amused at her obvious come-on.

"No, I'm not leaving. I've had a vision of a blue-eyed man now for a couple of years and you fit his description," Laurie said pointedly.

"That's a load of bull, woman," Peter said, grabbing her by the arm and trying to pull her off the bed.

"No, listen, he's a wonderful man–strong, capable. And the Lord has prepared him just for me," she crooned as she tried to pull him down. Peter jerked his arm away and snorted at her blatant sexual tactics. He'd had many, many women in his days as a sailor, before he took a vow of celibacy to become a Latter-day Saint. He wasn't about to fall for this line. Nevertheless, even at her age and thin as she was, Peter had to admit that Laurie was still moderately attractive. He set his jaw.

"Look, Sister Winder, you are obviously very upset. But I know the Lord doesn't condone this kind of behavior, so get your butt off my bed and out of my room!"

Laurie exploded. She sprung to her feet. Her red nails gashed his left cheek just below his eye before he could raise his hands to defend himself. She then struggled to press her mouth onto his. He shoved her hard, back onto the bed. She struggled to get back up, then threw herself on the floor at his feet, begging, "Please don't reject me. I can't take it. I can't. I'll die if one more man fails me." She burst into hysterical crying. Peter daubed his eye and looked down at her with disgust.

Just then Missy appeared in the doorway and stared first at Peter, standing over her mother, and then down at her mother prostrate on the floor. She said nothing, just turned and went back into the adjoining room. Peter could hear her voice soothing the frightened children.

Now with the tub nearly full, Laurie turned back to the bathroom in a frayed pink nightgown and robe and to the waiting razor blade. Missy had been cold and withdrawn all morning. Laurie could see in her daughter's eyes the same contempt she often saw in Nate's. "I've lost them all," she said vacantly, turning off the water and sitting down on the stool.

Laurie stared first at the back of her hands and chipped away at the nail that had lost its polish in the skirmish with Peter, then turned over her thin hands to consider the veins at her wrists. She felt nothing. She didn't move; a little tune began to play in the back of her mind, part of a Primary song: "...popcorn popping on an apricot tree...." *I was happy once*, she thought, *once when I was very young.* She sagged against the cold enamel toilet seat and tried to remember in which Primary class she'd learned that song.

There came a firm knock on the motel door. Startled, she got up and answered it without thinking. It was the motel owner. He handed over a bulky envelope addressed to her. He tried to strike up a conversation with her, but she didn't even thank him. She just shut the door in his face and greedily ripped open the envelope. Five hundred dollars in twenty dollar bills tumbled out onto the bed. She couldn't read the letter that accompanied it through her tears.

Sometime later her youngest son came up from the games in the gravel to go to the bathroom, accompanied by Missy. By that time the tub had been drained, razor put away, and Laurie was dressing. "Things are going to be okay now, honey," she said to the stone-faced girl. "Grandpa sent us money. He'll get us out of here any time now." Missy walked her little brother into the bathroom and set him on the stool. Laurie, now in mauve shirt and slacks, came into the bathroom. "I'll take over here," she said. With that Missy let out an audible sigh and hastily left to rejoin the other kids.

Out in the parking lot, Peter looked over at Missy and caught her eye as she returned from the room. "How's your mum?" he asked with obvious irritation in his voice. He'd had his fill of playing with the "little monsters."

"Better."

"Well, then, why don't you kids go ask her what's for lunch?" Peter said somewhat sarcastically.

Everyone but Missy hustled up the stairs. "What are you going to do now?" she asked him. "Leave us?"

Peter looked straight at her and said, "Yep. You bet. The guy at the desk told me he just delivered money to your mum, so I'm off the hook." He started up the stairs, but Missy followed close behind.

"But what will you do? You don't have a car," she asked protectively.

"Hitch."

"I'm going with you. Are you going to my dad's house?"

"Don't know. But, one thing is sure. You're not coming with me."

Missy hung her head and said softly but bitterly, "I hate her."

Peter did not respond. He felt sorry for her, but not enough to let her tag along. He slipped into his room and left her on the landing looking out at the hills dotted with scrub brush. He quickly stuffed clothing and toiletries in a navy-blue duffel bag, looked under the bed for stray socks, then knelt and closed his eyes. "Father, you've been good to me thus far. Please see me to St. George, Utah. Thank you, in Jesus' name," he prayed with his usual directness.

Tentatively touching the long scratch on his face, Peter could not decide if he was going to say something to Laurie. He hadn't seen her since last night. *Nah*, he thought. *I don't want to face that crazy woman again.* Quietly closing the door to the motel room, he crept out and tried not to clank down the metal stairs. It was about noon when he stopped to check out of the Bakersville Motel. "How far to the main road?" he asked the paunchy owner.

"Best you head down Highway 487 out there," he gestured to the right, revealing a stained underarm on a fading blue cowboy shirt. "It'll be a might easier crossing the border. You may have to wait a bit, but you'll find locals who won't mind takin' on a passenger as long as you's in the back of the truck and providin' you're willin' to throw in a couple bucks for gas."

Peter Butler headed out to the road. He plopped his duffel bag down so it stood up on end. He leaned against it as he shaded his eyes and watched for movement on the long stretch of asphalt that led back to the main highway. *Hell, I've been in a lot tighter spots than this,* he thought. *I've known blokes who's stood for days in the outback waiting for a ride. Just keep my head on straight, I'll make it. No worries.*

But in the ensuing hours as he stood next to the road, the one lone truck that passed didn't even pause. It got dark; he got hungry so he decided he'd eat at the cafe and then try again. Maybe someone there was heading into Utah. But the only folks in the cafe were the Winders. Peter, stomach growling, peered through the plate glass window and fought the instinct to turn on his heel.

"Hi!" the children said in chorus as he set his duffel bag down near the door. "Come over here, Peter," they said with enthusiasm. After the incident in the car, the children had been frightened of this man—so fierce, so unyielding, so unlike their dad. But all the game-playing in the parking lot that afternoon had put them somewhat at ease. Peter sat down at the other end from Laurie. Missy immediately changed seats, so she could sit across from Peter.

"Where have you been, Peter?" Missy asked.

"Out on the highway, trying to get a ride," Peter replied flatly.

He ordered from the wrinkled, two-sided plastic menu and stared out the window. The waitress finally strolled over with the hamburgers and French fries after a interminable fifteen minute wait. From then on Peter just chewed on the flat-tasting burger and continued to look out into the night to avoid Laurie's occasional stare.

Finally, when it was obvious that he was nearing the end of his meal, Missy begged Peter in a low voice, "Please take me to my father. I won't be a problem, I promise. I just want to be with him."

"N...O...O way!" Peter threw down a ten dollar bill and walked hastily back to the cafe door. "See, ya," he said with a quick wave. The chilly air felt invigorating, the stars began to appear overhead, and there was a hint of a moon. Peter decided to go back to his station on the road for a few hours. *I can always sneak back into the motel,* he mused. *We've been the only ones there for the past three days.*

About a half hour later, Peter stood up from his duffel perch to see where the bouncing, distant lights were coming from. They continued coming on up the road, so he decided to risk standing out in the middle and waving them down. The aging truck's brakes squawked and moaned as the driver brought the old Ford to a halt. He stuck his head out the window. "What's the matter?" the Ute Indian asked tersely.

"Got stranded out here. Wonder if you're headed for Utah." They agreed to take him for the $50 he offered. He climbed in the back, but didn't see the small figure that darted from the edge of the road at that moment and disappeared into the folds of the canvas covering of the truck bed. It wasn't until they were several miles away from Baker that Missy emerged from her hiding place.

"You're a tough little bird?" Peter asked, fighting back a grin.

"Yup."

"Well, now you're here, you have to do what I say, okay?"

"No worries, mate." Missy shot back with a smile and heavy Aussie twang. She tossed her pigtails defiantly over her shoulders. And Peter laughed and shrugged.

Laurie Whitmer Winder, seen by two psychologists in her teens, had been labeled histrionic by one, narcissistic by the other. But both agreed that she was short on empathy. Rarely would she role-take; and even when she did, it was a hollow performance. She neither had, nor cared to get, any sense of what the other person felt. So when Peter left without speaking to her, she immediately dismissed him as a woman-hater, probably a homosexual. Missy, however, was another matter. It wasn't so easy to just consign her to oblivion. Nor was it possible for Laurie to face the fact that her daughter loathed her. So Laurie set to work convincing herself that Peter had abducted the girl.

Upon reaching her brother's house in Holladay, Utah, a very exclusive suburban community complete with iron fences and long driveways guarded by men and dogs, Laurie called Interpol, almost before she put down her bags. Peter Michael Butler's name now made its way onto Hazrat Patel's most wanted list–listed as a kidnapper and child molester, to boot. In her rage, she gave Nate's parents' address to the policewoman with the hard voice. She regretted it the moment she hung up–for about sixty seconds. She really did not care what happened to Nate either. She just wanted her children back. Men were monsters.

Chapter Thirteen

I have just three things to teach
Simplicity, patience, compassion.
These three are your greatest treasures.
Tao Te Ching, Lao Tzu

Monday was both a good day and a bad day, as days go. The UWEN invasion force pulled out of Utah, which was greeted with spontaneous celebrations in cities across the state. But hard on the heels of that news came word leaked by ITN (International Television Network) that a confrontation with the Chinese in Alaska looked inevitable.

And two significant things happened for the Pah Tempe tribe: Nate Winder, who was able to slip across borders and bring his children and Bobby to his parents' home in St. George, was reunited with Missy and Peter. And Ben got a call from Robert Olson.

After arranging a sacrament meeting on Saturday at Pah Tempe, the bishop asked Ben if he would be available to meet with a couple of church representatives that afternoon.

"Tell me more, Bishop." Ben's first thought was that he might be in trouble.

"I'm not at liberty to say more at this time. Just that it is very important. Pick me up at 1:00." Because of his crippling arthritis, the bishop did almost no driving. So with Ben in the driver's seat, they headed south on I-15, making small talk. Ben's stomach was in knots. He couldn't even get their destination out of Robert Olson. *This was a man who knew how to keep a secret,* Ben thought. *It probably came from all those years of hiding his constant arthritic pain from everyone.* The bishop's ever-cheerful countenance did not betray the menace that had kept him from leading a normal life since adolescence.

Ben saw a tall, three-armed cactus growing on the traffic meridian. "That's a Joshua tree," the bishop informed him. "Where are you on the question about God directing a prophet like Joshua to do something so dramatic as bring down city walls, Ben?"

Ben glanced over at his mentor and smiled. "You know what my answer would have been. We've certainly gone over this ground before."

Olson smiled broadly as he remembered the many evenings he had spent with Ben beside the fireplace in the bishop's snug Sugar House home. He could still see Ben sipping a cup of hot chocolate in one hand, while he ripped through section after section of *Doctrine and Covenants*, wrestling with theory and obscure points of Mormon doctrine with the other hand. Bishop Olson had been moved (and also amused) by Ben's rabbinical passion, but he knew all along that it was a passion constantly at loggerheads with skepticism.

Ben's voice pulled him out of his brief reverie.

"You'll be pleased to know that since Moira's healing, I'm a changed man."

"Oh, how so?"

"I've experienced the miraculous. I can't deny it, Bishop. I can see the hand of my Father in my life."

"I'm glad," the bishop responded warmly. "I'm so glad, Ben," he said patting Ben on the knee.

He directed Ben to turn off in St. George and onto a side street adjacent to the vacant St. George Temple. They quickly walked down the sidewalk, headed for the door that had been the entrance to the baptistry. Ben was surprised to see that Bishop Olson had a key. Olson then led Ben into the temple down the pale green hallway, past a gaping hole where once plaster oxen had carried a copper baptismal font. (This and all other sacred objects had been removed by church authorities when the church was forced to shut down.) At the end of the long hall lay an office with lights dimmed. *This has all the earmarks of a spy thriller*, Ben thought.

Seated on high-backed chairs with aquamarine velvet seats were two apostles. The bishop introduced Ben first to Elder Charles R. Stewart, a tall, thin, elegant Scotsman with white hair. People said he reminded them of David O. McKay, only thinner. He had studied at Oxford and then headed an international children's advocacy program before the UWEN disbanded it. The other was Elder Joseph Dawahoya, senior to Stewart by only one year in the Council of the Twelve and shorter than Stewart by a head. He was a Hopi tribal elder and a decorated Vietnam officer.

Dawahoya still had a military bearing despite his seventy years. His tanned face was smooth, except for deep lines that ran down either side of his mouth. Those, along with his square jaw, made him look a little like a boxer dog. In fact, Stewart teased him and called him Bulldog Joe in private. But when Ben looked into the Indian apostle's eyes, he could see nothing but a mirror. It seemed like Dawahoya had been cleansed of all traces of ego. What was left was love. Ben was both surprised and disarmed.

The two apostles often teamed up with Church matters that required a high degree of sensitivity in international affairs. They were a good balance–Stewart, decorous and diplomatic; Dawahoya, plain-spoken and heartfelt.

Of course, Ben had seen these men's pictures in the *Ensign*–when it was still being published. And he and Peg had, on a couple of occasions, seen them from a distance on the podium in the Tabernacle. At first glance they had seemed like any other businessmen on the streets in downtown Salt Lake. What a good disguise for the Lord's servants, Ben thought.

Elder Stewart was the first to speak. "Brother Taylor, thank you for coming on such short notice."

Ben flashed a look to Robert to convey his shock at the level of church official he was being introduced to. *No wonder the bishop has been so tightlipped. These men are special targets of the UWEN's round-up. What could be so important that they would risk imprisonment?* Ben wondered.

"Ah...er...you're very welcome, sir," Ben stammered.

"We have had a recommendation that we interview you for a very special assignment, Brother," Elder Stewart continued on in a polished upper-class British accent.

"You have?" Ben asked. Dumb question, he chided himself.

Elder Dawahoya picked up the conversation. "Yes, we have, Brother Taylor. Of course, we would have checked to see that you held a temple recommend before things were shut down, but we cannot do that any longer, so would you mind if we ask you a few personal questions before we go on?"

The questions seemed similar to a temple recommend interview, but Ben noticed that the apostles leaned forward with each of his answers, scrutinizing him like surgeons, something he'd never experienced before. After the questioning, they relaxed. *What in the world is this all about?* Ben wondered. *The suspense is killing me.*

Elder Stewart said, "Something has come up where we need a good man whom we can trust on a special project. Robert Olson, as your former bishop, has let us know that he thinks a great deal of you." He smiled, leaned back and folded his fingers together.

Ben glanced at the bishop, but he was looking straight ahead at the apostles. *Come on,* he thought impatiently. *I can't take much more of this! Let's cut to the chase.*

"Ben," Elder Dawahoya said, placing his left hand on the scriptures in front of him,"the Church has come into the possession of ancient records lent to us by the Tibetan community near Mt. Nebo." Ben looked perplexed. "Mt. Nebo is in the middle of Utah."

"Yes, Elder Dawahoya, I know where the monastery is. And I know the rinpoche slightly. He wouldn't have anything to do with this, would he?

"If you are speaking of Sangay Tulku, he has everything to do with it."

Ben couldn't contain a few chuckles."Well, I'll be." *No wonder he was sizing me up on our hike in Zion.*

A bit puzzled by Ben's response, Elder Stewart, who had taken an immediate liking to him, said warmly, "We've considered several men, Ben, but you were the one recommended by both Mr. Tulku and Bishop Olson. We understand you have quite a facility with language."

Ben nodded modestly. "Well, I do have a Master's degree in linguistics and know a few languages fairly well. But I am very far from being a bona fide linguist, Elder Stewart, if that's what you mean. May I ask what are we dealing with here, sir?"

"Something in the Sino-Tibetan language base, we think. Very old, perhaps as old as 3000 B.C."

"The closest I've come to Sino-Tibetan is picking up some basic Chinese when I was teaching English in Shanghai ten years ago," Ben said, "but I never did get the hang of tonal language, to tell you the truth. Get one little tone wrong and you wind up saying, 'I jumped to the moon,' instead of 'I want some ice cream.'" The three men joined Ben in a good laugh. "Anyway, gentlemen, there are many Chinese language scholars who taught at BYU who know infinitely more than I do. I don't know that I can...."

"Ben." He was cut short by Elder Dawahoya. "Not only the rinpoche, but the Lord feels strongly about your participation in this."

Ben, never one with nothing to say, sat speechless. His mind went blank with the enormity of the offer. It took a couple of seconds to pull himself together. "Well, I'll do what I can, sir. I've never turned down a church assignment." He looked down shyly and picked at a gold button on his camel coat.

A fly buzzed around the room and landed on Ben's shoulder. He swiftly swept it off and it landed on the blue-covered Triple Combination Dawahoya was holding. Dawahoya gently moved it away, then continued, "Since you've accepted this assignment, Ben, we ask you not to say anything to your wife. These are dangerous times, and we would not want to put her in any jeopardy."

Ben agreed somewhat reluctantly. It was hard enough keeping the Interpol invasion from Peg. *Not again*, Ben moaned inwardly.

"Fine, then. We've arranged for you to meet with the other

man involved with the project today. And for the next few weeks, or however long it takes, we'd like you to consider this a regular job, if you can."

"Of course," Ben said with great emotion. While the other men talked about procedural matters, Ben leaned back in his arm chair and looked around the basement area. *It is amazing,* he thought, *that the Church still keeps up this temple and manages to use it under the noses of the UWEN brigade quartered just miles down the road. What a shame the L.A. temple is such a mess, between the earthquake and the looters.* Ben sighed. *It's still standing, but last I heard it had been desecrated—covered with obscene graffiti. Oh, well, nothing I can do about it...This is truly amazing. Just when Alex says I can stay as long as I like at Pah Tempe, for free, two apostles walk into my life and ask me to translate ancient plates! This is just too much.* "Oh, the Lord, the Lord," Ben whispered.

The conversation between the apostles and Bishop Olson wound down, so the apostles rose and walked over to Ben. Thinking they were leaving, he stood to shake their hands, but they indicated that he should sit back down because they wanted to set him apart. For the rest of his life, Ben would never forget that moment. The pressure of two sets of hands on his head, hands belonging to the Lord's most intimate confidantes—the distinct feeling that the Savior stood next to them—being made a high priest, then set apart as a translator of ancient texts, and the thrill of hearing Elder Stewart say, "Ben, if you pick up the plow and work at cultivating this field, you will finish what the Lord has given you to do, and you will be rewarded with the fondest desires of your heart." That last phrase had become his favorite.

On the drive home, Ben must have asked ten times for a description of the plates. But each time Bishop Olson told him that he hadn't seen them.

"I'm sorry, Bishop. I just can't wait for tomorrow. The suspense is killing me."

The bishop reminded Ben of another occurrence in that same

baptistry–that President Woodruff was visited by the signers of the Declaration of Independence.

"Amazing. Just amazing." Ben paused to let the import of that historical moment sink in, then continued, "But why me, bishop? That's another amazing thing. I am really puzzled."

"Ben, as I told you in Salt Lake when I blessed you, the Brethren are aware of you. You are to be a special servant of the Lord's."

Ben just shook his head. They rode along in silence for a while. He looked out at the red hills and cloudy skies, pierced with occasional shafts of sunlight. Then somewhere in the back of his mind, he remembered a rumor Peg had told him. Something about an apostle telling a group of missionaries that the time would come when they would have to pull their scriptures around in a little red wagon, so much new scripture would be revealed. He had dismissed it as cute.

"I wonder how many other sets of plates have been given to the church for translation," Ben speculated aloud.

"I've often wondered that myself," the bishop replied.

"I have to confess I've always wanted to know what went on behind the invisible curtain that seems to shroud the Church's hierarchy. Now it seems I'm going to get my wish."

The bishop smiled warmly. Ben always had the impression that Robert Olson knew far more than he would share. That was a great comfort to Ben.

When Ben got home, Peg pulled him into her arms as soon as he had taken off his coat and boots. She could not wait to hear everything about the meeting. He replied he had been called to help in an important project for the church, but could not say more. That really riled Peg. "Terrific! What happened to temple vows? What happened to equal partners?" She began working herself into a real state. But no matter what she tried to get him to tell her, Ben refused to say anything more. So they slept in separate beds that night.

He wore his only white shirt, coat and tie on Tuesday as he drove the thirty-five miles to St. George. He couldn't remember ever being this excited. *Miraculous!* he thought. *Incredibly miraculous!* There were no superlatives grand enough to express his joy. Ben smiled at the sturdy Joshua trees as they began to appear on both sides of the highway. He'd been given a key to the baptistry. He felt into his camel coat to see if it was still there. It was.

Ben's hand shook a little while turning the key in the lock at the baptistry door. He glanced furtively over his shoulder out onto the grounds for troops. No one in sight. *Here goes nothing,* he thought, as he stepped in and closed the door as quietly as he could.

Ben took long strides to the entrance of the same office that he'd been taken to yesterday. Now he was greeted by a plain, grey-haired matron in a severe maroon suit. To the jacket lapel was pinned a black tag which read Sister Janice Haglund. She wore no wedding ring, Ben noted. *Probably asked to help because there was no husband or children to mourn her if she got shot.* He knew he was being a little melodramatic, but he had goose bumps in the closed temple.

It reminded him of WWII movies where the underground communication station was manned by two spies and a woman who got coffee and was always gunned down when the Nazis broke down the door.

There were no apostles today. In fact, he saw no one else. *Surely I'm not doing this project by myself,* he worried as Sister Haglund led him down the hall to a large conference room. *Oh, no, that's right. They mentioned another guy yesterday.*

Sister Haglund ceremoniously opened the dark oak door. The forty plates lay on a square piece of red, yellow and blue silk on the conference table like buried treasure recovered from some sunken pirate ship. He paused in the doorway to catch his breath, then walked over to them, as deferentially as one might approach a newborn child. They reminded Ben of reproductions of other ancient plates he'd seen on Temple Square. The brass-colored metal leaves were about 4"x 5", the thickness of three or four sheets of paper, and they were held together by three small metal rings spaced evenly apart on the left. These rings had been pried apart. Additional rings had fit into the top and bottom, but they had been removed altogether. Delicately chiseled characters lay waiting to be deciphered.

Ben was so intent on the plates, he didn't notice someone walk quietly into the room. Standing at the other end, waiting to introduce himself, was Bill Hadley, a BYU scholar who'd done some cutting-edge work on the Dead Sea Scrolls in the 1990s and a major Iranian find a couple of years back. When Ben became aware of Hadley, he was startled and wondered how long the man had been hanging back in the shadows watching him.

Ben's first impression of Hadley was that he must take several showers a day—he appeared that clean—hair slicked back, shirt crisply pressed, nails which looked professionally manicured. Bill had a thin, pock-marked face and a moustache that drooped over the sides of just a slice of a mouth. His dark brown hair had receded halfway back on his head. The two shook hands somewhat woodenly. Then they heard the swish of a robe and the doorway was filled with the small but powerful presence of Sangay Tulku, wearing his usual red and yellow garb, but with a very different demeanor than the grinning imp Ben had encountered in Zion.

"Good morning, gentlemen," Sangay said as he shut the door. "I would like to give you a sense of the work that you have so graciously agreed to do, if you don't mind." As he strode across the room, Ben nodded to him. Sangay walked straight to the head of the conference table without returning Ben's greeting. Ben felt a little irritated and hurt.

"First, I will tell you, Mr. Hadley, that Ben Taylor is the man of my choice to be added to this project." Now Sangay nodded to Ben, who detected a slight twinkle in his eyes. "Next, I will tell you the background of how these plates came to be at our monastery." The two men remained standing where they were—Ben near the plates at the far end, Bill in the middle, leaning up against the conference table. Both men glanced involuntarily out to the waiting area. Sister Haglund was bent over her scriptures, reading, out of earshot.

"In 1957 before the Chinese took over our country, the Dalai Lama knew the time was growing short, so he sent older monks over the Himalayas with our most ancient records. I stayed behind with the Dalai Lama until we had to flee for our lives in 1958. The Indian government was so kind as to let us settle in Dharmsala, India," Sangay said putting his right hand over his heart as if in silent gratitude to the Indian nation.

That would make him at least sixty-five! Ben calculated. I thought he was maybe forty, on the outside. But there's hardly a wrinkle on his face!

"Among the records that we preserved were very ancient plates. Some you see here. I was sent to this country in 1973 to establish a monastery, which I did in Washington state. Then when the Dalai Lama came through the United States at the end of the last century, he told me he wanted me to move to Utah and entrusted me with these records. He said he felt they would serve a higher purpose being with me than at the Summer Palace where he lives."

I wonder what the Dalai Lama does know, Ben thought. He's such a spiritual old man. I wonder if he knows what is going to happen in the world, especially if he knew what was going to happen in Tibet more than fifty years ago.

Sangay lowered his voice, "I, of course, was very honored. When the monastery had been in operation about a year, a man came to study with us who was a former member of your church. One night, after a rather long meditation session, he told me about his disenchantment with his former religion, even to the point of telling me about the rites which I found out later take place in the inner sanctum of your temple."

Ben and Bill shifted uncomfortably.

"You cannot imagine my shock as I listened to him and realized that those rites that he was disclosing closely corresponded to some of the most secret and sacred traditions of my religion–traditions that go back before Buddhism came to our country." Sangay raised his eyebrows, took a deep breath and took the end of his robe and rewrapped it around his left arm.

"But that's astonishing!" Ben blurted out, looking from Sangay to Bill and back to the Tibetan master.

"Indeed it is, Mr. Taylor," replied the rinpoche with a gentle smile. "Your professor Nibley sometime ago wrote about the very ancient foundation of all temple worship...."

"That could account for some slight similarities," Ben cut in, "but the kind of correspondence you're talking about...it's just mind boggling."

"Well, Brother Taylor," Bill Hadley chimed in, stroking his dapper moustache, "perhaps, as the rinpoche has said, one clue might lie in the fact that Tibet, or San-Wei as the Chinese anciently called the region, has only been a nation of Buddhists since the seventh century A.D. Before that, they were more animists than anything. Except for at least one sect, who used the records you see before you as a basis of worship. What I suspect is that that sect may have had very close ties with these ancient temple rites."

"I see," Ben responded with a smile, taking an instant dislike to Hadley and his slightly arrogant tone. *Maybe it's a good thing I never got to defend my dissertation,* Ben thought. *I'm not sure I could have worked all day with guys like this.*

"So what did you do with what the Jack Mormon told you?" Bill asked Sangay.

"The Jack Mormon? I don't know that term," Sangay replied.

Ben interjected, "A former member of the Church."

"Ah, I see. Jack Mormon, I'll have to remember that. Well, I contacted a Mormon bishop near the monastery to see if this young man's story was true. After finding it basically was, I contacted someone in the administration of your church. I've had a series of meetings with Elders Joseph Dawahoya and Charles Stewart. You've met them, haven't you, Ben?"

Ben nodded.

Bill had been studying Ben's face as the rinpoche spoke. What he saw was an intense, intelligent man, but that didn't solve the mystery of who this guy really was. He'd been briefed about Ben's background: Master's in Linguistics, doctoral work in Education, Summer Institute of Linguistics aide in Central America—okay, but nothing terribly impressive. *I wonder why this guy and not ten other people from my department,* he mused. He hoped Ben wasn't some general authority's relative who had made it a hobby to study archeology on the side and wormed his way on to the project because of political connections.

"It was they who suggested that we work together to translate these plates," Sangay said, folding his arms.

Ben could only shake his head. He looked around at the pastel blue walls and wondered what other secrets these walls could tell. First Beethoven in the mud baths, and now a Tibetan monk in the St. George Temple! *Holy Guacamole, what next?*

As if he read Ben's thoughts, Sangay said, "We felt it was far too dangerous to meet about these matters in the Salt Lake City area, so we have come here in this building, which is now closed, to do our work. Perhaps Mr. Hadley, who was first selected because he is an expert in the Sino-Tibetan language, would like to say a few words. Mr. Hadley?" Sangay again rearranged the end of the ocher robe.

"When I heard of these plates," Bill said in what seemed to Ben to be a slightly superior tone, "I thought of a number of excavations by the Russians in the 1980's, which have confirmed both the antiquity and uniformity of steppe cultures. There is, for example, the Kelteminarian culture. You may be familiar with it, Ben," Hadley said pointedly, searching Ben's face for a response.

"No, I'm afraid I'm not familiar with it," Ben replied with a fixed smile.

Bill continued now a bit more imperiously, "In any case, it is beginning to look increasingly likely that there was once a uniform culture which extended with relatively minor variations over all of Asia, including India, and may have even reached into pockets of what is now Europe."

Sangay frowned slightly at Hadley, as if to say, don't get too professorial here.

Ben broke in, "I seem to remember reading that the linguistics department at MIT was doing some pioneer work in the late '90s along these lines. Wasn't it Fitzsimmons who was constructing theoretical models of a proto-language that would have been the root of not only the Indo-European languages, but of the major languages of central Asia as well?"

"That's right, Ben," Bill said, relieved that this fellow he had been given to work with seemed to have a grip on the basics of what had been going on in historical linguistics over the last twenty years or so. "So, really, the picture that is now emerging is a relatively straight-forward one, despite all the twists and turns that have led to it."

"Right!" Ben responded enthusiastically. "A single culture and a single language before the dawn of recorded history. Adamic, if you will." And a single temple ceremony too, he thought. "Perfectly in accord with what Latter-day prophets have been telling us from Joseph on!"

Sangay sat down in a chair at the end of the table, arms folded. He was enjoying this exchange. It confirmed what he thought about Ben; he could hold his own.

"Precisely." Bill nodded in assent. "And that would, of course, explain why these plates exhibit both Indo-European and Asian elements. We know that the Tibetan alphabet was borrowed from Sanskrit in the seventh century, but what was written or spoken before then has been a mystery."

Ben, who had been leaning against the dark oak table where the plates lay, unbuttoned his jacket, moved a straight-backed chair to the side of the conference table and sat down. *I'm not sure I belong here, but I sure as heck am not going to say anything to anyone. This is far too fascinating.* He glanced over at the plates. They looked like they were glowing from inside out, although there was just fluorescent tubing overhead.

"Despite their great linguistic significance, these plates would not be half so interesting to us were it not for the fact that Mr. Tulku has told us some of the oral teachings that accompany them. According to him, those teachings contain the creation story and tower of Babel stories, and an account of a tribe of people who were led by a man with a name similar to the brother of Jared. According to the oral tradition, he passed through Tibet and left teachings with the native population." He paused to let that sink in with Ben. Ben shook his head and exhaled loudly. Then he stole a glance at Sangay, who broke into a grin.

"Do you mean to tell me that some of the stories on these plates may have occurred before the Jaredites set sail for the New World?" Ben's voice went up. He could scarcely contain his excitement. *Why, oh why can't I share this with Peg? It's just too good to keep to myself.*

"Yes!" Sangay exclaimed with a toothy grin.

"It's possible Jaredites taught Tibetans while they were en route to the ocean?"

"Yes, yes!" Sangay clapped his hands.

"The Tibetans and Jaredites hanging out. Un-be-liev-able!" Ben blurted out.

Bill hurrumphed. He was determined to get through this briefing with some professional dignity. He looked to Ben, as if to say, "May I continue?" Ben nodded. *This guy is really beginning to get on my nerves,* Ben thought.

"The major reason for wanting these plates translated, Ben," Bill said, "is to see if what's written on them corresponds with the oral traditions that Rinpoche Tulku has told us about."

Sangay yawned. Bill was quick to get the message that he should draw this explanation to a close.

He took a deep breath and concluded, "Another reason relates to the fourth chapter of Ether where the Lord commands Moroni to seal up the plates. If you recall the Lord says, 'In that they shall exercise faith in me...even as the brother of Jared did, that they may become sanctified in me, then will I manifest unto them the things which the brother of Jared saw, even to the unfolding unto them all my revelations....'"

"These very plates before us could be part of what the Lord meant by 'unfolding my revelations,'" Ben said quietly, putting his hand to his mouth.

Motioning for the men to sit down, Sangay picked up the story, "Tibetan tradition says that these plates reveal the highest truths ever given to man." He paused for effect. "Ever given to man. Naturally we've wondered what could possibly be written on them. Secrets of prolonging life? Travel to other worlds?"

Ben watched Sangay and wondered what he knew about Joseph Smith.

"We are, of course, fascinated with the prospect of finding corroborating evidence for the *Book of Mormon*," Bill cut in.

Let it go, man, Ben thought. *We're talking here about a lot bigger things than proving the Book of Mormon true. We could be revealing to the world what Moses and Abraham learned before they were translated.* Ben felt a shiver run down his back as if the Spirit were confirming his suspicions.

Sangay walked around the conference table and leaned very close to them. In his Tibetan accent he said in a low conspiratorial tone, "Although we have been able to find a few consistent symbols from the plates, we have not, as yet, been able to build an alphabet. The writings are completely unintelligible to me. We need you two to translate these plates. What do you think? Want to give it a try?" he asked as he stepped back and broke into a grin.

Ben nodded his head vigorously.

"More than anything I can think of, Rinpoche," Bill said gravely.

"Well, then, what I'd suggest you do," Sangay said in an equally grave voice, "is take separate stations somewhere on this level of the building, divide up the forty plates and see what happens. I'll be back around five to see how things are going."

Ben smiled. *Sure, and we'll be here waiting for you with the answers to the universe.*

All three men bowed their heads and Ben offered a simple but powerful prayer for the Holy Spirit's inspiration. Then he took the top twenty plates from the pile and strode forcefully out of the room. He sensed the weight of Sangay's scrutiny as he passed and bristled. *If he is such a great meditator, why doesn't he use his powers to do this job?*

Ben felt the enormity of the task fall on his shoulders as he walked as far down the half-lighted hall as he could. He didn't want anyone looking over his shoulder. Never in his most outrageous fantasies (and he'd had his share), could Ben have imagined such a moment. To hold in his hands the very plates that the Lord Jesus Christ had prophesied about thousands of years ago! He was sure his blood pressure was up around 200/200. "I haven't a clue where to start," he said to no one, sitting down at a large desk and rummaging through the drawers. He found a yellow legal pad, then pulled his favorite zebra-striped pen from the interior of his coat and put on his lucky baseball cap.

Ben sat in front of the plates and stared at them reverentially for almost an hour, transfixed. The only thing he heard was the distant sound of swooshing blood in his eardrums. Finally he carefully laid out the small plates, which were heavier than they looked, in two rows, left to right, across the top of the desk. For nearly ten minutes he studied them, then got up and walked around to look at them upside down. Unsatisfied, he came around the desk, sat down on the corner and began to notate where he could see possible apparent syntactic similarities and what might be grammatical markers. *Does the system run up and down like Chinese? Right to left like Hebrew?* Frustrated with his inability to figure out any obvious system, he sat down in the swivel chair and sighed.

After a couple of moments, he sat straight up, turned his baseball cap visor around to the back, and laughed right out loud. *Surely the Lord has a sense of humor to pick me out of the litter,* he thought. *Oh, well, I always say, never doubt the Lord, especially when He takes you on such interesting rides.*

That first day flew by; Ben even forgot lunch. At one point Beethoven's *Pastoral* came on Sister Haglund's radio. He took it as a comforting sign.

At the end of the eight hours he returned to the conference

room with his portion of the plates and set them back on the brightly colored cloth. Sangay sat erect in a straight-backed chair with his eyes closed. Bill wasn't around. Without opening his eyes, he said to Ben, "Our mutual friend, Alex Dubik?"

"Yes," he stammered nonplussed. How to address a man with his eyes closed?

Still Sangay sat unmoving. "He has recommended I teach you meditation. How much do you want to learn?"

Ben didn't know which way to answer this question. There wasn't an inflection on either the "much" or "want" to help him make the decision. He couldn't figure out why he felt so uneasy with this man. It was more than just the rinpoche's strange behavior. It was as if Ben were being probed and he didn't know how to raise any protective shields.

Sangay opened his eyes and smiled broadly. "Do I mean what quantity or do I mean how intensely?"

Ben felt like the rinpoche was toying with him. A flash of anger erupted from his stomach. He restrained himself from saying something in spite of the fact that he had had a long and fruitless day.

"I see that you are angry. Would you like to learn to use that anger for higher wisdom? Perhaps to help you translate?" the rinpoche asked lightly.

For some reason Ben began to laugh. He laughed and laughed until tears came to his eyes. Sangay smiled broadly throughout the outburst. When it subsided, he said, "You have access to your emotions. That is very good. Most Western men do not. Alex had to work with me for several years to let his feelings flow through his body. I think you can see the results in his sculpture."

"I can. There really is a profound difference," Ben said trying to check his laughter as he wiped away a tear. "But that's not why I'm laughing, Rinpoche." He looked down for a moment, then lifted his eyes to meet Sangay's gentle stare. "It's because I realize that I'm in the presence of a much smarter man than I am."

"No, I am not much smarter than you. I am more efficient

because I can see and feel things with a greater clarity. But you have not answered my question."

"Yes, I do want to learn from you," Ben replied simply.

"I only ask you not to try to use your charm with me."

Ben immediately felt guilty. He had had a habit of emotionally seducing people to gain the upper hand, but this man's simple words suddenly stopped him dead in his tracks.

"And I want to work first on this automatic guilt button you have," he laughed.

At that point, Bill returned to the conference room. Ben and he shared what progress they had made–very little–then agreed to meet the next day at the same time. Ben hung back as Bill left. "When can I start learning how to meditate with you?" Ben asked Sangay.

"I am here now for some time. Why don't we try working together after you finish your day's work?"

"I can't stay late tonight, Rinpoche. I promised Peg I'd come home and take the kids off her hands."

"That's okay. What have you been practicing with Alex?" Ben told of the breathing exercise Alex had given him that night in the baths. He said he'd been practicing it with some regularity. Sangay then gave Ben a mantra (which were just a series of sounds to Ben's ears) to practice instead of breath counting. "Watch the effect each sound makes on your body. What we're looking for is a quieting of heart and mind."

"Thanks so much," Ben said touching his heart in a gesture of genuine gratitude.

As he stood to leave, Sangay reached out and indicated to Ben that he wanted him to sit down again. "I think, Ben Taylor, I'll also introduce you to the nature of mind," he said to his puzzled student.

"That's okay by me, so long as I can get out of here by six," Ben said looking at his watch and glancing over at Sangay who was taking a bell and small hand-drum from a satchel on the floor at his feet.

"Oh, this won't take long," Sangay said and smiled obliquely. He began to ring the bell with sharp, rhythmic strokes. Ben was fascinated, but drawn away by inner pictures of an angry Peg waiting at the gate. Besides, his growling stomach told him it was time to eat.

Sangay now began to beat the drum. Its hollow, plangent rhythm slowly, hypnotically drew Ben into an enchanted circle of pure sound. He felt his mental fists unclench, and gradually he let go all emotional and physical sensation. On the verge of completely giving himself over to an exquisite emptiness, Ben was startled to see Sangay's bright face emerge out of the void, his fiery eyes burning into Ben's eyes. In a quiet but forceful voice, the rinpoche snapped Ben's consciousness with the question, "What is mind?"

Paralyzed by surprise, Ben couldn't answer. He opened his mouth and shut it again. He felt his mind shattering as if an ax had been taken to an ice-covered pond–all those cobwebbed cracks and creaking sounds of water displacing ice. What bubbled up to the surface of his consciousness was clear, still, deep-blue water. How long he sat in this trance of amazement, in a state of no-mind, he couldn't tell. Next he knew, Sangay was pointing to his watch, indicating Ben needed to leave to get home on time.

As he stumbled out the door of the baptistry into the half-light of the desert sunset, Ben called out back to Sangay, "I'll try to think of the answer by tomorrow morning. Promise."

Ben heard Sangay's low chuckle from the depths of the baptistry.

That night was difficult for Ben, almost physically painful. He ached to share with Peg the astonishing events of this day. She sensed he was struggling, but in her frustration, she had begun to form a fantasy of him leaving her for a thinner woman, and his chafing only reinforced her suspicions. When he approached her in bed, she was icy. As he climbed back in the other bed and burrowed into the cold sheets, a phrase from his Salt Lake blessing came back to him, "You'll have to secure your relationship with your wife." He had a glimmering that this translation project might force him to do just that.

About four in the morning, he woke up, gurgling and crying out. He had been thrashing around in the covers and awakened Peg, who was frightened. "Ben. Ben, what's going on?" she called out across the room.

"I...I just had a terrifying dream." He struggled to bring himself to consciousness. "I was standing on the side of a highway, a four-lane one, trying to get to the other side. Halfway across I looked to my right and saw this roadster bearing down on me. It had bright red flames painted on the side. Hunched over the wheel sat Satan grinning, with this menacing, horrible look on his face. I wasn't sure whether I'd make it to the other side–he looked so determined to run me down." Ben shuddered. "Ho, that was the most frightening dream I think I've ever had. It seemed so real."

Peg was kind but cool. *I knew he had a guilty conscience*, she thought. But she let him come into her bed and held him until he started to drift off. "Thanks, honey," he said sleepily. She had already gone down to the river with the kids when he left for St. George.

The beginning of Ben's day was colored by the nightmare. It was like a hangover that wouldn't go away. It didn't help to find out when he reached the temple that Sangay wasn't there. Bill and he said little, took the same twenty plates. Ben walked back to where he had worked and Bill closeted himself at the other end of the basement hallway. Sister Haglund typed on an old blue electric typewriter and listened to classical music from the St. George station.

Before they split up, he and Bill were able to agree on several minor patterns of symbols on the plates, but neither man had a clue what they might mean, except for a few ideas about a possible tense marker, a direct object particle, and maybe a interrogative particle. But this was small change, and it certainly did not buy them one iota of insight into what the plate actually said. The project for the day would be to try to do a morphemic analysis of the text (an attempt to isolate the smallest meaningful units of a language that make up a word or part of a word, like morn/ing or un/use/able). Ben went at it in the best way he knew how, using what he could remember of Pike's Tagmemics from graduate school, even though he suspected that approach must be way out of date by now. *Who knows what linguists were doing these days!*

After lunch he felt tired and discouraged. His mind went to Joseph Smith. *It's not fair that he had the Urim and Thummin,* he thought. *What about that black seer stone he dug up? Maybe I'll go looking for one when I get home.*

After musing for a few minutes what his next step might be, he did a silly thing. He reached over to his blue book bag and took out his baseball cap, an old Yankees cap. He put it down on the table, gingerly picked up one of the plates and placed the precious object into it. Sticking his face into the hat, he waited to see if anything would happen. But all he encountered was dark and a musky odor. Nothing else.

Oh well, he mumbled to himself, *it worked for Joseph.* Worried that Bill or Sister Haglund might walk in on him, he stood up and placed the plate back on the desk. "I guess Joseph wasn't a Yankees' fan. Maybe it was a L.A. Dodgers' cap he used."

"But really, how did Joseph do it?" Ben wondered aloud. He reached for his copy of the *Book of Mormon* in the original format that Peg had given him as a wedding present. He thumbed through it until he found Ether. "Hey, did you guys dip south and visit the Tibetans on your way to the sea?" he said, hoping to wake the spirit of Moriancumer. No luck. Silence. Only the hum of a heating unit somewhere in the building.

He picked up a fake plant and pulled out a plastic leaf, which he began to chew on. *Okay, so I've eliminated hat tricks and raising the dead. What's next on the list?* He paced back and forth in the small, spare white-walled office. Flipping open his *D&C* to Chapter 9, he reread for the hundredth time: "You must study it out in your mind first...." The only conclusion he could come to was that Joseph had the ability to quiet and clear his mind, so that the Lord could whisper his messages.

So Ben leaned back, straightened his spine, and rotated his head, first to the right, then the left. He took a few deep breaths using the breath counting technique he had learned with Alex. In, one-two-three-four-five-six; hold, two-three-four-five-six; out, two-three-four-fix-six. He did that twenty times. That helped quiet his body. Then he added the mantra. The sounds vibrated in his chest and throat. His mind slowly returned to its deep-blue clarity. The background music from Sister Haglund's office stopped being a distraction, and after a little while he felt a calm but energizing feeling come over him.

His breathing had slowed way down. A half hour passed. Gradually he became aware of the total silence—the music down the hall had stopped. "Sister Haglund leaves at three," was the only thought that now kept circulating in his consciousness, almost like another mantra. Since he had dropped the thread of "no-mind" for a moment, he opened his eyes and gazed down at the top plate in front of him. Ben was astonished as, looking at the first line of the writing, he sensed an almost audible word which turned into phrase. It said, "I, Nawang, having set my hand to these plates at the command of the Lord...."

Ben fumbled for his pen, grabbed the legal pad and scrawled what he had just heard. Then he raised his head, eyes tightly shut, and strained to catch the voice. But it was quiet again. He strained to listen. Nothing. So he prayed, "Please, Lord, if this is your doing, please, please continue." He had to shove to the rear of his mind the image of Bill mocking him. Then..."do write these words for those who have been prepared in the last days to receive them...."

"Wow! This is really happening!" He nearly exploded with delight. The intense process of words, focus, prayer, words lasted about fifteen minutes. It might have gone on, but Ben was suddenly overcome with exhaustion.

Although aware of the meaning of each chunk of words as it

came to him, he hadn't put the chunks together into a larger message. Now he read what he had written. He was stunned to see that he had penned the creation story very similar to that in the Book of Moses.

Doubts immediately began to press in on him. *Come on, Bubba, you want to do this too bad,* he thought. *Why, this could all be nothing but a fluke of your imagination! Hypnotic self-suggestion, maybe, or automatic writing.* "You could be moving into a very weird area, my lad," he said aloud to himself in the still room, rubbing the back of his neck. Still, what if this was not a delusion of some sort? What if maybe, just maybe, his prayer had been answered and he was being used as the filter through which the impossibly obscure symbols on those ancient plates were being changed into modern English?

He stood up abruptly, jammed his Dodgers cap on his head and paced. *I'm sure as heck not going to show this to Bill,* he thought tearing off the sheets of legal paper, folding them up and shoving them deep in his jacket pocket. Then he plopped down on the chair and tried to return to his analysis of data, so he'd have something to bring to the day's end meeting. But he was spent, so he put his head down on the desk and fell asleep.

Ben slept for nearly an hour. Just before awakening, he began to dream again about the Satanic roadster. He moaned and jerked up his head—he was sweating. For several long moments, he couldn't remember where he was. *Boy, I must either be on to something big or ready to commit the biggest sin of my life. Either way, Satan sure wants me,* he shuddered.

Then he heard Sangay's chuckle down the hall and immediately felt better. As he hastily packed up his book bag and scooped up the plates, Ben said to himself, *Okay, no more games. I'm going to level with this guy and I'm going to get him to do the same.*

Sangay sat in a black leather chair in the conference room. His hands were folded, palm up, in his lap—one on the other. He was trying to calm a very upset Bill. "Look, Rinpoche, we're probably not going to crack this code in just a few days. I need my computer. This is really an impossible task, given the time constraints."

Ben walked in and asked, "What time constraints? I thought we had as much time as we needed."

"No, Mr. Tulku now says we don't have much time. It seems we are about to experience some cataclysmic, world-altering change," Bill said, trying hard, out of respect for the Tibetan monk, to fight back any signs of irony or anger.

But Ben could sense what Bill was trying to conceal. *So what's your problem with apocalyptic changes, Bill?* thought Ben. *Isn't that what Mormonism is all about?* Sangay looked knowingly over to Ben. Ben smiled. *This Tibetan is something else,* he thought.

Bill complained for a few more minutes, then left. After the door closed behind them, Sangay gestured to Ben to sit down. "I see you've had some success today."

"How can you tell?" Ben asked.

"There's no hiding anything. It is always on a man's face."

"Yes, Sangay, I did have an auditory hallucination today, but I don't know what to make of it. Can we just be straightforward here? Not play games?" Ben paused, expecting Sangay to respond. But he remained quiet and still, staring at Ben with the vague smile of someone who was watching a train disappear in the distance. "Look, Sangay," Ben finally broke the silence, "can we get on with this?" He felt foolish the second the words left his mouth.

"Of course, Ben." Sangay cleared his throat and sat up straighter. He reached up and rubbed his dark, short-cropped hair, what there was of it. His robes rustled as he repositioned himself. "What would you like to say or hear from me?"

"Well...ah...first, what time constraints?" he asked and sat down on the other side of the conference table.

"The world is coming to an end as we experience it, beginning with a war that will start in a few days on this continent. We will have little time to complete this project before you'll have to move on."

"Move on?"

Sangay nodded .

"How do you know that?" Ben asked.

"I just know."

"I thought we are being candid here," Ben said.

"We are."

Ben saw he was going to get nothing more about that subject from the inscrutable rinpoche, so he asked, "Okay, then, my second question is: why choose me? It's obvious I'm not the leader of the pack when it comes to Sino-Tibetan translation."

"Because you are a unique combination of several things. First, of course, you are a Mormon. You were on a short list Apostle Stewart gave to me. You got on that list because of some articles you had written about cross-cultural sensitivity to other religious systems, if I remember correctly. Second, you are a very religious man. Third," Sangay pulled down his index finger to his thumb to raise the three last fingers, "you are a moral man. And fourth, you have a very fine, well-trained mind. But most important..." Sangay spread out five fingers, "... you are a man given to visions."

Ben started. "Who told you? Alex?"

"Yes."

"About the Beethoven incident?"

"Yes."

"That was just a fluke. I was under a tremendous amount of stress."

"No, I don't think so. He also told me about an experience in a Catholic church."

"Oh, that. Well, maybe a few really exceptional times. But I wouldn't call myself a visionary man."

"Oh, I see," Sangay laughed. "Well, would you like to test out my theory?"

"How?" Ben felt a little frightened to hear the answer. He had not recovered from the question Sangay asked the previous day: "What is mind?"

Sangay watched Ben's face as his thoughts played across his

face. "I take that as a 'yes'? Do you have to go right home tonight or can you stay for awhile?"

"I guess I can stay." He felt like the man who inadvertently agreed to stay for dinner with a headhunter.

"Good!" Sangay smiled broadly. "Come sit next to me." Sangay pulled another black leather chair from the conference table and set it quite close to his chair. Sangay patted the seat and Ben sat down. Then the rinpoche closed his eyes and took several deep breaths. "Follow me. Do your breathing routine." Each man breathed in and out slowly for a couple of minutes. Then Sangay said, "Now quiet your heart. Make sounds with your mantra and let your body and mind come to a still point."

Ben settled back into his routine. Minutes went by. Then, just when Ben felt unusually peaceful, the rinpoche suddenly reached over and thumped on Ben's chest right above his heart. Startled, Ben opened his eyes, but instead of seeing Sangay, he found he could see through the wall of the conference room, then through the thick walls of the temple out to the foliage growing on the grounds. Electrified, literally entranced, Ben found he had 360° vision. Without moving his head at all, he could see a passing car on the I-15 behind him and miles away.

His body felt like it had been pulled down and rooted by the end of his spine to the chair. No, not just to the chair, but to the earth below the temple. He had stopped breathing, or so it seemed. Ben was sure he would never need to breathe again. Light seemed to be pouring in and out of every pore. He looked over at Sangay and the rinpoche's face dissolved into an energy pattern of golden swirling flames.

Suddenly the scene changed so he could see Peg, at Pah Tempe, piling laundry into the washing machine. His vision shifted again to the bottom of the Virgin River, where he followed sulfur bubbles floating up to the surface of the blue opaque water.

Joy, indescribable joy, flowed up the center of his spine–up into his head. As it reached his crown, waves of liquid, blissful light played in patterns in front of his open eyes. He watched fire burst into gaseous galaxies–greens, purples and iridescent blues exploded into yellow white golden clouds...Then, as suddenly as it had started, he took one big deep breath and the scene shut down, like a television zapped with a remote control stick. Ben closed his eyes and fell back against the chair. After a few breaths, he slowly opened his eyes and turned to Sangay. The rinpoche looked at him with tremendous tenderness.

Chapter Fourteen

To see the world in a grain of sand
And Heaven in a wild flower,
Hold infinity in the palm of your hand
And eternity in an hour.
"Auguries of Innocence," William Blake

"What...what was that?" Ben asked slowly and reverently as he rubbed around his heart where Sangay had thumped. His pupils were completely black.

"That, my friend, proves my point." Sangay leaned over and looked intently into Ben's eyes.

"I see, I think," Ben whispered.

Sangay sat back and there was a long silence.

"I feel so in touch with God," Ben said softly. "In fact, I almost felt like I was a god, if that's not blasphemy."

"The human body is designed to experience many more wonderful things than we ordinarily allow."

Another long silence ensued. The two men sat at the end of the nine-foot-long conference room—Ben in a tie and white shirt with the sleeves rolled up and Sangay in red and yellow robes. Sangay rose effortlessly from his chair and turned off the row of lights at their end of the room. At the other lay the plates, spotlighted on their brightly-colored cloth. The two stared at the treasure trove for quite a long while.

"So what was that rap on my chest? What did that do?" Ben broke the silence.

Sangay cleared his throat, then said, "It's a way of speeding up a natural process."

"Oh." Ben took several deep breaths and bathed in the delicious taste of the experience. It filled his body and head. "I used to think I'd like to go down to Mt. Nebo and learn to meditate."

"But you never did."

"So...if Mohammed doesn't come to the mountain..."

"Sangay comes to Ben." Both men grinned.

Several minutes passed. Ben continued to feel blissful waves begin at the base of his spine and flow up and over the crown of his head. "You know, I had the strangest sensation that I knew you from somewhere when you first came to the Dubiks'. Do I know you somehow?"

"Probably from what you call the preexistence. I have had a number of students tell me that."

"But what about you? Do you feel anything special?"

"I feel many things. Mostly, can I help? Will he learn what I teach him? Those kinds of things."

"Oh."

Long pause. The only sound, other than the heating unit that went off and on at five minute intervals, was the chirruping of a cricket that had found its way into the former baptistry. "I got a name today in that auditory hallucination," Ben volunteered.

"Oh?"

"Yeah, 'Nawang.' Storyteller about the beginning of the world."

Sangay was silent for awhile, then said, "That's good. I'll have to see what you've written."

Ben sighed and stretched out his arms, knitted his fingers and cracked a couple of knuckles. "I have to call Peg. It's really late." He struggled to get up. "Would you stay, Sangay, and talk if I can arrange it?"

"You must arrange it. There's much for us to talk about."

Ben didn't know what to say to Peg. He paused in the doorway of Sister Haglund's office before phoning. Considering Peg's mood the evening before, he was sure she was not going to be pleased with the news that he was not coming home. But Jed answered and said Peg couldn't come to the phone. She and the children were up at the Dubiks'. "Just tell her I've been tied up in St. George," Ben said. "It will be really late when I get back." He gingerly set down the receiver and breathed a sigh of relief.

He wasn't hungry, he wasn't sleepy–he was euphoric. His hands and feet were extraordinarily warm. In fact, he glowed. When waves of energy hit his heart, he felt enormous compassion for every living creature. *Ah*, he thought, *now I understand why Buddhism teaches that doctrine.*

And with his new vision of the composition of matter dancing in his head, he searched for what the Lord had said in *D&C*. "Oh, yes. 'All things unto me are spiritual.' I feel for the first time that I truly understand this."

Back in the conference room, Ben tried to describe what had happened to him during the meditation as Sangay put a hand to his mouth to hide a smile. At that moment, Ben reminded Sangay of a young boy who had just taken his first roller coaster ride. He was very pleased with Ben and told him so. "You're the man for the job, Ben. Translating will now come easier." Ben blushed and turned his head away to look to the other end of the table, to the bright silk cloth and the small square objects that might contain the mysteries of the ages.

Sangay said, "The plates, they not only contain the history of the world from the beginning, they also tell the end, according to Tibetan tradition. I am certain the Dalai Lama placed the plates in Utah to serve a very high purpose."

"It sure sounds like it," Ben enthused.

"And who knows what else," Sangay said with a twinkle in his eye. "The secrets of eternal youth? How to arrest time? How to fly unaided through space? Maybe small, insignificant items like that."

Both men chuckled, then fell silent. Time hung lazily around the pair.

"How can I stay this way?" Ben asked after another surge of energy flowed up his spine and filled his head with a warm liquid glow.

"You can't."

"Well, then how can I do this again, on my own?"

"That will come. For now, be content with knowing that your body–your nervous system to be more precise–has been through a process that will heighten your spiritual acumen."

Ben let out a long sigh. "Good, just so this isn't a one time thing."

Sangay shook his head.

Both men sat silently for what must have been five minutes. Then furrowing his brow, Ben turned to the rinpoche and said, "My wife. She's very unhappy with me, with her life right now. Can you help her?"

"You can help her by sharing who you are now. Be patient."

And so it went almost all night. Ben asked questions, Sangay answered them. They talked more about meditation, what Sangay thought was on the plates, the future according to Tibetan prophecy, things in that vein.

Throughout it all, Ben occasionally sat back to remember how he had longed for a spiritual teacher in his college days. He'd even had a series of dreams about a character much like Sangay. The dream character, a very old man, was as sprightly as an eight-year-old. He often grinned, revealing both an enchanting smile and several gaps between his teeth. Ben sensed he was a Zen master. Yet he carried with him a Jewish shofar, or ram's horn, which he sometimes blew. And instead of monk's robe, he wore robes that reminded Ben of Jesus' clothing. In these dreams Ben would always sense that the old man was preparing him for something. But whenever Ben started to ask what it might be, the old man would blow once on his horn, grin, and disappear behind a rock. Ben fondly named him, Rabbi Jeshua ben Roshi. *Now here I am,* thought Ben, *sitting here with a real life teacher.*

As much as he tried not to, Ben alerted Peg that he was home with the scraping of the bedroom door over the short shag rug.

"Can we talk?" she asked immediately as Ben stepped into their darkened room. He felt his stomach involuntarily tighten.

"I thought you were asleep."

"No, I've been waiting."

"I'm really tired. Can this wait until morning?"

"No."

Ben sighed and sat down on the adjoining bed. "What?" he asked in a flat voice.

"I want to talk about us," Peg began.

Ben groaned. "Peg, I've just been through the most remarkable night of my whole life."

"I bet you have."

"Oh, stop it, Peg. It isn't anything like you've imagined." Ben walked across the room, took off his coat and jacket and plopped down on the bed he had been sleeping in.

"So what have you been doing until this hour?"

"You sound like my mother."

"For Pete's sake, Ben, I'm worried that our relationship is changing, and I don't like what's happening."

Ben bent down and untied his shoes. He was determined not to get baited.

"It's not another woman, if that's what you think."

"I haven't known what to think. Why can't you tell me? I'd like to have some clue about where you're going until all hours of the night." Peg's voice was reaching the soprano range.

"Hold on, there, Peg, honey. Whoa." Ben held up a hand like a traffic cop. "I've just received permission from the head of the project to tell you what I've been doing there."

"Oh?" she asked with a slight sarcastic edge to her voice.

"Yes, and it's really amazing. I'd like to talk to you about it, but in coherent sentences, tomorrow." As he pulled off each shoe, Ben moaned.

"Well, for heaven's sakes, at least give me a hint."

"How about apostles and ancient plates?"

"Ben, how exciting!"

"More than exciting, my sweet. Way beyond that. Basically I'm helping translate ancient Tibetan plates with the help of a remarkable Tibetan abbot."

Ben was now into his pajamas. He knelt by the bed and signaled her to be quiet for a moment. Then, turning back the covers, he wearily climbed in.

"Okay, okay...tomorrow." Peg tried not to sound as frustrated as she felt. "But I want to talk about the kids, now. I don't want them to hear us."

"Can't that wait? Honestly, I am so exhausted I can't move." Then there was a long silence from his side of the bedroom. He lay like a statue since dropping his head on the pillow.

"You aren't going to sleep?" Peg asked in an irritated voice. She sat up straighter, leaned back against the bed board and folded her arms across her chest.

"Trying not to," he said sleepily.

"Ben, I want to be included with them. You run off and do things with them, and then, when you've had your fill and want to be alone, you leave them with me. We just don't do things together as a family."

"Twice. That's just happened twice, Peg," Ben replied, his voice betraying his crankiness.

"Well, it doesn't take much to see that you regard them as yours exclusively. Ben, that's just not going to work. I want to be part of this family, too."

Ben winced at the truth of her statement, his head suddenly filling with some very old and jumbled thoughts. *Maybe I'm afraid I'll be the odd man out. Don't want to live feeling like I did in my family. Families...those feelings cut so close to the bone...all so primitive...everyone desperate for love.* He felt himself leaving the conversation and fixating on a line from Yeats, "The foul rag and bone shop of the heart."

"I hate it when you don't answer me," Peg said angrily.

"I was just trying to decide what I do feel, Peg," he said evenly, returning to the room, the conversation. "This feels like such a loaded issue. I'd like to slow it down a bit, maybe talk about this, too, in the morning when we're fresh."

"That's a switch," Peg shot back with a small laugh that wasn't a laugh. "You're usually the one who wants to hurry through these discussions."

"I'm learning to slow my pace." He breathed in and out very

slowly, audibly. "Look, kiddo, it's obvious you have an agenda, but I can't do it. I'm pooped."

Peg rustled around in the bed.

Ben's voice began to trail off, "You want to be included. Okay, I'll be aware of that. I'm sorry. It's a habit I'll have to break."

"Okay." Silence. "Well," Peg finally broke through the dark. "Well...me, too. See you in the morning, sweetheart."

She turned over to face the wall, sighed and hugged one of the pillows. He lay facing away from her toward the windows. He didn't move for hours. But Peg woke twice and lay quietly, aching all over. *I'm losing him*, she lamented to herself. *We should have prayed before we went to sleep.* She listened to a coyote who howled intermittently on a narrow ridge above the sulfur river and finally fell asleep.

Ben dreamed he and Linda were walking in a park in a small Spanish town they had visited. Danny was just a toddler, Miriam not yet conceived. They strolled behind Danny whose blond head bobbed up and down, alternately checking out the pigeons swooping down from overhead and carefully putting his foot down so as not to step in pigeon doo. Ben felt happy, yet a melancholy tinged the scene. Later he and Linda made love–he caressed her small sinewy body–she was just twenty-three at the time. When he awoke, he felt embarrassed and guilty. He hadn't dreamt of his ex-wife for several years.

Peg got up early with the kids. It was the Rivers' turn to cook breakfast, so Jed and Jody banged around the kitchen with baby in tow. Ben woke to family sounds and the smell of bacon. Then he heard Peter Butler's unmistakable twang, so he put on his ratty bathrobe and stuck his head out to see what was going on. Danny and Miriam pounced on him. "Hi, Dad! I'm glad you're up," Danny exulted. Miriam squirmed into his arms.

"Hey, Peter. What's happenin', dude?" Ben asked over his daughter's head.

"Hey, Ben. I'm livin' here now."

Ben looked to Jed who said, "Yeah, he arrived last night. Alex said he could take the small cabin next to ours, the one nearest the gate."

"Great! That means the Winders got here safely. Everybody okay?"

"No worries. 'Cept Bobby Whitmer. He got called up for the National Guard yesterday. Seems every able-bodied bloke who's at least 18 and under 26's going off to fight the Chinese. They got 48 hours to report for basic training."

"No lie?" Jed asked and jumped up.

"Yeah. Don't you guys watch the news?"

"No, we don't have a television here," Danny complained.

"Well, it seems that the invasion is a real thing," Peter said flatly.

"Daddy, are you going to leave us?" Miriam cried out.

"No," Ben chuckled and hugged her tightly. "It's been a long time since I was 18, sweetheart. Or 26, for that matter."

Ben looked to Peg and then reached out for Danny and pulled him to his other side. "I'm so glad we took them," he whispered to her over his son's head.

Jed asked, "So what are your plans, Pete?"

"Got to go over to your bishop's house this morning. Going to talk to him about startin' up a solar conversion project for cars." Peter stuffed his mouth with pancakes. "Oh, yeah, and Nate told me to tell you Nephi Bingham was dead." He then downed a glass of orange juice in a few noisy gulps, got up, put his plate in the sink, and strode out. "See ya for dinner," he called out over his shoulder as he loped back down the gravel driveway to his cabin.

The adults sat stunned. Jody began to cry. Jed put Craig down and took her in his arms. "Nephi, dead," he repeated several times. "Nephi, dead."

Peg also moved to where Jody was sitting and gently stroked her arm. After a few minutes, Jody, wiping away the streaks that the tears had left on her cheeks, said, "Oh, well, at least he won't have to deal with the Chinese."

"That's exactly right, darlin'," Jed said, brushing back a few strands of hair from her forehead. "'Cause if Peter's right, we're in for some pretty weird stuff." He motioned to Ben that maybe the kids should leave the room now that the talk was turning to war.

Danny and Miriam already antsy, shot out the door and up the path to the Dubiks' when Peg told them that Moira and Alex were making homemade dolls and wooden toys. Alone in the dining room, Ben, Peg, Jed and Jody sat around the table for an hour sipping herbal tea and speculating about what might happen now that war was just around the corner.

Later Ben went out for firewood. When he returned with an arm's load of wood, the Rivers had left, and the door to his bedroom was closed. He tapped on the door with his foot. No response. "Honey, are you in there?" Still no answer, so he put down the wood and opened the door impatiently.

Peg sat with her back to him, facing the fireplace. He walked across the room and put the wood down on the ledge. He felt a flash of anger. *Why are you spoiling this for me?* he thought. *I finally have what I've hoped for all my life, a real teacher, and you have to pout.*

"So, Peg, what's up?" He could see tears in her eyes.

"You said you'd tell me what you've been doing."

So he told her briefly about the project. "I'm sorry I can't say more, honey. I didn't think I could say anything, but Sangay said it was all right to confide in you as much as I have. No one wants to put you in any jeopardy."

"I see," she said stone-faced.

"Peg, I can see you're upset. Maybe you're about to have your period. You get this way sometimes. "

She still sat without showing any emotion.

"Look, I'm going to work, Peg. I've told you what I can. I don't know what else to do." With that he walked out into the dining area.

She followed right behind, "Great. Walk out. Right when I want to talk...."

He wheeled around. "No, you don't want to talk. You want to make me feel guilty. Well, I'm not buying into it."

Peg stood with her arms to her sides, fists clenched, gathering her thoughts. "You think you're superior to me because you are a man and you have the priesthood. It's an old boys' network. 'Dear little sister Taylor, let's not tell her anything. She might blab it all around.'"

"Peg, you know I believe we share the priesthood." Ben's voice got considerably louder.

"That's a bunch of bull," she spit out the last word.

"Okay, that's it. I'm leaving."

She began to cry. "What's gotten into you, Ben? You act like you're this superior being."

Ben sighed, stopped and turned around. "Peg, sweetheart, you've got to get your act together. I love you and I want you as my wife, but you're really unclear at times. Maybe you should do that work on death with Moira."

"Well, fine. You think I'm crazy. That's just great!" Peg cried out, stomping off to Miriam's bedroom and slamming the door. "You're such a creep, Ben Taylor!" She threw herself down on the bed.

She had not lain there long when the outside door flew open and an upset Miriam appeared in the doorway to her room. "Don't you lay on my bed, Peg! You're so mean to my Daddy!"

"Me, mean to him? No way." Peg reached out to draw Miriam to her, but she would have none of it. "Did you hear us fighting, honey?" she asked softly.

Miriam nodded.

"It's not that serious. I'm just really tired and scared, and your daddy hasn't been around to hug me. Can you understand that?"

"Well, okay...you can lay on my bed, but just for a little while," she said, wheeling on her heel and returning to the driveway to pick up sticks for the doll project.

Peg sat up on the unmade bed. The white eyelets on the bedspread reminded her of one she had when she was young. She brushed her hair out of her eyes. *What has gotten into me? Am I going nuts?* The phone on the kitchen wall began to ring. Since she was the only one left, she slowly plodded over to it. It was the bishop looking for Peter.

"Peter just left, Bishop. Can I give him a message?" Peg tried to sound cheerful.

"Oh, no, he's probably on his way to my house."

"Bishop?"

"Yes, Peg."

Peg surprised herself by asking, "Could I meet with you sometime soon? Like today? I think I need a blessing."

"Well, I've been released as your bishop. I'm just a private citizen now, but I'd be happy to see you. And Ben?" he asked tentatively.

"No, just me." She felt annoyed that the bishop thought that her own need for spiritual comfort somehow had to include Ben. They agreed to meet at 3:00 at his house.

She left Ben a note, asked Grace if she would continue looking after the kids, took the Honda and drove slowly to the address Olson had given her in LaVerkin. When she arrived, she sat for a few moments in the car, staring at the black dashboard and struggling to decide what to ask for. *Lord, please speak through him,* Peg prayed. *Please let me know we're going to be okay.* As she opened the car door and walked up the sidewalk, she thought, *I guess that's what I want to know more than anything—that we're going to survive.*

Robert Olson sat, white shirt and dark blue tie, in the living room of the small rambler he had managed to rent. His navy suit jacket was draped on the overstuffed chair. He wondered what Peg needed. He hoped it wasn't their marriage. In fact, he had been sitting there for twenty minutes, mulling it over, a little anxious. "Occupational hazard of holding the priesthood," he said to no one in particular. Turning his eyes to one of his favorite pictures of Christ that he had placed on a bookshelf (it was the first detail that he had attended to in his new home) he sighed and asked very softly, "How do you do it, Lord, always giving perfect counsel, always knowing just the blessing the each one in your flock needs? How do you do it, Lord?" From the bookshelf, Christ gazed tenderly back at the bishop, as if in silent reply.

Now the former bishop was leading Peg down the hallway to the den. He gestured for her to sit down on a small wicker couch. Excusing himself, he put on his suit coat and stepped into the master bedroom to tell his wife he'd be tied up for fifteen minutes or so. Peg wondered where Sister Olson was, then remembered she was now an invalid. She could hear their muffled voices up the hall. She could also hear the giggles and laughter of two children in the backyard. Grandchildren, she guessed.

"What is on your mind today, Peg?" he asked in what Peg had critically called his "institutional, canned-warmth" voice. Now it sounded soothing and familiar. She felt guilty for having judged a good man—a good man who had been her bishop.

"I don't know, exactly. I know you gave my husband a blessing that he values a great deal, although I don't know the details. I just know I need a blessing," she sighed. "As you know, we have added to our family quite suddenly—maybe a few words from the Lord about that?" she looked up quizzically. "Or whatever." Her throat tightened. *I'm not going to cry*, she said fiercely to herself.

Pulling a chair from behind the desk, he motioned her to sit down.

"Frankly, I'm scared, Bishop. With this Chinese invasion, I'm really scared. Maybe you could ask the Lord what he wants me to be doing, now that everything is going nuts."

"Okay, Peg, I'll do just that. What is your full name?" he asked as he rounded the chair.

She sat up straighter as he placed his gnarled hands lightly on her head, "Margaret LaDawn Christen...ah, Taylor." She blushed. *Why did I almost say Christensen? Will he guess we're having problems?* Peg tried to calm down, took a couple of long breaths.

Olson remained quite still for ten seconds or so, then began, "Margaret LaDawn Taylor...I want you to know this morning that you are truly precious in the sight of your Heavenly Father."

Peg didn't get any farther without tearing up.

"You are one of his choice spirits here upon the earth."

Now big tears began to roll down Peg's cheeks. Her nose began to run, so she tried to pinch it shut. The bishop, realizing what was happening, stopped and handed her a handkerchief, then continued, "He allows those who would be His servants to be tested. Through this testing you have already faced many trials and tribulations."

If you only knew, Bishop, she thought wearily.

"The Lord is so very pleased you have been faithful in overcoming these difficulties, in keeping your promises to Him. Peg, you've asked about adding to your family. Know that these two children who have been put in your care are precious in the sight of the Lord." The bishop paused and listened to the interior voice of the Spirit..."you will have much posterity sealed to you and your fine husband."

When it was over, Peg knew she had been touched by the Lord Himself. Too often for it to have been a matter of chance, Olson had given voice to thoughts and described situations that only Peg knew.

The bishop embraced her in a great nurturing hug before she left. She nestled briefly in the warmth of this pure patriarchal energy, taking it in for all she was worth. And as she did so, she could feel barricade after barricade fall away from her soul—defenses that she had raised long ago to shield her from her harsh, rigid father—defenses she hoped she might never need again. She sat in the driveway and wrote in her journal as fast as she could, capturing on paper what the bishop had communicated to her about the will and wisdom of her Father in Heaven.

After about a half an hour of writing, she drove down to the interstate to the only gas station in the area. Their car, being eleven years old, still ran on gasoline, since they were too poor to pay for the conversion to electric. Peg had squirreled away the two gallons of gas that they had brought with them from Salt Lake in a storage area under the office and checked on them periodically. It was hard being dependent on gas stations.

"Still funny to think that gas is made from corn," she said aloud to herself.

While she was filling the tank, a mechanic sauntered over and struck up a conversation with her. She was always surprised to find how easily people outside of metropolitan areas fell into conversation. It was like being back in Idaho where she'd grown up.

"You live around here?"

"No, just visiting for awhile," she said carefully.

"You like it?"

"It's beautiful. Can you suggest somewhere I might go to get away that's an easy hike?"

"Have you been to Kolob?"

Peg laughed out loud. "Are you LDS?"

The young man clammed up.

"Oh, I'm sorry. I didn't mean to offend you. It's just really funny to hear someone ask that question."

"Kolob Canyon–about ten miles up the road toward Cedar City. Take exit 40 off to the right," he said taking her money.

I shouldn't waste the gas was Peg's first thought. But she found herself at the phone asking for Jody. "Hey, Jody, just tell him I've gone to Kolob without him. Okay? I'll be back by dinner. Who's cooking? You? Oh, great."

Peg hadn't been out in nature by herself for quite a long time. She was determined to go somewhere quiet and pull herself together. Her first surprise when she turned into the Visitor's Center was the color of the road–an almost ruby red. *Not quite the yellow brick road, but maybe it will lead to Oz,* she chuckled. As she slowly drove up Kolob Canyon Road to Lee Pass, she pulled the car off to the side several times, stunned at the grandeur of the "Fingers," a series of narrow canyons, each dramatically carved from a thousand years of erosion. They were tight, splashed with vibrant shades of red, emerald green foliage at the base, with a fork of the Taylor Creek rushing through each. Peg could see thin, wispy waterfalls slipping over the high canyon walls. *So this is Kolob,* Peg thought imitating Ben's reaction to the small town of Enoch. *It's gorgeous!*

From Lee Pass, she drove to the next turn-off and found herself in a scene of exquisite beauty. One of the "fingers" looked like an entrance to the womb of the Great Earth Mother. Peg decided she'd climb up the side of the hill across from the turn-off and try to get a grip on her emotions. Settling on a large, flat rock, she took a jacket out of her backpack, slipped it on and removed her precious journal from the side pocket. She took in several deep breaths and felt the peace of the place seep into her pores.

If Ben had read her journal, it would have confirmed his intuitions about Peg's great depths–depths that her vivaciousness generally concealed–depths that, despite her extroversion, she kept to herself. She might have said she was intimidated by his intellect, but really she savored having a secret life, one where her writing and sketches were just hers.

She had been influenced in her journal writing by seeing a piece about Carl Jung's Red Book, a highly personal and ornately illustrated journal. Before that, she had only written in her journal what she had been told to in seminary–accounts of important events, especially "spiritual" ones. Then when she was in therapy after Rachel's death, she began reading every self-help book she could get her hands on. In her therapist's office she saw Jung's *Memories, Dreams and Reflections,* and thinking it was a book about dreams, she asked to borrow it. She felt like Alice stepping through the Looking Glass from the moment she picked up and read the first page of this exotic, stream-of-consciousness autobiography. A psychiatrist with open visions, a man who had written his dissertation on the paranormal and mediumship, a student of ancient Tibetan texts and medieval alchemical manuals. She felt like she'd found her guru. And started her own Red Book.

Peg looked up to see a jay with a black crest hop across the rock next to her. She wished she had brought some bread crumbs. He surveyed her for a moment, then flew off. She smiled--the wrenched heart was feeling better. She quickly sketched the bird. Peg was pretty good--she had a slightly abstract style which, with some work, could develop into a distinctive one. She felt a little guilty not saying more to Jody about where she was going, but she wanted to annoy Ben. He always hated it if she was late or if he didn't know where she was.

Peg opened the pages to the last entry and read what Olson had said. "Peg, there are more trials ahead, but because of your faithfulness, you have been given the priesthood in your home to protect you from the fiery darts of the adversary."

The Lord has given me Ben, she thought. A rush of desire for him flooded her mind. *I hate fighting.* She wanted to go back right then and snuggle in his arms, but she knew she'd come for more than a reminder of how much she loved her husband.

"He promises you to perfect your power of expression, and you will have power over the elements." These two passages were directly from her patriarchal blessing. She shivered. *How could the bishop know that? Really miraculous!* Especially because they were the two parts of her blessing that she had most puzzled over.

"How could I have power over the elements? Isn't that a priesthood function? Power over the elements? Parting the Red Sea? Healing the sick? What?" She never got an answer. So she contented herself with the faith that the Lord would make the interpretation obvious in His own good time.

Still, she couldn't help imagining what perfecting her "power of expression" might mean. Secretly she hoped that He might help her with her writing. During her fifth year in teaching training, she took a creative writing class, even though it hadn't been required for her degree in literature. She ended up in a class of mostly published writers, and she felt very intimidated.

It took her an entire quarter to write "Arch Disturber of Tranquility," a short story at the turn of the century in Ireland.

Kathleen O'Toole, the main character, was a high-strung, mystical girl who, disgusted at her crass groom, flees the church where she is to be married and finds sanctuary in a nearby monastery. There she has a transfiguring vision of Jesus. Peg's professor selected it as the best short story of the term. He also asked her permission to publish it in the university's prestigious literary journal. She had never told Ben about it.

Writing fiction had been an ordeal for Peg and had left her limp. But poetry—well, that was another matter. It came easily to her—the sounds of things, the rhythm and flow, the images. She loved to let outrageous pictures percolate up from her subconscious and lay them alongside other equally unorthodox ideas.

She read aloud a few notes she had written on Ben's birthday, last September: "The man who died printing the Bible deserves a purple heart....meandering through the Middle Ages (40-50)...God sends his blue-blooded Hound to hunt down dream children in soup kitchens and lazy wine deaths."

They weren't really poems, but they gave her pleasure because she was free to write the way she thought. Her professor encouraged her to keep writing. She'd stopped when first her father died of a heart attack, then her divorce, and hard on the heels of that was Rachel's accident. No images, no rhythm, no hope. Mute.

She reread the last of her blessing notes: "Go now, become a mother and queen unto your husband in Zion, and you will see the hand of the Lord in your life. Rise up and rejoice and look forward to each new day, for glorious blessings await you."

She read it again—slowly—out loud, savoring the image of the hand of Lord being made visible. *Maybe I'll be like the brother of Jared*, she thought. *Glorious blessings.* "Glorious blessings!" she shouted down the canyon.

"Glorious blessings!" the canyon replied.

Oh, thank you, for answering my prayer! she exulted silently. It felt like iron filings on a paper being magnetized—suddenly all the parts of her being falling into place—in a lovely geometric pattern. "Hallelujah!" she shouted and hugged herself.

"Hallelujah!" echoed the mountain chorus.

Peg took out a cheese sandwich and nibbled on it. Then she carefully wrapped it up, half-eaten, and slipped it into her pocket. After taking a sip of water from the bottle she had brought, she picked up the journal and began doodling in the margins--took the bird figure, stylized it and ran down the left margin for half a page in various positions. She imagined for a moment that she was an Irish monk 700 years ago on some small island illustrating the margins of a page of the Bible. Then the gypsy woman from the dream she worked on in the therapy group appeared in her mind's eye. *Crazy old woman, what are we going to do with you? I really want to go to Paris with you to find your favorite tree. But I want to live, not die.*

She pulled out a well-worn paperback anthology of poetry and began thumbing through her favorites. She felt like she could write again today after that blessing, but didn't trust that she could produce her own structure, so she had decided to try to imitate the style of someone she admired--Dylan Thomas or William Butler Yeats. She spent some minutes trying to get Thomas' "The Force That Through The Green Fuse Drives The Flower" to fit her mood but couldn't. At last her eye fell on a stanza from "Sailing to Byzantium" by Yeats. She felt a mounting thrill run through her body--growing and expanding--almost like waves of erotic delight, as she wrote:

> Oh, aging Carmen standing in Charon's deadly bark
> As in a plumed, tattooed wagon of a gypsy queen,
> Come from the bark, snatch me from my misery
> And become the staccato-dancer of my soul.
> Consume my disbelief; for I am stopped up,
> Sick with fright and fastened to a dead father.
> Gather me to your sweaty breast and hie me to your tree.

Peg titled it "Under A Parisian Oak."

She was so intent on the poem that she hadn't noticed a mule deer who had come up to the road in the late afternoon. He stood several yards away and looked at her with those animal eyes that see reality without distortion--clear, brown, steady. She guessed he was about four years old—a three-point buck, she remembered from Idaho hunting days. He didn't move, not sure what she might do. When she did discover him, she dropped her pen and fell back with a little shriek. He jumped back on skittery, spindly legs, but held his ground.

"Hi, there, fella," Peg said extending her hand. "What do you want?"

She immediately loved his white muzzle with its contrasting black nostrils. The deer simply stared. Peg got goose bumps. "Are you from my gypsy woman?" The deer nodded his head slowly. "And you've come to say what? That she's real? That I'm for real?" She couldn't be sure she saw him move his head. The mule deer stood so still it could have been a statue. Finally it moved a flank. "Well, I thank you for the message if it was one. I'll cherish it no matter what." With that, the deer turned and bounded back down the hill into the brush.

Peg felt the adrenalin pound through her chest and neck. She shivered in the misty shadows. *What an afternoon! I surely got what I came for. Thank you, Beloved Savior.* She got up, brushed herself off and watched a bird land on a nearby rock, flex its legs up and down, suddenly peck at the ground and fly away with an insect in its mouth. *It's time I went home to my children,* Peg thought proudly. *I too have babies to feed.*

And it's time I did death.

With that, she felt suddenly free. "I will face that which I most fear," she said dramatically, stretching her arms high over head. She lowered them; then with a circular motion, she scooped up the last of the sun's rays with her hands and placed them first on her eyes, then on her mouth.

It was well past five by the time Peg drove up to the Pah Tempe gates. She knew she was in trouble. The hollow twitch in her stomach reminded her of a time when she was about eight. She had decided to go back into the Saturday movie and watch *Bambi* a second time. Her furious father had to bend over and search row after row for her. *I think I knew all along that he was looking for me,* she thought. *I just wanted to get back at him, just once.*

Ben emerged immediately from the bed and breakfast at the sound of the Honda. Storm clouds swarmed around his head. "Where have you been?" he demanded.

"In Kolob Canyon," she said evenly. "I called and left you a message. Didn't you get it?"

"I got a message that read you'd gone to Kolob without me."

"Exactly."

"What was I to make of that?" he asked angrily. "It's nearly dark."

Good, Peg thought. *I like this, Mr. Smartypants. Now you're on the defensive!*

"I went hiking in Kolob Canyon," she said evenly.

"Alone?"

"Of course," Peg shot back jauntily.

"You've never done anything like that before," Ben said incredulously.

"Oh, yes, I have, many times, but that was before we met. I needed some space to get my head together, that's all. Have you eaten?"

"No, we've been waiting for you," he lied.

"It's not six yet. Why would everyone be waiting for me?"

"I dunno. Maybe you're to help out with dinner."

Peg smiled back unperturbed. "I don't think so. I talked to Jody and she said she was cooking."

Ben knew he'd been caught in a lie. Exasperated, he scrambled to regain the upper hand. "Well, it sounded like some kind of suicide note."

"Oh, really, Ben," she said with a great deal of disgust. "Don't be so melodramatic!"

"'I've gone to Kolob without you!' What kind of a message is that?" Ben said raising his voice. "I mean, really. Think about it. You scared the kids to death."

"What? What did you tell them, Ben Taylor? I hope nothing

about a suicide note!"

"Of course not, but they were worried about you."

"I hate it when you get hysterical," she said acridly. "Maybe you should work on your death issues with Moira," she said stomping into the bedroom.

What Ben really wanted to say was, "I thought you were lost and I was frightened."

What the children heard was yet another argument today. Sure they were to blame, Danny and Miriam slipped away from the house on the pretext that they wanted to get their clothes down by the river.

"Are you really going to try to call Grandpa?" Miriam asked Danny worriedly as they entered the office next to the bed and breakfast.

"I sure am. This is a dumb place. I can't stand it here," Danny said. "I don't have any friends and I want to go back to school. Besides, I miss Grandpa and Grandma. "

He was the quiet one, who had learned to guard against expressing his feelings, because of his grandfather's explosive temper. Danny was the recipient of regular beatings, which his grandmother was too frightened to try to stop. Ben knew nothing of these incidents which left Danny swollen and bruised. Miriam carried the burden of not telling, or she would "get it worse," Abe Breyerson had warned.

"I miss things too," Miriam added, "but I don't want to leave Daddy, do you?"

"I don't know. I just want to go home, that's all." Danny sat down at the desk and dialed the seven-digit number he knew for his California home. He got someone who said he had dialed the wrong number. Before she could hang up, Danny asked, "Is this California?"

"No, this is Utah. You have to dial the prefix for California."

"How do I do that?"

The friendly woman on the other end asked where he was calling in California.

"Ukiah."

"I'll look it up. Hold on, sweetheart." There was a pause. "That's 1-7-0-7 and your number, okay?"

"Thanks," Danny said and smiled as he hung up. "I bet Dad and Peg thought we couldn't figure this out, but we did!" He walked around the oak desk, sat down in the swivel chair and put his feet up on the desk. The chair nearly tipped over and he sat up quickly, red-faced.

Miriam looked worried. "I think it costs a lot of money to call California."

"Tough," he replied.

When he got through to his grandmother, she broke down sobbing. His grandfather took the phone and asked gruffly, "Where has that maniac taken you?"

"I don't know. I know we're in Utah, Grandpa, and it's a place called Pah Tempe."

"Is that a town?"

"No, it's just a place where a few people live."

"What big town is it near, Danny?" his voice softened. He didn't want to scare him away. The Breyersons had heard from the radio station that the kids were safe but didn't really believe it.

"We've only been to a place called 'Hurikun.'"

"Are you kids okay?" he asked in a voice that was growing louder.

"No, we want to come home."

"Is your dad there? I want to speak to him."

"No, he doesn't know we're calling."

"Let me talk to Miriam...Hello, honey, are you okay?"

Miriam began to cry. She felt torn.

"Do you want to come home?"

She said yes because she knew Danny would be mad if she didn't.

"Okay," her grandfather said, "we'll do something about it right away. Don't you worry. What's the phone number there?"

There was nothing written on the phone.

Abe vowed under his breath he'd kill Ben when he found the kids.

"Listen, sweetheart, give the phone to Danny. Okay?"

Miriam handed over the phone, tears running down her cheeks.

"Don't you tell Dad or Peg, do you hear me?" Danny said fiercely. "Promise?"

"I promise." Miriam hung her head.

"Yes, Grandpa?"

"Listen, Danny. I need you to find out the phone number where you are. Can you look around and see if there is a paper with the number on it?"

"Okay. Hold on." Danny rifled through some of the papers stacked on the desk until he found an invoice for art supplies Alex had ordered. On it was the phone number. He gave it to his grandfather and again threatened Miriam if she told. He had a nasty streak, something like Edmund's in *The Lion, The Witch and The Wardrobe*.

Peg did something she hadn't done since she was in college and worried to distraction about her love who was away on his mission–she locked herself in the bathroom and wrote a letter to God.

"Heavenly Father, I know you're really busy, but I've got to get Your ear just for a few moments. You see I love my husband and I hate to fight, but it seems that we are getting into more and more arguments, and I think I'm the problem."

"I know that You know that we're in a really tight situation, and so far, You've been great about keeping us safe and sending angels to protect the kids so they could get to us."

"But you see, I want more:

I want them to love me.

I want Ben to love me.

I want You to love me...."

Peg put her head on her arms and leaned against the sink. She began to weep as quietly as she could.

She really didn't care if someone heard her—she felt completely and totally unloved and unlovable. Gone was any recollection of the day's wondrous high. She had been brave in front of Ben when he blew up on her return, but afterward she was devastated.

"Why can't he be a dad to me sometimes?" she picked up the pen and continued to write. "It feels like it's always about him. Never about me."

She knew that wasn't true. Ben did spend time listening to her, holding her and reassuring her, but not since Pah Tempe and especially not since the plates.

Chapter Fifteen

He rais'd a mortal to the skies,
She drew an angel down.
"Alexander's Feast," John Dryden

The children slipped back into the bed and breakfast through
Danny's bedroom and walked into the dining room, trying to act
like nothing had happened. In the clutter and noise of dinner-
making, they went unnoticed. A couple of times Danny looked
over at Miriam, who avoided his eyes by looking down. She knew
intuitively (as young children often do) they had done
something that could cause real problems for everyone there.

Danny's blond hair had worked its way out of Peg's morning
attempt to lacquer down a very stubborn cowlick. It stood
straight up at the back of his crown. His cheeks were a little
hollow and his body looked thin through the blue turtle neck he
was wearing. The enormity of what he had done began to weigh
on him, but he was used to keeping secrets, particularly the
blows he received at the hands of his grandfather.

This secret felt about the same. He didn't think that his
Colorado City rescuer, Alex, would get into trouble. Just the
people who lived at the bed and breakfast–specifically his dad. He
was unconsciously angry at Ben for not spending the time with
him that he wanted. He was also disappointed with this bookish
father who preferred reading to swimming in the river or hiking.
And he was jealous of what he perceived as Ben's favoritism
toward Miriam.

And Peg–he didn't know what he felt for her. He wanted to
relax into her hugs, enjoy the games she tried to play with him,
but he was old enough to remember his mother and felt he had to
be faithful to what memory he had of her. But mostly, he was
just afraid of losing another mother.

Not more than an hour after Peg came back from Kolob, Peter
arrived for dinner with Bobby Whitmer, who had come to say
goodbye before leaving for basic training at Hamilton Air Force

Base in Marin County, California.

"Well, Bobby, this is it," Jed said slapping Bobby on the back and pulling him into the middle of the dining area. "Wish I could go with you, get some trigger time, but I'm too old," he said in a creaky voice, while he bent over and pretended to be walking with a cane.

Bobby managed a smile.

"I know you've been dying to get into battle. Got all those knives and junk you were always saving up and squirreling away?" Jed poked him playfully in the ribs.

"No, not really. Just a couple of knives stored in my boot," Bobby said weakly. Jed leaned down as Bobby pulled up his pant leg to reveal a small dagger strapped to the outside of his lower left leg.

"Hey, you'll be great in the field," Jed said trying to cheer him up. "Real gung ho. But they won't let you keep extra hardware."

"Really? Why not?" Bobby asked.

"That the rules—just military issue," Jed said matter-of-factly.

Peg noticed Bobby's lower lip quiver, so she whispered to Jody, "Where are his parents?"

"They're on a welfare mission in Louisiana," she whispered back. "Helping refugees move north, away from all the coastal flooding."

"Oh, it must be really hard to leave without seeing them." Peg felt like taking him into her arms and holding him while he had a good cry.

Jody whispered to her, "Let's see what we can do to make his last evening a good one." She handed the baby to Peg and moved in among the men who were gathered around him. Peg smiled at Jody's tomboy frame and how she elbowed Ben and Jed aside to get to Bobby. "Hey, Bobby, join us for dinner. Why don'tja? I've just cooked up some outrageous enchiladas."

Bobby's expression went from repressed terror to temporary relief. The women led him to the head of the table while everyone else sat around on chairs and stools from the kitchen.

"This is a grand reunion of the Ukiah Third Ward," Peter said, sweeping his hand to include the whole gang. Peg wanted Bobby to feel comfortable, and he was. He was spirited away into a sense of normalcy with this group of outlaws–with the smells and taste of the Mexican food, children's high-pitched chatter, the joking back and forth between Ben and Peter, who had made a practice of telling really bad jokes to each other. Ben was forcing a new one on Peter, "The Tells, you know William's family, took up bowling for charity. They'd become rich after the apple and arrow incident–speaking engagements, things like that. So one day, some guy asks a friend which charity the Tells worked for on the bowling circuit, and the other guy says, "No one knows for whom the Tells bowl."

It took Peter a moment to get it, then he burst out laughing, spitting food in Danny's direction. "Ha, ha, HA! That's a good one, Benjy."

Bobby's eyes eagerly took in every bit of the scene. He'd at least have these memories to hold onto in the battlefield. Then Ben asked Peter, "What happened in your meeting with the bishop?"

Peter took a long drink of water, wiped his mouth with his sleeve and said, "It was real good. He's gonna to put up the money and I'm gonna to do the work. We sent to Salt Lake for the supplies. Should start tomorrow convertin' the cars over to solar."

"How do you know how to do that?" Bobby asked.

"Oh, I built cars for the great Solar Races in the outback for years. But the Japanese always beat me. They had the money. That's why I went to the Yanks, but they just lined my pockets and didn't build a bloody thing. Frustrating, really."

"So they paid you off not to build what you knew? Why?" Bobby asked.

"Corporate hogs," Peter said and looked down sadly. "But," he brightened up, "now that there's no more America, I can do what

I like."

"Aren't you being a bit premature?" Ben asked.

"Well, a little. But I tell you it won't be long till there ain't no more electric batteries in stores for you Yanks, much less gas at the pump. Solar's king, in my book."

"How much you gonna charge us, Peter?" Jed asked teasingly.

"Nothin'. The bishop's shoutin' for everyone's car."

"Shouting?" Peg asked.

"Payin' outta his own pocket."

"No way!" Peg said. Touched by the bishop's generosity, she remembered the blessing and the bishop's hug and felt a gentle surge of warmth.

While the men continued discussing the solar conversion project, Jody came by and served Bobby a third helping of enchiladas swimming in hot sauce and mounded with brown-crusted white cheese. This he ate with relish, wiping the plate clean with his index finger. Then he sat back in his chair for the first time since sitting down.

Jody asked, "How's your uncle Nate?"

"He's good. He's with his parents and the kids in St. George. He told me to tell you they'll be up here on Saturday for the sacrament meeting."

"Oh, that's really good," Jody replied.

"Yeah, we were really relieved to get here in one piece."

"It's really treacherous out there," Peter interrupted. He fingered the slight, white scar under his left eye and tried not to think about Laurie Winder and Room 206 in Baker, Nevada.

Finally it came time for Peter to take Bobby to St. George–to the high school football field–where he would be joined by nearly one thousand young men and women who were to be flown to Salt Lake and then on to the Air Force base in Marin. Standing in the dining area in old Army surplus fatigues that he had saved from before his mission, he looked terribly vulnerable, but he stood very straight as his friends gathered around to wish him well. Everyone, except Peter, took turns hugging him. Bobby struggled to hold back tears.

No one except Alex and Jed had been to war. This was the first time for the rest of the "tribe" to stand with a friend, a young friend, who might be marching off to his death.

Then Bobby was gone. While Jody and Peg washed up and sniffled and talked, Alex wandered around the kitchen eating left-over enchiladas. "Do you think Bobby will have to kill anyone?" Peg asked Alex in a mournful tone.

"Depends on the Chinese. Yes, if they make the move to invade Alaska and the UWEN decides on a ground war. No, if the UWEN nukes them. No one knows what will happen at this point."

"Hey, Tubby, doesn't your wife feed you enough?" Jody tried to lighten the mood as she wiped down the turquoise-tiled counter.

"Uh, uh," Alex grunted, cheeks bulging. He was finishing off the remains of one of the large pans. Both women laughed. They knew that Moira was easily the best cook around.

Up at the big house, Moira and Grace moved from the kitchen into the living room. Dressed in a long beige caftan she had borrowed from Moira, Grace built a fire in the large open fireplace and motioned to Moira to sit in the brown leather occasional chair. Moira wrapped a soft wool blanket over her lap, while Grace sat down on a matching ottoman and began to rub her daughter's feet. Moira said in Maori, "Oh, that feels so good, Mom. Is being pregnant usually this tiresome?"

"After a few babies, you get used to it. But you've got to remember you're 44 and even though you're in good shape, your body goes through a lot."

They sat there for some minutes talking about simple matters. Then Moira said, "I've really put off asking this question, Mom, because I haven't wanted to know. But I know that my son is going to make it, I do want to know what's going on out there in the world, and I suspect you know a lot, don't you?"

Grace looked down.

"Come on, Mom, I know that look when you're holding back things that you think you can't talk about."

The square-faced seeress put down Moira's left foot and picked up the right one to begin massaging the heel. "Well, let's just say the world is pregnant, dear. And once it goes into labor, it passes through a few stages."

"Yeah, I know: the beginning, the middle and the end," Moira said wryly.

"Well, something like that," Grace said, defusing her daughter's irony with a soft smile. After you've been in labor for hours and hours, you come to the place where the nurse says, 'Okay, Mrs. Ihimaera, you can start pushing now.' That's where we are now—the world has begun to push into the very last stage of labor before the Lord comes."

Moira pulled her foot away and sat up. "Oh, come on, Mom. Level with me! I'm your daughter, remember? I know you know more than that." Moira put her hands on her sides. "Come on. What do you know?"

Grace stared for a long time into the fire. "Okay, okay," she sighed and sat motionless, gathering her thoughts about her like the green shawl draped over her bony shoulders. "When I was quite young—nine or ten, I read the Bible cover to cover. I didn't understand very much, but when I reached the Book of Revelations, something came over me and I could see scene after scene as John described them, and I heard a voice say, out loud, 'You, Grace, will see the end of days.'"

"You never told me that, Mummy." Moira sounded both surprised and hurt.

"No one knew except my mother and husband," she said pointedly. "And since that time I have studied the signs and prophecies both in scriptures and in Maoritanga (Maori culture)."

Moira couldn't keep her eyes off her mother's face, which was alternately lighted and darkened by the dancing flames. Grace looked like Hestia, Greek goddess of the hearth—one with the stones, the sacred fire and the ash. An ember from the fire flew out of the fireplace and onto the Oriental rug. In one swift movement, Grace picked it up and threw it back in.

Moira sat very still.

"So I've always known some things," Grace continued, "but since the Visit, I've known a great deal more."

"The Visit?" Moira asked quietly. She scarcely breathed fearing she'd say something to cause her mother to shut down. Grace gestured to her to put her right foot back up on the ottoman. She quickly obeyed.

As Grace began to press down on the instep, she closed her eyes and began to speak, "Gordon, your dad, came to see me. He does that sometimes, when I'm half asleep."

"Mom, he came to me too! That night in the hospital. In a dream."

Grace opened her eyes, smiled broadly and said, "Oh, sweetheart, I'm so glad. I told him to keep trying–that he'd get through one of these days." She dropped Moira's foot and reached out to give her daughter a quick hug. "What did he say?"

"He was young and healthy!"

"Uh, huh." Grace said, sitting back down on the ottoman.

"He told me to carry on the work that we had started. Only to work now for all Lamanites. That I had the *mana*. Then he disappeared."

"You see, you do have these abilities. Admit it, Iwi".

Moira hung her head, "O...kay, but nothing like you."

Grace, with a satisfied smile on her face, returned to her massage and asked, "And, so, what do you make of the message?"

"It felt like a big piece of me slipped back into place. Since I left New Zealand and came here, I've been happy with Alex, but I certainly haven't been able to use my political skills. Not in this small area and not in these political times." Moira leaned back and sighed. "It feels really good to think the Lord can use what I've learned. I just wish I knew how it's all going to come about."

Grace laughed softly.

"Okay, Mom, enough of this. What happened when Dad came to you?"

"Well...this time he came with a Visitor, a very tall man with hair hanging down over his broad shoulders. He was all in white, very handsome."

Moira sucked in her breath. "An angel?"

"An angel." Grace said in a low, controlled voice. She worked around Moira's swollen ankle, then looked up and said, "You're holding onto too much water. Cut down your salts."

"Yes, Mummy."

Nothing was said for a time. Moira didn't know if she should prod her mother to continue. Finally she couldn't stand it any longer and blurted out, "So who was it?"

"A friend of Gordon's. You know when you have the priesthood over there, it's a very great advantage. Gordon can talk to many important spiritual people."

"Yes...s...s?"

"He introduced himself as Timothy."

"Timothy? Timothy? As in First and Second Timothy?"

"No, Timothy as in *Book of Mormon* Timothy."

"Wasn't he one of those who was translated?"

"That's what I asked him."

"And?" Moira felt like she was trying to swim in a river of heavy molasses.

"And...he didn't say."

"Well, did you ask to shake his hand, like Joseph suggests in *D&C*?"

"I didn't have the presence of mind to do anything, except to take in what I was being told."

Moira let out a sigh of disappointment. "Okay, then, let me make sure, before we go any further, so that I understand. My father appeared in your bedroom with one of Christ's New World apostles," Moira said, unable to conceal a trace of incredulity.

"Well, it sounds preposterous when you say it like that, but you asked and that's what happened," Grace replied testily. She glanced up at her daughter, then looked down as she continued rubbing the swollen ankles. "And that's when he told me about my grandson and many other things which I promised I would not tell anyone, not even you."

Moira struggled to sit up, pulling her feet from her mother's supple hands. She took a poker from the black metal stand near the fireplace and pushed around a log which had been blocking the progress of the burn. She broke the silence. "Well, what can you tell me?" she said trying to contain her frustration.

"I can tell you that you and Alex and Israel are going to live through it all and thrive in Zion. I can tell you that the Chinese will invade the United States and when that happens, that will truly be the beginning of the apocalypse. Oh, and I can tell you that, in a little while, construction will start on the temple in Jackson County."

"Unbelievable!" Moira was breathless. The fire was now in full force, casting its warmth over mother and daughter. "But will you be with us?" Moira asked tenderly.

"Yes, for a while."

"And then?"

"Oh, child, it's more than you could ever imagine—more than the mind can take in! It's...it's...glorious! And really, little one, I won't say any more than just that. You'll have your turn to learn these things, I'm absolutely certain." Grace breathed in deeply and stretched out her arms to her daughter. Moira moved forward and slid into the welcome harbor of her mother's arms. The widow warmed Israel as well.

Later, Ben and Alex, stomachs full, stood outside on the back porch under a crescent moon. "That Bobby, did you know him well, back in California?"

"No, I just heard from Nate that he came back early from a mission in England. Stayed with the Winders."

"Seems like a really nice kid," Alex said warmly.

"He is. I sure wouldn't want to be in his shoes right now, going through his rites of passage."

"Me neither."

Both men fell silent, trying not to think what these next days might bring. Ben always felt protected in his athletic friend's presence. He still wasn't that comfortable living in nature and wondered to himself if cougars creep up silently or give out a warning growl before attacking their prey.

Alex let out a couple of long sighs. "I think extended family is a lot healthier than the way most of us live."

"Me too. This feels really good." Ben said letting go of the cougar attack fantasy and patting his belly. He sometimes joked that he was getting a little too thick in the middle and a little too thin on the top. Behind the joke lay the niggling fear he would end up looking like his bricklayer father. "Now I just wish the world would go away. Actually, you know what would make this really perfect? A Balkan-Sobranie."

"What's that?"

"Used to be a top-of-the-line British cigarette. Came in tins of ten. Eight bucks a tin."

"Do you still have a hankerin' for a smoke, old buddy?" Alex taunted him.

"Yep, gotta confess that I do. Only after two events, though–a good meal and you know what else."

Both men chuckled. The moon continued to rise above the narrow cliffs. "Reminds me of a silver comma," Ben mused," or Aphrodite's eyelash...ahhh, 'swear not by the moon, the inconstant moon...'"

"Make that a period," Alex cut in. "I'd like time to stop right now, this night." Alex blew out into the misty air. He could see his breath, so he tried forming a ring with his fog breath, but couldn't. "Let's go take comfort in our women's primeval embrace."

"A brilliant notion, Professor Dubik–and a penetrating one at that," Ben said, patting Alex on the back.

On the way to his bedroom, he worried what he'd have to do to get into Peg's arms. Not much as it turned out. After an exchange of "I'm sorry's," Peg shared her blessing from Bishop Olson and her experiences in Kolob. She even risked reading him her poem. When she finished it, Ben, surprised at the poem's high quality, said, "I had no idea that I had a real poetess on my hands."

Peg beamed. "You really liked it? Really and truly?"

Ben smiled back. "It shows a lot of promise. However there's one thing I would suggest..."

Peg winced and placed her hand firmly over his mouth. "Don't," she said, close to tears. "Don't do that. I just want you to enjoy where I'm at. I'm not looking for an editor." She folded her arms around her chest and turned her back on him. "I'm not planning to submit it to some stuffy journal. Don't ruin it for me," she said over her shoulder.

"I'm really sorry, sweetheart," Ben said reaching out to her and gathering her in his arms. "That's another habit I'll have to break." He pushed away the errant curl that fell over one eye and kissed her on the nose. He was particularly pleased when she told him she had decided to do further work with Moira. And he had to admit he had been a bit haughty lately, swept up with the romance of being translator of ancient plates. (*Lately!* he thought to himself...*how about all my life?*) *Yet Peg always manages to keep pace with me*, he thought. Later, after they had made love, he laughed to himself and mused, *No, a lot of the time she's one step ahead of me.* As they fell asleep in each other's arms, Peg sleepily asked, "What would you change?"

"In the poem? Really? You're not going to hit me, are you?"

"No, I promise."

"'Hie me to your tree' doesn't work."

"Oh...thanks, I think." Peg laughed softly as Ben pulled her to him.

Chapter Sixteen

To suffer one's death and to be reborn is not easy.
Gestalt Therapy Verbatim, Fritz Perls

The next day was Thursday, the day scheduled for the Garden Club to meet. Women gathered in the Dubik kitchen, pouring and sipping herbal teas and cocoa. Moira had not seen most of the women since her healing, and she was worried about confronting Dr. Hunter's wife. She wasn't sure just what reaction she'd get, since she knew from the last meeting, the miscarriage was still a loaded issue with Sandy. Grace and Jody who had never been in a group hung around the edges. Peg, scared and eager to work on her gypsy woman and death, talked a little too loudly to anyone within reach. She tuned into the middle of a conversation between Patricia, the former concert violinist, and Sandy Hunter.

Sandy had just asked, "Why? Where's his wife?"

Patricia responded, "She's refused to come here. She and her other five children are in Salt Lake. He's already gone there a couple of times. It seems the marriage was strained before this rather radical move." Peg guessed they were talking about Nate Winder.

"Why doesn't he just move there?" Peg asked, warming her hands on the sides of the beige ceramic cup Alex had made.

"To tell you the truth I don't know," Patricia replied, turning to Peg. "My husband guesses Brother Winder really needs to make some rather big changes–to live out more in the country, maybe."

"She's a general authority's daughter, did you know?" Sandy volunteered.

"Who?"

"His wife."

"I saw him in the store yesterday. He sure looks like his grandfather," Grace said, joining the conversation.

"His grandfather?" Peg asked.

"President Nathan S. Winder, you know, counselor to several presidents some years back," Grace responded.

"Oh!" Peg exclaimed, her eyes widening. "I didn't know that Nate was President Winder's grandson."

And so it went. To an outside observer, it might have looked like gossiping. But to someone who really knew this group of women, it was clear that they were simply doing what came naturally to them—expressing concern for the community.

Peg mentioned that Ben wanted to join them. "How come," he had asked, "there are just girls in the group?"

The women looked to Moira. She raised an eyebrow and said,"That's just the way it is. We have to have our private club, too."

The women laughed in relief. "No men allowed" felt good.

The attention stayed on Peg. Everyone agreed she looked much better, had more color in her cheeks. She shared that the Gestalt work had done her good. She wasn't letting her fear of death get in the way of loving her stepchildren.

"I've done a lot of soul-searching this week, and I want to finish what I started last meeting—I want to face death," she said dramatically, throwing her arms in the air.

"That's great," Peg heard from several women now taking their seats in a circle in the living room. The mood was upbeat. Moira had placed freshly arranged wildflowers in vases on various tables throughout the spacious room. The sun shone through low-lying clouds after a short shower.

But before Peg could go any further, Sandy spoke up. A natural blond with startling green eyes, she looked like a Miss America candidate dressed in a tailored beige pant suit. "Sorry to interrupt, Peg, but before we get started," Sandy said turning to Moira, "I don't want any tension between us to get in the way of the group process today."

Moira blushed.

"I know what happened to you was really a miracle, because my husband was part of it." The women in the circle grew silent as all eyes turned to Sandy. "What I want to say is I don't hold it against you. Really, I don't." She uncrossed her legs and leaned forward. "I admit I had a few very bad days wondering what I did to offend God, but I thought I had really worked it all out." She paused to daub tears that had begun trickling down her cheek. "But it seems I had only worked it out in my head."

Fiddling with a small pearl earring, she continued, "Then I had this nightmare that's really bothered me. Do you mind if I could go first? I believe I know what it means, but I'd like to see what you all think."

Moira looked to Peg, who shrugged. She'd get her turn.

"Go on, Sandy, please," Moira said warmly. She could feel her body relax. She was grateful to Sandy for bringing up the subject of the healing.

With sorrow creasing her young face, Sandy began. "There is a raft in the middle of the ocean. I'm on it with David and a baby. Suddenly sharks begin to circle us. One big white one forces the raft to tip over. I'm thrown into the water. I'm terrified because I can't swim very well. All of a sudden I'm above the scene looking down on us, and I see the baby being carried off in the mouth of this same shark. David manages to pull me back onto the raft, but he's helpless to get the baby back."

The women in the room sat very still–supportive yet tense. Sandy dropped her head in her hands. Moira moved next to her and put her hand on her shoulder. "Sandy, I imagine you need to get out some of the feelings left over from your loss. As you said, it's one thing to work things out in your head; it's quite another to take care of your heart." Sandy nodded, but didn't look up.

Jody, who was becoming agitated with the rising tension, raised her hand. Moira glanced at her. "If you can wait a few moments for Sandy to share what she wants to say, okay?" Jody lowered her arm, but continued to look anxious.

Quiet gripped the big house. Finally Sandy raised her eyes to meet the group. "I can't have any more children," she said in a monotone then lowered her head. Tears fell like drops of acid into her hands which lay palms up in her lap.

"Oh, no!" escaped from Jody. Several women gasped. No one

moved during the brief silence that followed–a silence disturbed only by an early-season fly buzzing across the room.

Jed's voice suddenly cut through the air from the garden. "Hey there, little guy, you be careful!" Craig's muffled complaining response brought Jody to her feet and across the room to the doorway. She listened for a moment but couldn't hear more, so she reluctantly sat back down and asked, "Now can I say something, Sandy?"

"Sure."

"We don't know each other very well, but I want you to know that we'll be glad to let you have Craig whenever you want to play with him. I wish I had more to share."

Sandy smiled weakly. "Thank you, Jody. It's just that I waited nearly six years to have a baby while David finished medical school and established his practice." She patted her heart as if to stem the sob that was trying to force its way out. "And now–well, I feel like God must hate me."

"He doesn't!" Jody said vehemently.

Moira put her hand out to signal Jody to be quiet and then said to Sandy, "Maybe that accounts for the sharks in the dream. Do you feel that you're being punished by God?"

"Well, the prophet has said that we shouldn't wait, but have our children right away. Maybe I'm being punished for having waited. Frankly, I don't know and I don't care." Sandy sat back and crossed her legs. Her voice went flat, dull. "I don't want anything to do with religion. Any god who would let this happen doesn't deserve to be obeyed or worshipped."

"I can really understand how you feel," Peg offered. She related how, after losing Rachel, she had been inactive for two years. Finally, when she did return to church, it was the very Sunday she sat in front of Ben in that Sunday School class. "When I first met him, he was so on fire about the *Book of Mormon* I couldn't resist his passion for the gospel."

Sandy remained stiff and pale in her chair, hands folded almost primly in her lap.

"Sandy, would you be willing to face that white shark?"

Moira asked quietly. "I'm afraid if you don't, you're going to be so bitter, it will sour your relationship with David, your work, everything."

"It already has," Sandy said acidly and tightened her jaw.

Grace, who had never seen her daughter at work, was moved by the powerful calm Moira exuded. "I don't know the rules here," Grace interrupted, "so I'm just going to butt in because this seems to me to be a crucial moment. Sandy," she said leaning forward and lowering her head slightly as she stared at Sandy with piercing tenderness, "I am an old woman. And I've watched bitterness eat away at the souls of many people like a tapeworm. I don't want that to happen to you. You don't have to be consumed. But you must be willing to do what my daughter is asking of you." Grace leaned back and folded her arms.

Moira flashed a grateful smile at her mother.

"All right," Sandy agreed reluctantly. "It can't make things any worse than they are now."

As Moira dragged two chairs across the room, Peg moved to the edge of the couch. *This is exciting!* she thought. *Death, I'm coming to do you real soon.* She smiled warmly at the attentive group of women–glued to their seats–all focused on the doctor's depressed wife.

Sandy sat straight in the chair facing the couch. She gripped the arms of the chair, her knuckles turning white.

"What are you feeling right now, as you see the shark sitting in the chair across from you?" Moira began.

"I feel like I want to pass out."

"Your breath is really shallow? Stomach in a knot?"

Sandy nodded.

"Okay, now I want you to speak to the shark. Let's give him a name."

"Oscar."

Moira motioned to her to look at the chair and begin speaking. Sandy wrapped her arms around her chest and began, "You scare me to death. Why did you take my baby?" She began to tear up. "How could you be so cruel?"

"That's good." Moira interrupted. "What's going on in your body?"

"I feel like crying."

"And you've knotted up your hands to make fists?"

"Well, I'd also like to smash his face in."

"Tell him that."

"I'd like to smash your horrible, toothy face in!" She slammed her hands down hard on the arms of her chair, her face distorted with anger. She began breathing heavily, which caused her face to flush. After a few moments, Moira signaled to Sandy to move to the other chair.

"You know how to do this," Moira said in a low voice. "You're to just see what happens. Don't try being a shark."

Several of the group held their breaths. Then it seemed like Sandy had actually changed. Her jaw line hardened, her voice dropped nearly an octave. As Oscar, she coolly replied, "I really don't care what you think. I do what I do." She rustled around in the chair, then stretched out her arms to the side and let out a long yawn.

"Could you tell me what you think about Sandy as you see her sitting over there, Oscar?" Moira asked.

"A piece of meat. Dinner," she said with a sneer. "Weak, pitiful...not really worth my time."

"I see," Moira said. "Well, thank you for your candor."

Sandy let out a sigh of relief when she was allowed to drop back into the original chair. She ran her pearl pink nails through her short bob.

"What do you think, Sandy? Who does he remind you of?"

"No one in particular. Some men's attitudes toward women, I guess."

"How are you feeling now?" Moira asked.

"Better. He's not quite so frightening."

"Could I suggest we look at the idea of fate for a moment?" Moira turned to the group. "Each of us has to find a way to deal with impersonal disasters in our lives, don't we? Everyone here could tell us a tale of accidents, illness, the law—cutting us down indifferently, not caring who we are or what pain we're in."

Nearly every woman nodded soberly. But Jody, now very uncomfortable at the turn of events, stood up and walked to the door again. And Peg struggled not to cry as an image flashed into her mind of Rachel in a turquoise blouse on a merry-go-round at her first circus.

Then Moira continued, "We often blame God for such occurrences. But he was a man himself once. He is a loving father. Would he deliberately create circumstances in which we would be so terribly wounded?"

This question led the women into a discussion of the origin and purpose of pain. Moira kept her eye on Sandy to see how she was handling this intellectual interruption. She seemed engrossed in what the women had to say. So Moira got up and walked over to Jody. "Is this a bit much for you?" she asked kindly.

"Yeah, it is. I'm having enough trouble handling my own life."

"Would you like to leave?"

Jody looked up into the nonjudgmental expression on Moira's face. "Uh, huh," she admitted.

"Well then, this would be a good time to slip out."

Moira gave the young woman a quick hug and shut the door quietly after her, then turned back to Sandy, who said, "I want to talk to the shark again, Moira."

"Okay, let's do it."

Sandy leaned forward toward the other chair. "I want you to know, Oscar, that I now understand more who you are. I don't blame you for what you did, but I hate you for how you did it. In short, I hate your indifference."

Moving to the other chair, she responded in the shark's voice, "I just do what I do. I really don't care what you think."

Then back as Sandy, "I've got it! I know what this is about. This is just exactly how I felt when my parents got a divorce. I thought my father was really so cruel. He didn't seem to care who he hurt."

"Would you like to talk to him?"

"Yes!"

Moira pulled up another chair and set it next to the Oscar chair. Sandy didn't wait for Moira's cue. "You are a filthy man who walked out on your family and you didn't care who you hurt. I hate you for that!" she said vehemently.

"Now be your father."

Sandy grimaced, then slowly, reluctantly moved to the other chair. As she sat down, her expression softened, "Honey," she said tenderly as her father, "you weren't old enough to understand what your mother and I had been through, trying to make that marriage work. Finally I had to save my life. I was literally going crazy. I was suicidal. I cared enough to get away from the marriage so I could still be your dad. I hope you can understand that."

She slumped back into her original seat and said nothing.

"So, what are you feeling now?" Moira leaned close to her, speaking softly.

"I don't know. I suppose I'm being selfish. I don't want to give up my anger at my father. If I do, I don't know what my purpose in life might be."

Moira looked at Sandy and asked, "What is it now?"

Sandy smiled. "To hate my father, I guess."

The two women's gazes met and merged. Sandy laughed quickly and said, "I know what you're going to say. 'Why not try forgiveness on for size? Right?'"

Moira smiled and nodded.

Sandy sat for a minute or two, biting her lip and looking down at her lap. Finally, exhaling deeply, she said, "Okay, this is just a game, so I'll try."

"No," Moira said sternly, "if you aren't sincere, nothing will be accomplished. You have to commit yourself emotionally to the moment."

"That's the part that's terrifying," Sandy almost whispered, her pupils so enlarged that her eyes were nearly black.

"Uh, huh," Moira said.

Then there was a heavy silence. Grace cleared her throat several times. *I'm not sure where Iwi is going with this,* she thought, somewhat uncomfortable with the tension.

Finally Sandy began talking to her father. And as she did, the other women in the room leaned forward, crossed their arms or adjusted their positions. Each, in her own way, heard in Sandy's voice echoes of her own secret dialogue with her father.

Sandy began timorously, "Dad, I...I forgive you for leaving us." She put a hand on her heart.

"Good, now how does that feel?" Moira asked.

"I feel detached, powerful like I did as the shark," Sandy replied coolly. "I thought I wasn't supposed to feel this way. All my mom did was cry or look hurt all the time after my dad left. I guess I decided that was the way I had to act as a woman."

"And?" Moira asked.

"I can see–no, I can feel–that I don't."

"Good. In that powerful detached place, I'd like you to talk to one other person."

"Who?"

I don't know if I should push this, Moira thought. *No...I have to risk it. Mom says we're not going to have the leisure time to sit around and do Gestalts. Got to take care of business here while there's still time.* Moira took a deep breath and said, "Your baby."

Shocked, several of the women sucked in their breaths. They looked askance at Moira. One turned to another and whispered, "How could she be so cruel?"

Sandy's head jerked up, and she too looked with disbelief at the composed therapist. "My baby?"

"Yes." Moira didn't move, but looked directly at her.

The sad woman stared back.

"Do you think I'm cruel? More cruel than the shark?"

"Yes, I do. I think it's a horrible thing to suggest." Sandy glared at Moira. "You who can sit there with your baby still growing and kicking inside."

Moira winced but held her ground.

"What's going on in your body right now?"

"I feel angry!" Sandy shot back. Then after a brief charged pause, she added, "And a little excited, too."

"Good, and I think you know this is the door you have to pass through to be free. Are you willing to push pass the door? To risk it?"

Peg suddenly understood what had happened in her own work. This is the point where she had stopped with the gypsy woman. What Moira wanted from Sandy made perfect sense. "Oh, come on, Sandy. Do this for all of us," she chanted under her breath.

Trancelike, Sandy slowly turned to the empty chair where Oscar had sat. Slowly she spoke to her daughter. "Susanna, sweetheart, when I see you sitting over there, I want to reach out and take you in my arms."

Moira pulled a red and blue throw pillow from behind her back and placed it on the empty chair. "Go on, take her," she said pointing to the pillow. "Hold her."

Sandy reached out tentatively to the pillow, pulled back, then lunged forward, gathering it to her breast. A primal sound something between a loud sigh and a sob, swelled up inside her and then burst out.

Everyone sat in reverential silence.

"You just stay there with her as long as you want," Moira said tenderly. "I'm going to talk to the group." Moira turned and looked into the faces of the women she cared so much for. "Most of us stop at the 'death layer' as Fritz Perls called it. If we have the courage to push through, to do the unthinkable, then we are no longer split between body and mind. Or, in other words, we're no longer neurotic."

They nodded and looked to one another. Peg said, "I've got it, I've got it," several times to herself and rocked back and forth on the big beige couch with the Indian blanket thrown across the back.

Moira stood up and said, "If you will excuse me, ladies. I need to take a brief break before we continue with Peg." With that, she stretched and walked slowly toward the bathroom off the kitchen. The group gathered around Sandy, hugging her along with the pillow.

With one arm around Sandy's shoulder in a maternal, protective gesture, Peg asked her, "So how do you feel? You okay with all of this?"

"Surprisingly fine. I feel quiet. The bitterness is all gone," Sandy said. "I feel kinda detached–but in a good way."

Grace watched her daughter head for the bathroom. She wanted her to stop now, send the women home, not tire herself out. But she knew it was useless to argue with her. *How does my Iwi do this for a living?* she asked herself and shook her head.

Moira paused for a moment in the bathroom and looked into the mirror. She looked very tired. Dark circles shadowed her eyes. She wished someone would work with her, just once. "But this is really important work. I've got to remember that," she said drying her hands.

Moira walked back to where her mother stood with her arm around Sandy's waist, while she talked with Patricia and Peg. *Maybe I can get my mother to rub my feet again,* she thought as she was poked with a twinge of jealousy–Grace was mothering someone other than herself. Then she looked at Sandy's face and the jealousy instantly dissolved. She knew the therapeutic push had been worth the pain. Sandy looked profoundly relaxed. Little sad lines still sagged around her mouth, but she moved lightly, as if she had just laid aside a hundred pound weight that she had been forced to carry, as in some Greek myth.

Chapter Seventeen

This conflict between the claims of the Soul
And the ego may be expressed more powerfully
At the period of transition to middle age than
At any other time in life.... (A man who) is
Inwardly dominated by the fears caused by
Childhood subjection to his mother...needs
To challenge his manhood.
Man and His Symbols, Carl Jung

After Jody walked out of the group, she started down to the garden where Jed had been hoeing, but he and the children weren't there, so she decided to go back to their cabin to take a nap. She had just stepped on the small bridge over the Virgin River when she was startled to see a lone figure making its way down to the gate. Jody stepped up her pace. As she drew closer, she could see it was a woman in high heels picking her way through the gravel and rocks.

The woman had not seen Jody, so when she reached the gate, the woman shouted in the direction of the bed and breakfast, "Hey! Hey! Is there anyone here?" in a high, annoying voice.

Jody gathered up her courage and, as she reached the gate, asked, "Yes? May I help you?"

"Is this Pow Tempie?" the woman asked.

"This is Pah Tempe (Paw Temp)," Jody corrected her.

"Whatever. I've come to speak to Benjamin Taylor. I'm his mother, Esther."

"Oh, hi!" Jody reached out to shake her hand, but Esther kept her hands to her sides. She was sixty-eight, had dyed camel-colored hair, wore red lipstick and nail polish and carried a large, brown alligator bag which matched the heels. From the smell of her breath, Jody guessed she smoked. And drank.

"He's not here right now. His wife is, though." Jody took a step back. "Would you like to talk to her?"

"No, I wouldn't," she hissed. She didn't want to speak to Peg. In fact, she hadn't spoken more than ten words to her since she and Ben were married. With that Esther whirled and wobbled back up the long drive.

"Trouble, major trouble," Jody said under her breath, and started to walk, then ran back up the path to the Garden Club meeting. She burst in just as the group was ending the break. Peg was settling in opposite the Chair.

"Ben's mother was just down at the gate," Jody tried to say quietly to Moira, but she was out of breath and her voice carried across the room. Peg jumped up to join them.

"Where are the kids?" Moira asked firmly.

"I thought I heard them down playing in the river with Jed," Peg replied, obviously worried and angry.

"Go! Now!" Moira pointed to the door and gave Peg a loving push on the shoulder.

Peg hurtled out of the room and turned left up the path, jumping over boulders to get down to the river bottom. She could hear the kids' voices coming from around the bend. They were squealing and laughing at Jed who was playing crocodile. He'd disappear under the murky water, then pop up and grab them and try to pull them under, while they tried to wriggle away. Craig sat on the bank and clapped his chubby hands in delight.

"Jed! JED!" Peg cried out, as she ran up somewhat breathless. "Ben's mom is here!"

"That's bad?"

"That's horrible! It means they've found us." Peg's face was chalk white. Jed scrambled to his feet. Danny looked to Miriam, who began to cry.

"It's okay, honey," Peg reached down to comfort her. "We won't let them take you away."

"What do you want me to do?" Jed was pulling on his shirt over his mud-caked chest.

"Can you keep the kids here for a few minutes? I'm going down to confront her."

"I want to come too," Danny said, but neither adult would let him, so he sat down in the silt and sulked.

Peg made a dash down the path to the bridge. By the time she reached it, it was blocked by police. *At least they're local,* Peg thanked the heavens, as she slowed to a walk and tried to muster her wits for the imminent locking of horns.

"There is the woman who kidnapped my grandchildren!" Esther screeched and pointed a thin, accusatory finger at Peg. "Don't look like that. You know what you did! For shame!"

Peg stopped when she reached the gate, uncertain how to respond. She half expected Esther, whose face had gone cherry red, to explode on the spot.

Just then Moira appeared on the bridge. She marched across it with the same martial force that she had displayed on the night of Robert Olson's arrival. With or without a gun, this Maori woman was formidable. "What are you doing on my property?" she called out in a commanding voice. The police took a step back. In a few more long strides, she was on the scene. Moira walked up quite close to Esther. Even in high heels, Esther was a good half a head shorter than the warrioress. "I asked you a question, madam. What are you doing on my property?" Moira's New Zealand accent grew stronger, more stacatto-like, as it often did when she was very angry.

Somewhat feebly, Esther gestured to the three policemen, sitting in their black and whites to get out of their cars, but they kept their distance. "My grandchildren have been kidnapped," Esther raised her voice so the policeman could hear, "and we have every reason to suspect they're being held here against their wills." Esther jutted out her chin in Moira's direction.

Ignoring her, Moira walked over to the closest squad car, looked in and said to the driver, "Hey, Ron, how's the little one?"

"Fine," the policeman blushed.

"Ron, Benjamin Taylor is visiting us from Salt Lake with his two children for a few days. He and Alex go way back. But I think you'll find, if you check, that he has visitation rights."

Ron Highland stepped out of his car and walked over to the other police car twenty feet away. Moira, Esther, Peg and Jody all stood like statues while the policemen conferred, glanced over at the foursome, then huddled again, discussing the situation in low tones. Finally Highland walked over rather stiffly to the waiting women. "I'm so sorry, Mrs. Taylor, that you've come all this way from Chicago..."

"It's not Taylor," Esther snapped. "It's Hirschfield now."

Ron raised his voice a notch and continued, "Considering what Mrs. Dubik has explained to us, Mrs. Hirschfield, we can find no justification for arresting your son, or your daughter-in-law, for that matter."

Esther gave him a scathing look and wheeled back to Peg, "Look, you, you tell my son I'm not leaving without the kids," she said leaning right into Peg's face. "I'll stay here until hell freezes over if I have to. The Breyersons are worried sick."

Peg did not retreat. "I'll let Ben know you're in town, Mrs. Hirschfield," she replied cooly.

Esther tore off a piece of paper, wrote the name of the motel in St. George where she was staying and shoved it into Peg's hand. She dug a brown stiletto-spiked heel into the ground, spun around and stomped over to the nearest police car where she fell heavily into the passenger seat. As the policemen turned their cars around and headed back up the hill, the women could hear Ron Highland getting the brunt of Esther's complaints about grandparent's rights.

The three women hugged each other, then stepped back and slapped hands together above their heads. Then Jody began to sing, "Ding, dong, the witch is dead..."

"No, we're dead." Peg said in a mournful voice as she fell to the earth, put her arms over her head, and began to rock back and forth.

Moira put out a hand to pull her back up. "Come on, Peg. Don't do that. It doesn't help."

On her feet, Peg wiped off her back side then stood staring up the hill. "Come on," Moira repeated. "Let's go back up to the house."

The three walked in silence—each trying to take in the enormity of the situation. Peg fought back tears. *Poor Ben,* she thought, *just when he's involved in a lifetime dream. Now what next,* she moaned to herself. *Oh, God, can't we have any peace?* In her mind, she began packing.

When they reached the Dubik house, Moira excused the women in the Garden Club, claiming fatigue. She hugged Sandy at the door. They held each other for awhile, then Moira said, "The Lord will provide for you and David. I just know He will." Tears flowed down both their cheeks.

Sandy then turned to Peg. "I'm so sorry you didn't get to do your work on death. Maybe next week?"

"Yep, well, we'll see," Peg said averting her eyes away, so she wouldn't tear up with Sandy's sympathetic look.

When everyone had gone, Grace, Moira, Peg and Jody sat down in the living room and stared off into the distance. Grace finally broke the silence with, "Where's Alex?"

"Gone to town. He should be back in a couple of hours," Moira said. She turned to Peg, "Can we get ahold of Ben?"

"No. He's not due here until six. But he's often later, as you know."

Suddenly the cries and whines of a child reached them. Peg jumped up and opened the door just as Jed, carrying Craig on one hip and hanging onto Danny's ear with the other, reached the doorstep.

"Danny did it!" Miriam cried out when she saw Peg in the doorway. "He told me not to tell!"

"Ow! Stop it! You're just like my grandfather," Danny screamed at Jed as he struggled to get away.

Marching Danny into the front room, Jed shoved him down on the big couch near the fireplace. Danny defiantly folded his arms over his chest and gave Jed a cold stare. The women gathered around.

"Tell them what you told me," Jed roared.

"No! I won't," Danny said, pulling his lips in under his teeth and clamping down his mouth. He wrapped his arms tightly around his body and stood stock still as if he was expecting a blow.

"What?" Peg turned to Jed. "Tell us, for Pete's sake."

"He called his grandparents. They both did."

A wave of shock passed through the room.

Grace bent down to Miriam and asked, "Why did you do that, sweetheart?"

"I didn't. Danny did." Miriam struggled to move away from Grace, but she grabbed the little girl's arm and pulled her back down on the couch next to Danny. Sensing they were in Grace's inescapable grasp, both children suddenly became teary.

Moira moved in to play good cop to Grace's bad cop. Like her daughter, Grace was no one to be trifled with. "Danny," Moira asked, "please tell us what you were thinking when you called Ukiah?"

Slowly the story emerged–all of it–the phone call, the beatings Danny suffered at the hands of his grandfather, all of it. Peg cried and tried to hug Danny, but he wouldn't let her. "Why didn't you tell us, sweetheart? We would have done something about it years ago if we'd known," Peg said tenderly.

"I didn't want to bother you. Besides, if my father really loved me, he would have known that something was wrong." Danny began to weep so hard that he began choking on his sobs. Slowly he allowed Peg to first hold him and then rock him. Miriam scooted over next to the two of them, and Peg reached out and pulled her close.

"You know, we've been so excited for your dad to finish school, so we could come to Ukiah and get you to live with us," Peg said, kissing the top of Danny's head. "You guys know that, don't you?" Both children nodded. "So why have you taken us to this ugly place?" Miriam asked, looking for her share of the attention.

"I don't think this is ugly, Mimi," Peg said. Miriam let the diminutive stand without protest. "We've come here because Alex and Moira said we could stay here for a while. Then we're going to take a pretty long trip to our new home."

"Well, I want to go now," she pouted. "There aren't any kids to play with. And besides Danny wants to go back to school."

Peg looked up to the circle of concerned faces, hoping someone would have something to say. Moira knelt down to the kids' level, "Hey, you weren't safe in Ukiah so we had to bring you here. There are a lot of bad things happening in the world right now."

"Oh, we've got to tell Grandpa and Grandma!" Danny burst out. Peg quickly explained that they knew what was going on and would take care not to get hurt.

Jody whispered to Jed, "How can he be worried about them, when they were so awful to him?"

"Kids are like that. Just like puppies. They love their care-takers—even if they misuse them."

Peg stood up and untangled herself from the kids. "You guys, we've got to talk to your dad about all this when he gets home. Why don't we go down to the kitchen and cook up some sugar cookies?"

"Okay," they agreed reluctantly.

"Hey, let's do it right here," Moira chimed in, trying to raise some enthusiasm. "We don't get kids cooking around here, and it's about time we did." With that, everyone crowded into the kitchen and began the cookie production. Moira kept an eye on the clock. She wanted Alex, and she wanted chocolate chips to put in the dough. (Chips had not been available in the store for a long time now.) Chocolate was a comfort to her.

About ten minutes later, the phone rang. It was Ben. Phone in hand, Peg slipped around the corner to be able to hear him over the din. He told her that he'd been busy at the translating project, when he had the distinct impression he should call home. "Boy, are you psychic!" She paused, hoping to be able to tell him the news without upsetting him too much. *Silly*, she thought. *Why do I always feel like I have to protect him?*

"Why? What's up?"

"Ah, ah, Ben, honey...your mother showed up at the gate this afternoon."

"No!"

"Yes, I'm afraid to say that Danny called the Breyersons.

And because they're too old to travel on a moment's notice, I guess they called Esther to come from Chicago. Though how she got permission to travel from there so quickly is beyond me."

"Money," Ben mumbled.

"What? I didn't hear you."

"I said 'money.' You can do anything in this world if you have enough money."

Peg thought she could hear him sit down. There was a long pause. "Are you there, honey?" she finally asked worriedly.

"Yeah, just trying to think."

"She's in a motel in St. George," Peg volunteered. "She brought the police with her, but they were local and refused to do anything. She's waiting for your call."

"I see," Ben said flatly. "Okay, give me the phone number."

"Honey, I'm so sorry."

"So am I."

Ben sat in the office on the couch, staring at the wall. He tried to sort out the jumbled pieces of the intense day he'd had. When he'd come to work that morning, he was greeted by Bill Hadley, who was seething with frustration. "Tulku's shutting down the project. No reason. Just taking the plates and going back to Mt. Nebo."

"Where is the lama now?" Ben asked.

"You just missed him. Told me we should continue on with what we're doing. He'll be back later this afternoon." Ben commiserated with him, but Sangay had told him that time was short, so he consoled himself with the thought that he had seen the plates, touched them, translated a few lines. One day, in Zion, he'd get another crack at it.

After Ben heard what Peg had to say, he knew he couldn't continue to work on the translation. After she hung up, he kept hearing her say, "Abe's been physically abusing Danny–for years now, it seems. According to the kids, Danny's had beatings that have left him with bruises all over his body at one time or another." Ben sat with the receiver pressed against his forehead. He was immobilized like a deer on a dark road hit with a truck's high beams. Guilt washed over him. *I should have known–somehow–about what had been happening to my own son. I should have been there!* Tears sprang to his eyes. He wiped them away with the back of his hand and turned to the quiet matron at the desk. "Sister Haglund, I've got to use the phone one more time, if I may," Ben said in an even tone even though he felt like tearing out someone's throat. He couldn't decide who he was more angry at–Abe Breyerson or his mother. His fingers felt like lead as he dialed the Ramada Inn. They agreed he'd come in fifteen minutes.

As Ben drove into the nearly empty motel parking lot, his heart was beating erratically. He put his hand over his camel coat in an effort to slow it down. It didn't help. He was directed to the smoking section of the motel. When Esther opened the door to 179, he was struck by the fact that she looked like an old woman. *She certainly doesn't look sixty-something,* he thought, *more like eighty.* The room smelled of her cigarette smoke layered on top of the old, rancid smoke film that had permanently impressed itself into the walls, the furniture. The curtains were closed. He asked her to open them as she led the way to a small table near the air conditioning unit. It was too cold to turn it on, but Ben wished for some circulation of air.

Esther sat down with a pack of cigarettes, a round, glass ashtray with the Ramada Inn slogan stamped on the bottom, a bathroom glass filled with Scotch and water and her habitual cigarette holder, which she insisted took out much of the tar and nicotine. She had been in a bathrobe, but quickly changed back into the beige suit with her initials monogrammed on the pocket, in rhinestones.

She was a worthy adversary.

"So, Benjamin, it's come to this, has it? Negotiating for the health of the children in a motel room in God-knows-where."

"What do you want, Esther?" Ben tried to sound slightly annoyed. If she thought he was at all intimidated, things would be much more difficult.

She winced and lit up the second pack of the day. Through

the exhaling smoke, Esther surveyed her first son. *He doesn't look at all like Pete. I can't find much of his dad in him at all,* she thought sadly. *Petros Totak, Ben's great-grandfather, changed the name to Taylor at Ellis Island proud to be an American. Now this. What would he think of an offspring who kidnaps his own children? He'd weep, tear his shirt...Doesn't look like his brother either. How two boys could end up so different is beyond me—Michael, the government's pride and joy, and here's Ben! A failure at everything,* she thought bitterly.

"So what do you want, Esther. Let's get on with this." Ben continued with his slightly superior tone.

"I want the children returned to their home in Ukiah. It's not that difficult, I don't think.

"They belong here with us."

"You've taken them without permission," Esther retorted.

"I've taken them to save their lives!" Ben nearly shouted. If these two had been pit bulls, they would have been up in each other's face, growling and salivating.

"Has your wife put you up to this?"

"Her name is Peg, Esther. No, Peg has not put me up to this."

"I never liked her. Not from the beginning."

"That was obvious," Ben rejoined. "That's your problem...and your loss."

Esther sat back to inhale deeply. She wasn't going to get an upper hand this way. Ben looked too well-fed, too content, somehow. She'd always been able to get him on her side when she'd start in on Linda. But this Peg person. The woman seduced him into a bizarre religion, turned him against his own mother.

"Mother, I'm not going to tell you in detail what is happening with us, because I don't want you to be harmed."

She snorted, "That's a novelty," and took another drink of the Scotch and soda.

Ben looked away, then back, composed. "I'm on Interpol's list."

"Oh, Ben, no!" She threw her hands to her face. Instinctual concern for her son surfaced for the first time in years. He then proceeded to tell her about the Mormon underground and its breakdown. She listened, but wasn't particularly sympathetic to the culture's problems, just the survival of her son. However, when he got to the part about Abe Breyerson beating Danny, she called him a liar.

"Why would I make up a thing like that, Esther?"

"To have an excuse to take the children, of course." She sniffed. "Who told you? Miriam? Danny?"

"Both of them, in some detail. Just today."

She grew quiet, put out one cigarette and put another in the holder.

Ben pulled himself out of the chair and paced the small room. "Do you think that I would leave those children there, with that bastard, now that I know?"

Having gauged his performance for veracity, she stood up, turned her back to him to look out at the parking lot and dry hills beyond. She was torn. *He has abandoned me and our faith to become a Mormon, of all things! Why not become one of those guys who shaves his head and begs in the airport? That would be better than to be a....*She couldn't think of word bad enough for what she thought about his religious choice.

Esther looked back just as Ben shut the bathroom door. *No,* she thought. *I'm taking them with me. I've decided. He's lying,* she whispered petulantly to herself. She poured another shot from the flask in her suitcase and caught her expression in the fake mahogany mirror. Yet...something about Abe Breyerson rings true. She shuddered in her bitterness.

Ben came out, drying his hands. His stomach felt like lead. He tried to read her, but, as usual, she was inscrutable. He didn't dare say anything else. Esther was now judge and jury. He also knew she would take all the time she wanted to weigh it out.

At last she turned to her oldest and brightest son and said, "I won't say a word. I promise you."

Ben let out a deep sigh, made his way across the room and pecked her on the cheek. He knew she would keep her word. Her family history included many members who had lost their lives in the concentration camps in Poland. She knew what it meant not to betray one's own.

He sat down heavily on the bed and put his head in his hands. She didn't move. "What will you do?" she asked.

"Move on. Probably to Colorado. Peg has friends there," Ben said lifting his head. "What will you tell the Breyersons?"

"That I arrived too late." Esther picked up the glass on the table and finished off the drink."I'll say you had moved on to parts unknown. No one knew where you had gone."

"Thank you," Ben said softly.

Esther started to move over to him, to reach out, to take him back from the Mormons, from Peg, from the nightmare, but she stopped herself and asked guardedly, "Will I see you again?"

"Not for awhile, at least."

She looked very old the last glimpse he had of her, as he shut the door to the smoke-filled room. She had poured herself another drink and slumped into the plastic-covered arm chair next to the television set, her cigarette holder stuffed with yet another "cancer stick."

Ben found himself grinning as he walked out into the sun-drenched parking lot. He felt like he'd been released at the last moment from a tiny, white cell with a stroke of the governor's pen. His step was light. *I'm not a bad person*, he thought. *I'm not!*

Halfway to the car, Ben's warm exuberance changed into burning indignation for his son. *My poor, sweet guy*, he half-cried out in the empty lot. He wanted to run home and scoop him up in his arms, but he knew he needed to go back to the temple and make his excuses before driving back to Pah Tempe.

He had just closed the outer baptistry door behind him, when Sangay walked up behind him. "Oh, Sangay, I'm glad you're here. I had a call from my wife. I have to go home."

"I'm sorry, Ben. Let me speak to you for just one moment before you go." Sangay took Ben by the elbow and, without word, escorted him into the inner office where Ben first had met the apostles. Sangay shut the door and indicated he wanted Ben to sit down. Softly placing his hand on Ben's shoulder, he looked intently into Ben's face and said, "Ben, the Chinese have overrun the U.S. border. There's war."

"Oh, my God," Ben moaned. "My God." He sagged in the chair.

Sangay sat on the corner of the table and waited for the news to sink in. "Listen, my friend, as I mentioned the other night, I have plans for these plates." Sangay pointed to a small, white cardboard box on the other side of the desk. "I want you to take them with you when you leave here."

"What do you mean? How could I possibly do that, Rinpoche? I mean, I can't guarantee their safety or that someone at my house won't get into them." Ben's mind reeled.

"Ben, listen to me," Sangay said earnestly. "You know Alex's mother-in-law." Ben nodded his head and played nervously with a button on his coat. "I think you know she has developed some capacity to know the future." Ben nodded again. "Well, I have been fortunate to do the same, so I know these plates have a destiny with you, not me now. I've known this since the day I first met you at Alex's home."

Ben was stunned. "What about Bill? What about the apostles?"

"Let me worry about that," Sangay said, handing the box to Ben, who opened the top to see newspapers which had been stuffed around the silk cloth. The forty plates felt quite heavy.

"I have to trust you, Rinpoche. After what we've been through, I'll do what you ask, of course." Ben looked into Sangay's face and searched for the meaning of it all, but Sangay revealed nothing more than what he had just said. So Ben stood up and put out his hand, but Sangay reached out and embraced him and said, "I will see you in the not-to-distant future, you'll see."

Then Sangay raised his hand in a kind of benediction and said, "Be at peace." A line from Eliot's *Four Quartets* seized Ben as he looked into Sangay's wizardly face,

> I caught the look of some master
> Whom I had known, forgotten, half recalled
> Both one and many, in the brown-baked features...

"Thank you," Ben said simply, calmly, lowering his head. After a few moments, he raised his head, smiled at the monk, and stood to leave. When he reached the door, his hand on the knob, Ben turned back to ask Sangay a question he had wanted to pose for some time now, "Why don't you become a Mormon? With what you know, Rinpoche, why not come be part of us?"

Sangay laughed affectionately. "Thank you, Ben, but I have my own path—one that will intersect with you Mormons once again, I assure you." He then opened the office door, bowed respectfully to Sister Haglund who'd returned from lunch, and disappeared down the hall. Ben could hear his robe swishing back and forth as his small figure took a right turn and headed toward the conference room and a very disappointed Bill Hadley.

Peg leaned on the gate as Ben drove down the long driveway. She had been waiting there almost since Sister Haglund's phone call that he was on his way home. His heart went out to her as she pulled back the gate and searched his face with worried, brown eyes. The car had scarcely come to a halt when she pulled open the Toyota's door and asked, "What happened, honey? What happened with Esther?"

He managed a big smile. She shrieked and pulled him out of the car. "It's okay," she called out to a crowd who had stood at the doors and windows of the bed and breakfast.

Everyone poured out into the driveway, laughing and hugging each other. Everyone but Danny, who stood waiting for his dad to notice him. Ben immediately began searching the crowd for his son. He pushed his way gently through all his friends, finally asking Miriam. She pointed to his thin figure, his arms held stiffly down at its sides, in the shadow of the building. When Ben got close enough, he crouched down and held out his arms. Danny ran to his father and buried his head into his shoulder.

"Don't hate me, Daddy. Please don't hate me," he cried.

Ben squeezed him tightly and rocked back and forth. "I love you, you silly guy. And I love you more than ever now that I know what you've been through. You've been very brave, you know."

Danny, who expected blows for his disobedience, pulled back and furrowed his brow. "Really? I'm not in trouble for calling Ukiah?"

"No. I really understand and I'm really sad I didn't know what that bast..., what your grandpa was doing to you. Will you forgive me for not knowing?"

Danny let go of Ben for a moment and looked away. Just then Peg came up to hug the two of them. Danny looked up into her face and back to Ben, then said slowly, "Okay, Dad, I guess so."

Ben threw Danny over onto his back and carried him to the spot where everyone was gathered. "Folks, it's great to think we're safe from the law, but...," Ben dramatically changed the tenor of his voice, "I'm the bearer of some really bad news. The Chinese have invaded Alaska." The celebration melted into a funereal silence.

"I can't believe it," Peg muttered. "It can't be." She looked to Ben in hopes that he was somehow telling a macabre joke. But he shook his head, so she reached for his comforting frame.

Ben held her a moment then said with urgency in his voice, "Jed, let's see if we can get some news on that radio in your cabin." He, Jed and Alex headed off to Jed's place, where Jed fiddled with the set for a few moments until he found a news station that was broadcasting the news. He turned the volume up full blast so that everyone out in the driveway could hear the newscaster say, "Let me repeat: those in the lower 48 states need not panic. UWEN officials insist that this incident will be contained and that there is no chance of it spreading to the continental U.S."

Alex looked at Ben and said with great irony in his voice, "Yeah, sure." Jed, in protest, spat on the ground.

Chapter Eighteen

It was the best of times,
It was the worst of times.
Charles Dickens

Ben walked out of Jed's cabin and gathered Peg, Danny and Miriam as close to him as he could while they listened to the news broadcast. "It's not long now," Ben said, stroking Peg's hair as he gazed up at the clouds moving slowly overhead. "Surely the Lord is coming soon." Peg snuggled in close and gazed up into his face. She felt safe with him, like a small ship finding harborage in his spiritual certainty.

The rest of the group began to move off somberly in different directions. Suddenly Alex clapped his hands and proclaimed, "I'm starved. Let's rustle up some grub." He began herding everyone toward the bed and breakfast.

Ben excused himself. He said he needed to get something out in the car. He could hardly keep himself from breaking into a run across the parking lot, because he'd left the white box containing the plates on the front seat of the battle-scarred Toyota.

When he got there, he quickly looked to see if the box was still there. It was. Gingerly Ben lifted it out of the passenger side and paused, looking up the hill to the highway and down to the baths. *Where to hide these? What if word gets out that I have ancient plates, like Joseph? Will I be beating back neighbors who want to kill me for them?*

Ben revered Joseph Smith more than anyone, next to Christ himself. Once, at a fireside in the Bryan Ward, a speaker said that Joseph's true identity and ultimate stature were probably beyond what any Latter-day Saint could imagine. Joseph's nobility and loyalty, his power and gentleness, his likeness to the Savior himself–Ben carried all of these very close to his heart. And now, to find himself, like Joseph, responsible for plates and in peril because of it!

"Lord Jesus," he prayed, leaning against the dusty car, "I am a weak and proud man. Please give me even a small portion of strength and humility which thou didst give to thy dear prophet Joseph, so that I may do Thy will with these sacred records." Straining to hear the Spirit's voice, he heard, instead, Peg calling from the bed and breakfast to come wash up.

"Peg, would you come out here for just a moment?" he called out. She turned to say something to one of the children, then walked across the fifty-foot gravel driveway, looking perplexed. Ben's heart quickened as he watched her come toward him. A round, fleshy woman, she walked like the earth was hers. In the dusk, he imagined she was a Reubens' peasant come to scatter evening seed to the chickens.

"What, honey? I've got to help set the table," Peg said a little impatiently.

"I've got something here I want to show you," Ben said mysteriously.

"What?" Peg laughed as she walked near enough to see a mischievous grin on her husband's face.

Ben held out the box, then placed it on the hood of the car. She knew he was teasing her. "Did you bring sweet rolls from the bakery? How thoughtful." She laughed and reached for the box.

"Uh, uh. You have to guess first," Ben said, grabbing her hand. "It's not so edible or so sweet. Although Ezekiel might think it is."

"Come on, Ben. Tell me. I don't want to play this game."

"Come on. Guess."

"Dinner rolls. Okay?"

"Nope." Ben put her hand on the box, nodding to her that she could open it. She peered in, then pulled herself to her full height. "Oh, Ben, this is not funny. Newspapers? Wadded-up newspapers?"

He shook his head. "Go on. Look inside."

As she pulled out the newspaper balls, the brilliant silk cloth began to emerge like a gem being cut away from the dull, protective stone that encrusted it. Ben's eyes sparkled. At last he could share this tremendous secret with his wife. Nothing had been worse than feeling that he had been separated from her unconditional love that he so counted on. Looking at the contours of Peg's sweet face, Ben knew that the Lord wanted him to share this blessing with her.

"Oh, honey, how beautiful." Peg reached in to take out the cloth but it wouldn't budge, so she carefully laid back the folds of cloth, exposing the plates.

Peg jumped back with a little shriek. She quickly folded her arms over her breast, then put her right hand over her mouth, looking at the plates as if they were some exotic animal behind glass. After a long silence, she slowly moved over to Ben, leaned against his side and, raising her eyes to him, whispered, "Ben, are these what I think they are?"

He nodded gravely.

"What...I mean, what are they doing here?"

"Sangay gave them to me. He said they belonged with me; that they and I have some important destiny together."

"I can't believe it!" Peg put her hand to her heart. "How old are they, did you say?"

"We think thousands of years old."

The couple stood transfixed, overcome with the enormity of the situation. Peg nervously pulled at a silver necklace Ben had given her. Finally she asked, "Can I pick one up?"

"Go on."

"Are you sure?"

"Go ahead, darling," Ben said nodding toward the plates.

She tentatively reached in and ran her finger over the engraving on the top plate. Then she delicately separated it from the one below and held it like a newborn babe–tenderly–afraid of its fragility. "Uh, this is heavier than I thought it would be," she said slightly bouncing the plate up and down.

"Yeah, I know," Ben said, as he put the plate back in the box. "So, honey, are you happy? Are you happy that I've shared this with you?"

She beamed, then frowned and said, "And I'm scared. Where are you going to put them to keep them safe?"

"Haven't decided. I was just saying a little prayer, when you called to me. Have any ideas?"

She thought a moment."You know, I have my precious boxes of Kate's drawings, genealogy and that sort of thing under the office in the storage area. How about there for now?"

He agreed and the two, furtive as cat burglars, tiptoed around the bed and breakfast without being detected and crept down the stairs to the small storage area near the river's edge. After they placed the white box in a plastic storage bucket, covered it with newspapers and snapped on the lid, they pushed the bucket into the back corner and shoved a couple of boxes in front of it.

"No one will find it there," Peg whispered as she locked the door.

As she turned around, Ben gathered her into his arms. "You are every bit as precious to me as those plates are, you know, sweetheart. I'm so happy we're finally in on this one together."

She kissed him a long time, put her head in the crook of his neck and sighed. Then she pulled back and asked worriedly, "Aren't you going to get in some of kind of trouble for taking the plates without permission? Weren't you called to translate by apostles?"

Ben shrugged. "All I know is that Sangay just handed me the plates and said, 'End of project.' And they were his plates, in a sense. I mean, they came from his monastery."

Peg looked apprehensive. Ben smiled. "Don't worry, honey. I'll discuss all of this with Bishop Olson when I take the Toyota in tomorrow. The bishop will know what the next step should be, I'm sure."

For the first time since she had seen the plates, Peg felt that she could exhale. *Yes, Bishop Olson. He will know what to do.*

Early the next morning, Ben drove with Peter to the Olsons'. The bishop's house sat a couple of blocks south of the main road in LaVerkin next to a horse pasture. The large detached garage out back had been converted into a solar engine machine shop. Peter and his crew had already converted Ben's Honda. Now they were taking in the Toyota. This was the third lightweight car to be worked on. As they drove along, Ben encouraged Peter to talk about his project. Peter was obviously in his element. It took very little coaxing to get him to talk about his innovation–a highly efficient photoelectric battery. Actually, it was a photovoltaic battery made from several different semiconductor materials, each sensitive to a different portion of the solar radiation spectrum. This allowed a car's engine to make optimal use of all kinds of solar radiation, whether the sunlight was direct or obscured. He sold his patent to American car makers, but they did not use it for solar-powered cars as he had hoped.

"In converting to solar, we first pull out the engine." That was as far as Ben was able to follow him. The rest of Peter's explanation immediately turned into a jumble for Ben, whose understanding of cars extended no farther than changing tires and checking the oil. "The battery power is located in the trunk...lead acid battery very heavy...charge to weight ratios...." Ben just stared out the windshield and shook his head. *The Tibetan plates were easier to translate than this foreign language*, he thought laughing to himself.

It was a chilly, grey morning and Ben had not worn his down coat. He shivered in the green windbreaker and wool sweater he wore. He had never adjusted to desert cold. Trying to take his mind off the cold, he said, "So, Peter, go on. This is fascinating."

Encouraged, Peter continued, "What you do is put a motor on each wheel so you can have four-wheel drive. The motor is connected through a double helical reducer."

"A what?" Ben burst out laughing. "You're joking. You made that up."

"Nah, mate, it's a gear that's cut on an angle. Gives you more contact area for your teeth to mesh. Prevents tooth fracture. Also helps prevent noise." Peter grinned at Ben. *Now it's Benjy's turn to play catch-up*, Peter thought, with just a touch of malicious glee. Usually it was Peter struggling to keep up with Ben during their many theological discussions back in Ukiah. Peter playfully punched Ben's shoulder. "Now, listen up, Benjy Taylor, brain child. You'll get a hang of this if you just stay with me here."

Ben shrugged. "I'm a captive audience. Go on." As they entered the outskirts of La Verkin, Ben struggled to remember just where the turnoff was to the Olson's. A large water tower on the hill had served as a marker his one other visit there.

"Okay, so through a rectifier we convert the power to DC and we use a VFD, that's a variable...frequency...device," Peter said very slowly. "It can allow a DC motor to operate at different speeds. Otherwise you're limited to just the frequency cycle in your electricity. But with the VFD you're not limited to 1800 or 3600 rpms or whatever. You can make it infinitely adjustable. Basically you can control your speed–you can start slow and accelerate rather than have fixed speeds."

"I see," Ben said. He'd begun to wish they could just drive straight through La Verkin, down to the highway and on to the St. George temple. He missed Sangay already.

"So you need to make modifications to the wheel well areas...got to use as much of the existing linkage as you can."

"That's very nice, Peter. You are most informative," Ben said sardonically. "One question, if I may break the flow of this gripping narrative. How much time is this conversion going to take?"

"First time we did this, it took us 250 hours. Now we've got it down to 75 manhours, now that we have standard components and a really efficient crew."

"Where did you get the components?"

"Bishop Olson. He was in defense contracting, you know. He had been manufacturing a composite and ceramic motor, so we just drop it in where the engine was, and we use the trunk for all the batteries. The key is superconductivity. Drops the weight of the engine. As you know," Peter said with a wry grin, "silicon has been tamed as a conductor–somebody finally produced the magic mix—just the right amount of gold mixed with silicon, resolving the low temperature requirements. Anyway we've got superconducted windings that are really lightweight."

"Turn here!" Ben barked.

As Peter waited for a truck to pass on the other side of the road, he glanced out his side window just in time to see several deer run across an open field a few hundred yards away. "Ah, isn't that great?" he asked. Without waiting for a reply, he turned on Bishop Olson's street and asked, "Okay, where was I?"

"I have no idea," Ben said, shaking his head. "Peter, my boy, I have *no* idea where you left off."

"Oh, yes, now this isn't as powerful as a gas motor, but it's okay. The electric motor just uses magnetic currents, and once you get your windings moving past your staters, you produce power...."

Ben's head was swimming.

"Now this bit should be easy enough for you, Mr. Philosopher, to understand." Peter gestured broadly. "We have a coating we put all over the surface of the car to collect solar energy. This is directed toward the motor with a portion maintaining the battery. That way, it's even charged for night driving. We're able to use moonlight to a limited degree."

"No kidding?" Ben said, not sure whether he was surprised by the possibility of night driving on solar or by the fact that Peter had finally said something he understood.

"Nope. Works best on small light cars because of the limited power capacity. That's why we're workin' on your cars, along with Nate's."

"I actually understood that, thank you," Ben shot back.

"Good," Peter retorted. "Guess there's hope then for every ape in Africa, eh, mate?"

Both men laughed.

"Anyway," Peter continued, "we've got 95% conversion from the solar to the electrical, so once you figure out how much horsepower you get on a bright day then, as long as you remain below that power requirement, you can drive clear across country.

You can pretty much drive 90-120 mph indefinitely, varying with the terrain."

They were now pulling into the Olson's driveway, and Ben was out of the car almost before it stopped. *If I don't get out of there, my head will definitely explode,* he thought, holding his hands to either side of his Dodgers baseball cap.

Ben made his way back to the garage before visiting the bishop. To his surprise he found that Peter's work crew consisted of Jed and Alex. "Hey, guys, since when were you solar mechanics? Correct me if I'm wrong here. But Jed, I seem to recall that you're a nurse. And Alex, let me see...." Ben said putting his finger to lips in mock puzzlement. "Oh, yes, I remember! Someone mentioned that you've gone in for sculpture. So which is it? Are you Michelangelo or a mechanic?"

Both men guffawed. "Hey, Ben, come on and help. Or are you afraid of chipping your nails?" Jed called out and grinned.

"Jed, my good man," Ben said, walking over to Jed and putting his hand on his muscular shoulder, "I guarantee you that if you let me at that engine for ten minutes, you'd spend the next ten hours undoing the mess I'd make!"

"That's for dang sure!" Alex laughed. "Get him out of here. And make it quick."

"Yeah, intellectuals need not apply to this club. They're bad luck!" Jed said, making a cross with his index fingers and pointing it at Ben as if to ward him off.

"Gentlemen, gentlemen," Ben responded in his best Count Dracula imitation, "I am deeply wounded. Just allow me a moment to remove this stake from my heart."

"Go on, professor. Isn't there a book you should be reading?" Peter joined in and laughed.

"Okay," said Ben, slipping into an imitation of Richard Nixon with cheeks bulging and fingers forming victory signs, "You won't have Benjamin Taylor to kick around anymore!" The men chuckled and returned to their work.

Peter showed Ben around. Assembly tables, soldering irons, overhead winches, strange components laid out in piles on the floor. It was surprisingly clean considering the oil, grease and discarded car parts that had to be dealt with. Ben was impressed that the bishop had put up so much money. *Of course, with the Chinese invasion, gas and electric batteries will probably be rationed,* he thought. *But, geez, this is a whole lot of cash.*

Ben thanked Peter for the guided tour and walked back down the driveway. He climbed the couple of front porch stairs to shake the hand of Bishop Olson who stood smiling at the open screen door. As they walked through the sparsely furnished home, a sudden fluttering in the pit of his stomach alerted him that something important was about to happen, but whether it was good or bad he couldn't say.

The former bishop, in checkered work shirt and beige work pants, led Ben down the same hall Peg had traveled to the study. He left Ben on the wicker couch while he spoke to Elizabeth in low tones. Then he returned, pulled up a chair and looked intently into Ben's face.

"How's Elizabeth?" Ben asked warmly.

"Holding her own, thanks. We need to talk, Ben," said the bishop as he leaned forward, brow furrowed.

"I know." Ben felt like he'd been called to the principal's office.

"I've heard about your mother's visit yesterday."

"Word travels fast," Ben said with a vaguely guilty smile.

"In spite of her promise to remain quiet about your whereabouts, the local police now know, and that compromises your position, doesn't it?"

Ben was afraid he'd hear these words. He had hoped that he and his family could still go on pretending everything had been smoothed over. He leaned forward and put his chin on his palms. "I guess it does, Bishop," he said with a long sigh.

"Well, Ben, I have a proposal for you." The bishop's voice grew lower and more resonant, more protective and paternal. He put his hand on Ben's knee. "The prophet has asked Elders Stewart and Dawahoya to go to Jackson County to prepare the land for the return of the Lord."

Ben felt an electric shock go up his spine which forced him upright in the couch.

"We have discussed using the solar-powered cars for that purpose, in light of the invasion," Bishop Olson continued. "The apostles would need to take along Brother Butler and Brother Rivers as mechanics. They could also serve as security. Since you are in the middle of translating plates, we felt it might be prudent to offer you and your family another location and see that you get there safely. We have such a place in Puerto de Luna, New Mexico. There you would be safe and could continue on your work."

"Did Sangay tell you about giving me the plates?"

"Of course. And you haven't been released from your calling, if you're worried about that."

Why do I think all this is happening in isolation, Ben thought. *These men—the bishop, Sangay, the Brethren—they know everything ahead of time. I'll miss Pah Tempe, but if we could get settled somewhere else, somewhere where the police, the Breyersons or Esther couldn't find us, well....*"Yes, Bishop, we'll do that," he heard himself say. He was uncomfortable speaking for Peg, especially about something so big as a move to a place in New Mexico that he had never even heard of. But these were critical times and they called for dramatic decisions.

Just then a car drove down the driveway past the study. Ben glanced out the window and recognized Nate Winder with his son, Cannon. He hadn't seen either of them for several years. A smile crossed his face. Good old Nate. "Do you know Nate Winder, Bishop?"

"I knew Neddy when he was a boy. He was his grandfather's favorite. Used to bring him up from St. George to general conference, introduce him all around as an up-and-coming general authority. I think Neddy, ah, Nate liked it, but was embarrassed by it, as boys often are."

How does this man know so many people—people in high places? Ben wondered, certainly not for the first time.

"In fact, we had him and his grandparents for dinner nearly every time he came up, as I recall. My Elizabeth is a Winder, you know."

"No, I didn't." Aha! Suddenly the picture was coming clearer.

"Yes, she and Nate Senior are–or were, I guess I should say–brother and sister."

Okay, now it all makes sense. Ben felt something release in his brain, probably in the hindbrain, something primitive about survival. *By some miracle I've somehow found my way into this circle of righteous and powerful people who will see that I survive, unless the Lord wants to take me home.* How he had longed (the recent Jewish convert) to have been born into such circles of established security. *Amazing!* Now he felt a tremendous rush of energy flow out of his heart toward the bishop. It extended throughout the house, into the garage and his friends, on and on until he felt he was washing the entire world with love.

Robert Olson watched Ben as the visionary moment flashed across his face. This was not the first time that the bishop had witnessed Ben being caught up in a moment of ecstatic awareness. It had happened before during those fireside chats in Sugar House. Bishop Olson, from quiet and conservative Scandinavian stock, was amused and even a little envious of Ben's capacity to be seized, his countenance transfigured, by sudden insight into a line of scripture. *He's like a Hasidic rabbi,* the bishop said, chuckling to himself. After a long moment, he reached out and patted Ben's knee. "You okay?"

"Yes, bishop. I just need a moment." The two sat in silence while Ben struggled to rein in his feelings.

"We're also relocating Nate and his children," the bishop said.

"Oh? Not Laurie, his wife?"

"No, sadly, she's filed for divorce. It seems she's met another man. Nate will be taking the older children. They'll be going to Puerto de Luna too."

Ben's heart leapt up. "Fabulous!" he exuded. "Then we won't

be alone."

"No, and I assure you there are other wonderful folks just waiting for you to arrive."

"By the way, where is that in New Mexico?"

"About ten miles south of Santa Rosa."

"Is that where the New Mexico temple was?"

"No, that's Santa Fe. This is in the eastern part of the state."

"The town's not that big," the bishop said as he watched Ben struggling to see a map of New Mexico in his mind. The two men had spent so many hours together with the bishop trying to guess and anticipate Ben's objections to this or that point of theology, Robert Olson had become quite good at guessing what was going on in Ben's mind.

"Boy, I don't look forward to telling Peg," Ben said looking to the bishop for commiseration—and maybe even a little advice.

"Women do have a hard time moving, sometimes. My Elizabeth has had to go from home to nursing home to LaVerkin all in the last six months. It's been really disorienting for her. I feel so bad that it's had to happen, but what could I have done?" The bishop was talking less to Ben and more to his absent wife.

"I just hope she doesn't hate me for it," Ben sighed.

"She'll love you for wanting to protect her. Just give her a little time to get used to the idea. That's all the advice I can give you on the matter of moving women," the bishop said with a twinkle in his eye. Both men shared a laugh. "Well," Olson said standing up and offering his crippled hand to Ben, "let's get this show on the road. The Lord is waiting."

When Ben walked back into the garage, the crew had gathered around a small portable radio in the middle of an oily table that was covered with tools, gears and metal filings. He could tell by their strained postures that what they were hearing wasn't good. Jed looked up, nodded to Ben and loudly whispered, "UWEN troops being massacred near Nome. Hundreds of thousands of them Chinese pouring over the border."

The announcer's voice on the radio intoned, "In an emergency

UWEN meeting at Zurich headquarters this morning, leaders met to consider the possibility of using nuclear force. From unnamed sources, we have learned that Brigadier General Hazrat Patel, ground commander in Alaska, has suggested that limited nuclear bombing be used to contain the advancing Chinese troops, which now number close to 350,000 according to unconfirmed reports."

Peter snapped off the radio and put it on the refrigerator against the back wall. "Bloody hell, boys. Let's get these cars done and on the road. We're gonna be runnin' ahead of a giant mushroom cloud." The three men soberly returned to work on Ben's car.

Ben backed outside and walked up to Nate, grabbed his hand, and the two shook hands warmly. "I hear we're going to be neighbors," Nate said beaming. Even though he had dark circles under his eyes and had lost at least fifteen pounds since Ben had seen him last, Nate seemed happier, stronger.

Ben certainly understood the horrors of ending a marriage. Yet he was also aware that, unlike Nate, he didn't carry the weight of disappointing generations of pioneers and general authorities. Nate's was the first divorce in a line of Latter-day Saints stretching back to Hyrum Smith.

"Ben, did you ever meet my nephew, Bobby?"

"Yes, at Pah Tempe, just the other evening."

"Oh, of course. Well, he's north of San Francisco now. Basic training. Don't know how much time he'll have to get trained, though. Rumor on ITN has it that the damn Chinese are preparing to attack all West Coast cities in the northern hemisphere, and soon."

"NO! Really?" Ben hit his forehead with the palm of his hand. "It's really hard to believe this is happening, isn't it? I mean, as Latter-day Saints we've been preparing for this for almost two hundred years. But now that it's happening, now that prophecy is unfolding before our eyes in such concrete ways...it's both wonderful and terrifying, isn't it?"

"It is," Nate replied mournfully. "My only consolation is the thought that the whole blasted thing is going to end one of these days." Nate let Ben see past his confident facade just long enough for the dark, depressive gloom that lurked just beneath to surface. Ben tenderly patted Nate's arm in a genuine display of empathy.

Nate and Cannon drove Ben back to Pah Tempe. Along the way, the two men caught up with each other's lives. They had been quite close in Ukiah, and both felt the bond between them reestablished on that sunny afternoon in early March. As Ben got out of the car, Nate said, "Thanks, Ben. It means a lot to have you back in my life."

Ben smiled and banged on the top of the car as he turned to leave. "Hey, the four older kids and I will be here Saturday for the sacrament meeting," Nate said warmly.

"Great," Ben said, reaching in to ruffle Cannon's hair. "Can't wait to see how the rest of the Winder crew has grown." He walked around to Nate's side of the car and leaned in, "I also can't wait for some serious spiritual comfort in the face of all this horror."

Nate put his hand on Ben's arm and said soberly, "I couldn't agree more."

Ben stood back and said exuberantly, "All right then. Saturday, it is. And Monday morning–we're on the road!"

Chapter Nineteen

All is clouded by desire
As fire by smoke
As a mirror by dust,
As an unborn babe by its covering.
        Bhagavad Gita 3:37-38

The sacrament service was scheduled for noon. Around eleven Peg walked across the bridge toward the Dubiks' house. She was dressed in a white baggy T-shirt and jeans, carrying her brown corduroy backpack over one shoulder. But she didn't get past the open door of Alex's studio. She looked in and found Alex sitting across the room in a director's chair in blue work shirt, jeans and his fancy cowboy boots propped up on the window sill. He was staring out the west window. His arms crossed, fists tucked under his armpits, he looked as forlorn as one of his statues. Sensing her presence, he turned and she saw tears glistening on his cheeks.

"Hi," she said shyly.

"Hi, yourself," he replied quickly brushing back the tears with the back of his large square hand. "What can I do for you, Miss Peg? Like the studio."

"This is really a...." Peg couldn't find words.

"A mess?" Alex tried to respond cheerily.

"No," she said very seriously. "A...a catharsis."

Alex laughed. "I don't think anyone has quite used that word before to describe my work."

Because she wasn't sure that she hadn't made a fool of herself, she winced and quickly changed the subject. "I've come up to see if I can help getting things ready for church."

"I don't know. Check with the girls next door."

"Alex?"

"Yeah?"

"Ah...I'm not trying to be nosy, but you seem down."

"I'm going to miss you guys, that's all." Alex stood up and strained to smile. Alex made his way through the work tables to where she was standing. She reminded him of his aunt, Lidia, who was also a Czech. *There is something of the peasant in Peg, something earthy and reassuring,* Alex thought. *I can see why Ben would be attracted to her; I guess opposites really do attract.* He felt a warm protective feeling, like he did with his younger sister. "Want to come in? Take a guided tour?"

"Yes, I'd really like that," she said forcefully. Even though she'd been in and out of the Dubiks' house, she had had only glimpses of the studio through a half-open door. Alex took her from table to table, talking about his artistic process, describing what he was trying to say with each piece. She was moved by his kindness and his obvious talent. "How do you dare expose yourself this way?" she asked in a kind of innocent surprise.

"I can't help myself. I need to express the passion I feel for certain truths. If I don't, I start feeling almost sick. It drives me that much."

"You know, whenever I start to...ah...come out with what I feel, this kind of terror starts to fill my throat." Peg put both hands around her throat.

"Sounds like a fifth 'chakra' problem."

"Excuse me, what?"

"Chakra. It means 'wheel' in Sanskrit. According to Hindu philosophy, there are seven ascending levels of energy centers in the body. The fifth level relates to creativity.'"

"Hmmm," Peg responded and shifted her position to come to rest against the pottery cabinet. "Could chakra relate to the term, 'mandala?' Jung wrote about that."

"Yes," Alex said in a surprised voice. "I didn't know you were acquainted with Jung."

"I've read a few of his books."

"Well, I'll be. Me, too." Alex's eyes twinkled as he looked down into her freckled face. "According to Eastern spiritual systems, we evolve through those seven levels of consciousness, from one stage to another, much like western psychology's stages of psychological development, only there's a spiritual component. At stage five, right here at the throat, (Alex pointed to his Adam's apple) one has to learn to communicate who one really is."

Peg gently, tentatively touched her throat with the tips of her fingers.

"And most people get trapped, stopped up, blocked there—much like you described. That's sometimes called the death layer." Peg felt a warm rush of energy run up the back of her neck. "So this isn't some therapeutic problem, as much as it's the need to communicate who I really am?" Peg's eyes grew larger. "And the terror is what comes up when I risk revealing who I really am?"

Alex nodded sagely. "That would be my guess," he said.

Peg furrowed her brow. "Well, well. You know sometimes I feel like a moth flapping at a street lamp. I'm afraid if I connect with the light source, I'll fry."

"That's a beautiful image for the fear."

They exchanged smiles. "You know, I'm so thankful to you, Alex, for taking the time to be so kind to Danny and Miriam."

"They're great kids. I'll really miss them."

"They'll miss you, too. Would you mind if I showed you something I was going to show Moira?" she said impulsively. Peg slowly drew out the journal. Her heart began beating rapidly. "This is kinda scary. I've only shown this to Ben. And, well, you know... Ben's so smart..." Her voice trailed off. Alex took the blue flowered book, untied the strings holding it together and opened it carefully. She held her breath and studied his face intently. He thought he'd see an ordinary sketch book or a few amateur poems. He was shocked to see the depth and richness of both the writing and drawings. Peg pulled the book away from him, turned to the last page and pointed to the poem.

"Remember the dream I told you about the gypsy woman?"

"Ah, yes, I think. Remind me where we were."

"At breakfast, last week."

"Oh...ah...sure," he said enthusiastically. "You were on your way to Paris. I remember thinking it was quite archetypal." He looked to see if Peg picked up on the Jungian term. She smiled back in acknowledgment.

"Well, I did some work with Moira on it, but then I had an experience hiking in Kolob and wrote this poem:

> *O aging Carmen standing in Charon's deadly bark*
> *As in a plumed, tattooed wagon of a gypsy queen,*
> *Come from the boat, snatch me from my misery*
> *And be the staccato-dancer of my soul.*
> *Consume my dread away; for I am stopped up*
> *Sick with fright and fastened to a dead father,*
> *He knew not who he was. I beg you gather me*
> *To your dusky breast under a Parisian tree.*

This time she got what she wanted–an audible expression from Alex. As he read the poem, his eyes widened and he let out a long whistle. "Girl, you can write!" he exclaimed, dropping into a Southern drawl.

Peg glowed. "Well, it isn't entirely original. I tried to copy the structure from Yeats' 'Sailing from Byzantium.'"

"Another one of my favorites."

Peg stood awkwardly silent for a moment, then said, "Alex, could I ask another favor?"

"Sure. What is it?"

"I see you have a lot of books." Peg pointed across the room at the floor-to-ceiling book case, next to the director's chair."Do you think you might have something about these Eastern stages of enlightenment? If you do, I promise I'll return them before we leave."

"You bet. Let me see," he said, squinting at the books as he guided her back through the worktables to the west alcove.

As he looked through this highly personal collection of books he used as inspiration, she spied *Memories, Dreams and Reflections*, by Jung. "Oh, I love that book," she cried. "It's made such a tremendous impression on me."

"Me, too," Alex said warmly. "Me, too." He pulled two books from his shelves. The first, a narrow little volume by Swami

Muktananda called *Kundalini, The Secret of Life*, he handed to her, saying, "This will give you a basic philosophical background. And this one," he said pointing to *Yoga and Psychotherapy*, by Swami Rama, "might be more than you want, but I've found it a good tie-in to Western psychology."

Peg took each one almost reverently and beamed. "Thank you so much, Alex. You can't imagine what it means to me to think there may be an alternative to spending ten more years on Freud's couch. I'll take perfect care of them," she said hugging them to her. "I promise."

He watched as she walked the few feet to the porch, opened the big oak door and called out to Moira. *I wish I were just on the verge of some new psychospiritual insight*, he thought to himself bitterly. *Try as I might, I think I've pursued God as far as I can go. Maybe Ben's right about me working through my eastern European Catholicism.*

Alex fell back into his canvas chair–and into his Angst.

Later Alex stood in the doorway of the studio and watched the parade of Mormons pass by, filling up his house. To cover for the large crowd that would be at the sacrament meeting, he had told people in town that he was having a birthday party. He put his hands on his hips and thought, *I can't understand what motivates these people to persist in such a...*(he struggled to find the right word) *such a provincial religion. I can understand the need for belonging, and I can understand the innate need for a god and perhaps a savior, but why this form which brings such persecution on their heads?*

The Pah Tempe members had already gathered in the living room when Bishop Olson, his daughter and family walked up the road and paused to shake Alex's hand. The bishop greeted him with such warmth, he blushed. They were followed by Nate Winder and his four children. They all picked their way through mud puddles that pocked the path. Nate introduced himself and thanked Alex for his hospitality. Next came Dr. Hunter and his wife, Sandy. About five minutes later the last of the group left their cars down at the gate and crossed the bridge. Patricia Young, her lawyer husband, Jim, and their four children hurried up the road.

"That makes twenty-eight in all," Alex muttered as the last group passed by. He wandered back into the studio and halfheartedly resumed work on a crucified black man. He pushed a thumbnail into the willing clay as a crown of thorns began to emerge, circling the agonized Negroid features.

As the service began, Alex could hear most of what was being said and sung, although he tried to tune it out. The chocolate Dobie turned over and groaned in her sleep. After a little while, Alex left the studio and, without being detected, looked through the crack of the half-opened front door. He watched Ben play hymns on his guitar for a minute or two, then shook his head in disgust. *I never thought he'd go so soft. Maybe it's his Jewish need to be a lily-white Protestant*, he thought bitterly.

The bishop, in a tweed suit, red vest and bow-tie, conducted the meeting standing next to the fireplace. Everyone else sat around on couches and chairs except for Jody and the bishop's daughter, who stood in the back of the room with squirmy youngsters. The bishop cleared his throat and said, "Brothers and sisters, although this is not the sabbath that we are accustomed to, we can gather today, as do those of the tribe of Judah on Saturday, to give thanks to Heavenly Father for his tender mercies." He warmed his aching hands behind his back on the low fire. "I am grateful to the bishop and stake president of this area for allowing me to conduct this meeting, since I am no longer in an official position of authority. We join many Latter-day Saints worldwide as we take the sacrament and share our testimonies in these troubled times."

He cleared his throat again. "Since we have no piano, Brother Taylor and Brother Rivers are going to accompany us on the guitar and the harmonica as we sing "I Stand All Amazed." If you have a hymnbook, would you please share it with others around you." Ben picked up the guitar. His fingers were slippery and his hands shook as they began, but once into it, he relaxed. He was actually quite an accomplished classical guitarist, but he hated performing in public. He could speak in front of 10,000 people without a quiver, but playing his guitar in front of five people filled him with dread. "Only for the Lord," he kidded the bishop before the meeting.

Ben and Jed did a passable job of accompanying the group. Then Jed took off on some jazz improvisation of the hymn and Ben laughed to himself—*Bob Dylan, he ain't*. Ben glanced at the bishop to see if he disapproved, but the bishop appeared to be happily soaking in every bit of the scene.

After the sacrament and in the middle of testimonies, Ben stood up from the couch and began speaking. Passionate, verbally adroit, Ben was able to galvanize the room with a spiritual electricity. "I wouldn't be here today," he said, "were it not for my wife, a light who has shone in many of my darknesses." He smiled down at Peg. "Danny and Miriam, you are Heavenly Father's message of joy to me. I love you both. And I want you both to know that your Daddy loves the Lord and this Church." While Ben was speaking, Danny shyly slid behind the nearest couch. Miriam, on the other hand, sat straight up and beamed at the crowd when her name was mentioned. "The bishop," Ben went on, "has also been a spiritual exemplar for me." He turned to Robert Olson and said with great tenderness, "You embody true spiritual leadership and humility."

It was at that moment that Laurie Winder walked by the studio on her way to the house. Angelina jumped to her feet and made for the door, growling. Only Alex's quick moves kept the dog from nipping at Laurie's leg. She was dressed in a navy and white pant suit. Her gold earrings and necklace sparkled as if they were new. A grim, fixed look on her face darkened the effect.

Laurie barely acknowledged Alex and the Doberman, she was so set on getting to the meeting. She had just driven six hours to St. George only to find her family had left for Pah Tempe. Now, as she paused in the doorway of the Dubiks' spacious home and looked around for Nate, she was swept up with Ben's delivery.

Ben stopped briefly. His heart began to pound loudly in his chest as he saw the figure of Laurie backlit in the doorway. For just an instant he thought she was Linda, come back from the dead. Laurie had the same coloring, small figure and carried herself with the same tight, controlled mannerisms as his ex-wife. He shook his head in an effort to collect his thoughts, then took a deep breath and continued.

Laurie was electrified. The last time she had seen Ben, he was a sunken and burnt-out man who was obviously struggling just to survive. And back then, he was a novice in the church. Now here was a powerful, impassioned man, like her father. She sat down on a wooden chair near the door and crossed her shapely legs.

Fighting against being flattered by her obvious attraction to him, Ben quickly finished his testimony and sat down. It didn't take Peg very long to pick up on the electricity crackling between the two. She wrapped her arms around her breast and looked glumly out at the river. When Ben tried to whisper something soothing to her, she scooted down the couch away from him.

Laurie found Nate and sat down next to him, but she looked over seductively at Ben a couple of times. Both Peg and Ben pretended not to notice. Ben struggled to reel in his desire and felt both guilty and disoriented. The Lord's stern injunction, always such an agonizing one for men, started echoing in his mind, "But I say unto you, that whosoever looketh on a woman to lust after her hath committed adultery with her already in his heart."

This exchange was cut short when Jed, with a red, flushed face, stood to proclaim, "The Lord is coming! We all know it. Unless we repent and love Him more than any other thing in this life, we will not be spared." He paused for dramatic effect. "There is an anti-Christ in the world today prepared to slaughter innocent lambs."

"No, not the lambs!" Miriam cried out. "They're so cute." She began to cry.

Ben reached over, hugged her and whispered in her ear, "It's okay, sweetie. He doesn't mean it in that way. Nobody's going to hurt any of those little lambs. Don't you worry, pumpkin. Daddy won't let them." Miriam sniffed a few times, then leaned over against Ben's side.

Silence filled the room. No one spoke. The truth of Jed's declaration bore into them. The room became so quiet that people could clearly hear the rush of the Virgin River as it ran its course. The sun broke from behind low-lying clouds and flooded in through the tall west windows. It struck a crystal glass on the kitchen counter and spread dancing rainbows throughout the living room.

After the meeting, Peg hurried back to the bed and breakfast, trying to hold back tears. She threw herself on a bed cluttered with boxes and clothes. "I know it isn't Nate's wife he wants," she cried, "it's Linda. Will I ever, ever get rid of her? "

Back at the Dubiks', Ben tried to avoid Laurie, but she pushed her way through the crowd to stand inches away from him. He tried not to inhale her perfume. "Ben Taylor, that was truly marvelous. I'm going to tell my father, Elder Whitmer, about you." She grabbed his arm. "You are definitely general authority material, you know." Ben tried to remove his arm, but she tightened her grip. "Look," she said looking up at him intently with her large brown eyes, accentuated with black mascara, "I have a lot of connections in Salt Lake. Why not call me and I'll arrange for you to do fireside speaking."

Ben shook off the spell and pulled his arm away. "I heard you were getting married when your divorce is final."

"Oh, how did you hear that?" Laurie was flattered.

"Bishop Olson."

"Oh," she said flatly, realizing Ben was probably in Nate's camp since he knew Olson. "Well, I think it's a bit premature to talk about marriage. I've met a really nice man, a ski instructor at Solitude, in fact. We've discussed marriage, that's all."

Ben had now regained his wits and was thoroughly repulsed by her obvious come-on. "If you'll excuse me," he said icily, pulling his arm away and moving through the crowd.

Angry, she tightened her jaw, then whirled and smacked into Nate. "I want to talk to you now. Outside!" she said in a loud whisper. Out on the porch, she spewed her venom in Nate's direction. He deflected it as best he could. "I want Neddy and I want him now. He'll be eighteen shortly and I don't want him going off to fight." Her breath smelled of mouth wash covering a bad acidic stomach. "I've got connections to get him out of here and underground."

"No," Nate insisted.

"Yes!" she hissed.

"I'm leaving here and I'm taking him with me."

"Where?" she asked in alarm.

"Where he'll be safe."

"I demand to know where you are taking my son."

"You can demand all you want, Laurie, but I won't tell you where we're going." Nate knew he didn't have to worry about his son leaving with her. Neddy really did not like his mother.

She was not accustomed to such resistance from a husband whom she had worn down and made more and more pliable over the years. "We shall see," she said in a steely voice. Furious, she stamped back into the house, looking for Neddy. When Missy saw her come through the front door, she ducked down behind a couch and waited for Laurie to walk through to the kitchen. That done, Missy slinked around the couch and out the door. Halfway down the path, she exhaled noisily–she had escaped detection. She didn't want to go through another scene with her mother demanding she return to Salt Lake.

A couple of minutes later Laurie picked her way down the path, trying to avoid the mud puddles in her new white shoes. She could just see Neddy in profile as he turned off the bridge to Peter's cabin. She tried to call out to her son, but he was out of hearing range. He was walking down with Peter and the other teenagers to look at a device Peter had put together to convert motorcross bike engines to solar.

Somehow she had missed seeing Peter in the sacrament meeting, and as she approached the first cabin, the laughter of the kids covered Peter's voice. Then, within a few feet of the cabin, she recognized his Aussie twang. *What? What is he doing here?* Laurie said furiously to herself. Burning with a memory of the humiliation she had experienced in Nevada, Laurie stalked off to her father's Mercedes and slammed the car door. She sulked in its leathery interior for a few moments, trying to devise a plan.

She decided rather than disturb the group and show her hand, she'd go to St. George and wait for Nate and the kids at his parent's home. She hoped the elder Winders could be reasoned with. Neddy had to come with her to Salt Lake, for his own good. As she sped up the long driveway, a smile slipped across her face. She knew she had to make just one stop along the way—to the Interpol office. There she would let them know that a notorious Australian criminal was living right under their noses...at the former Pah Tempe Resort.

Chapter Twenty

The night has been unruly...
Lamentings heard i' the air;
Strange screams of death,
And prophesying, with accents terrible
Of dire combustion and confus'd events
New hatch'd to th' woeful time.
Macbeth II.iii, William Shakespeare

Bobby Whitmer sat in the tall grass on Mt.Tamalpais, which is not really a mountain but the highest hill in Marin County, and watched through binoculars for incoming planes. This was a fruitless activity since a milkshake-thick cloud bank obscured the Pacific shoreline. He, along with hundreds of National Guard recruits who had had just a scant two days of basic training, found themselves on high alert after word had come that a Chinese aerial invasion was probable. They were scattered over the straw-colored hillside, idle yet terrified. Some of the seasoned officers leaned on hand-held Dragon-16 anti-armor missile launchers that could blow a hole in just about anything at 2,000 meters. Together with these impossibly green recruits, they made up a contingent of soldiers spread throughout the San Francisco Bay area. They had been told virtually nothing, except that the Chinese were expected to storm San Francisco and surrounding communities. Anytime now.

Bobby couldn't imagine it was possible. He inhaled the scent of bay leaves and felt the almost tangible brush of moisture in the air. He was lulled by the rustle of the long grass in the morning breeze. "This place would be great for a picnic," he said aloud as he looked out over the small towns and bay that lay below. Lowering his glasses, he walked away from his buddies, who were eating breakfast consisting of MRE's and canteen water. He wandered down a knoll into a deer "nest," a protected, grassy area below several trees. There he thought he could see the rounded outline in the packed-down grass of where a deer had lain. He too wanted to lie down in it, curl up and dream about the girl in Gloucester he had met on his mission. But instead of lying down, he knelt, pulled out a small copy of *The New Testament* and opened it to Matthew and read, "Be ye also ready: for in such an hour as ye think not the Son of man cometh." Then he paused. "Lord, if this is not your hour, please protect me until you come." He said it with such heartfelt force that one would think this prayer, of all prayers, would reach the Lord's ears.

After a few moments he pulled himself up and walked around the back of the hill to look out at the Golden Gate bridge through the binoculars. Suddenly a large cloud of smoke appeared across the bay at what he assumed to be Oakland—down near the water's edge. He couldn't tell what had caused the explosion, so he moved the glasses higher up into the hills. There he could barely make out what he guessed was the spire of the Oakland Temple. *Too bad I never got to go in there before it closed*, he rued.

Then a blast echoed across from San Francisco and more billowy white clouds began to appear. Startled, he scrambled back to his squad. "What was that?" he yelled as he got near.

"We don't know!" came the anxious reply. The men huddled around the radio operator waiting for some kind of report or command from headquarters, but nothing came, so they turned to watch helplessly as more and more white clouds dotted the hills on both sides of the bay. Fires could be seen leaping up in some parts of the city. Through his binoculars, Bobby could see traffic at a dead stop on the Golden Gate. It appeared the same thing had happened on the Bay Bridge leading to Berkeley.

Finally the radio crackled and they heard, "Delta 6 Actual, this is Kennedy, over. Delta 6, Chinese have taken the airports. They've begun an assault outward from Oakland, Palo Alto, San Rafael. You're to cut them off between San Rafael and the Golden Gate bridge. Over?"

"Roger, Kennedy. It's a done deal. Over and out."

The order was given by the beefy platoon commander to move out. "Okay, listen up. First team stays here. Second, third and fourth, you head out down that road. Let's go. Let's go get those commie bastards!"

The troops set out down the winding, scenic route, past million-dollar homes into downtown Mill Valley. Bobby kept shifting his rifle from one shoulder to the other. He was still getting used to it, since he and his unit had been issued the battle gear only yesterday, after just two afternoons on the rifle range.

Other than the occasional command from the platoon sergeant, the area was eerily silent. People who hadn't tried to flee inland had been told to barricade themselves in their homes. The troops came to a stop for water and rest near the interstate. "We'll take ten here," the platoon sergeant barked. "See that interchange over there?" he asked pointing to a freeway bridge. "Gleason here is a guy who can blow up anything. We're going to head over there and provide security for him and second platoon while he does his job. Understood?"

Several of the boys nodded. "You girls can perform as soldiers," the Arkansan hollered, "even though y'all only had a couple days of basic. Is that understood, Ladies? Let me hear you!"

"Yes, sir!" responded the ragged chorus.

"Once Gleason does his magic, we're headed about ten clicks down the highway to a tunnel. And we'll waste it the same way we're gonna do this concrete monster. Believe me, those yellow zipperheads are going to find themselves in a world of trouble. And I don't want any of you dumb broads gettin' your heads shot off, is that understood?"

"Yes, sir!"

The squad moved down to the ramp leading into Mill Valley, hearts beating, fear in beads of sweat, dripping down brows and off upper lips. The closest most of them had come to battle was a virtual reality arcade.

"The name's Scooter," Bobby said to the newly-shorn boy

marching on his left.

"Beetle Juice. Where are you from? "

"Cedar City."

"You?"

"Brigham City."

Bobby had chosen the nickname Scooter, which was what his sisters had called him as a toddler. He wanted to use the name Joker, a character in Kubrick's *Full Metal Jacket*, a movie he had watched at least twenty times, but did not in deference to the character and the director. He was addicted to war films.

"Just exactly how far is this ten clicks we're supposed to run?" BJ asked.

"I think he said it was about four kilometers. I can't remember."

BJ, sweat beginning to run down his sides, asked, "I mean, how many Chinese troops could have invaded? Couldn't be more than a few plane loads, I wouldn't think."

Bobby just shrugged.

They stood guard as Gleason first planted a shape charge to blow a hole in the ground where he placed the TNT, then let it go with the enormous boom. The steel-reinforced concrete groaned, split and fell in a tangled heap. A cry of surprise and joy rose up from the small crowd.

M-18's slung over their shoulders, they then began their march down the highway, boots clacking on the concrete. The sixty men, most in tan uniforms and battle gear, had marched a couple of miles when they heard a terrifying sound–screams of advancing Chinese who had been lying in wait on either side of the highway. In seconds they were spilling out onto a stretch of highway near the swampy lowlands. Some were in dark blue uniforms, but many were not. For the invading troops had been joined by thousands of Chinese smuggled in freighter cargo holds into the Bay Area. Once there, they lived in secret, waiting for this great moment to liberate America for Chinese expansion.

"Take cover, take cover! DO it!" yelled the swarthy second lieutenant who had been trotting near Bobby. But there wasn't time. Chinese rushed the troops, shooting as they ran. The National Guard unit fired back. In an instant the UWEN troops were falling, screaming, running for the sides of the highway, ducking behind concrete highway dividers. Bobby froze for a second, standing on the double yellow line in the middle of the highway–unable to run or breathe. *This isn't how it's supposed to be*, he thought fiercely. *Where's the organization? Where's the charge, the bayonets, the flag?*

The kid from Brigham City grabbed him by the shirt and dragged him down an incline. They flopped on their bellies. "What are we supposed to do?" Bobby asked breathlessly.

"I dunna know!"

"Well, I want to know what my orders are." Bobby's mind hadn't caught up with the reality.

A spray of bullets tore up dirt near Bobby's left boot. He instinctively doubled up. He had drunk too much water in Mill Valley and now he had to urinate. "Pull back! Pull back! Do it! Do it!" rolled over the heads of the novice unit. But before Bobby and BJ could respond, they saw two Chinese soldiers approaching. Luckily the Chinese had not yet seen them but probably would in a second or two.

Something told Bobby to lunge forward. The boy next to him had the same impression. As they pitched forward, frantically tearing through the loose dirt, Bobby pulled out one of his illegal knives from his boot and tossed it to BJ. (There had not been enough time to strip the recruits of their illegal caches.) In another swift motion he had pulled another from his other boot, and when he hurtled into the soldier, he plunged the fancy dagger into the man's neck. Blood spurted like a stream of deep-red tomato juice. Bobby turned to see his friend plunging the borrowed stiletto again and again into the other Chinaman's chest to the sound of loud cracking as he struck ribs.

Bobby and Beetle Juice whirled around and began to weave and dodge down the ditch through pickle weed and chord grass. Bamboo-like plants with long, slender leaves were blown into the air, cut loose by the pursuing bullets. The two Utah boys, along with several other men in their platoon, ran a short distance to a strip mall, zigzagged through the parking lot, alternately hiding behind abandoned cars, and then covering each other as they ran toward the back alley and into the nearby housing development. The Chinese fanned out and pursued them for blocks, but lost them when they hid in a drained swimming pool under the blue plastic tarp.

"I really have to go," Bobby panted an apology to the men, as he relieved himself in the pool's drain. Suddenly the reality of what he'd done—cut a man's throat—caught up with him and he vomited down the front of his flak jacket.

Similar pitched battles were occurring all up and down the Coast with the National Guard retreating in the face of superior numbers of Chinese. In all they captured Forts Richardson and Greeley and Wainwright Air Force Base in Alaska and took out nearly every airport from Seattle to San Diego—some they overran with suicide squads.

A general call went out all over the country for help. Men and women, armed with everything from Saturday night specials to Uzis, began reporting to designated stations up and down the Pacific coast. Mormons were conspicuously present in organized quorums. Many of the citizen militia squads were headed by Latter-day Saint men and women who had seen service under the UWEN flag. But the Chinese were better armed and there were many more of them than the UWEN forces and U.S. volunteers combined. The Chinese rolled through town after town in captured UWEN tanks. They launched missiles into downtown business districts with savage regularity. Refugees began fleeing in cars and on foot eastward to the mountains with the Chinese not far behind.

Each man at Pah Tempe wanted to drop everything and join the fighting. But, with the exception of Alex, they had been called to a very different front. The fourth vehicle would be solar ready sometime Monday for their departure to Puerto de Luna.

Contrary to Ben's fears, Peg had taken the news of their move quite well. She welcomed the opportunity to finally settle down somewhere and begin making a home. She always felt like a guest with the Dubiks.

But Moira was unhappy. She wanted to go with the party to Puerto de Luna. Now just into her sixth month, she was feeling much better. Since her blessing and her mother had assured her that her son would be fine, she was anxious to get back into the thick of things.

Alex, on the other hand, withdrew more into his shell. He and Moira had always joked about going to Jackson County, but for him it had been just that–a joke. How else to deal with the wild visions of the future this Mormon wife of his was prone to? Now, with the news that the apostles were actually headed to Missouri, he had to face the fact that his wife might really want to move there, to be with her people. And worse, that the Mormon apocalyptic scenario might be unfolding.

On Sunday, late in the afternoon, Moira and Grace stood in the kitchen warming a pot of hot water for tea. Moira again tried to cajole her mother into sharing what she knew about the near future. "Come on, Mom, I need to know," she begged. "Now of all times, with everything falling apart around us, I really do need to know."

"What I've been told is very general, sweetheart," Grace replied. "I really don't know specifics. I've been told you three will prosper in Zion, but I don't know how that will come about. I guess it would take away everyone's free agency if I did."

Moira sighed and shrugged. Then, rubbing the back of her neck with her long brown fingers, she said, "Alex is even talking about going to L.A. to help fight. I don't think he'll go, because of the baby, but frankly, Mom, I'm worried about our marriage. I know what I'll do if I'm asked to go back to Jackson County. But I don't think Alex knows what he'll do. It's really setting off all kinds of alarms inside him--about God, Mormons, everything."

Just then Alex walked in from the studio. "Hey, that looks good. Got some extra?" he asked pointing to the tea.

While Grace poured, Moira pulled at Alex to sit down with her on the couch in the living room. "Al, can we talk about Zion?"

He stiffened slightly.

"You and I seem to go round and round," Moira said evenly. "I thought if we included Mom, it might help get us out of the deadlock we're in."

Grace glided across the room and sat down opposite the couple on the ottoman. She smiled warmly at her son-in-law, so he relaxed a bit.

"Okay, sure," he said folding his arms across his chest and crossing one leg over the other knee. Seeing the state his black boot was in, he reached down and brushed dried clay from around the edges. Moira furrowed her brow and folded her arms. With her hair wound up in back, she looked a younger version of her mother, only much fiercer.

"You two look like a couple of sumo wrestlers ready for a match," Grace said lightly.

"It's not funny, Mother. Come on. We don't need a comedian, we need a referee."

Grace took the time to put a hot pad under the cup she placed on the coffee table, arrange her shawl around her shoulders, and retie the knot in her hair. Then drawing a deep breath, she finally said, "Okay, let's see what we can do. Alex, you go first."

"Thanks, Mom," Alex said. He glanced a little nervously at Moira, then, returning his mother-in-law's soft smile said, "I never thought that Moira really believed this story about Mormons going to Jackson County, Missouri to be sheltered from nuclear attacks or whatever. I guess I thought that it was some kind of myth that went with the religion."

"And I...," Moira broke in.

Grace held up her hand, palm toward Moira, indicating that she should wait her turn.

"Go on, son, please," Grace said firmly.

"Well, frankly, I don't know what to do with Iwi's insistence that we begin packing up to go. In the first place, I don't see any evidence whatsoever that this migration is going to happen. And second, I'm not convinced it would help, anyway."

"But I told you...." Grace again cut off her daughter, giving her a very stern look.

"The Chinese are invading," Alex said bitterly. "We're a pale version of the great United States of the last century. The way I see it, we're on the road to becoming a Chinese territory."

"That's a really pessimistic view, Alex," Moira shot back, tears starting to form.

Alex, who had been a champion boxer in college, could sense he had really stung Moira with that last jab, and his frustration spurred him on. "Yeah, or even worse, we might just get carved up and parceled out to invading countries the way we were when this country was first discovered."

Grace took a sip of tea and looked at both of them. *You're both so powerful and stubborn,* she thought. *What to do with you two?* She sighed and asked, "Okay, son, is that basically your point of view?"

"Basically. I say stay here, live off the land, keep our heads low and ride out the political winds. Stick with the known." He tightened his jaw and narrowed his eyes, as he exhaled and leaned back against the couch.

"Round two. Your turn, Iwi," Grace said and smiled at her daughter.

"First, Mom, I don't think you're taking this seriously enough. Our marriage is on the line here."

Grace remained impassive.

"Well, I told Alex, in all seriousness, the first time we met that I thought we were living in the very last days, and that, if we were going to get married, I needed him to respect that position. I feel betrayed. Now that the apostles are leaving for Zion to prepare it for the gathering, he cops out." Her voice quavered.

"Is there more?"

"Yes, there's our son. In the healing blessing, Ben said he'd be a great warrior for the Lord in Zion."

"He did?" Alex asked surprised. "I didn't hear that."

Grace nodded. "You probably stepped out of the room when that happened. I know you were pacing back and forth." She waited while Alex mulled over this new information.

"I don't know. I just don't know," he said sadly, running his hands through his hair.

Grace cut to the chase, "Alex, I think you're attached to being sad and unsure. Every time you have a happy period, it seems like you find some reason to make yourself miserable."

Alex started to protest, then sank back into the couch with an involuntary grin. "You got me there, Mom. Attached to my existential despair. Yup. It makes the blows of life less painful. I beat myself up first."

Rather than laughing with him, Grace became upset. "I know you weren't raised a Mormon, but this attitude of yours is really the devil's work. You play right into his hands when you think like that."

Alex immediately rose to his feet. *I've sat through enough lectures from my own mother about the "devil's handiwork," and I sure as hell don't have to sit here and take that off of this old lady,* he thought bitterly. "Well, I can see this discussion is going nowhere," he said, heading for the door. "Now that it's two against one!" With that, he walked out the front door, slamming it behind him. The dogs, who had been lying in the sun, struggled to their feet, happy to see him. They wanted to go for a run. Moira and Grace could hear him loudly complaining to them about his lot in life. He put on his coat and cowboy hat and left to hike up the canyon in the last hour of daylight.

"Iwi, you must have faith," her mother said in Maori, patting her on the leg. *"This is a very good man who must work out his faith in his own way and in his own time."*

"Yeah, but will it be in time for me? For Adam? For Zion?"

"Yes, I believe it will," Grace said in a very comforting voice and took a sip of her half-chilled tea. "The Lord willing."

Jody sat at a small desk writing a letter to her parents while

Jed tiptoed around their small cabin putting everything they owned into the backpacks and a couple of suitcases they had brought with them. Craig was asleep on the bed.

"What are you saying to your parents, luv?"

"Oh, just letting them know what's what," she replied obliquely. "Why don't you go for a walk? It's not dark, yet."

"Good idea," he said and pulled a bulky woolen sweater over his light-blue long john top. He stepped out and took a long whiff of the sulfur-tainted air. He saw Alex leave the studio with the dogs and called out to him. Alex turned and waved, so Jed took off in a trot to catch up with him.

Jody wrote, "You were so sure that I had married some dumb jerk. Well, I hope you're sorry now. Jed is going to guard two apostles! On their trip back to Jackson County. We were right about selling all our things and coming out here. You guys don't always know everything!"

Peter was away, working on the last car at the Olson's, and the Taylors had just put potatoes in a big pot on the stove to feed themselves and the Rivers. Ben was playing Bingo with the two children, while Peg fussed over the fact that there probably was not enough room to take several boxes of memorabilia she had brought from Salt Lake.

Then everyone, to some degree, became uneasy.

Grace froze in mid-conversation. "Where does Alex keep the guns?" she asked Moira.

"Why?" asked Moira alarmed.

"I don't know. I just sense danger," Grace said, squinting her eyes. At that Moira jumped to her feet and made for the gun cabinet in the study.

Jed and Alex were not more than a hundred yards up the canyon, when the dogs went crazy and began barking, then tore off running back toward the house. The men ran as fast as they could after them.

Jody stopped writing and listened. The barking in the distance alerted her to a sound she had become accustomed to, the "thump-thump" of cars crossing the large 30's style bridge a thousand yards up at the top of the hill. Although she did not know why, she sensed now the sound meant trouble. She grabbed Craig, who sleepily fought her, and the .45 they had in the desk drawer and walked quickly away from the gate to the bed and breakfast. Both Ben and Peg whirled around nervously when she came through Miriam's bedroom door.

"What's wrong, Jody?" Peg asked.

"Don't know. Something. The dogs are going crazy." The three stopped talking to listen to the dogs barking wildly just across the river. "Have you guys got a gun?" Jody broke the brief silence.

"Two in the dresser drawer," Ben said and walked quickly into the bedroom, pulled open the top drawer, took out the guns and began filling the clips with ammunition. His hands were shaking. He was relieved he had acted on his intuition about arming the family. Without the children noticing, Ben handed one gun to Peg. She stuffed it into the pocket of the red cardigan she was wearing. Although she wasn't sure what all this meant, she did know how to use the gun. Ben had taken her up the canyon target shooting, and she had shot her brother's shotgun a few times growing up.

Ben sent her a loving glance, even though she had been giving him the cold shoulder for his flirting with Laurie. She shooed the kids into Miriam's room, carrying Craig on her hip. She muttered a prayer for the Lord's protection.

Not more than ten seconds later, Ben heard the crunching of tires through the speaker as cars approached the gate. At that very moment, Jed burst through the side bedroom door, carrying his shotgun and two boxes of ammo. "There must be about 15-20 men in the three cars nearing the gate," he said breathlessly. Their faces are blackened and I could see shotguns on a few of them."

Ben bounded over to the phone and called the big house. Moira picked it up almost immediately. "Yes, we know," she said in her thick New Zealand accent. Peg gathered the children in the walk-in closet in Miriam's room, where she laid out blankets. With the light on and the clothes pushed to one side, she hoped they would ride out what might happen by playing house.

Before shutting the door, Ben said to Danny, "Son, you've been through a big battle before, right?"

Danny nodded soberly.

"Well, it looks like we might have another one, and I need you to take care of your stepmother and sister—oh, and the baby. Think you can do that, son?"

"Yes, sir. But I'd like to call her Mom, if that's okay?"

Tears welled up in Peg's eyes. What a time to decide that, she thought tenderly. She pulled Danny to her.

"I'd really like that," Ben smiled, tousled the boy's hair and slowly shut the door. His hand shook on the handle as he bent his head for a quick prayer. He then joined Jed and Jody, who were shoving furniture against the door that led to the outside in each of the children's bedrooms. That done, the three raced to the big bedroom where they pushed the two beds out from the wall. Ben unlocked the outside door, then jumped behind one of the beds. The Rivers knelt behind the other.

"Okay, let's sucker them in here," Jed panted. Taking a handful of shotgun ammunition out of the box, he handed it to Jody, who pocketed it without looking down. She was too terrified to take her eyes off the door.

Ben whispered loudly, "At least we've got the advantage of surprise."

The three knelt, steadied their shooting arms by resting them on the bed, and strained to listen for the oncoming peril. Beneath the waves of fear, Ben had to admit that a part of him relished this opportunity to show his son, and himself, that he was a man.

There were eleven intruders, all heavily armed. Six headed for the Dubiks' and the other five black-faced men made their way straight down the gravel driveway toward the bed and breakfast, talking in low tones. These were men who had been released from prison by Interpol and given a list of homes and businesses to hit–to take what they wanted and kill anyone who got in their way. Government orders. A tidy way to both free up limited cell space for political prisoners and eliminate people on Interpol's most-wanted list. The group had been told the people at Pah Tempe had stashes of gold and jewels, but that they were armed and probably would resist–particularly an Aussie with an attitude.

First they tried Peter's cabin, then Jed and Jody's. But both were uninteresting–essentially bare. Now they were nearing Miriam's room. One of the men rattled the door. Another did the same at Danny's door. Peg had to put her hand over Miriam's mouth to keep her from crying out. Danny was doing what his father asked. He was entertaining Craig by running a small car back and forth over the blanket on the floor.

"Good," Jed said when he heard the rattling. He tilted his head toward the small bedroom. "The goons are right outside." His adrenalin was pumping away like crazy. Sweet and sour pork, he loved the high.

Jody hadn't moved a muscle. Her heart was in her throat. She kept repeating, "Lord Jesus, have mercy on us," over and over, half aloud.

Then the group of intruders stalked around to the master bedroom. It was really hard for the trio behind the beds to stay still as they watched the men's shadows slink across the curtains.

"Try the window," one rough-voiced man said to another.

"Locked too," the other said as he rattled the lock.

Jody thought she was going to scream. Jed put his hand on her arm. She exhaled several times.

"Okay, then, we're knocking down this door," the first one said pointing at the outside door to the master bedroom.

Why? Ben screamed out in his mind. *It's open, you idiots. Try the knob!*

"One, two, three...." Two men rammed their shoulders on the

door, but it did not give way. "Again, you stupid grunts!" another shouted. This time it flew open. As soon as the first two men stumbled forward into the room, Jed, Jody and Ben fired almost simultaneously. The intruders fell back with the blast, then crumpled to the floor. Two more thugs, propelled by their forward motion, fell into the room. Before they could raise their sawed-off shotguns, they too were shot at close range. The last man yelled and scrambled back out the door and down the driveway. Ben jumped up and ran after him. He shot twice but missed.

The noise of the gunfire in the bedroom had been deafening. Jed jumped up, ears ringing, and pointed his gun at the four on the floor. Two men lay sprawled face down, blood beginning to seep out of their fatal wounds and run in rivulets toward the bed "fort". The other two were badly wounded. They moaned. One with tattoos on both arms cried out to Jed to help him.

At that point Ben came back into the room. "You, okay?" he shouted at Jed.

"Got it covered."

Ben stood immobilized for a moment. The memory of his childhood nightmare, the one that emerged when he first drove down the road to Pah Tempe's gate, leapt to the surface of his mind: the pungent smell of gunpowder, the gruff exchange between Jed and himself. It was nearly exact. And this was the exact moment in the dream where he'd wake up terrified.

Then gunfire rang out across the river. Nearly twenty shots were heard. Then screams. Ben froze in fear for the Dubiks. He ran into Miriam's room, called out to Peg just as he opened the door. Peg's eyes were as big as saucers as she sat trembling, the pistol cocked and ready to fire. "Oh, honey, it's you," she said lowering the gun as Ben appeared in the doorway. Her arm went limp. Craig was crying as he clung to Danny, and Miriam, hiding in among the clothes, stuck her head out at the sound of her father's voice.

Ben took the baby from Danny and tried to comfort him. "We're not out of the woods, yet." His voice rose over the baby's cries. "But we got some of those bad guys."

"Did you kill a bad guy?" Miriam asked, running out from behind the clothes and grabbing him around the waist.

"Honey, I did what I needed to, to protect my family." Ben had so wanted to impress his children with his fighting prowess, but now that he had his kill, it tasted bitter, even foul.

Danny pressed him, "Yeah, but did you kill any bad guys, Dad?"

"Yes, I did," he said softly.

"Yeah! My dad's not a coward. I told you, Miriam," Danny crowed. "I told you he could do it!"

Ben put his hand over Danny's mouth. "Shh, son, we've got to be quiet. We still have to chase away some more bad guys. You kids stay here with Peg, ah...Mom, (He smiled at Danny to acknowledge Peg's new status) until I come for you. Won't be long."

Then leaning close to Peg, he whispered, "It's pretty gory in there, honey. Make sure the kids don't go in until we've had a chance to mop up—at least get the bodies out." Glassy-eyed, Peg took a quieted Craig in her arms, slowly nodded her head, but grabbed Ben with her free arm for one last comforting hug before he left.

At the big house, Angelina and Renoir barked furiously as the raiders approached. Alex grabbed the two shotguns that Moira had loaded and sent her and her mother to the second floor with handguns. He crouched behind the couch with the Indian blanket and waited. *At least I'm not out running down irrigation ditches in the middle of the night,* he thought.

As the gang approached the house, Angelina streaked out from behind the studio and lunged at one of the men, taking him down. His gun went off and tore into Renoir, who was right behind the Dobie, seriously wounding her. Angelina bit deep into his flailing arm, while the other five threw open the oak doors. They were met with a hail of bullets—the ones from the women on the balcony were especially accurate.

Three men were killed instantly, the other two turned to run. Angelina was momentarily distracted, so the man on the ground was able to struggle to his feet and run toward his companions. But she quickly recovered and, fangs bared and foamy, began to chase her prey. Then Alex stepped out onto the front porch. Planting his feet as if he were on a firing line, he raised the rifle and stared down its sites. Then he took aim, gently squeezed the trigger until the round broke with a sudden boom. The man that Angelina was chasing grabbed his thigh and fell with a loud cry. When Angelina caught up with the young Hispanic, she began circling him with a growl that was punctuated by the sound of her teeth clacking together. Alex spurted past her on a dead run after the other two men who were dashing for the gate.

Moira went to the phone and called the bed and breakfast. Her voice crackled with alarm, "Are you guys okay?"

"Yes," Ben nearly shouted. "And you?"

"We're all okay. Three men here are hit and Alex's got another outside. Two are headed down to the gate." He could hear Grace in the background saying something about Renoir.

"Jody, you keep your gun trained on these guys, okay?" Ben barked as he returned from the phone call.

She shakily agreed, and Ben and Jed sprinted out the bedroom door headed for the gate. The two ex-cons had arrived at the far side of the bridge by the time Jed and Ben had reached the last cabin and flattened themselves against the adobe wall. Jed jumped out shooting. He hit one man dead center in the chest, who pitched forward and fell with a thud the fifty feet down to the river bed. The other man dropped to his belly and returned Jed's fire. Jed jerked back just as bullets tore chunks out of the wall next to his nose.

Then Ben whirled out of his hiding place and shot off two rounds. The second hit its mark, crashing through the skull of the other gunman. His head dropped without a sound. Ben jumped back to the safety of the cabin, but not before he saw the blood and brains oozing out the back of the intruder's head. It reminded him of the scene he used to play over and over again in his mind when he was very depressed–Kennedy in the back of the open car, lunging to the left as a crimson flower of brain obscenely blossomed out of his shattered right temple.

Alex reached the bridge just after the last shot was fired. He stopped to stare down at the convict who had fallen from the bridge. He lay still, face up, his chest ruby red from the massive wound Jed had inflicted. Then everything became very still. The river gurgled as it passed under the bridge. Ben stifled an exuberant war whoop. The scene he never wanted to dream had played itself out. And he was alive! He turned and gave Jed a bear hug, which Jed returned, nearly squeezing the breath out of Ben.

"Damn! We were good," Jed said, setting Ben back down on the ground.

"Real good," Ben said, wheezing and rubbing his ribs. He grinned broadly. *And I'm free from dream demons!*

Chapter Twenty-One

He straight obeys,
Not knowing to what Land, yet firm believes:
I see him, but thou canst not, with what Faith
He leaves his Gods, his Friends, and native Soil
Not wand'ring poor, but trusting all his wealth
With God, who call'd him, in a land unknown.
Paradise Lost, Book XII, 126-134, Milton

Alex gazed at the dead man, sprawled and twisted, on the river bank below. He struggled to swallow the bitter acid coming up his throat. But along with the acid came memories that he could not fight back: Vietnamese villagers–some of them children–like human candles exploding in pain as napalm fire crawled over their flesh; parts blown off bodies littering the road; legs still twitching on torsos without heads. And then the homecoming: college kids in ragged jeans with Indian beads around their necks and smirks on their faces, spitting on the ground and screaming, "Fascist! Baby killer!"

Alex shook his head to rid himself of the visions, like a stallion trying to shake off a too-tight bridle. Then, seeing Jed and Ben across the bridge, he shouted, "You guys okay?"

"Yeah, we're fine here," Ben hollered back.

"How many dead at your place? What's the count over there?" It was as if Alex were standing outside himself listening to his own voice. It sounded flat, foreign. He couldn't connect with it. This had happened before–but not for a very long time.

"We got four dead, one wounded and one got away, unfortunately." Jed's voice carried down the canyon. "How about you?"

"About the same. Listen, one of you men call Dr. Hunter. I'm going back up to the house to check on my women."

Alex turned up the collar on his windbreaker, turned and walked hurriedly back up the path. Halfway to the house, he saw that Angelina was still standing guard over the wounded thug.

"Good girl," he called out to her. She wagged her tail wildly in response.

As he got closer, he could see that the man was bleeding profusely from the thigh. Maybe an artery, Alex thought. The young Hispanic man moaned and called out to him, then lapsed into semi-delirious cursing. Alex leaned down, zombie-like, hauled the man to his feet and summarily threw him over his shoulder.

"Shut up. Shut up!" Alex muttered in a low voice filled with murder. Alex repeated in Spanish, "Callate. Callate! Voy a matarte!" The man briefly opened his eyes very wide, stopped swearing, then lapsed back into unconsciousness.

"Iwi?" Alex called out breathlessly as he neared the house. "Moira, open the door!"

She was at the door in seconds. "Watch this guy, will you?" he said as he dropped him with a heavy thud in the entryway, trying to stay on the parquet and not stain the rug. "You okay?" he asked worriedly.

Moira looked flushed, still high from the adrenalin. "I'm fine, you duck, and so is Mom. They make tough birds where we come from," she said tenderly. The couple stood suspended in time for a few moments, talking as if there were no carnage scattered around them.

Just then Grace came into the living room from the kitchen, wiping her hands on the green and white apron she wore. "Is he going to live?" she asked. She was torn between wanting to help the man and wishing him dead.

"I don't know," Alex said flatly. "We've called Hunter. He'll be here any time."

Moira stood menacingly over the unconscious intruder, her pistol pointed at his head.

"They've got some wounded down below, too," Alex said as he stepped over one body to get to his art collection hanging on the far wall. "I can't believe it!" he roared as he put his finger through a bullet hole bored into one of his favorite paintings–a landscape by an English friend. Waves of molten anger began to fill his stomach. One of his own pieces of sculpture lay on the floor, the torso of a nude man had been pocked and chipped by a spray of bullets. Now he felt like lava had begun to flow throughout his belly.

Alex took off his windbreaker and threw it over one of the dead men's faces. Then he dragged another to the door. As he did, he left a trail of blood all the way across the off-white carpet. That wasn't the only blood. Alex's boots swished through the sodden, dark-red mess left by the dead men's wounds near the couch.

He hauled first one, then another corpse outside, up the hill, a little ways from the house. On the third trip, as he looked down at his striped cowboy shirt soaked with blood, Alex began to unravel. But it was finding Renoir seriously wounded that was the final yank on the thread. Having finished his ghoulish task with corpses, he walked back to the studio. There he found the golden retriever in a heap near the door. He knelt down and tried to scoop her up in his arms, but she moaned in pain. As he pulled his hands away, he found even more blood on his arms and hands. Gently he laid her back down, then something inside Alex snapped. He stood up, put his head back and began to scream—no words, just a guttural scream of pain, feral and outraged.

Moira was out the door in seconds but could only watch helplessly as her husband pulled up an axe stuck in a stump near the house and began flailing it up and down like a madman. After a dozen blows, he missed the stump and smashed at the ground. Shouting at the top of his lungs, he turned to a nearby tree, a small one that he had recently planted, and swung the axe so hard, he nearly chopped it in half in one stroke. Finally he doubled over coughing.

Ben had just hung up the phone with David Hunter when he heard Alex. He rushed onto the porch that fronted the river to see what was happening, all the while dreading what horrible scene he might find at the big house. But he didn't need to see more than his friend hacking away with the axe and Moira in the doorway with her head down and arms folded, to understand what was happening. Peg ran to her husband and breathlessly asked, "What is it, honey? What in the world is going on?"

"It's all right. It's Alex," he said pulling her around in front of him and hugging her from behind. "It's just Alex," he said sadly, "and some old ghosts that have finally decided to pay him a visit–on his own doorstep."

Dr. Hunter was at Pah Tempe in less than ten minutes, bag in hand. Before he left, he called the Olsons and told them what had happened. Robert Olson immediately grabbed Peter and Nate Winder who had been there to help with his car's conversion. They arrived at the gate at Pah Tempe almost at the same time as Hunter.

The doctor hurried to the Dubiks', moving in long, labored strides. After examining the man in the entryway, he went to the phone in the kitchen and called for an ambulance. "No sirens, please," he instructed his friend who ran the service.

Peter jumped out of the car, his face contorted with anger, his fists clenched by his sides. He ran ahead to the bed and breakfast, furious that he hadn't been there to help defend the place. He came in through Miriam's bedroom where he could hear moans coming from the master bedroom. He threw open the door and found Jed and Ben standing guard over the two injured thugs. The dead men lay in two crumpled heaps, with their eyes wide open as if death were the ultimate surprise.

The three man nodded to each other, then Peter lunged toward the nearest injured man. "I'll kill you! You frickin' waste of flesh!"

Nate, who had just entered the room, grabbed Peter from behind and held him back as Peter struggled to get free."Take it easy, pal," Nate said in a low, authoritative tone. Finally getting free, Peter straightened the sleeves of his work shirt and ran a hand through his thick curly hair. He was breathing heavily.

The bishop appeared in the doorway and stepped on the beige rug. His shoe made a squishing sound. "Dr. Hunter will be down in a few minutes," he said, quickly picking his foot up off the large pool of blood.

"What did you think we had here?" Peter leaned down and yelled at the heavier of the wounded two. "Gold, silver, guns, ammo, what?"

Peter started to kick at the ex-con's head. This time it was Bishop Olson who stepped between him and the man on the floor. He put his crippled hands on Peter's shoulders. "Now you calm down, Peter. Things are bad enough."

Peter stepped back and took a deep breath. His face was crimson. "I'd kill 'em if I could. I swear I would," he muttered under his breath.

"What do you think we should do with the dead ones?" Ben asked the bishop.

"I'll take care of that," Nate said calmly. He gestured to Jed, who took the corpse's shoulders while he took the feet, and they dragged the body outside. Ben and Peter did the same with the other dead man. They laid them in the courtyard, next to the office and under a tree. After they finished, they milled around awkwardly, waiting for the doctor. They tried small talk but fell silent. All the violent movies and television shows had not prepared them for the feelings that arose at that moment.

Finally, Dr. Hunter along with Ron Highland, the sheriff's deputy, appeared on the scene, responding to a neighbor's concerned call about screams and gunshots coming from Pah Tempe.

"I'll have to take statements from you all," the deputy said in a friendly voice to the assembled group. His husky frame seemed to fill the small dining room. "I understand this attack was unprovoked. Is that right?"

Ben spoke for the group. "Yes, sir, that is correct."

"Then how is it that you were armed and waiting for them?"

"We weren't. The dogs alerted us."

"I see. Do you know any of these men?" he asked the group.

Everyone shook his head. The deputy paused, then pulled the sheet off the clipboard he was writing on. He knew these intruders had been sent by Interpol. Everyone there knew that. This attack was typical of what they did to people on their hit list. Finally Highland said kindly, "I'm going to treat this as attempted robbery."

There was a collective sigh of relief, and Jed stepped forward to shake his hand vigorously. "Thanks. Thanks very much," he said.

Ben moved in to do the same. "We've become quite popular at your station recently," he said apologetically. "But we'll be moving on now." Highland gave him a sad look and shook his head.

As soon as the officer left and David Hunter examined the injured men, the ambulance sped away to St. George, and the place became a beehive. The group decided they would try to leave Pah Tempe by 10:00 p.m. While Peter took up a guard station at the gate to wait for the coroner's office (and the thugs, he hoped), everyone else cleaned and packed. Jody went out to the dead men and covered their faces with napkins so the group didn't have to see the expressions on their faces. It was her way of dealing with the numbing reality that she probably had killed one of them. No one knew for sure when there would be another Interpol attack—just that there probably would be one. Rarely was anyone lucky enough to get the jump on these hardened criminals. They'd be back.

Later, after Robert Olson had gone to take Renoir to the vet, Alex returned to the studio. He walked slowly across the darkened area and turned on a lamp in the study. As he slumped in the director's chair, sobs rose from his belly. He rocked back and forth. His great grey mane, now loosened, fell in his eyes, then back down his shoulders as he rocked. As his cries pierced the walls of the house, Moira decided to broach his sanctuary. They had a tacit agreement that when he needed space, he took it in the studio. She rarely followed him there, unless asked. But she had never heard such sounds come from Alex, so she went next door.

"Sweetheart?" she called out as she opened the slatted door.

"Iwi, go away."

She remained in the doorway not sure what to do. "Alex, I'm concerned. We all are."

Alex did not respond. Finally she turned and walked back into the house. Her mother stood in the living room, worry lines running across her forehead. Moira shrugged. "He wants to be left alone."

"What shall we do?" Grace asked, reaching out to embrace her daughter.

"I don't know," Moira said fighting back tears. "We've got to get out of here by 10:00." She glanced over at the ornate grandfather clock which stood against the wall leading to the upstairs and read 8:15.

Grace took Moira's arm and sat her down on a padded stool in the kitchen. She looked deeply into her eyes. "I know what we've got to do," she said in Maori. "We've got to pray to the Lord. He's got to soften Alex's heart." Moira nodded, so the two women folded their arms, bowed their heads, and Grace, in her husky voice, begged the Lord for his intervention.

After Moira left, Alex got up and locked the door. Then he walked over to the first work table where two nearly finished statues of crucified men lay. In one swift motion of his outstretched arm, he wiped the table clean. The hardened clay figures smashed into pieces, dust flying as they hit the concrete floor. Mechanically he went to the other three tables and repeated the same ritual motion. Then he walked back across the broken pieces on the floor and ground them into powder with his cowboy boots as if he were killing some deadly insects.

His face was expressionless. He looked like a wind-up toy soldier. He strode woodenly, purposively to the south wall, took in a deep breath and pulled over a cupboard of greenware waiting to be fired. The noise from the crash brought Moira running. She pounded on the door until he opened it. Looking over Alex's shoulder, she could see into the studio and the debris.

"Alex! What in the world?"

"Honey, go away. I'm fine. I just have some business to take care of."

"What business?" she asked alarmed.

"Go. Away." He gently pushed her back.

Moira folded her arms around her stomach and began to cry. "Why? Honey, why? All your beautiful work."

Alex took her by the elbow and escorted her next door. "Please leave me alone," he said firmly. "Okay?" He looked into her large, frightened eyes.

"Okay," she said hesitantly.

He wheeled around, entered the studio and locked the door again. He was shaking. The only light shown from the study. The studio held pockets of dark anger. "Damn you!" he said to no one in particular. "Damn you!" he shouted as he picked up a broom from the corner. On the shelves on the north side of the studio, clay-sculpted faces creased with shadow stared ghoulishly out at Alex. In three big strides, he was upon them. He swung the broom handle, and head after head flew off the shelves. They sailed across the studio several feet before smashing into shards and dust on the floor. Methodically, Alex cleared off each shelf along the wall, like an angel of the apocalypse, using the broom as his instrument of destruction. Then he headed for his office area and the book shelves. But something stopped him there. It was the memory of Peg, hugging the two books he'd lent her.

Suddenly he felt spent. He leaned the broom up against the bookshelves, letting his arms sag to his sides. Then he dropped his head to his chest. "Damn you," he whispered, "damn, damn you," and crumpled into the director's chair.

The tears returned and as they did, so did memories of his father standing over him, his breath reeking of alcohol and vomit saying, "This time you're really gonna get it." Alex could see his father, swinging his alligator belt over his head, and then aiming blows to his youngest son's buttocks and back. Sometimes the belt buckle would hit too high and nick a piece of Alex's head or ear. He still had several small scars from those attacks.

This was one of those rare times when Alex had let himself

remember these scenes. But now, like a serpent wriggling out of its hole in the ground, paralyzing images forced themselves on him--images he had held back all of his adult life. With all of his mental might he had submerged the memory of the horrible night when he was ten. But it was the violence of this day, here at Pah Tempe, that propelled those memories past his psychological censors. He now was floating in a troubled void.

He could feel the night's beating begin. He registered once more the awful knot in his stomach, the throat raw from trying not to cry. Always before, after his father had spent his frustration on him, he'd tire and go away. But this time was different. It seemed that each blow fed his father's fury, and he hit harder and harder and harder until the belt buckle smashed against Alex's head–not once or twice but three times before Alex passed out from the pain. When he awoke in the hospital, he could not hear out of his left ear. He was covered from head to toe with welts from the beating that his father had continued, even after his son had collapsed into unconsciousness.

In those days a parent could swear the boy fell downstairs and the doctors and nurses, even if they knew it wasn't true, had no way of reporting the abuse. Alex's mother took him home and nursed him until his injuries healed, then moved her belongings to an attic bedroom where she slept the rest of his boyhood. His father went to AA off and on for several years and never beat him with a belt again. But the abuse continued–not physical, but verbal, until Alex believed he must have committed a sin so awful that his father was God's avenger.

Later, in Vietnam, as a gunner on a helicopter gun ship, he completely lost the ability to hear out of that ear. It probably saved his life; he was sent home with a medal and an honorable discharge.

Alex turned off the only light. He sat very still. Specters from his past mingled with fresh fiends from this night's shoot-out. Both horrible, both invasive. Then he rustled around in his chair. He knew he and his family and friends would have to leave

Pah Tempe. No matter who told Interpol, they now would not leave them alone. His private paradise was no more. He thought back 25 years when he was traveling through Asia, living in bleak rooms, wrestling with suicide. He remembered going to the Zen monastery, Ryoanji, and staring out at the Zen rock garden. Nothing moved there—ever. The realization that he would now have to leave had that same feel of rocky inevitability.

Finally he got up and unlocked the door. "Iwi? Iwi?" he called out.

After a moment, Grace yelled out that Iwi was upstairs.

"Grace?"

"Yes?"

"Could you come over here?"

"I'll be right there."

Grace pulled her shawl over her shoulders and hurried over to the turmoil next door.

"Tell me again about Zion," Alex said meekly as he stepped out of the studio.

Grace sucked in her breath trying not to betray her joy. "You come next door and let's take care of that," Grace said, slipping her arm through his. "You must be starving."

He came like a lamb, head down, leaning on her strong arm.

"They came for the bodies an hour ago," Grace offered.

"I'm sorry I wasn't there for you," Alex said sitting heavily on the stool in the kitchen. "It seems I was having a nervous breakdown," he said with the slight hint of a smile.

Grace returned the smile and warmed milk to make hot cocoa along with the rice and beans dinner she and Moira had eaten. He slowly sipped the brew and stared straight ahead. Finally he said, "We have to go now, you know. If they'll take us, maybe we can go with the party to New Mexico. I hope they'll consider me, crazy renegade that I am."

"We've already talked with Bishop Olson, and he's made us the offer. You included."

For the first time, Alex looked into Grace's face and realized that she and the bishop, and probably Moira, had been busy planing their departure with or without him.

"You were going to leave without me, weren't you?" he asked somberly.

"Yes."

"I see."

"But, my son," she said holding up a finger, "everyone will be so truly happy and grateful to know that you will be with us." Grace beamed at him. Then she told him about the city of refuge with its temple, and how the Lord would appear to His people before He comes to the world, while Alex slowly ate his rice and beans. She wanted to take him in her arms and rock him—he looked that vulnerable.

"Thank you, Mom. Those are comforting tales." He took a last sip of cocoa, put the cup on the counter, stood up and said, "Okay, then, let's pack."

What Grace had not told Alex was that the two women had worked most of the evening doing just that. In fact, Moira was not sleeping upstairs, but resting from the packing.

"Any word on Renoir?" he asked as he headed for the stairs.

"She'll pull through, from what the vet said."

"Good. We'll have to leave her with someone until we can send for her."

"The Olson's have already volunteered," Grace said. Alex smiled in relief. He stood still for a moment, hand on the banister. This move away from Pah Tempe was more than he could imagine. He would have to trust his wife and mother-in-law—something that felt both uncomfortable and comforting at the same time. Then he took the stairs two at a time to get to his sweetheart. He could see light coming from under their bedroom door.

The folks at the bed and breakfast were finished packing by 9:30. Grace had kept them posted on the drama as it played itself out across the river. They let out a collective whoop of joy when she called at 9:55 to say Alex had emerged, ready to move on. That news helped raise their spirits somewhat as they waited, cars packed, places scrubbed down, ready to slip furtively out into the night to yet another hideaway–the next way station to Zion.

The Taylors and the Rivers sat around the dining table. Peter had gone on–borrowed the truck to get back to the Olson's to work on Nate's car. Jed, with a shotgun in his lap, finally voiced what the others had been thinking since the shooting. "Ben, I'm sorry it had to come to this."

"Me too," Ben replied. "I wish we could have left quietly."

"No, I mean that your mother...."

"My mother, what?" Ben's voice rose dramatically.

"Well, we just assume she called Inter...."

Ben pushed back the high-backed chair from the dining table and jumped to his feet. "You assume what? My mother gave her word!" he shouted.

Peg tugged at his hand to get him to sit down. He jerked it away. "Honey," she said, "maybe she didn't call them, but the local police did, after she was gone."

"She didn't do it," Ben said menacingly. Along with the shock of killing two men, it was nearly too much for Ben to imagine he had been the cause of the bloodbath. But instead of feeling guilty, for once he angrily defended his mother. "Get that idea out of your minds right now. She did NOT do it!"

Everyone sat back in their chairs in silent shock. Finally Peg said quietly, "Okay, sweetheart. It's okay." She patted the chair for Ben to sit down.

He glared at the three. Jed spoke up. "We're sorry, Ben. Of course she didn't call them. I don't know what we were thinking about." Ben wasn't sure if Jed really meant it, but Ben breathed in a few times and changed the subject.

Peg, who had been nearly hysterical right after the shooting, had now quieted down and was doing needlepoint. At the bottom of her knitting bag lay the ancient plates carefully covered with cloth, then yarn. Each time the image of a dead man lying on the floor in her bedroom formed in her mind, she pushed it back with the thought of Zion being only one stop away. She was sure angels had protected her and the children during the battle. How else could any anyone explain how they came out unscathed while seven wicked men lost their lives?

All three children were in bed now, asleep, but Craig cried and fussed even though Jody had laid down with him. Miriam wet the bed, something she had not done for a very long time. And Danny wanted to go through the day's events again and again before dropping off to sleep. He was very disappointed that he had not been allowed to see the dead men piled up in the driveway waiting for the coroner.

Moira was just rising from her knees, as Alex opened the door. He swept her up in his arms and kissed her and held her tightly to his chest, but said nothing. He didn't say what he had decided. He did not have to. She ran her hand through his thick, grey mane. He pulled her up and picked up the large red throw pillow on which she had been kneeling and tossed it on the bed. His eye fell on a list in her hand-writing lying nearby and began to read: "Tents, sleeping bags, lantern, cookware, water purifier, first aid kit, army knife...." He looked lovingly into her eyes and said, "My dearest Iwi, how I love you. You even remembered my Swiss Champion Army knife with the magnifying glass, saw, ruler, screw driver and corkscrew. Not that I'll need a corkscrew anymore–not where I'm going–not surrounded by Mormons!" They both laughed. "It looks like you two have been really busy here. What's the plan?"

"We decided we'd wait until 10:00 to see what you were going to do." Alex glanced at his Mickey Mouse watch which read 10:03. "And as you can see, you were very prompt." Moira grinned and kissed his eyes. "Need I say how much I've prayed that you'd see your way clear to come."

"No. Say no more." He put his hand over her mouth. "I'm here. What can I do?" Then he patted her stomach. "And how could I leave Junior here?" he said in a low, loving voice.

"It's Israel."

"Adam."

"Okay, compromise–Adam Iharaira."

They laughed. Moira pointed to the pile of belongings on the bed and said, "Help carry this last load to the car. I'll grab your clothes and bathroom stuff while you do that." After Alex had descended the stairs with the heavy load, Moira again fell to her knees. "Lord, forgive me for ever doubting you."

Alex did not look back at the darkened house and studio as they drove down the road and across the bloodied bridge. If he did, he might think about staying. For the first time his mind went to the Jeep Wagoneer. Even though it had not been fitted with solar; the battery was fairly new. *It should get us to New Mexico,* he thought. *But what about a DAI?* he worried. What he didn't know was that Grace had called Peter, who at that moment was working in the machine shop behind the Olson's house to outfit the wagon with one.

The seven adults embraced one another as Moira, Grace and Alex emerged from the packed car. Angelina sat quietly in the back. Peg hugged Moira for a long time then said, "Well, I guess I've just done death." Moira managed a wan smile. "I'll have to remember to finish the Gestalt when the therapist tells me to," Peg said wryly.

"You just have to be brave enough to meet Death wherever he presents himself," Moira replied gravely.

"I'll remember that." Peg felt certain she would recognize that skull and hooded cape when next they met.

Finally about 10:30, they put the sleeping children in the cars. The tires crunched on the gravel as the cars crept up the long driveway to the highway. Jed and Jody were the last to leave. Jed got out to lock the gate behind them and then realized how futile that act was. Along with everyone else, he suspected that the thieves would return as soon as they had licked their wounds sufficiently. Looking mournfully down the driveway past the bed and breakfast to the baths, he said, "What a wonderful little place." He tried not to imagine it stripped, looted and maybe even burned to the ground. That was Interpol's signature, especially if there was any resistance.

The women and children went off to the Hunter's to sleep. The men left for the Olson's to work through the night to finish Nate's car. Sandy Hunter was very pleased to play hostess to the group. She thought about Emma Smith taking in Saints and somehow felt she was doing the same work for the Lord.

Peg and Jody shared a bedroom with twin beds as did Moira and Grace. The two kids were allowed to sleep in the family room. It was agreed that if they were good, they could watch television in the morning. They were so excited, they had difficulty settling down. It had been weeks since they had seen a cartoon.

Dr. Hunter gave each woman a sedative, knowing the shock of the day would most likely cause their sleep to be fitful and riddled with nightmares. A night of dreamless sleep would help. But he gave nothing to Moira because she was pregnant. She insisted she would let him know if she needed anything.

She lay awake listening to her mother's soft snoring. She worried that Alex would have a change of heart once he got away from the immediate danger. She could not know what he had been through in the studio—what memory had been loosened from his heart and flushed through his system to make way for another Father, this one both powerful and loving.

Once she got up to go to the bathroom and found David Hunter dozing in a chair in the living room, a shotgun draped across his lap. Finally she drifted off toward morning and she had a remarkable dream. She found herself walking up a small hill. When she reached the top, she looked down on a wide bay. The tide had gone out, exposing a muddy shoreline. Gnats rose in the air. Then her eye fell on two figures out near the water's edge, standing in the mud. Both had their backs to her. One was a boy about 10 or 11, who was looking eagerly up at a long-haired man. What was striking about the man was that he had taken off the white robe he was wearing and wrapped it around one shoulder and his legs, like an Indian dhoti. He and the boy were skipping rocks across the water. As the man turned to speak to the small boy, Moira saw that it was Christ. Her heart began to beat wildly. She didn't know what to do. She was afraid she might disturb Him and He would disappear. Now, as happens in dreams, the young boy was gone. She could see her Lord in profile. His face was etched with loneliness. Great loneliness. She burst into sobs. "How can this be?" she cried out. Suddenly He was at her side, walking briskly beside her, his robe now untied, flowing down to his ankles. She glanced down at his left hand. There she saw a large scar at his wrist and another in the back of his hand. She felt her heart pinch tight with empathy for the great pain he had suffered.

Moira had to lengthen her stride to keep up with Him. They traveled a worn path over a green hill covered with wildflowers. The Lord exuded such waves of intelligence and physical intensity, it was like walking next to someone who operated at a higher energy frequency than she did. Wordlessly, the Lord conveyed to her that He missed her, that they were friends who had been separated. Her heart, thudding in her chest, seemed to burst, spreading liquid joy throughout her body. She stumbled; He caught her elbow and helped steady her. They walked on over one hill then another. Finally Moira found the courage to ask, "Master, may I speak?" He nodded. "Whom shall I marry?" The question surprised her.

"You must choose from one of my servants. It is not appropriate to love me in a husbandly way."

Instantly Moira's joy turned into shame. Jesus lovingly touched her arm again, letting her know that He understood how a woman frustrated with her man might turn her passion to Him instead.

Then He showed her Alex in a big, bright studio with high windows. He was in a blue jean shirt and pants, absorbed in his work on a new sculpture of Christ. But this time it was a vibrant, triumphant figure, not a tortured and mangled one. Moira turned to her Master and said, "I understand. I'll choose him. Alex and I have been through so much already, it's as if our hearts are intertwined."

She looked into Jesus' loving face and saw that He was clearly pleased. Then He said enigmatically, "There will be a Wednesday wedding." But the sound of early morning cartoons filtered into her dream, and in spite of her desperate efforts to get Him back, the Lord had disappeared.

Chapter Twenty-Two

Outside, the freezing desert night.
This other night inside grows warm, kindling.
The continents blasted,
Cities and little towns, everything
Become a scorched, blackened ball.
The news we hear is full of grief for that future,
But the real news inside here
Is there's no news at all.
                    Open Secret, Rumi (d. 1273)

In the dead of night, the lights in the Olson's garage illuminated a scene reminiscent of a late 1960s space shot at Cape Canaveral. Men were wired tight in hurried purpose. A costly countdown in command headquarters was underway. But this time the focus of attention was not a slick 100-story missile, hissing gases in great clouds out into the spotlighted Florida night, but Nate's old station wagon, the last of the lightweight cars to be converted to solar.

The work lights on the walls of the garage cast their garish light on the ragtag group of men, who were hunched over the station wagon. Peter, who had been called a mechanical genius by more than one professor, was in charge of this group–men who certainly were not mechanical geniuses. But he was relaxed and so good-natured in his role of mission commander that he put the men at ease. He was everywhere–doing his own work, stopping to help Nate or Jed or Alex with a task he'd given them–his Aussie sarcasm lightening the mood, prodding men along. He even kept Ben busy sorting and cleaning parts and tools.

When they stopped for a break about 6:00 a.m., Ben went into the Olson's to use the bathroom. The rest gathered around a pot of boiling water to pour themselves a hot drink and warm their hands on the cup. The small space heaters barely managed to take the chill out of the air.

"I don't care what he says," Jed said watching the garage door for Ben's return. "It had to be his mother who called Interpol."

"Not necessarily," Nate cut in.

"What do you mean?" Alex asked, stomping his feet to warm them. Cowboy boots with pointed toes and a slight high heel did not make the best work shoes. "When Laurie came down for the sacrament meeting she was after Neddy, who'll turn eighteen next week. When I refused to let him go with her, she flew into a rage. In front of my parents she called me a number of pretty nasty names and accused me of breaking up the marriage. When I said I'd see to it that Neddy did his duty for his country, she threatened to bring us all down." He stopped to sip the hot bouillon.

"Whew," Jed whistled, "she's a real hard cookie."

"You know she called Interpol before, don't you?" Nate asked, ashamed.

"No, when?" Ben asked, returning from the house. The men had been so involved in the conversation they hadn't noticed him. They looked to Jed, who shrugged as if to say, let's keep going.

"She called Interpol when Missy slipped out of the motel room in Baker. The police tore through my parent's house with the finesse of the Abominable Snowman, demanding to know where Missy was. Of course, my parents knew nothing–the kids and I were still at the Bingham's ranch. After Peter and Missy showed up, I called Interpol and contradicted Laurie's report."

"Man!" Jed said under his breath. "Is she trouble!"

"So am I on some government bad guy list?" Peter pulled himself up so quickly from the interior of the car he bumped his head on the hood. He rubbed his head and started counting to himself to keep from boiling over.

"Frankly, I don't know," Nate said slowly. "I didn't want to worry you, Pete. I thought the case was closed. But after the scene in my parents' house on Saturday, I took her threats seriously enough to move me and my kids to a friend's house in Cedar City, until we came here tonight."

"I'm sorry I missed the first part of this," Ben said. "Are you saying you think it was Laurie who brought Interpol down on us?"

"I'm sure of it," Nate said and hung his head.

Joy played across Ben's face, but he restrained himself from whooping out loud. *I knew it. I knew she didn't do it,* he said to himself. *Esther wouldn't tell.* He hummed as he went back to his post near the door and as close to a heater as possible.

Having finished their drinks, the crew returned to their work with renewed purpose. Peter ran the Laurie conversation around and around in his mind. It wasn't like him to hold grudges, so after muttering to himself for awhile about Baker, Nevada and friends asking too much, he let it drop. *Besides, we'll be out of the government's clutches soon enough,* he thought.

They were done with Nate's car about nine, at least four hours ahead of schedule. As they cleaned up, Nate voiced what the others were thinking. "You know, it felt like we had extra helpers with us all night. Any one else feel that way?"

They all agreed.

"I've never been that good at putting things together," Nate continued. "It was like someone had his hand on mine, guiding them."

"And another thing is that I'm not that tired," Alex chimed in.

"Me either," Peter said. "You'd think we'd be dead on our feet, wouldn't ya?"

"I know I made it through the night, and that's a miracle," Ben said. "Gentlemen, I suggest we give thanks to the Lord." He bowed his head. The four others followed suit. "Father, thank you for your everpresent help. See us safely to our destination, in the name of Jesus Christ."

After the group concluded with a hearty collective "Amen," Jed piped up and said, "Let's get this show on the road. I'm hungry enough to suck oil." The four dirty and hungry friends snorted and shook their heads at him.

No sooner had they turned to cleaning up the remains of the mess, the apostles arrived in the old Honda wagon. The car had scarcely stopped when Apostles Dawahoya and Stewart jumped out and disappeared into the house. Nate, visibly worried, slipped out to talk to them.

"Why does he have special privileges?" Jed asked wiping down oily tables.

"Because they've probably got a message for him from Elder Whitmer, his father-in-law," Ben said with a little irritation in his voice. "He's Laurie's father, remember?"

"Oh, yeah, yeah. I knew that," Jed lied. "Winder, Whitmer, schmitmer," he muttered to himself, "too many W's if you ask me."

"That Laurie woman," Alex said as he swept up the debris around the work tables, "boy, does she have some karma to work off." He whistled. "Uh, uh, bad news."

Ben could see the apostles and Nate through the window, deep in conversation. Nate's kids sat around the kitchen table. They looked glum. They were learning that Laurie had created a string of scenes, trying to get Elder Whitmer to divulge her family's itinerary, but he refused to tell her. He knew his vindictive daughter well enough to know that she would jeopardize the sanctuary in Puerto de Luna. Although he hoped she would tire of her ski instructor and reconcile with Nate, he wasn't sure how she'd take living in a small farming community without a mall, or any public building for that matter. The other message from Elder Whitmer was that he would see that the younger children were cared for, no matter how long it took. Ben could see Nate's body relax as the last message was delivered.

While Peter put finishing touches on the Suburban's DAI, the rest ate, then drove to pick up the women and children at David Hunter's home. After a flurry of packing and deciding who would ride where, the Pah Tempe tribe was ready. The group decided the cars would leave at ten-minute intervals, headed to Colorado City and on to Tuba City, where they'd stay the night with Dawahoya's people. The two apostles left first, the Dubiks with Grace, then Nate and his children.

While the Taylors waited the requisite ten minutes, Ben and

Robert Olson stood in the living room. "I'm not sure we won't be following close behind you," the bishop said to console Ben who was obviously struggling with having to say goodbye to the bishop a second time. "This place may become as inhospitable to us as it has been to you." Ben had left the beloved bishop in Salt Lake, but had miraculously recovered his mentor in southern Utah. It was too much to hope he would now come to Puerto de Luna.

Finally, the time came. Ben backed the solar-equipped car slowly out of the driveway and turned down toward the main road. He and his family waved at the Rivers and Peter, who would bring up the rear of the caravan. Ben kept his eyes on the thin figure of the bishop until he couldn't see him any longer standing and waving on the porch.

At that exact moment, a half a continent away, Hazrat Patel paused before pressing the four numbers on the secured videophone. *Allah willing,* he thought, *we'll get out of this mess. If not, we'll die in battle and find our reward in Paradise.* Les Hackmann's stolid face appeared on the screen.

"Good morning, Les," Hazrat said, "the situation here is critical. If we don't act immediately, we'll be overrun."

"I'll make a couple of calls and get back to you," Les said curtly.

The screen went blank and Patel, pushing away the list with yesterday's casualty figures, looked out into the inky sky. It had been light for a little more than four hours before the sun set at 2:30 p.m. As he toyed with his handgun, he could hear booming sounds coming from the fierce tank and artillery battle less than a mile away. Hazrat wanted out of Alaska. He wanted to go home to Pakistan--the sun, the hills, to his family. He hadn't counted on dying in the tundra.

Hackmann immediately phoned the Alaskan director of emergency management, Irwin Graves in Fairbanks. "What happens if we decide to drop a couple of one megaton nuclear devices–surface blasts–on the Chinese up there?"

The director froze. His mind raced to getting his family on an airplane. "When are we talking about, sir?" he asked as he rifled through his desk for his URMAP (UWEN Radiological Monitoring and Assessment Plan). He found it in the bottom drawer, dog-eared and coffee-stained.

"Now!" Hackmann shouted into the receiver.

Graves gulped. "Well, sir, obviously we've done any number of computer simulations since the land bridge formed. Best case scenario is summertime—winds travel over Canada, Greenland. There will be little fallout over the major cities. But now, General Hackmann, sir?" He voiced betrayed his alarm.

"Quit stalling, man, tell me!"

"Well, sir, there's a high pressure cell stalled off the coast of San Francisco—a really big bulge. That means we've got a major storm in the works. The jet stream dipping into the Dakotas, Chicago and on to the East Coast of the United States would carry massive radiation."

"What about Europe?" Hackmann asked gruffly, so the man on the other end of the phone wouldn't know it was a very personal request.

Graves pushed a few buttons on his computer and brought up the European screen. "Right now any fallout would probably pass over the Scandinavian Peninsula, sir. But with a nuclear blast, who knows what might happen. It could just as easily cross over London, Berlin and Moscow."

Seconds after Hackmann hung up, the frightened emergency management director threw a few folders and documents into his briefcase, phoned his wife at work, jumped into his car and sped home. If he had to, he'd pay for a single engine plane to get out of there. He hoped he'd be in time.

Hackmann lit another cigarette and took several long puffs before calling Patel. He had called UWEN Central Command in Zurich and apprised them of the situation. After what felt like several hours, they called him back with the order to drop the bombs even though it would indiscriminately wipe out both the

Chinese invaders and the UWEN forces. The burden of informing Patel sat in Hackmann's stomach like a poisonous apple that he was about to throw up. He stared at the UWEN motto hanging on the far wall which read, "World Peace through World Government."

Still he did not call, his hand hovering over the phone like an old gnarled bird uncertain about landing on the black branch below. Finally he punched in the code. The strain on Patel's face was obvious to Hackmann as he answered on the first ring. "Have they made a decision?"

"Yes. We're going for it. It will dust the eastern half of the U.S. and Scandinavia. Can't be helped. If we don't, those places may be Chinese colonies before we know it, anyway."

"Yes, sir. Thank you, sir." Patel, whose voice usually had a haughty undertone, now sounded sincerely humble.

"And you get clear of there, Haz, you hear? Pronto! We don't want to lose you."

"Yes, sir." Hazrat had no intention of going down with his troops. After a long pause with an uncharacteristic heaviness in his voice, Patel continued, "Les, this may be the largest instance of friendly fire in the history of warfare."

"I know, Haz, I know," Hackmann replied tersely.

In the enormity of the moment, both men said nothing. Finally, squaring his jaw, Les looked into the screen and barked, "Okay, let's do it. Let's drop 'em."

Four UWEN bombers appeared on radar about 4:00 p.m. The troops had been ordered to pull back from their artillery positions, but still there was ragged fighting near Nome, in spite of the dark. Hazrat Patel and his entourage were on their way south, following the west coast of Canada to Vancouver, where Patel would help combat the Chinese invasion there.

The two bombs were spaced a minute apart. The first warhead ripped open a crater 200 feet deep and 1,000 feet across at the rear of the Chinese forces. The second was dropped on the enemy troops near Nome. The blast wave produced winds of several 100 miles an hour, and nearly all 55,000 men around ground zero were killed at once. Some melted, burst into flames or were charred in the military hardware which melted into shapeless masses of metal. A mile away, at vacated mission headquarters, the walls were blown out of all the buildings and most cars were destroyed. Of the remaining 400,000 troops (both UWEN and Chinese) in that mile to two mile perimeter, more than two-thirds died, killed by flying objects or being hurled against buildings, tanks, trees by gale force winds.

Because it was winter, the fire storms were less severe than had been projected. The surface blast tossed tons of radioactive debris into the atmosphere and because of the winter blizzard that was already roaring down across Canada, highly toxic radiation descended on Calgary, Minneapolis, Milwaukee and Chicago, in the delicate form of flakes of snow.

The travelers from Pah Tempe stopped briefly in Colorado City about 11:30 a.m. after passing through the border crossing at Hildale without incident. Everyone praised Peter under their breaths for his DAI expertise. Alex wanted to see Todd Barlow to thank him again for his help with the kids, but when he checked at the motel, he was told Todd and his cousins had gone to the San Francisco Bay area to help with the fighting. So the caravan headed into the empty Arizona desert, where the women drove while the men slept.

Ben couldn't put the seat back all the way to get a really good rest, because the kids were playing on the back seat, so he leaned his head against the window and dozed off and on. Sometime mid-afternoon, in a vivid, hypnagogic dream, he saw, suddenly appearing over the North Pole, the head of a giant serpent. Mottled brown and green, it flashed horrible iridescent yellow eyes. The snake draped the top portion of its hideously scarred body over the top of the globe, first on Alaska and then on Russia.

Ben jerked awake with a little yell. The children who were wearing headphones listening to children's CD's couldn't hear him, but Peg jerked her foot off the gas and asked worriedly,

"What, honey? Are you okay?"

"I just had a really bad dream," Ben said and shuddered. "I think something really awful is about to happen."

"Oh, no," she cried and pressed down on the brake pedal. Fearfully she began guiding the car toward the shoulder of the road.

"No, honey, not to us. To the world," he said quickly.

"Oh." She let out a loud sigh and speeded up. "Like what to the world?"

"Promise you won't think me weird." They both laughed simultaneously. "Okay, you know I am weird, but more than usual?"

"Promise."

"I feel like old Ben Kenobe in *Star Wars*. You remember the part where he grabs his heart or head and moans."

"I do," Peg said seriously. "Something about a disturbance in the Force."

"Well, that's how I feel. I think that experience with Sangay has somehow sensitized me to the world's vibration. I know that sounds all woo-woo, but I just feel like something really bad is going to happen to the whole world."

Ben leaned over and put his head in his hands. Peg drove on in silence. Several miles later Ben looked back to see that both children had conked out in the back seat. With that he pulled the Tibetan plates from the needlework bag and gently placed the top two plates on the bottom of the pile of forty or so plates. *I need to concentrate on something positive*, he told himself.

He placed Plate #3 on the door of the glove compartment, opened his backpack and pulled out a yellow legal pad, which he laid on his knees. Having written "Plate Three of Forty: Tibetan Scripture," he looked over at Peg. She seemed lost in thought.

"Lord, bless me with the power to translate what you would have me know," Ben fervently whispered.

Silently he waited. Peg glanced over at him, then to the plates. Then he began to feel a warm surge, which seemed to fill the interior of his spine. It made its way slowly up to his heart.

That sensation brought blissful tears to his eyes. It snaked its way through his throat where it felt a little like menthol, then on up to warm the interior of his head. He felt light, yet powerful. He opened his eyes and focused on the plate.

The story of the Flood spilled out just as the other stories had. Then Nawang, as narrator, interrupted to tell how it was that Moriancumer could converse with the Tibetans. There had been a pure language, remnants of which remained in their language. And because Nawang had been a merchant who traveled the trade route, he had been exposed to variations of the language.

Ben furrowed his brow and broke the spell.

"What's the matter, Ben?" Peg asked. She had been in awe of seeing her husband in a kind of trance state, writing rapidly, then listening, then writing again.

"I'm not sure that these are the real thing."

"Why?" Peg's voice rose in alarm.

"Because they give us the brother of Jared's name. The scriptures don't do that." Ben peered out at the dry, mountainous terrain. His heart sank.

"What's the name, honey?"

"Nothing you'd know," he said dejectedly.

"Don't you do that, Ben," she said somewhat angrily. "You promised me that you wouldn't pull your 'I'm-superior-to-you-in-intellect' routine."

"Okay, it's something like More-an-comber," he said slowly translating the script.

Peg burst out laughing. The children stirred in the back.

"Shhh," Ben said.

"Sorry. But that's Mahonri Moriancumer."

"How do you know?" Ben asked, surprised.

"Everyone know that's his name."

"From what source?"

"I don't know. Joseph told people that was his name."

Chastened, Ben fell silent and shook his head. Then he said under his breath, "Forgive me, Lord, for doubting you. Please,

please don't take away my abilities."

He needn't have worried. When he returned to the translating, he read that the Jaredites were going to the land most precious above all lands. Nawang's people wanted to go. The brother of Jared inquired of the Lord. As Nawang watched, a cloud descended, covering the two men. A voice spoke to both. Nawang fell to the ground, overcome. Moriancumer helped him to his feet. The voice said no, Nawang's people were not ready, but one day they would be counted among the ten tribes and come to the New Jerusalem.

Ben's attention was diverted to the back of the car when Miriam coughed and kicked her crayon box to the floor. Both he and Peg froze.

"Daddy," Miriam said in a weak little voice, "are we there yet?"

"No, sweetheart. You go back to sleep. We'll be there soon."

"I'm thirsty."

Ben pulled a plastic bottle of water from under his seat, turned around and gave her the bottle. She took a long drink. Ben and Peg looked at each other hopefully. Miriam handed the bottle back to her father, curled into a ball against the door and stared ahead for a while. No one spoke. Peg lovingly glanced in the rear view mirror at her stepdaughter. Finally, the tired little girl, who hadn't slept much during the night while she waited for cartoons, closed her eyes and nodded off.

"Coast is clear," Peg whispered and squeezed Ben's leg.

Ben put the third plate on the bottom of the pile and began reading the fourth one. This one opened with the brother of Jared teaching the Tibetans about baptism and the gift of the Holy Spirit.

The narrow two-lane road became wider at Fredonia. Peg pulled into Jacob Lake around one o'clock and searched for familiar cars at the three restaurants in town. It was at the last one, the High Chaparral, that the three cars sat parked. Ben and she woke the grouchy, sleepy children and helped them into the restaurant.

The apostles sat at a booth with Nate and three of his four kids who were hungrily eating burgers and fries. Missy sat with Jed and Jody, playing with Craig while they ate. Ben wasn't sure if they should acknowledge everyone, but when he and his family reached the middle of the restaurant and Alex caught sight of them, he bellowed out, "Hey, there, slow pokes, sit over here," pointing to a slightly torn-up, red naugahyde booth.

After they had ordered, Ben excused himself to go the men's room. On the way back, he stopped at the apostle's table. His face was still flushed from the remarkable experience of peering into 3,000-year-old scriptural history. His eyes were even dilated. Elder Stewart sensed he wanted to speak to one of them, so he slid away from the table and disappeared with Ben back into the men's room.

"Sir," Ben began, then choked up. "The plates...." Tears filled his eyes.

Elder Stewart laid a large hand on Ben's shoulder. "Yes, go on."

"Sir, I'm fairly certain they are authentic." Ben was so filled with the Spirit, he felt he might be transported to Kolob at any minute.

Charles Stewart took Ben's hand and shook it several times and said, "I'm so pleased." Then he glanced out of the small opaque window which was open for ventilation and asked, "May I ask you to speculate on something, young man?"

"Of course, Elder Stewart. Anything." Ben was pleased to be called young, for at that moment he felt timeless.

"From what you've been able to read, can you ascertain why these plates might come into our hands at this moment in church history?"

Ben thought for a moment then shook his head. "What I've read so far provides us with some pretty overwhelming evidence that the *Book of Mormon* is an ancient record. And that is exciting in itself. But you must realize, I've only read through three or four plates. I suspect there is a great deal more once I get farther along."

"I see. Well, good work, Ben." The apostle took Ben's hand into both of his large ones and shook it again. "The Lord is most grateful to you for your ability and worthiness, Brother Taylor," he said looking deeply into Ben's eyes. In that moment, Ben felt as though the Lord himself were speaking to him.

"Thank you, sir," he said most humbly.

The caravan pulled into Tuba City about 5:30 p.m. (3:30 Alaska time). They checked into the Trading Post Motel run by Elder Dawahoya's nephew. Danny and Miriam threw their backpacks down on the bed and disappeared next door to play with Missy. While Peg showered, Ben sat down on one of the sagging beds with a faded quilt and snapped on the television to check out the local news. Now it was a few minutes before six and Peg emerged from the bathroom, towel around her head. "Whatja doin', tiger?" she asked lightly.

"Watchin' the six o'clock news to see about the road conditions into New Mexico."

"Oh, okay. But let's go eat. I'm starved." She disappeared back into the steamy bathroom.

A couple of minutes into the news broadcast, the announcer began covering the top of the international news. "And now let's cut live to Johnny DeWitt of ITN who's outside Nome."

Ben felt a burning rash suddenly cover his arms, then his chest. Distracted, he scratched at his upper body through his checkered shirt. *Now what have I got? Measles?*

The reporter began, "You can see in the background the flashes from the artillery exchange in a battle that has seen very little UWEN progress." He opened his mouth to report on the ground fighting nearby when a blinding flash obliterated the scene.

Ben thought they had lost transmission when, to his horror, the light faded and an enormous mushroom cloud began to form over the scene.

The reporter just had time to shout, "What the...?" before he and the cameraman were pitched against the hotel wall by the force of the 150 mile-per-hour winds.

"Peg, come here!" Ben gasped, but his words came garbled.

She peered around the door from the bathroom. He could only point to the television screen, which now was only showed static. Ben swallowed hard and managed to get out, "They nuked them," before doubling over.

Peg rushed over and pulled up his head. "Who nuked who?" she nearly shouted into his face.

"I'm not sure, but I think the UWEN just nuked both the Chinese...and their own troops," said Ben, trembling and trying to shut out the scene from his mind. He remembered a quote that had stuck in his mind after the first nuclear device was detonated in New Mexico. One of the scientists who witnessed the mushroom cloud had said, "I am sure at the end of the world–in the last millisecond of the Earth's existence–the last human will see what we saw."

Then Ben and Peg could hear people shouting in the street below. In moments, Jed was at their door. "They dropped a couple of bombs on the Chinese in Alaska!"

"We know. We know," Peg cried out. "What about fallout? What will happen now?"

No one in their party knew the answer to that question, but they talked about it incessantly as they went down to eat in the back dining area of the motel's cafe and picked at a Mexican meal that had been prepared especially for them because they were in the apostles' entourage. Ben told of the rash he had just before the bomb, and how it left as quickly as it had started once the bombs were dropped.

When they were through eating, the apostles called everyone to their table and signaled to Elder Dawahoya's nephew to pull shut the large accordion doors so they could have privacy. The apostle had arranged to have the younger children taken out and entertained, but Nate's four teenagers, Neddy, Cristina, Andrew and Cannon were invited to stay. They sat, very quietly, in the tall wrought iron chairs that had been placed in a semi-circle around the apostles. Everyone else pulled their chairs as close in as they dared, like travelers huddled together against a wintry blast, free to warm themselves at the spiritual fire of these special messengers of the Lord.

Elder Stewart began, his Scottish brogue particularly thick. "My brothers and sisters, how momentous this trip is becoming. Our little journey to Missouri now has taken on grave significance."

Ben looked over at Peg, who sat staring into the wise, kind, craggy face of the apostle. He picked up her hand and placed it between his. *What would I have done if all of this had happened while I was married to Linda?* He recoiled internally as memories resurfaced of fights they had had about religion. Peg turned her head and he mouthed, *I adore you.*

She smiled and turned back to hear, "We have been in contact with the prophet, who has instructed us to continue on to Jackson County, in spite of the possible nuclear retaliation from the Chinese. We are to wait, though, for further instructions in Puerto de Luna before proceeding."

Alex leaned over to Moira and asked, "Is he getting his instructions from the prophet or from God?"

"Both," she whispered as she tried to hold back a smile of delight. What a miracle to hear those words from her much beloved agnostic.

"Rather than colonizing Puerto de Luna," Elder Dawahoya now began speaking in a low, authoritative voice, "the prophet has asked if you would consider settling in Jackson County."

Moira turned to her mother and squeezed Grace's hand. It took a couple of seconds for the two women, and the rest of the group for that matter, to take in the magnitude of the offer.

Then a thrill ran through the small group like a string of firecrackers at a Chinese New Year celebration. The two apostles sat back and smiled warmly while everyone slapped each other on the back and whooped, "I can't believe it!" over and over again.

Jody gave Jed the thumbs up sign. "Your blessing was right!

Craig is going to grow up in Zion." Alex sat quietly in the middle of the turbulent scene. He had at least one major question to ask the apostles–about the practicality of declaring Independence, Missouri, suburb of Kansas City, Missouri, approximate population 175,000–the New Jerusalem. Somehow he didn't think the natives would take kindly to the news.

Because the fallout was trapped by the moisture of the severe winter storm, radiation dosages (rem doses) exceeded 300 in Calgary. Most people had sufficient warning to get indoors before the deadly storm blanketed the city with six inches of snow. They were told not to venture out for at least three days. Those unfortunates who were exposed to the radiation, suffered nausea, vomiting and severe loss of white blood cells, making them susceptible to hemorrhaging and PDS, "the plague." Causalities were low in the Canadian city, at least the obvious causalities were low. Only time would reveal the long-term effects on humans and animals, plant life, even the soil.

American cities were less affected, because the rem doses were less. By the time the storm had blown itself out over the Atlantic, it was not the lethal cloud bank that government officials had predicted since the 1950s. But there was the real problem of the tons of debris in the atmosphere. It wasn't until morning in the northeastern United States that people became aware of the grey-brown filter over the sun. No one dared to guess what this blast had done to the nearly depleted ozone layer over the North Pole.

The Chinese government responded as expected by withdrawing its troops from Alaska, but with a threat of nuclear retaliation. The invaders along the West Coast were told by their leaders to redouble their efforts. So the fighting intensified. More and more Chinese suicide squads were used to smash through UWEN barricades and into nominally secured areas up and down the West Coast.

Although the day's emotional roller coaster ride had left him exhausted, Ben awoke about 3:00 a.m. He was sure that someone had called his name, but the room was quiet. Peg lay beside him, sound asleep, curled around a pillow. The children slept like daddy-long-legs, limbs outstretched and bent at odd angles. They each clutched stuffed animals Peg had bought them for the trip. And although they had not been told about the bombing, Miriam had pieced most of the story together through dinner conversation and had to be rocked to sleep.

Ben felt rested and wide awake. He took a flashlight, pad and pencil from a canvas bag, and picked up the top plate (#4) hidden under the needlepoint and skeins of thread in Peg's sewing bag. He sat down as noiselessly as possible at the small table near the window. A large truck rumbled by. Then it was silent.

"Lord," he whispered, "I am here. I am your humble servant. Please, guide my work." Eyes closed, he waited for that intense peace he had experienced with Sangay, to help settle his breath. That accomplished, he opened his eyes and heard the translation resume. Now there was another speaker, a man named Tenzin, called by the brother of Jared to be the leader of this group of ancient Christians. Ben heard him say, "I have been told by the Spirit of the events to come...." He paused to write, then listen "...in the end of time."

Ben sat up straight and opened his eyes. As he wrote "in the end of time," he felt a great shiver run through him. *Could these plates give some detailed description of the days that lay ahead? Could this be the reason the Lord had preserved these plates until now?* Excitedly he returned to focus on the plate and strained to hear "...then deadly winds and black clouds of destruction will fill the sky and sweep the land, leaving only the...(come on, come on!)...stench of illness and death in their wake."

Next he heard a description of what could only be the Chinese invasion of America. The new land bridge, the opponents with blue eyes and yellow hair, the geography of the final battles–it all matched with chilling accuracy.

"Whew," he whistled out loud.

"Daddy, what are you doing?" Danny sat up and asked sleepily.

Ben quickly covered the plate. "Go to sleep, son."

"No, Dad," Danny got to his feet, "whatja doing?" He was now wide awake.

"Shhh, son, you'll wake up Mom and Miriam." Ben got to his feet to tuck Danny back in bed. But Danny squirted around him and lifted up the pad. He sensed Ben placed great value in the small, square, metal object lying on the table.

"What's this?" the boy asked wide-eyed.

Ben paused, trying to think what he should say. *Should I tell my son, a ten-year-old boy, the truth and swear him to secrecy? Can he keep a secret like this? Surely Joseph did his translating before he had children,* he moaned.

"Come on, Dad," Danny whispered impatiently.

"That is," Ben scrambled to hear the Spirit's voice, "...ah, an old computer chip...way back in the 1950s they made them that big. Isn't that weird?"

Danny stared at the his dad, but Ben made no move that gave away his lie. "So why do you have it?"

"Because Peter gave it to me and I was trying to make sense of what was written on it," Ben volunteered, showing the pad with translation written upside down.

"Oh," Danny said flatly. "I was dreaming that we had angels in the room who were writing something down, but I couldn't read it." He rubbed his eyes and smiled sleepily at Ben.

Angels? My son? Ben was surprised. He quickly recovered to say, "Hey, that's an interesting dream, bucko, but you've got to go to sleep."

"So can I read it in the morning?" Danny persisted as Ben helped his son slide back into bed.

"Well, we'll see. We're going to be arriving in Puerto de Luna to-morrow." He kissed Danny on the forehead. "I'll turn off the light and try to sleep, too."

Ben didn't feel guilty about the lie. It would be too much of a burden for Danny to bear, he decided. He lay awake in the dark at least an hour, anxious to get back to the translating, but fearful he'd wake the family. *How odd,* he thought, *that Danny would dream about angels writing. What was that in Joel? Your sons will dream dreams, your old men...no, it's the other way around. "...your sons and your daughters shall prophesy, your old men shall dream dreams...."*

Finally his curiosity got the best of him, so he slid quietly over to the table and slowly turned the switch on the lamp so that it only made a low click. He pulled out the stack of plates from the bag and pushed them together with his hands so they were in perfect symmetry. Then he slipped #4 back in its place and sat back to look over his prized possessions. *I wonder how far in the future these plates go,* he asked himself. Then impulsively, he pulled a plate from the middle of the pile and prayed, "Lord, I'd like to know more about the mysteries. But I know you won't let me translate without your Spirit's help. So, if it's all right, I'm dying to know what's farther down the road." Ben held his breath and waited.

After fifteen seconds, which seemed like an eternity, he heard, "Everything is illusion." He quickly grabbed the legal pad and began writing. "Geshe sat before his master, having been sent to Badrinath by the emperor, Ashoka. In this holy place, site of many pilgrimages, high in the Himalayas...."

"Whew," Ben said as quietly as he could. "What is this?" Fascinated Ben skimmed down to the end of the plate, concentrated and then heard, "Geshe entered into that state where his physical body ceased to age and sparkled with a golden lustre of divine incorruptibility."

That was the last that he remembered until Peg shook his shoulder about 7:30 in the morning. "Honey, hurry," she whispered. "Wake up! Get rid of these things," she said stuffing the plates in the knitting bag and pad into Ben's backpack. "The kids will be awake any minute. Did you read anything interesting last night?"

"Yeah, I did," he said rubbing the back of his neck to try and get a kink out. "I was reading about prophecy last night. It was really miraculous! The Tibetans predicted the Chinese invasion of the country."

"How fantastic!" she whispered loudly. "I can't wait to hear."

"You will, I promise," Ben said, pulling her to him and kissing her nose. Then he headed for the bathroom. After showering, he looked into the mirror and tried to focus, as he attempted to bring the motel soap to a lather for shaving. *What was that last night? Geshe? A translated body?*

He struggled to remember if he had had a dream about immortality. Then suddenly, halfway through shaving, he was able to focus on the legal pad in his backpack. *I'm sure I wrote something down before I fell asleep!* With soap bubbles still clinging to the left side of his face, he peered around the corner of the bathroom. Peg was outside doing her morning stretching exercises. The two children still lay sprawled on their beds, fast asleep. He wrapped a towel around his waist and tiptoed to the table and the backpack. With shaky hands, he slipped the yellow pad out and read, "...entered into a state of...incorruptibility." He wanted to shout hallelujah. Instead he grabbed the towel so it wouldn't fall off and did a little jig back to the bathroom. *Oh, the Lord, the Lord! What next?*

Chapter Twenty-Three

There lives the dearest freshness deep down things;
And though the last lights off the black West went.
Oh, morning, at the brown brink eastward, springs--
Because the Holy Ghost over the bent
World broods with warm breast and with ah! bright wings.
"God's Grandeur," Gerard Manley Hopkins

Visibly relieved, Hazrat Patel flashed a smile exposing his gold-capped teeth on ITN as he disembarked from the blue and white UWEN executive plane. He arrived in Vancouver just in time to watch the same television transmission from Nome as Ben did. Patel watched the ghastly mushroom cloud billow into the Alaskan sky and muttered a quick prayer of thanks to Allah for helping him get downwind and thousands of miles away. As images of his own decimated troops swelled in his mind, he steeled himself with the thought that the Muslims among those who died were now in Paradise.

As Brigadier General, Patel's assignment was to coordinate defense efforts to take Vancouver, then sweep south with UWEN and Canadian volunteer forces. UWEN naval resources were being moved into position all along the West Coast of the United States. From Central and South America, Buck Fredericks' units would arrive in Baja California within 24 hours, ready to push up from San Diego north, using the Navy destroyers up and down the coast as cover.

Within twelve days, UWEN forces had ruthlessly pressed forward, north and south, in a pincer fashion, virtually destroying two Chinese armies of more than one hundred thousand men. Patel's troops and American volunteers took to the ridges of the inland mountain range where they succeeded in cutting down Chinese troops trying to escape. Despite their smaller numbers, the volunteers knew the terrain and used guerrilla tactics to ambush one Chinese company after another. The few Chinese troops who managed to escape were summarily hunted down and captured by Air Cavalry helicopters.

The decisive battle occurred in the Sierra Nevada Mountains, west of San Francisco. The Chinese, forced into the Bay area from the north and south, began fleeing east into the hills for one last desperate stand. Many troops in the volunteer army positioned high above Sacramento were from Utah, Idaho and Nevada. Over half were Mormon, and Bobby Whitmer was among them. Now, after several skirmishes and a handful of kills, he was not the greenie who had thrown up in the swimming pool drain. He looked older, thinner. A set jaw and sad eyes replaced the gung-ho idealism that had animated his face as he left Pah Tempe.

The sun set in a surreal blaze, all orange and pink and maroon, and Bobby and BJ sat with their patrol and other troops they had not previously met, huddled in among brush and trees twenty miles east of Grass Valley. Tired troops grunted to each other as they chewed on beef jerky and crackers and shared whatever MRE's the regular troops still had.

Bobby, who bordered on being hyperactive, stood up and shook off the crumbs of the peanut butter sandwich a woman had pressed into his hand as the troops marched through Auburn. After he had relieved himself behind a nearby pine tree, he wandered around looking for conversation and sat down next to a freckle-faced kid from Pocatello. The teenager intently stared at a crumbled piece of paper that he had unfolded and now held a few inches in front of his face. This potato farmer's fourth son, who went by "Hairy Monster," mouthed the words as he read.

"Whatcha readin'?" Bobby asked.

"A letter from my girlfriend," Henry Monsen replied, peering at Bobby over the top of the letter.

"Well, if it's that interesting, there must be some juicy parts in it!" Bobby said, smiling and looking around at the other men for support. "Let's hear some, Monster!"

BJ and a couple of other guys in the circle piped up. "Let's hear what Miss Idaho's got to say for herself!"

"Yeah, c'mon, lover boy. Share the good word!" chimed in the ragged chorus.

Henry cleared his throat and looked over at the other men. "Well, guys, to tell you the truth, it's not romantic or anything like that. In fact," he said turning red as he fingered the page, "it's a poem against war. I can read it to you if you want."

Silence quickly replaced the good-natured jeers. Many of the men fell back to chewing on the remains of their rations.

"Well, I'd like to hear it," Bobby said in a low, friendly tone. The other men seemed to hunker down even further into their silence.

Henry smiled at Bobby and said, "I'm not used to reading out loud, much less a poem, so hang in there with me, okay?"

"No sweat," Bobby replied.

"Here goes. It's by a British poet who died in the First World War. His name was Wilfred Owen. It's called 'Anthem for Doomed Youth.'" The carrot-topped kid read slowly, stumbling over large words:

> What passing-bells for these who die as cattle?
> Only the monstrous anger of the guns
> Only the stuttering rifles' rapid rattle...

"Okay, Monster, that's enough," BJ said angrily. "Sorry we asked. I mean, that stuff's depressing. I guess your girlfriend never went out for the cheerleading squad, huh?" He mimicked a girl leading a cheer. The other men burst into laughter, relieved by BJ's buffoonery.

But Bobby decided to resist this wave of nervous laughter. He didn't know quite why, but it seemed to him almost as if his buddies were being irreverent--like telling jokes in the back pew during the passing of the sacrament. "I agree with the man who wrote that," Bobby said soberly. His words went like a knife to the heart of the laughter, which died again into silence.

Booing came from several quarters.

"Listen, when I started out in Cedar City, I thought this fighting was going to be great fun."

Hollow laughter erupted from the weary men.

"Well, now I think the Lord is preparing a place for anyone

who is tired of fighting. In Zion," Bobby continued, his jaw set, his voice even. "And those who enjoy war can stay away from Jackson County and kill to their heart's content."

"Ah, you're full of it, you stupid kid," said an older man with leathery skin from Las Vegas, taking a deep draw off his cigarette. "That's absolutely crazy."

"No," Bobby said, digging in even further. "No, it's not. It's a promise from the Lord that when things get so bad that peace is impossible, He will provide a sanctuary."

The former black jack dealer hurrumphed, leaned back against his pack and pulled his navy knit hat down around his ears. A freezing wind rustled the bare branches.

Talk became divided between Mormons and non-Mormons. The Latter-day Saints talked about scriptural prophecy, about the experiences they had had with garments protecting them in really tight situations, even patriarchal blessings that promised them they would live through the darkest hours the world has ever known. The others shot back by ridiculing the Mormon boys' naivete, their health code, their virginity before marriage. The LDS soldiers didn't return the jeering. They just moved closer to the fire.

Just one figure sat in no-man's land between the two factions—Todd Barlow of Colorado City, Arizona, a polygamist. He was the man who had helped Alex in his plan to bring Ben's kids across the Arizona/Utah border. Todd was torn, as he often was, between the two world views. He sat silent. He didn't want to say anything that might betray the fact that he came from his father's third wife of four, or that he had seven children back home by his own two wives. Suddenly he found Bobby Whitmer bounding up and plopping down next to him.

"The name's Scooter," Bobby said heartily shaking his hand.

"Mine's Todd. Todd Barlow. Where you from?"

"Cedar City."

"Hey, that's not too far from me. Colorado City."

"You a Mormon?" Bobby asked.

"Not quite. It's a long story," Todd said reaching down to get a drink from his canteen. "Probably one you wouldn't like hear told, since I assume you are a Mormon."

Suddenly Bobby remembered that polygamists dominated Colorado City and laughed. "Never mind, man, I understand." As their conversation continued, they searched for common places and people they knew.

"You wouldn't happen to know anyone from LaVerkin, would you?" Todd asked.

"Not quite LaVerkin, but close. Do you know where Pah Tempe is?"

Todd's face lighted up. "Alex Dubik?"

"Yeah! Alex!" Bobby almost cheered. The two talked into the night about the people at Pah Tempe. Even though it had only been a little over two weeks, Bobby felt like he'd been gone for years and was hungry for news. And when he heard that Todd was involved in the rescue of Ben's kids, he hung on to every detail of his friends' exploits.

"Hey, when this is over, I'll give you a lift back home," Todd volunteered. "I drove my truck to Reno and left it with a cousin of mine."

And so the two kept close together in the days ahead–grotesque and triumphant days–in which many of the men died that had lain against trees that night outside of Grass Valley. In fact, Donner Pass proved to be just as deadly to the troops as it had to those pioneers trying to make it to California too late in the season 160 years or so earlier.

It was far deadlier, however, for the Chinese. It was not so much the snowstorms that caused the Chinese war machine to sputter and stall; it was the fact that they were cut off from supplies. Hungry, cold, out of ammunition and broken in spirit, they were just a skeleton of an army by the time the fighting had reached the decisive battle of Truckee in which over 22,000 Chinese troops either died or were captured. The combined UWEN/US forces, on the other hand, lost 4,876 with another 9,328 wounded.

And Bobby, now sick to death of fighting, was sent home with a bullet embedded in his rib cage. He drove back with Todd, only to find that his uncle and the Pah Tempe tribe had disappeared, so he was taken by the Mormon underground to his grandparents, Elder Whitmer and his wife, Dorothy, hiding on a ranch outside of Kamas. There he joined the four younger Winders, whose mother decided they were too much to care for while she started a new life with the younger, handsome and definitely blue-eyed Dan Magleby. This Solitude ski instructor was a noted womanizer, but Laurie was certain she would be more than enough for him, now that they were wed.

For Ben the trip across New Mexico was a frustrating one–he wanted to get back to the plates, but Peg was very tired and frightened about fallout, so he drove. He didn't tell her what the new plate had hinted at, but he did share with her that whenever he turned his attention to the translation, he felt Sangay's presence. He swore sometimes he could even hear the rustle of his robe or see a flash of saffron fabric out of the corner of his eye.

And it wasn't until he was the only one awake in the early dawn hours of the next day, that guilt descended on him like an acid bath. *What was I thinking about reading the plates out of order? How could I lie to my son? To my own dear wife? Am I so blindly ambitious? What an egotist!*

He tried practicing his breathing technique, made low melodic mantra sounds, and finally quieted down–for a few minutes. Then the inner assault began again. *How I was ever able to read on in the plates was just a fluke. God is going to severely punish me for this, I just know it.* On and on like that for miles and miles.

It was nearly sunset (another brilliantly red and pink one) as the four cars kicked up a dust cloud on their way down the rutted road to Puerto de Luna (the locals called it PDL). Ben smiled to see the juniper trees mixed with yucca and mesquite. They reminded him of the drive to the St. George temple and his time with Sangay. He was grateful to be at the end of his sentence of miserable guilt which he had stirred up for himself the last two hundred miles.

Peg stared out across the muddy Pecos River at the small farms spaced at odd intervals. The only good land for growing alfalfa, chiles, corn and cantaloupe was along this river bank. Here in the Pecos Valley fruit trees, now bare, would blossom to produce pears, apples, plums, even peaches in a good year. Cottonwood trees, just beginning to give birth to dark buds, lined the banks of the river. At the southern end of the valley, between two tall mesas, came the glow of the moon about to rise over the cliffs. "You know that man I talked to in the restaurant in Santa Rosa?" Peg asked Ben.

"Uh, huh."

"Well, he told me how this little place got its name." She looked to him to see if he was interested in hearing the tale. He was looking out at the clumps of field hands standing together talking and pointing at the four cars.

Danny leaned up and hooked his arms over the seat and around Peg's neck. "I want to hear, Mom," he said. Delighted that he had taken to calling her that, she kissed his arm. He pulled it away and wiped it off in mock disgust.

"Looks like we're expected," Ben said distractedly. Peg remained silent, so he glanced over at her. "Hey, honey, I do want to know about this place. How did it get its name?"

So Peg continued, "Well, years ago people used to call this place El Puerto de la Luna or de Los Lunas," she said in her school teacher voice. "Many early Spanish and Mexican settlers, maybe going back to Coronado, believed that the moon passed through that point or door," she said pointing to the glow above the mesa at the end of the road, "as it passed on its way westward. It looks like we've come on a good night to see it pass through the gateway."

Ben, whose Spanish had improved greatly during a four-year stint teaching English at the University of Costa Rica, asked rather gingerly, "Shouldn't that be Las Lunas—not Los Lunas, honey? I think the noun 'lunas' needs the feminine article, 'las.'" He had been trying hard lately not to use his book learning in any way that would even seem to diminish Peg. He had done that with Linda for many years and had anguished when he heard about Linda's death, fearing that his constant put-downs contributed to her heart failure. Now he valued this precious wife and friend whose tenderness to him was so constant, so genuine, and so unlike Linda.

"No, it shouldn't," she replied, beaming back at Ben like a jokester who, alone, knows the punchline. "They called it that because there were two groups who settled this part of the States, the vaqueros, who were some of the original cowboys roaming the *llano* or plains, and the farmers whom the *vaqueros* called Los Lunas because they followed the moon's cycles in everything they did." Peg put her hands together and smiled. "So, see, it should be 'los', because they are talking about men, my dear." She leaned back, turned to Danny, and gave him a conspiratorial wink.

They were interrupted by the loud barking of at least a dozen dogs chasing after the slow-moving vehicles. Miriam began to cry, but Ben soothed her with, "Hey, honey, don't cry. It's just our welcoming committee. They're just super happy to see us."

She looked out cautiously at the dogs whose tails were wagging furiously. "Okay, Daddy, but I want you to get out first." Ben laughed and squeezed her knee.

Peg, determined to finish, quickly added, "Anyway, to finish this little story, the settlers here worshipped the moon, in their way, even though they were Catholics."

Danny pointed out the window at the people gathering near adobe houses. Even though they knew that the villagers had been expecting them, the Pah Tempe group was a little unnerved when everyone stopped work to gawk at the newcomers as they drove in a slow processional parallel to the Pecos. At the end of the road, the apostles turned their car away from the river, onto a long tree-lined drive that led to a large adobe home out near the mesas. The other three drivers followed suit. But before they could stop and get out, Elder Dawahoya had disappeared into the house, with Elder Stewart a few steps behind.

"Where are we exactly?" Danny asked, the grouch creeping into his voice.

"Yeah," Miriam chimed in, matching Danny's mean voice inflection. "Is this where we're going to live?"

"No," Peg said steadily. "This is just the last place we're going to stop before we get there. We're going to be here just a few days." She looked out over the bare, brown fields freshly plowed and suddenly found herself caught up in a sweep of nostalgia for the sugar beet fields of southern Idaho.

"We're just following what the apostles have told us to do," Ben said trying not to get testy. "And that's what we as a family will always do. Right, guys?"

"I guess so," Danny said looking glumly at the spot on the ground where he was grinding his heel.

"I guess so," Miriam echoed her brother.

"That's great, troops, because that's the way we are Jesus' special helpers!" Ben knew his gaiety was a little forced, but he was determined that this message lodge itself deep into the children's minds, and he did not want to color it for the children with his present fatigue. He was tired, hungry and ready to stay somewhere for awhile.

"Well, I want to be in my own bed, go to my own school and play with my friends," Danny responded with a definite whine in his voice.

Ben took a very deep breath and ground his teeth. He was searching for something to say when he was rescued by Peg who said, "Oh, look!"

The children turned as she pointed to the house. Elder Dawahoya was emerging with a small, white-haired man who, though he shuffled from age, dazzled them with an enormous, nearly toothless smile and a large circular wave of his bony arm. "They want us to come in. You guys, be nice when we get in there, okay?" she asked.

"Okay, Mom," the two said. "We'll try."

The man who waved was Brother Hugo Martinez, patriarch

of the Santa Rosa Stake. The oldest living member in the area, he and Elder Dawahoya were long-time friends. Martinez and his wife, Inocencia, had played host to several visiting authorities over the years. But this request from the Brethren to hide important fugitives from Interpol excited them as nothing had in recent years.

Ben slowly opened the car door and gently shoved back the cold-nosed dogs who tried to get into the car. His plaid shirttail hung out of the back of his jeans. As he opened Miriam's back door and pulled her into his arms, the dogs jumped up and his glasses slipped down until they were nearly off his nose. Miriam stiffened, but when Ben laughed as he began wading through the mangy greeting committee, she relaxed and clung to him without complaint. Meanwhile Angelina barked wildly from the back of the Jeep Wagoneer.

They walked into a courtyard complete with a tinkling fountain. Peg held onto Danny's hand with one hand while she licked her other hand and tried to paste down his cowlick. No success, so she turned her attention to the Martinez' house. She instantly loved the blue and yellow-tiled walls and cobbled floor. Ben turned to smile at Nate who had walked up behind him. The two men slapped each other on the back. "We made it!" Nate exulted.

"We sure did, buddy," Ben exulted. "We sure did."

The party of sixteen–road-weary, dusty and hungry–clacked across the entryway into a spacious living room filled with large pieces of mahogany furniture, black velvet paintings in ornate gold frames and at least thirty wrought-iron candelabras complete with tall white candles scattered on tables around the room.

Brother Martinez gestured to them to continue on into the large dining room dominated by a twelve-foot-long mahogany table. As the group took their seats in high-backed carved chairs, he called out to the kitchen, *"Niñas, ahorita!"* and several young girls, his granddaughters, emerged carrying glasses of milk and cookies. Brother Martinez's English was never that good, but he managed to convey his delight that they had come. While the group warmed themselves in the company of this charming old man and his shy wife, Nate and Ben stepped outside to speak with the apostles.

"We've arranged for each family unit to stay with one of the LDS families in the community," Elder Stewart said.

"The only Latter-day Saint families," Elder Dawahoya said laughing. "Ben, you and your family will stay here with Brother Martinez. Nate, you and your kids will stay with the widow Cordova. She raised twelve children and joined the Church just last year at age 79. You'll enjoy her, I promise."

Elder Stewart picked up the conversation. "The Rivers' along with Peter Butler will stay with a young Anglo couple, the Reynolds, who moved here from Los Angeles a few years ago. The Dubiks, well, we've decided to have them stay with Señora Flores. She's not LDS, but my guess is that she and Grace Ihimaera will hit it off. She knows everything about herbs and is a trained midwife. She's delivered many of the children around here. This is just in case Moira goes into labor while you're here."

While Nate talked about a few personal matters with Elder Stewart, Ben pulled back mentally to take in what had just happened. Here were very busy, important men with huge responsibilities on their shoulders, yet they were taking time to see that each family was well-cared for. They could have delegated this problem, but they didn't. In his mind, he saw the Savior kneeling on the floor, head bent, dipping a towel into a worn basin—then washing Peter's large and calloused feet despite the apostle's protests. *To be the servant to all people*, Ben thought pensively. *I've got to work on that.*

The Pah Tempe tribe barely had a day to settle in when they were asked to help with spring planting, starting with alfalfa and hay. For most of them, it was a refreshing novelty—hard work, but a diversion from their worries about Interpol and a shattering world. Even though it was now unseasonably warm, in the high 70's, it had been a normal winter, and the Pecos ran swift and muddy on its way to the Rio Grande.

In the middle of planting, the apostles left. They said they would be back soon. But they didn't return. After a few days, Ben asked Brother Martinez if he knew where they had gone. He just shrugged and said, "I don't know. The ways of God are not the ways of man." Ben was disappointed and it showed. He had expected this wise old man, this "Sabio," to be able to give him at least a clue to the apostles' whereabouts.

Brother Martinez grinned his toothless grin, put his brown, wrinkled hand on Ben's shoulder and said, *"Escuchame. El Señor sabe todo. No te preocupas, mi hijo. No te preocupas."* (Listen to me. The Lord knows all. Don't you worry, my son. Don't you worry.) Ben put his hand over that gnarly and comforting hand on his shoulder. Comforted, he said, *"Gracias, abuelo."*

One night, a week later, after a long day in the fields, the group gathered at the Martinez's house. After dinner, the Pah Tempe men sat around on old overstuffed couches and chairs on the back porch. They were happy to be alone in each other's company. Squeals of laughter and high-pitched shouts of the kids playing in the large front yard filled them with contentment. It was dusk. The air was filled with the rich smell of newly-turned earth. Sipping lemonade, they talked of Pah Tempe, Bishop Olson, the solar car conversion, but not the bombing or the war on the West Coast. It seemed unreal. And it would have seemed almost a sacrilege to mention that madness in the innocence of this village sanctuary. Then Alex asked in hushed tones, as if to guard a secret, "What can you tell me about Zion? What can we expect to happen?"

Trying hard not to betray his excitement, Ben answered evenly, "I'll need my scriptures for that," and sauntered back into the house until he was out of Alex's sight. At that point he took long, loping strides to get to the bedroom for his and Peg's scriptures. As he passed her on his return, Peg was talking animatedly with the Pah Tempe women around the dining room table. He leaned over to her and whispered in a conspiratorial voice, "Alex wants to talk about Zion." She broke into a grin and flashed him a two thumbs-up sign.

Back on the porch, Ben gave one of the books to Nate, who opened to *Doctrine and Covenants*, Section 45, and read, "And it shall be called the New Jerusalem, a land of peace, a city of refuge, a place of safety for the saints of the Most High God...." Nate, sunburned from the day's work in the sun, flushed even redder with the great emotion he felt as he read the passage.

"Just the Latter-day Saints?" Alex cut in.

"No, Al," Ben answered. "Listen. Let him finish the quote." He passed his book over to Alex and pointed to Verse 71.

Alex slipped on a pair of blue-rimmed reading glasses and followed along, 'And it shall come to pass that the righteous shall be gathered out from among all the nations, and shall come to Zion, singing with songs of everlasting joy.' "I don't hear any difference between one and the other–I mean, just who are the righteous?" Alex's tone was a mix of tentative irony and gentle concern.

Peter, in a stained work shirt and dirty jeans, took over. "Listen, mate, one of the early prophets said, 'Those who will not take up their sword to fight against their neighbor must flee to Zion for safety.' I take that to mean a lot more than just Mormons. There's goin' to be your Baptists and Catholics, Hindus, Buddhists. Everyone who's got some love of God."

Alex ran his hand over his mouth and nodded his head, "I see, and how is it that you guys all know these quotes?" he asked.

"Oh, it's the standard fare in Sunday School classes," Ben interjected.

"Well, I want to read more. Where do I start?" Alex asked, pushing his glasses to the top of his head.

Ben relinquished his *Book of Mormon*, which had pencil scribbling in every conceivable space and margin, and padded to the kitchen to get a glass of milk for his ulcer which had finally begun to heal. He came back in time to jump into a passionate discussion about what would have to happen to Jackson County for it to be free of its existing population. The men were evenly divided between nuclear war and natural disaster. But either way they felt sure that Brigham had said that the western boundary of the state of Missouri would be swept so clean that there would not be "left so much as a yellow dog to wag his tail."

As the days wore on, they worked side by side with the locals. Ben got a straw hat, grew a beard, and, because of his command of Spanish and quick wit, made friends with the residents like Juan Gallegos. Juan took to him at once, with that beautiful and tenacious warmth so characteristic of Hispanics. He helped Ben go back over what he had planted to realign a row or make deeper holes for seeds, since this was definitely not Ben's natural element.

The Pah Tempe tribe labored hard beside their new comrades for hours each day and waited for the apostles' arrival. By now everyone assumed they had returned to Utah to get instructions from the prophet and would come back with orders to move on at any time.

Ben did not get much translating done because he was sore and tired at the end of the day. But he figured the planting wouldn't last that much longer, and it seemed more important to plow and plant so they could eat. Now and again, though, he managed to shed his role as fledgling farmer and furtively return to translating the plates in the middle of the pile. A quiet library; a single, simple candle, its flame bright and still; his spirit calmed and set in order by the breathing that Sangay had taught him—"in, hold-two-three, out, hold-two-three"— these were all Ben needed. Soon, all that remained for Ben of Puerto de Luna was its pungent earth smells. The rest drifted away with each steady breath. Then the translator found himself whisked away to the ancient world of Tibetan lore.

Chapter Twenty-Four

Our birth is but a sleep and a forgetting:
Not in entire forgetfulness
And not in utter nakedness,
But trailing clouds of glory do we come
From God, who is our home.
"Intimations of Immortality," Wordsworth

That weekend, Peter and Jed went into Santa Rosa to get supplies and did not return when they had said they would. As the afternoon, then the evening wore on, everyone became quite worried. The Pah Tempe men decided if they weren't back by eight, they were going to town to look for them.

Grace, Moira and Jody sat in Rosa's small and crowded living room. Large mahogany pieces of furniture, too large for the space, ran together around each wall. A tall credenza behind the front door was loaded with framed photos of Rosa's large extended family. The dark red velvet curtains were half-closed.

"I couldn't handle it if anything happened to him," Jody lamented as she leaned into Grace's comforting embrace.

Grace ran her hands through the young woman's long brown hair. "Now, now," she cooed.

"And besides, I've missed at least one period."

Grace pushed her gently away and asked earnestly, "Really? How many?"

"Probably two, although the last one was due to come when we had the big shooting incident, so I don't know," Jody said looking to Grace like a child needing solace from a mother.

"Well, well," Grace said, again pulling Jody against her breast and crooning to her in Maori. "A baby born in the new land of Zion."

Jody relaxed and asked, "Where is he? Why isn't he home?" Looking off in the distance, Grace suddenly spoke in English. "You know, I don't think anything bad has happened to Jed–or at least nothing he can't handle."

Moira, sat in a nearby rocker, struggling with her first attempt at a crocheted baby blanket. She had finally come to look like she was pregnant now that she was eight months along with that round, flushed face look that settles in on mothers-to-be. She said in low, comforting voice, "You can trust Mother, Jody. She knows things. I can tell by the tone of her voice."

"I sure hope so," Jody said with a lump in her throat.

At 8:10, Nate, Ben and Alex headed for the Jeep Wagoneer with Angelina in tow. Just then the old brown station wagon bumped into sight. The three men stood stock still in the driveway, hoping Jed and Peter were not injured or bearers of bad news.

As the errant twosome crawled out of the car, the three men hurried toward them. They could see Peter daubing his head with paper napkins, while Jed waved and mumbled, "We got jumped."

"Where?" Alex asked alarmed, as he reached the driver's side of the car.

"Santa Rosa restaurant parking lot."

"I told you guys to mellow out about wanting to leave here," Ben said. "If you're not careful," he went on, turning to Peter, "you'll leave here as dog food, all neatly wrapped up in cellophane. I can just see the sticker on the package: 'Ground Aussie, $1.59 a pound!' And you," he said pointing to Jed, "round rump of redneck, same dang price!" Everyone burst into laughter.

Peter joined them, holding his side. "Hey, mate, don't make jokes. My side is killing me."

The five walked slowly back to the house, Jed and Peter describing the scene as it had unfolded. It seemed the two had decided to stop to buy dinner and hang around in town. It was Saturday night and they were a little stir crazy, having been farmers now for two weeks. Someone must have heard them in the restaurant talking about the Sabbath or sacrament meeting, they weren't sure. But before they reached their car in the darkened parking lot, they were met by ten locals, armed with tire irons and sticks, whose breaths betrayed the fact they had been pounding down drinks all evening.

Jed and Peter jumped into the car and tried to gun it out of the parking lot, but the ruffians had blocked the entrance with a large pickup truck. Trapped, Jed and Peter watched as the men gathered around the car, pounding on the hood. They proceeded to beat on the windshield and broke a side window. It was at that point that Jed and Peter kicked into action, being scrappers themselves. (Jed had spent two years as a Navy Seal and Peter was a third-degree black belt.)

"We got our licks in," Peter crowed. "Jed, here, he's all right."

"Those bozos aren't going to be shouting anti-Mormon slogans any time soon."

"Was anyone badly hurt?" Nate asked worriedly.

"Nah, don't you worry none. They're just local boys checking us out," Peter said daubing at his head. "They won't mess with us again. We've made our point."

"And what might that be?" Ben asked.

"That Mormons ain't no wimps," Jed said, moaned and reached for his jaw. He opened his mouth slowly and wiggled at a loose molar.

"Jeddy here, though, is in a little need of some dental work," Peter said. "Oh, sorry about the car, Benjy," he added, lightly touching the wound on his temple. "I'll make it right first thing tomorrow, promise."

Ben put an arm around his shoulder and said, "Hey, you big dummy, I'm just glad you survived." The men had now arrived in the courtyard. As soon as Jody heard their footsteps echoing on the tile, she flew to the door to embrace Jed and pull him into the house to nurse him. Peter's minor wounds were cared for in an excessively emotional fashion by Sister Martinez, while Brother Martinez apologized again and again for the Santa Rosa men's behavior. Having neither wife nor child, Peter had up to now felt like the odd man out--as he often did around his fellow Mormons with their large families. But now, in his newly emerging role as the group's mechanical whiz-kid and all-purpose body guard, he felt more at one with the Pah Tempe gang, more a member of the communal family.

The very next day another vehicle came bouncing down the dusty, pot-hole infested road, escorted by the caravan of mongrel dogs. The apostles had returned. It was as the group had guessed: the men had gone to see the prophet in hiding to receive further instructions. The apostles wasted no time putting those orders into action. They first called Nate from the fields and talked with him privately in the Martinez' library. They told him of Laurie's marriage, the health of his children. Then they called and set him apart to be branch president of the newly formed Puerto de Luna Branch. His first duty was to see that Ben's children were baptized.

"Why are you doing this? Organizing this branch?" he asked puzzled by their news. "I thought we're only here for a short spell."

Elder Dawahoya smiled and reassured him the Lord wanted this done. In the course of further conversation Nate learned that the prophet was seriously ill and it looked like the President of the Quorum of Twelve, A. Lawrence Ueda, would become the next president before too long. Both the apostles and Nate expressed their satisfaction with him as their future leader. "It's about time we had a non-North American leading the Church," Nate said.

Next they called for Peter, who thought for sure they had heard about the fight in Santa Rosa, but they wanted to call him to be their assistant and travel with them as a mechanic and security guard. Peter felt a thrill of electricity run through his bruised body. What an honor to guard the apostles on their momentous journeying! History had touched Peter Butler. The Lord had touched Peter Butler, and Peter Butler knew it.

In his patriarchal blessing, which he had received ten years earlier, it said, "You will be called on a mission for the Lord which will not now be revealed. If you prove faithful, you will be called up to help the Lord using your great creative gifts." Even as a boy in Queensland, before Peter found the fullness of the gospel, he loved New Testament accounts of the Savior's life. He would push off on his homemade catamaran, sail up the Great Barrier Reef with its diaphanous, turquoise waters, and fantasize that Christ would get out of a sailboat and walk across the water. He'd call to him, arms outstretched, inviting the fourteen-year-old to walk out onto the waters. In his reverie, Peter would jump out of his boat and slosh eagerly to his Master. And now, here, of all places, in a little farming town in some dusty corner of New Mexico, the call had finally come.

"Brother Butler, can you be ready tomorrow morning? We'll be leaving again at six a.m."

"No worries, Elder Dawahoya. I travel light," Peter said beaming and shaking the apostle's hand vigorously.

Their next act was to call for Ben and Peg Taylor. Nate passed them on the way back to the fields and told him of his call. "I'll bet you're going to be called to be high priest leader and Relief Society president," he said. "Peg, better dust off your Jello mold and casserole recipes," he joked. Peg punched him playfully in the arm. But that was not what the two tired apostles had in mind. Ben and Peg sat down across the desk, trying to scrape mud from under their fingernails and sweaty dirt from their faces. Elder Dawahoya looked pointedly at them for a long moment before asking, "Brother Taylor, how's the translating going?"

Ben hung his head. "Slow. I've just been so tired...."

Elder Stewart cut him off with a wave of his hand. "We thought that might be the case. The prophet sends his greetings and is quite interested in this translating project, as you can imagine."

Ben's face turned red and he gulped. Are they going to ask what I've found? Am I going to have to confess my poking around where I probably wasn't supposed to be?

"And so," Elder Stewart continued, ignoring Ben's squirming discomfort, "he has asked us to call both of you to full-time translation."

Peg's head shot up and she let out a small gasp. "Both of us?"

"Yes, Sister Taylor, both of you." Elder Dawahoya looked at

her with great love and care. She noticed, as Ben had, how the Hopi apostle's eyes looked like fathomless, dark pools. "We want you to act as scribe. There is certainly a precedent for it in Emma Smith."

Peg couldn't speak. Ben reached over and tenderly took her hand.

"Ben," Elder Stewart said, "we've spoken to the Martinez family and they have volunteered their library here for that purpose. We want you out of the fields and back to work on this most important project." Elder Stewart's emphasis on the "most" gave Peg goose bumps.

"We'll start this very morning, sir," Ben said solemnly.

"Great. And, oh yes, Sangay Tulku sends his greetings."

Ben brightened. "Please tell him I think about him all the time and that he's always in our prayers."

There was only one more official call–that of Sister Martinez as Relief Society President. The apostles spent private time with everyone else. Ben and Peg guessed that the apostles had told everyone about the translation project, because no one said a word when they didn't return to the planting that day.

Jody was asked to be an unofficial school teacher to Miriam and Danny while their parents worked, since she was caring for her baby anyway. And Jed was to teach Nate's teenagers about survival tactics and medicine.

Grace spent a long time in the library alone with the two general authorities. She emerged with a face bright with obvious spiritual pleasure, and the men blessed Alex and Moira before they left. It seemed that this small group of Latter-day Saints was being primed for their calling into Zion, but the time had not yet come. Nate said it reminded him of the children of Israel's wandering the desert as spiritual preparation. Ben laughed and said he hoped it wasn't going to be any forty years. At that rate he'd be long past his prime and he'd have to give up hope for several young nubile wives.

Spring rushed into a very hot, very early summer, and it came time for Moira to give birth to her son, Adam. It was just after sunrise on June 11th, Moira awoke to the songs of mockingbirds and to cramping. As she started to get out of bed to go to the bathroom, her water broke. Her cry brought Alex, then Grace from the other room. "Today's the day. I told you he couldn't wait for your birthday," Grace kidded her daughter gently. Moira's birthday was two weeks away.

Grace didn't want to wake Rosa just yet. She usually rose at six anyway as Grace knew, for the two older women had spent the early part of the previous day walking in the hills, one carrying a shovel, the other a gunny sack. In that early morning renewal of earth and sky, they searched for fresh herbs to assist in the birthing. Grace and Rosa were amazed to find how similar were their approaches to plants, to children and to many other sacred duties saved for the older woman in a tribe. Grace tried to explain to Rosa that she thought they might have Lamanite ancestors in common. A storm cloud washed over Rosa's face–she would hear nothing of it and crossed herself. Nonetheless the two women formed a deep bond of respect. Each wished they spoke the other's language well, rather than using English as a second language. Grace told Rosa they would have to wait for the pure Adamic tongue to be blood sisters.

Before digging up a prickly plant growing in the damp arroyo, Grace said reverently, "Thank you. You will be good medicine for my Iwi." She smelled the roots, then held the plant to the newly rising sun to examine it before gently placing it in the sack.

Rosa, a plain Hispanic woman in her 60s with narrow black eyes and quick smile, knew where every plant grew. Peg said she reminded her of the gypsy woman in her dream. That day she was out looking for an especially potent plant, yerba del manso, which would help stanch the bleeding if there was any hemorrhaging after the baby came. She panted as she waddled in a black dress and white apron, leaning over plant after plant. She would pinch off a leaf and taste it for potency. Finally she spoke quietly to a healthy-looking light green plant with smooth leaves, then indicated to Grace she wanted the shovel. "This one

is a good one," Rosa said as she pushed her black boot down on the
shovel and pulled gently at the plant. Grace nodded in
agreement.

Now, on the morning of the birth, Rosa emerged from her
stark room–adobe walls painted white, dark-beamed ceiling, bed
with dark wood headstead and white comforter, and a large
crucifix on the far wall. "I dreamed we will have a baby boy
today," the rumpled matron said, yawning and running her
finger over her teeth, before Grace could inform her about the
water breaking.

"And you are surely correct," Grace beamed and wrapped her
green shawl around her bodice.

"Bueno, this is a good day for a baby to be born. All the signs
are good."

The two women worked unobtrusively around the birthing
scene as Moira's contractions grew more intense and shorter in
duration. Alex, whose stomach was so knotted he could not eat,
was soothed by their maternal movements. They had decided
that Grace would supervise the delivery of the baby, as she had
so many of her offspring, with Alex catching his son as his head
crowned.

It wasn't until the sun had gone down in a blaze of glory and
the full moon stood at the port of the sky that Adam Iharaira
Dubik made his entrance into the world. He emerged quietly,
staring intently first into his father's flushed, exuberant visage,
then into his grandmother's brown eyes, and finally into his
mother's wondering face. Everyone waited for the blood to stop
coursing through the throbbing, electric blue-purple cord and the
placenta to be flushed out to end his miraculous journey–a
journey that was nearly disrupted in its fifth month.

Afterwards, Rosa carefully wrapped the afterbirth in tissue
and laid it on a small altar in the bedroom–an altar on which
Alex had placed the small statue of the boy and his collie dog.
She crossed herself and quietly gave thanks to the Virgin Mary
for her friend's grandson. She prayed for the Holy Mother's
protection of this baby who was born into such a mad world.

Alex, a little shaky, stood up from the straw-backed chair next to the bed, where he had sat rubbing his wife's back for the last four hours of labor. He reluctantly left a room vibrating with the energy of new life to go outside and shout the news of Adam's birth. A great hurrah rose from nearby houses. Porch lights came on and people poured out into the brightly moonlit night, arms filled with fruits or vegetables or small colorfully wrapped gifts. Most people knew that Alex had lost his fortune right after the bomb in Alaska had been dropped and the international market bottomed out. The UWEN closed down access to foreign bank accounts, and the Dubiks were suddenly quite poor. Alex had dealt with his new Spartan circumstances gracefully, and the village admired him for it. Now they crowded into Rosa's small sitting room and waited impatiently for the presentation of the *niño*.

Beaming, Alex emerged through the curtain dividing the living area from the kitchen with the small blue bundle held awkwardly in the crook of his arm. "*Mi amigos, my hijo!*" he announced proudly in his pidgin Spanish, holding his son up in the palm of his right hand. As the crowd said their Ahh's and Ohh's, one old woman pulled dirt from the field from a small sack. She reached out and crossed Adam's forehead with it. Alex didn't mind, but it seemed that Adam did, and for the first time he began to cry.

Everyone laughed as a loud wail from the Lord's future warrior pierced the night air.

"Boy, he's got strong lungs," Jody said and kissed Alex on the cheek. "Jed and I are going to have another one, I think," she whispered.

"Congratulations, Jody! I highly recommend it," Alex said laughing lightly. He, who had become a favorite of this tight knit community, then kissed all the brown-skinned women who gathered around him and whispered, "*Gracias,*" in their ears. He hugged the farmers with one arm and said in heroic, comic Spanish what they meant to him. They laughed and slapped him on the back and filed out back into the night. Then, with a lump in his throat, Alex disappeared with his son back to the wide bed, the soiled sheets now changed by nurturing, shadowy grandwomen. Moira lay propped up on powder-blue pillows. Her dark unbraided hair splayed out like undulating chocolate water. She was pale but exuberant. Tenderly the couple moved to form a half shell around their precious pearl.

Jed went to the ham radio and called Clinton Rasmussen in Cedar City, who was now the church's contact person for the Brethren. The Puerto de Luna community had decided to pull the plug on all media except for the ham radio. If the Chinese arrived or a bomb was dropped on them, they didn't want any advance warning. They just wanted to live from day to day—"*paso a paso.*" Jed provided them with daily briefings, when they wanted them. Now it was his turn to send a joyful message to the Brethren and Sangay that the Dubik's son was out and healthy.

But the message he heard in return was a sour one. Although the Chinese had been routed out of the West Coast, the intelligence community reported a disturbing trend worldwide. Many of the terrorist groups had interpreted the nuclear bombing in Alaska as a green light to do the same. The UWEN had acted as a strict and punishing father, to which the world community had given its allegiance in the name of social order and prosperity. But now the father had done the unthinkable. He had killed his own children. Power crazy warlords now saw their chance to challenge the morally weakened paternal figure.

One particularly disturbing figure, Dmitri Gornstein, a rabidly patriotic and paranoid Ukrainian, had began rallying forces in northwestern Afghanistan for a march across Eastern Europe and down into Israel. Gornstein, a small, wiry Russian Jew on his mother's side, had spent a lifetime disavowing his mother and her ways. A twisted and tortured logic led him to the bizarre conclusion that the way to be "cleansed" of his Jewishness was to destroy the Holy Land. He'd made his intentions known as a media attention grabber over the years, but the UWEN, judging Gornstein a light-weight and unwilling to dignify him and his ragtag terrorists with a response, left him alone, fully expecting his improbable group to self-destruct within a year or two.

A Russian colonel, Gornstein had stayed behind when the Russians invaded Afghanistan some twenty years earlier. And what he stayed behind to do was to form an alliance of disenfranchised Russian soldiers and so-called freedom fighters from neighboring countries. He had done his homework and lined up arms, bombs and maniac men with nothing to lose. With a rallying cry of "Down with tyranny," he and his fanatic friends began their bloody march.

After a victory in Turkey–which caught every major strategist at UWEN headquarters off guard–Gornstein's forces swelled like a sudden spring torrent, fed by currents of the disaffected (from Bosnian peasants to Iraqi intellectuals) and began to wash like a flash flood towards Jerusalem. That's what Rasmussen had to report to Jed, who didn't want to tell it to anyone. It sounded too close to Biblical prophecies about Armageddon. He wanted to take his wife, baby and friends and plunge on into Zion. But it didn't exist. Not yet.

August–time for harvesting what had become a bumper crop. The unanticipated summer rains and the strange humid heat that followed produced beautiful fruit from both fields and orchards. People worried about high radiation dosages, but it appeared that there, in New Mexico, they had escaped most of the effects of the fallout. Pickup trucks droned as they moved from field to waiting barns. Villagers put out apples to dry in the sun, along with chiles. The women boiled vats of tomatoes, pears and peaches for canning. Sweet jellies stuck to the small jars labeled and cooled in the shade outside many of the houses. Corn was ground into meal, and hay and alfalfa were harvested for the cattle and sheep as had been done for centuries.

Near the end of this laborious, yet satisfying ingathering,

Miriam reported she'd seen a man down near a large cottonwood tree near the banks of the river–a white man she'd never seen before.

"How was he dressed?" Peg asked nervously.

"I don't know. Pants, and ah, a white shirt," Miriam said casually.

"Did he hurt you?" Ben was more to the point.

"No, I told you, Daddy, he was very nice and he talked to me about rock n' roll."

Peg pulled Ben aside. "We're not getting anywhere here. I know she isn't prone to making up stories. Maybe we haven't given her the attention she needs lately. We really have been preoccupied with the translation project."

Danny, who'd begun to look very healthy with a dark tan, came in the bedroom and guessed from the position that Miriam had assumed on the bed (arms crossed with a pout on her face) that his parents were interrogating her again. He immediately guessed what it was about and decided to come clean. "I saw him, too," he said in low tone.

Ben and Peg whirled around. Ben tried not to sound angry when he said, "Why didn't you tell us that before? You've got half this community locking their doors thinking there's some kind of crazy guy creeping around in the bushes."

"When I saw that you didn't believe Miriam...." Danny cried.

Immediately Ben knelt down and pulled his son into his arms. "I'm sorry, pal. I really am. I just get really protective of you guys."

Danny sniffled then said, "I think he was an angel."

Peg now knelt down beside Ben, "An angel, honey?"

"Well, first he wasn't at all dirty to be climbing around down near the river. Even his shoes weren't dirty. And second, I believed him. He had such a nice face and he knew my name."

"Did he also talk about rock and roll?" Ben strained to keep calm.

"Well, kinda. He told me the earth was going to rock and roll, but he was talking about a giant earthquake."

Ben sat back on his heels. "Ah, hah, well, at least that makes sense." He shuffled on his knees over to the bed and said to Miriam. "Sweetheart, I'm sorry for doubting you."

Miriam reached out and ruffled the fringe around the bald spot on his head. "That's okay, Daddy. You had to be there." The family shared a relieved laugh for the first time in days. Then the import of the news hit both the adults. Peg pulled Miriam's sun-bleached hair back behind her ears and asked, "An angel?"

Ben again remembered that passage in Joel, "Your young men shall see visions...."

"I knew you were special, all along," Peg said hugging her children to her breast. She whispered to them, "An angel. Can you believe it?" The family looked out across the river at the round yellow bundles of hay set in the amber fields. Ben, still a little doubtful, wondered why the children would have an appearance and not he or Peg. If it had really happened, it was (he decided) because the children needed to be comforted and assured about the terrible days that were surely bearing down on them all.

A day later, Brother Martinez awoke with a very vivid dream about a massive earthquake. It was disturbing enough to wake him at 4:23 a.m. Then, as was his custom when he had dreams about the last days, he put on his bathrobe and slippers, went to his large oak desk, turned on a small Tiffany lamp and wrote down the vivid, cataclysmic scene of great destruction in his journal. He carefully noted the date, August 26, looked up scriptural references in his well-worn black leather *Bible* and matching *Book of Mormon*, and placed those notes next to the entry, in small, neat Spanish. Then he locked the journal with a key he wore around his neck and opened the drawer quietly next to his bed.

"One of the benefits of being a patriarch," he muttered to himself as he placed the journal under two other books for safekeeping, "is that the Lord lets you dream His dreams...so long as you keep them safe and to yourself." Inocencia snored softly next to him as he took off the worn maroon robe and lay back down. But he couldn't sleep. He knew his dreams well enough to know this was about to happen, and it was just around the corner.

Later that hot afternoon, a certain eeriness filled the air. The sky filled with large, dark, threatening clouds. Dust devils spun like errant tops on both sides of the river. People left off the last bit of harvesting and gathered around their homes. It felt like a giant finger had drawn a low pressure cell on a weather map directly overhead. And a good thousand miles away in southeastern Missouri, in the middle of the North American Plate, on a fault line that ran from Arkansas northeast toward southern Illinois, the first of the great tremors hit at 4:23 p.m. local time.

Chapter Twenty-Five

And in that day shall be heard of wars,
And rumors of wars, and the whole earth
Shall be in commotion,
And men's hearts shall fail them,
And they shall say that Christ delayeth
His coming until the end of the earth.
Doctrine and Covenants 45:26

The earth trembled for only a few seconds underneath the feet of the folks in El Puerto, but it was enough to cause the bell in St. Rose of Lima, the 17th century adobe church, to clang abruptly several times–as if the dead were being peremptorily summoned to some invisible Mass. The storm which had hovered ominously moved on eastward toward Texas without the expected hailstorm. And then it was quiet–in New Mexico.

But this first quake, that registered 8.5 on the Richter scale, was felt from Denver to Detroit, even to Boston, Houston and Charleston, South Carolina some thousand miles away. Cities like St. Louis, Little Rock, and Memphis lost thousands of buildings, and hundreds of thousands of the people perished.

There were reported sightings of eerie flashes like lightning as the earthquake tossed cars off highways. Geysers of sand and coal dust gushed from the ground for miles around. At the epicenter in New Madrid, Missouri, great crevices, like subterranean beasts with diabolical hunger, opened up. Homes, cars, and trees were swallowed whole. The entire region around there was covered with either sand a foot deep or waters from the Mississippi River. All up and down the river, the banks collapsed, islands disappeared, and waves swamped river traffic.

All this was reported to Jed on the ham radio in his bedroom, along with the fact that the quake registered 8.5. Jed remembered from a geology class he had taken in college that an 8.5 quake would have almost a billion times the magnitude of a mild quake of 2.0. A billion times greater! He suddenly felt like he was going to faint. He quickly put his head down on the table in front of the now-crackling radio until the room stopped spinning. Then, after taking several deep breaths, he sat up, slapped his knee and said, "Okay. Thy will be done, Lord." He flipped off the radio switch, said into the silence, "Gotta tell the guys," then headed for the front door.

The first person he met was Alex, who was coming by for his work gloves. Alex, who now adopted a simple wardrobe of Levi shirt and jeans, took the news calmly, but by the time he had walked over to the Martinez' house to convey the news to Ben and Peg, he'd become very agitated. "It's starting to happen," Alex said in an awe-tinged voice as he stood in the entryway. "It really is. The end is near!" He had begun to read everything about the last days that his LDS friends gave him. He was making his way through Brother Martinez's library, reading everything there in English about prophecy. Ben kidded Alex that he was becoming a Zionophile.

"Al, it reminds me of what Yeats wrote in "The Second Coming," '...The center cannot hold...,'" Ben said putting his arm around Peg and drawing her close. "Want to come in and talk about it?"

"Nope, I've got to go tell Grace," Alex said turning around to leave. "She and Rosa are just headed home from herb collecting. I saw them down the road."

Ben and Peg sat and stared out into the courtyard for awhile. Ben played with a pearl ring on Peg's right hand. Peg asked in a worried voice, "Ben, sweetheart, who was it that wrote about how the Saints would begin to think in the last days that the Lord had abandoned them? Begging Him to return soon? I think I remember He answers them that even though nursing mothers might forget their children, he would never forget them. Who wrote that? Do you recall?"

"That was Isaiah, honey. It's also in First Nephi, Chapter 21, I think." Ben looked out at the shimmering sunset and his voice grew a little husky as it always did when he recited scripture. "'Yea, they may forget thee, yet will I not forget thee, O house of

Israel. Behold, I have graven thee upon the palms of my hands; thy walls are continually before me."

The couple embraced silently and gently kissed each other's cheek. After a few soothing moments, they returned to the translating of Plate Nine which Alex had interrupted. It took Ben awhile to get tuned back in but he finally succeeded. He sat at the end of a large wooden table with the plate. The rest of the stack was covered with the silk cloth, off to the left. Pad in hand, Peg sat near him to his right in one of the high-backed wooden chairs. When the words formed in his head, he spoke slowly. Although Peg knew no shorthand, she was able to keep up. After a few minutes, Ben stopped. "You know, Peg, I heard from someone in town that thousands and hundreds of thousands of mice carrying the PDS virus are moving up the Mississippi."

"Yuck! How awful! Oh, I hate feeling so helpless," Peg said, throwing her hands to her cheeks. "Grace says these times are like the very last stage of childbirth, when your body is doing what it wants you to do. It's so spooky, absolutely nobody has any control."

Ben stared out of a long narrow window crossed by a black wrought-iron grill. Missy, Danny and Miriam were shouting to one another as they kicked a soccer ball across the lawn next door. Jody sat nearby with Craig in her lap. "When we get to Zion, this whole thing is going to change," he said in a low menacing voice. "No more Mr. Nice Guy, none of this being on the run. It's going to be ours!" Suddenly agitated, Ben left the window to pace the length of the library. "So many people have such a prettified picture of Jesus. What they don't know—or don't want to know—is that in addition to everything else, He is history's greatest revolutionary. He is going to create a society that is invincible, fair, and ...."

Redfaced, he shook a closed fist into the air, then wrapped his arms around his waist. Peg pushed back the chair, walked over to him and hugged him. "I know, sweetheart, I feel the same way."

Then out of the corner of his eye, Ben could see Alex loping back their way, so he untangled himself, went to the door and opened it without Alex having to knock. "Grace already knew," Alex said as he pulled off his boots at the door and laid them down on the red tile. "I didn't ask how. With her you never know." The two men walked into the library. Peg had returned to rewriting the last bit of dictation, but quickly slipped the plates into the knitting bag at her feet.

Alex stood at the end of the long table next to Ben, and said to the couple, "I came back to tell you I'm beginning to believe it. I really am."

Peg stood up and walked to Alex as if to embrace him. "Alex, how wonderful!"

Alex took a step back. "Maybe it's just because I want a place of refuge so bad. I don't know," he said.

Peg, not wanting to press him, smiled softly and came to rest beside Ben. Picking up on similar vibrations, Ben said circumspectly, "I can imagine you feel a real urgency now that you have Adam."

"Yeah, I do. It's changed my perspective a lot," Alex said. He walked to the window where Ben had stood and looked out. Then he whirled around to say, "You know, all that Joseph said—it fits together. I'm finding that it's really hard to dismiss him as a prophetic voice."

Inwardly, Ben was cheering like an avid fan whose team was two yards away from a Super Bowl victory, but outwardly he appeared calm. He knew his old Czech friend well enough to just let him talk. But Alex caught a slight smile at the corner of Ben's mouth and said, "Wipe that grin off your face, you young whippersnapper. I'm only telling you this, so long as you don't have any designs on dunking me in the Pecos, like you did your kids."

"Only at your request," Ben said bowing to his grey-maned friend, "*Para servirle*." Images rose in Ben's mind of Danny and Miriam in white clothing emerging from the shallow baptismal waters of the river.

That night, after the kids had gone to bed, Ben and Peg went back to the library to finish up Plate Nine. They worked until nearly two. "...and thus will the people of the most High God come into a place of hills ...uh...formed by His almighty hand." Ben sat back, stretched and rotated his head around on his neck. "I'm bushed, honey. Read that to me again, will you?"

Peg read back to him the account of the earth's upheavals, transfiguring the land, preparing it for the new Zion. "Do you ever get the feeling we're reading tomorrow's headlines?" Peg asked as she pulled her fuzzy blue robe more tightly around her bodice.

"That I do, sweetheart—with each verse! It's like having a 3,000-year-old newsmagazine." Ben rubbed his eyes with the palms of his hands. "Well, that finishes that." He yawned and stretched. "I wonder what's up next. I can't wait till we get to the section about the temple building and Christ's appearance there." Ben leaned over and kissed Peg on the cheek. "I love your curly hair."

"And I love your straight, balding hair," she laughed, reaching over to rub his bald spot. "I like to rub it for luck."

"Okay, enough of that," Ben said in mock anger. "Can you get that in a readable form by tomorrow? I think Joseph Romero is due in."

Peg said she could. As usual, the couple would send a sealed handwritten copy of the plate's text to Albuquerque with Romero, a trusted LDS trucker, who would pass it on to another LDS trucker, who would place it in the hands of the Brethren.

When am I going to tell her about the plates? Ben worried as he lay awake in the dark staring at the ceiling. *Maybe I won't. When we get to those plates, I'll pretend I haven't seen them.* He tossed and turned for a few minutes, but then he was gone—it never took very long for Ben to fall deeply asleep.

As Peg started to sleep, horrifying images of the dead and dying from the earthquake filled her mind. Unfortunately Jed had been quite graphic in his description of the catastrophe. Finally, when she had just dropped off about an hour later, she was awakened by the sound of clothes rustling. Thinking it was one of the kids, she rolled over and sat up. Sangay, replete in brilliant red, yellow and black patterned robes, a black hat crowned with green and yellow topknot, stood at the end of the four-poster bed.

"Sangay?" Peg couldn't believe her eyes. "Is that you?"

"Yes, dear Mrs. Taylor, it is Sangay Tulku, your humble servant." He bowed slightly.

Peg started to get out of bed. "I didn't know you were coming. I'll see where Sister Martinez wants to have you sleep."

But Sangay held up his hand. "There is no need to find me a bed, good Peg. I'm just here for a few moments."

"Okay," Peg said and sat back somewhat confused. "What's happening?"

"I can't get through to your stubborn husband who's decided only children can have supernatural visitors. Maybe if you wake him now, I can talk to both of you about the plates."

Peg, suddenly glassy-eyed, her mouth open, leaned over and shook her husband by the shoulder, all the while keeping her eyes glued to Sangay.

"What? What is it, Peg?" Ben grumbled. "I've got to get a good night's sleep. I told you that." He rolled over, pulled the covers up over his ears and started to snore again.

Sangay indicated she should try again. Peg threw up her hands in mock resignation, smiled sheepishly, then tried again. "Honey, someone is here to talk to you."

"Take a message," Ben mumbled, sounding now definitely annoyed.

"No, Ben, you don't understand. Sangay is here."

"What?" Ben threw off the shiny beige comforter and reached for his glasses on the small night table. "Where?"

Peg pointed to the end of the bed.

His mouth dropped open. "Sangay!" he exclaimed groggily. "What are you doing here?"

"Why aren't you practicing your meditation? I couldn't get through to you." The Tibetan rinpoche had a stern look on his face.

"Oh, geez, don't you get on me too," Ben said in a mock whine, knowing Sangay was half-teasing him. "I've been working on being a farmer, Rinpoche."

"Enough of these pleasantries. I was performing a sacred dance at the monastery just a few moments ago, when suddenly I was called away to deliver you a message."

Now Ben's mouth dropped open too. Perched there on the bed, he and Peg looked like astonished bookends.

"Are you awake now?

Ben nodded as if to indicate to a hypnotist that, yes, he was now in a deep trance.

"You must take the plates to Jed Rivers immediately."

"Why?" Ben's voice rose in alarm as he snapped out of it, throwing off the covers and swinging his legs off the bed.

"Men, wicked men, from town will be here soon to take them away from you."

"How do they know about the plates?"

"After the fight in town, many of the men in Santa Rosa have taken an interest in you newcomers." Sangay waved his hand impatiently. "You, Ben, wrap the plates tightly to keep them out of the water, and Jed will show you where to bury them, until it's time to go."

"To Zion?" Ben and Peg asked hopefully in unison

"Yes. No time. Go." Sangay pointed in the direction of the bedroom door. "And Peg, you must help. Now hurry." Ben was shaking as he slipped his jacket and sweat pants over his grey-striped pajamas, jammed his feet into his thongs, and headed for the front door.

Peg ran to the kitchen for a plastic garbage sack, while Ben grabbed the knitting bag. Suddenly he turned back to ask, "Just one thing, Sangay. If we hide these, will anyone get hurt?"

He heard a disembodied voice say, "No, not if you hurry," but Sangay had already disappeared. Ben hardly had time to process the miraculous nature of the moment, before Peg came back with the sack and they shoved the plates into it. Then Ben bolted out the back door, stumbling over his thongs as he ran down the Martinez' driveway. After he tripped and nearly fell, he threw them off into the bushes when he reached the Reynolds'. "This is the last time I'm going to run away from bullies. I swear it," he muttered.

When he reached the back of the adobe house, he tapped on Jed's bedroom window. No reply. So he rapped again, as loud as he dared. Finally Jody pulled back a lace curtain and peered out. When she saw who it was, she struggled to pull up the old wooden window and leaned out. "Ben? What are you doing out there?"

"Get me Jed. Quick!" Ben could hear Jody trying to rouse Jed who mumbled several choice words before she could make him understand what was happening. It seemed like a century had passed before Jed finally stuck his scruffy, unshaved face out into the night.

"What?" Jed said, too loud for Ben's taste.

"Shhhh! Listen, I know this doesn't make much sense, but Sangay was here and said men from town were headed out here after these plates." Ben held the bag up for Jed to see. This was the first time he had acknowledged openly what Pah Tempe folks already knew–Ben had ancient records.

"Geez, what are you, some kind of Joseph Smith?" Jed teased as he struggled to get his leg into his work pants. "Where did he hide his plates?"

"Under a log. Under the house. I don't remember. Come on!" Ben said insistently while Jed struggled to get into some clothes. Then he pulled impatiently at Jed to help him through the window. Ben felt like they were two escapees from a maximum-security prison.

After Jed reached the ground, he turned back to take his trusty pistol from Jody. "Don't worry," he said reaching in and patting her on the cheek. "Just a little Porter Rockwell business to take care of."

The two friends ducked down in the shadows of the house and listened. No sound of car or horse. "Come on, soldier," Ben said roughly, "Sangay didn't have me get you for nothing. What should we do with these?" He dangled the bag in front of Jed's face.

Jed scratched his head. After a short pause, his face lighted up. "Hah! I know just the place!" He laughed and headed off to the river, crouching low, zigzagging his way to the river bank fifty yards away. Ben barely managed to keep up. Stepping on an occasional sharp rock in his bare feet, he hopped on one foot then the other muttering, "Ow, ow" with each misstep. They scrambled down the bank and followed it upstream until they came to a bend in the river. There the path was blocked by cottonwood trees growing so thick along the path, they made a tangled impassable net.

Jed stopped. Ben pulled up out of breath. "Is this it?" he asked, panting and pulling a sticker out of his big toe.

"Yeah," Jed said leaning back on the steep bank to catch his breath. The slow-running muddy waters slipped by. "Last summer Juan Gallegos told me about this place. The locals believe this is where witches gather. He said people sometimes see balls of bright light." He looked around the hiding place. "I've seen similar phenomena at sea. Lights at the top of masts. Probably has to do with static electricity. Something like that."

Ben began to tear into the earth high up on the side of the bank. "Can't let the river rise suddenly and sweep these away," he said with great determination in his voice. When done with the excavation, Ben let out a sigh of relief–Sangay was right. Jed did know what to do. When am I going to stop doubting these guys?

"That's a good idea, putting them high up like that," Jed said as both men shoved the heavy plastic bag into the hole behind the tangle of roots. "Some day I hope you'll show me what they look like."

"When I get permission, you'll be the first to see them. Promise." Ben slapped Jed on the back. Ben had baptized Jed, so their bond went deep. It was not all strange then, without saying a word, they simultaneously dropped to their knees. "Oh, Lord,"

Ben prayed, "protect these plates and our families. In Jesus' name, Amen."

Jed was on his feet and halfway up the bank before Ben could stand up. "Come on, Brother Ben," Jed said extending a hand. "We've got to alert the others."

After they returned to Jed's house, they split up. Jed took one side of the river and Ben headed for Rosa's house. Mongrels crawled out from under porches and set up a barking frenzy. When Ben told Rosa and the Dubiks that burglars had been seen prowling in the area, Rosa said angrily, "They try to sneak in and steal our food, our treasures. They come here all the time." She scowled. "But they will dare not attack us if our lights are on. People here are very close, and those thieves from Santa Rosa, they know it."

"Thank you, Rosa, that's a great idea," Ben said, as he and Alex and Angelina on her master's heel rushed out the door. He had borrowed a pair of Alex's moccasins so he could keep up. Along with Jed, they ran up and down the valley, like some latter-day Paul Reveres, knocking on doors, asking people to turn on their lights.

They were nearing the end of the settlement near the Gallegos' house when they spotted the outlines of two darkened trucks slowly making their way up the dirt-packed road. Angelina bared her teeth and growled.

"That's got to be them," Alex hissed, crouching down behind tall shrubbery in the Gallegos' side yard and pulling the dog down next to him. The two men watched as the trucks slowly moved to the bend in the road.

"Did I tell you Sangay was in an elaborate black hat of some kind?" Ben asked in a whisper.

"Oh, really? Must have been a black hat dance costume."

"What's that?"

"It's a ceremony that celebrates the Bodhisattva driving evil out of Tibet."

"Oh."

Just then the trucks arrived at the bend in the road and pulled within sight of the homes. The drivers, shocked by the blaze of light that suddenly swept over them, froze, then put their hands to their eyes. Ben and Alex heard angry words, in Spanish, carried downwind to them. The drivers then pulled an abrupt U-turn and bumped back down the darkened road, like cockroaches disappearing down a kitchen cabinet crack.

"Yes!" Ben said and jumped up. The two men slapped each other on the back and let out several hoots. As they turned to walk back to the homes to let the residents know they could turn off their lights, Alex asked, "If I become a Mormon, do you think Sangay would come to me?"

Ben thought he could detect a subtle note of jealousy. He didn't know what to say. He felt bad. *I don't want to get in between Alex and Sangay's long-time friendship, but Sangay is on the Lord's errand,* he thought. "I'm sure he'll come to visit soon," Ben said weakly. He secretly noted that this was the second time that day that Alex mentioned becoming a Latter-day Saint.

Alex suddenly grabbed Ben and rubbed the bald spot on top of his head. "Ah, well, you always were a weird, mystical kid, Benjy my boy."

Ben smiled and tried to wriggle out of Alex's grip. "Yeah, that's true, and right now I'm an angry one, Al." He pulled free and brushed down his hair. "I sure as hell don't want to be driven out of here like we were from Pah Tempe."

"Exactly!" Alex said, surprised at the fierceness in his own voice. Angelina barked, as if in agreement.

The second tremor occurred a few days after India dropped a nuclear bomb on Pakistani troops massed at its borders. Once again the world held its collective breath while the deadly fallout traveled around the globe, this time at lower latitudes. And once again it appeared that only the immediate area and those downwind a few thousand miles would be affected. But, Earth, her breast shattered, began to writhe in pain.

And this second earthquake, striking the Midwest region on October 10, was not one of the many aftershocks from the New

Madrid quake. Centered in Davenport, Iowa, on a previously unknown fault, this latest monster weighed in at 8.6–a thousand times more deadly than the first. It wrenched the mighty Mississippi off its course from Davenport to Burlington like a wrecked freight train whose cars lay zigzagged off the tracks. It nearly leveled Chicago, St. Louis and Milwaukee. And another flood plain, this one farther north than the last one caused by the August quake, covered half of Iowa and nearly all of Illinois.

Chicago dropped several feet, while the updraft from the quake pushed Lake Michigan that much higher. This created a tidal wave that washed all the way down the Wabash River into Indiana and the Ohio River, swamping everything in its path.

People who survived the quake and flood began fleeing west across the open plains with just what they could cart or carry. Roads in the affected states were impassible–torn up or flooded. More deadly aftershocks rocked the area. Even after the flood waters had receded somewhat, Lake Michigan remained double in size.

Poisonous snakes slithered over roads and into back yards. One could see them hanging from children's swing sets or coiled on cold barbecue grates. Not far behind the fleeing populace came both cholera and mice, in the millions, with black clouds of mosquitoes in their wake. The "plague," which took only twelve hours to go from cough to collapsed lungs, cut down many of the refugees in mid-flight.

More earthquakes began to erupt throughout the world along unknown fault lines. Volcanoes blew their tops with terrifying regularity–like some infernal planetary game of dominoes. The planet staggered under the blows. Finally just when things had quieted down somewhat in late November, the Chinese detonated two nuclear air bursts over Tokyo. Immediately the Japanese retaliated by bombing Beijing, and millions of Asians died.

In the midst of this collective psychosis, Dmitri Gornstein, who had by now fully aligned his forces with Middle Eastern terrorists, took Iran. Drunk with this and other recent victories,

Gornstein reckoned that it was now time for one of his most daring and improbable guerrilla feats. With this single stroke he would etch his name in history.

Exploiting the underground expertise of his Arab cohorts and capitalizing on their suicidal fanaticism, Gornstein's group was able to wire an Iraqi volunteer with a very small nuclear device, send him into the UWEN compound in Zurich as a Saudi Air Force colonel where he obediently blew himself up–along with four square city blocks. Several top UWEN commanders died, including Les Hackmann. And the world like an exhausted woman, panted between birth contractions–or death rattles, depending on your point of view.

After Adam was born, Grace was flooded with rich and satisfying grandmotherly feelings for this newest grandson of hers. She warmed herself on the family fires, pleased that her sacrifice of selling her country store and leaving family and friends had been worth it. Now that Adam was nearly four months old and Moira more than acclimated as a new mother, Grace had time on her hands. She and Rosa enjoyed each other's company, but they viewed each other over a yawning religious gap that separated them in essential ways. This put a check on how far their friendship could develop. With Moira, Alex, and Adam absorbed in one another and Rosa enveloped in her Catholicism, Grace began to feel alone. Her mind turned more and more to the ghastly events gripping the world, and she fell into a severe and uncharacteristic depression, one she could not seem to shake. She would walk in the barren fields by herself for hours, accompanied only by the specter of millions of people suffering and dying. She was so attuned to their cries, a blinding headache seared her forehead each time a nuclear device was detonated.

One night, when Grace felt deadly fallout begin to rain on the north island of New Zealand, she dropped to her knees beside her bed and cried out, "Oh, God, where are you? How long will you allow this to go on?" She then fell forward in a heap on the floor and began to weep loudly, her green shawl flowing out around her like a waterfall of tears. Although Rosa was not in the house (she had gone to stay with relatives in Cuervo), Moira and Alex were. Moira had just nursed Adam and rocked him to sleep, when the wail pierced through the white adobe wall of their bedroom.

The couple froze and listened. "Mom?" Alex asked tensely.

"Uh, huh. I've been really worried about her lately. She just hasn't been herself."

"What do you think is wrong, Iwi? Is she lonely for her friends, for family, for New Zealand?" Alex asked, moving over to the bed.

"I think it's something that goes far, far beyond that," Moira said, slipping into an expression that Alex called her therapist face. As the sobbing continued from the room down the hall, they looked to Adam who lay on his back in light-blue sleepers. He made a deep sleepy sound.

"Don't have to worry about him waking up," Alex mused. "He's like a bear in hibernation."

Then the house grew quiet.

"Sounds like she's finally gone to sleep," Moira said, relieved.

But Grace had not. She had picked herself up and lain on the quilted bed, when suddenly she was pinned to the bed by a shooting sensation like a heavy electric shock that ran through her body, and she heard a voice say, "Now you will experience the evil of *las brujas del llano* (the witches of the plains)!" Then Grace found she could not move a muscle of her tall, strong body. She opened her mouth to scream but nothing came out. Beginning to suffocate, she panicked.

Just when she thought she would die–in a flash–she was released from the black oppressive current, and what seemed like a giant invisible hand plucked her up into the air and threw her the full length of the long bedroom. She landed in a heap, hitting her head on the corner of a large ornate dresser. She was immediately knocked unconscious.

Alex was on his feet and down the hall the instant he heard

the crash. As he approached Grace's bedroom door, he felt a terrible chill in the air. The hairs on his arms and head stood up. Fighting back waves of terror, he pulled down the door handle but it would not open. "Grace?" he yelled. "Grace, are you okay?" No answer. He yanked again on the handle. Nothing.

He put his shoulder to the door and after several resounding thumps it gave way. What he stumbled into was something he had never experienced before. It felt like he had stepped into a deep freezer and at the same time slowed to half speed. It took all of his will power to somehow move across the ten-foot span, pick up his limp mother-in-law and get out of that room. He was sure that the devil himself was going to reach out and grab him at any moment. Struggling down the hall to get back to the sanctuary of his bedroom, he looked back over his shoulder a couple of times to see if he was being pursued by demons.

Grace let out a moan as he laid her on their bed. Moira was immediately at her mother's side. "What happened?" she asked as Alex quickly shut and barred the sturdy wooden door.

"Darned if I know. I felt like I'd walked into Satan's lair. I found her sprawled unconscious on the floor."

"Go get the priesthood!" Moira barked the order, forgetting momentarily who she was talking to.

Alex winced. She glanced up from her ministrations to see his hurt and perplexed look, but she didn't care. At that moment her mind was solely on saving her mother. "Go get someone who holds the priesthood—Nate, Jed, Ben, somebody! Hurry!"

He jammed on his boots and grabbed his leather coat. Out in the chilly, moonless night Alex felt tears well up. I've been sent out into the night to go get another man to help with my family, he moaned to himself. He felt utterly useless.

Nate, at the widow's house, was the nearest priesthood holder. He sent Andrew and Cannon to get Jed and Ben, while he and Neddy ran back with Alex. The three men's hurried footfalls echoed off the houses as Alex tried to describe the experience he had been through.

Nate knew immediately what he was trying to say. "A similar thing happened to one of my missionary companions in Ireland when I was there. We had been praying especially hard about finding converts," Nate said in a soothing voice. "My companion was a really sensitive guy. I used to think there was a spiritual umbilical cord between him and the collective Brasilian soul. Anyway, one night after we'd gone to bed, I heard this crash and he was on the other side of the room. That happened about five times during our mission. It was really frightening."

"Boy, I really know what you mean!" Alex said soberly as they reached the front door of the house.

Moira had bandaged Grace's head, but the aging grandmother lay motionless on the bed. "Oh, thank God, you're here," Moira said taking Nate's jacket, motioning him to sit next to Grace.

Taking her limp hand in his, Nate said to Grace, "I've sent for Jed and Ben," even though he knew she probably could not hear him.

"Heavenly Father, let them hurry! Please!" Moira prayed and paced. She glanced over at Alex, who sat in the rocker looking down quite disconsolately.

Without knocking, Ben rushed into the bedroom, with Jed close behind. The three Winder boys followed and pressed themselves against the back wall in a posture suggesting both terror and excitement.

"What's happening? Is she ill?" Ben asked, out of breath.

"I think she's been attacked by evil spirits," Moira said in a low voice.

Ben took a quick step back. It was one thing to bless someone to be well, but quite another to take on the legions of the underworld. He gulped, then declared, "Okay, let's get on with this," sounding much more confident than he felt.

Nate gestured for Ben to go to the other side of the bed. The two men laid their hands on Grace's head, her face pale and jaw sagging. Jed gestured to the boys indicating they should fold their arms and bow their heads.

"Our Father, Almighty and All-knowing, we thy humble sons do beseech thee that thou wouldst grant our prayers in behalf of Sister Grace Ihimaera." Nate paused and felt a rush of the spirit fill him, so he raised an arm in the air and said in a loud, commanding voice, "In the name of Jesus Christ and by the power of the Holy Melchizedek Priesthood which I bear, I command all evil to depart."

Immediately Grace let out a long sigh and sank beneath the weight of the men's hands. Nate and Ben slowly removed their hands and waited. Her breathing became even; she seemed to have slipped into a profound and peaceful sleep. The group fell silent. Finally Moira said, "There's not much here we can do now. We'll have to wait for the doctor from Santa Rosa to come tomorrow to see if she has a concussion." She showed the men to the door. "And thanks," she said, wiping the tears from her face with the back of her hand, "for being righteous men who honor your priesthood." Moira looked intently at each one before shutting the door and returning to sit with her mother.

On the walk back the boys followed silently behind the older men. Their esteem for their father had just jumped twenty notches. Ben wanted to talk about what had happened, so instead of going home, the five went to the Martinez' where they could find a quiet room to discuss the powers given to the priesthood. What the young men learned was this great gift from God is far stronger than anything Satan can muster.

Grace felt herself leave her body right after the blessing. Gordon with his kind, smiling face greeted her as she floated up toward the ceiling. She had had this kind of out-of-body experience before with her deceased husband, so she felt little fear.Wordlessly she questioned him if this was her time to go home permanently with him. He shook his head.

They floated higher and higher until they reached a green meadow. An exquisite lightness and peace permeated Grace's being. From behind a hill, she looked to see the Visitor, who had identified himself as Timothy when he appeared to her in Pah Tempe, walking toward the couple. When he got close, he extended both hands and took hers, then Gordon's. "Welcome, both of you. I've been to your home; now I welcome you to mine." With a sweep of his arm, she and Gordon suddenly found themselves standing next to him on another hill now overlooking a vast valley.

"What is this?" Grace spoke for the first time.

"This is the location where newly arrived souls are greeted and oriented back into the spirit world. You see, the world is rapidly returning to its paradisiacal state. Only a tenth of the people presently on the earth will remain. The rest are gratefully returning to their home base."

As they watched, people clad in white opened their arms to welcome the new arrivals who were streaming over the hill. The faces of the newly released spirits shone with relief.

"They had only a moment of suffering at death, and now they are safely home," Timothy said. He looked to see what was playing across Grace's face.

"I think I understand where I've been in error," she said softly. "Women are the bearers of life. They feel responsible to keep everything nourished. I've not been able to accept the deaths of so many." Grace put her hand over her heart. "I've been caught up with the dying and not the living. And I've been terribly angry that so many of my brothers and sisters are suffering. Angry at God, I guess." She watched as more and more souls filled the valley, shouting hosanna to God for his tender mercy in guiding them home.

"I think she's coming around!" Moira exulted, near tears. She leaned against the ornate dark wood headboard of her bed, rocking Adam who had finally awakened with all the comings and goings. Alex, on the other side, sat holding Grace's gnarled, brown hand. Her eyelids fluttered. She tried to focus but she was disoriented, not sure which plane of existence she was on.

"Mom?" Alex asked tenderly. "Mom, we love you."

"I love you, too," she replied weakly. "Can I have a cup of water?" Grace struggled to sit up. "I'm fine. Really," she said somewhat annoyed when Moira tried to restrain her.

Moira stroked her mother's forehead. Grace looked peaceful for the first time in weeks. "Mom, you look better. I've been worried about you," Moira said, gingerly brushing back a strand of hair from Grace's face.

"When I'm feeling stronger, I'll tell you all of what happened, Iwi. But I want you to know this," Grace said, her voice rising. "All of the tragedy in the world right now is part of the Lord's plan." She grabbed at her daughter's sweater sleeve. "Don't make the same mistake that I have."

Moira took her mother's hand between her two warm hands. "What mistake, Mummy?"

"I have been mother to many, many souls, as you know," Grace said and smiled at the thought. "Some from my body and some from my soul. What I learned tonight is that I must not allow my maternal needs to lead me into Satan's claws."

Moira dropped her mother's hand in surprise. "You? In Satan's grasp? Come on, Mom. How could you be a candidate for such a thing? You had that attack because you are so good!"

Grace knit her brow and said sternly, "Listen to me. The Father-of-all-resistance takes anyone into his clutches–anyone who, in anger, curses God for His plans. They are not man's plans, nor woman's, for that matter, Iwi. They are eternal and wiser than anyone in a telestial body can possibly understand." Tears began to roll down her cheeks. "And tonight the Lord has shown me how I have been in secret opposition to Him. I thank him for this experience."

Moira handed her a tissue from a box by the bed. "With possible cracked ribs and a concussion?"

Grace laughed, then coughed and held her side. "I told you I was a tough old bird. Some of us need a little more talking to than others."

"Mother, you're a such miracle to me," Alex said tenderly. "I really don't what I'd do without you and your cosmic adventures. Life would be so mundane."

Grace smiled and sipped the water Moira brought to her lips. "Son, you will soon be on your own cosmic adventures far grander than I've ever had."

The Maori seeress turned and looked deeply into Alex's eyes, and he knew she had seen a future for him he couldn't imagine. Then Adam brought all of them back to the moment with a loud burp and a quirky smile.

Chapter Twenty-Six

Ye shall not go out with haste
Nor go by flight; for the Lord will go
Before you, and the God of Israel
Shall be your rearward.
    Book of Mormon, 3 Nephi 20:42

Three months later, right after Christmas, Ben went down to the hideout in the cottonwood tangle to check on the plates. As he jumped down the bank onto the rocky path that skirted the Pecos, he thought he saw a flash of orange in the direction of the plates. But when he arrived there he found nothing and breathed a sigh of relief. He and Peg had been very nervous and prayerful about the condition of the plates.

As he began to pull back a few of the branches, he became aware of someone or thing behind him. He whirled around and there stood Sangay, in his usual ocher robes, not the ceremonial ones Ben had last seen.

"I'm glad to see you are being a conscientious guardian of our ancient plates," he said to Ben, who was thoroughly disconcerted. "When the time comes, which is very near, I want you to take them with you when you go to Independence, Missouri."

"Hello, Rinpoche. Thanks for scaring me to death." Ben grinned at Sangay who grinned back.

"You needn't worry so much about this treasure, Ben. I'd know if anything were to happen to the plates." Sangay wrapped the end of his robe around his left arm.

"Well, that's really good," Ben said. "But how would you know? Honestly, Rinpoche," Ben went on with a small sigh, "I'm a little confused. I need you to explain a few things to me."

"That's why I've come."

Even though Ben was wearing his black down jacket, he shivered, leaned up against the bank and folded his arms. "First, are you real? Can I touch you if I wanted to? Are you dead?"

Sangay put up a hand to staunch the flow of questions. "Yes, I am real. Can you touch me? You could try, but would fail. Am I dead? Not when last I checked."

"I can see I amuse you with my questions," Ben said, looking chagrined. "I'm just trying to find out how you can appear to me if you're not dead."

"You do not amuse me, Ben. But you are so deadly serious, I'm just trying to lighten the mood." Sangay smiled and with broad gestures explained, "At this moment my body is seated in meditation on Mt. Nebo. I have learned to attain a deep state of concentration which allows me to cast a long spiritual shadow, you might say. There are many things in heaven and earth that are not dreamed of in your doctoral program, young Horatio, to paraphrase the great Mr. William Shakespeare."

Rather than laughing, Ben said somberly, "I never know if you're toying with me."

"That I would never do," Sangay said, shaking his finger at Ben. "You are much too important a student." He rewrapped the robe around his left arm. "Ben, you asked me to teach you to meditate, back when we were in St. George. I take that charge very seriously."

Suddenly a voice from the lawn above cut through the interview. "Daddy, who are you talking to down there?" Miriam asked.

Ben looked up and tried to think of quick way to get her to go away. "Honey, I'm talking to myself." He knew if he asked to be left alone, it would produce the opposite effect so he said, "Want to come down and help me work?" She paused for a moment, then said, "Nah, I'll see you later." Her brown curly hair caught a glint of gold as she shouted to Missy and darted across the lawn.

"She can't see you?" Ben asked Sangay.

Sangay shook his head and said no. "Oh, I see. I think." Ben was hungry for answers. He was not sure when he would have another chance to speak to Sangay. "Before I ask any more questions, I have to confess something to you–I have been reading ahead in the plates." Ben looked to Sangay, but the lama's expression remained unchanged, so he continued, "On Plate Twenty the initiate is given certain words to bring the dead back to life." Ben sucked in and noisily let out a sigh. "And if that weren't enough, Plate 22, which I started to read before I had to bury it, starts with a description of a person whose body has been immortalized."

Now Sangay's eyes widened in interest. "Oh, really. The first is something I know from our oral tradition, but the second, I only guessed might be in these plates. Well, that confirms what the Dalai Lama told me--these plates may very well contain the mysteries of the ages."

Ben let out a low whistle.

Sangay leaned forward so that his face was very close to his student's. "And you're absolved of your need to feel guilty," the lama said lightly and poked a finger in the direction of Ben's ribs. "You don't always have to do things in an exact order, you know." He rocked back on his heels and flashed a smile.

"Once I tried to walk around a track counterclockwise," Ben confessed. "But a quarter of the way around, I got so nervous I wheeled around and ran a mile the other way, just to get the queasy feeling out of my stomach."

Sangay chuckled, then the pair fell silent. Ben finally worked up the nerve to ask, "Rinpoche, will you teach me what's on Plate 20, about raising the dead. I'd settle for that right now so that I could save a lot of people who are dying tragically and unnecessarily."

"Oh, so greedy and ambitious," Sangay said half seriously. He turned his head and looked at Ben out of the corner of his eye. He let Ben squirm in the long silence that ensued. Finally he said, "First you must learn to have a beginner's mind."

"Really? You will?"

Sangay nodded.

"O—kay!" Ben rubbed his hands together in glee. "What's a beginner's mind?"

"That is the willingness to experience each day, each moment as a young child would, without preconceptions or boredom. You occasionally experience great joy, Ben, but only rarely. Your mind moves forward to the future or back in time, but you see very little of what is actually around you." Ben opened his mouth to protest, but Sangay put up a hand to stop him, then continued, "Ben, you think there is movement in your life, but in reality you are living in one dimension."

The wind rustled the bare branches on the cottonwood tree, and Sangay raised his voice, "Your mind is caught in so narrow a pattern, you experience very little of what actually happens in a day. Ben, you plan your day before you get out of bed.

Ben blanched. "I don't!"

"You do! Let me give you an example: Why couldn't I get through to you the night I appeared to Peg?"

"Because I was sleeping," Ben said defensively.

"I should have been able to communicate to you in your dreams. But you had decided the scriptures say young men and old men had dreams and visions, so that left out middle-aged men."

Ben could not keep a grin from slipping across his face. He knew Sangay had him.

"So you concluded there was no fun for you in this realm. Ben, you are too literal and much too rigid in your thinking. If you want to experience the extraordinary, your lesson, for now, is to approach each day with the kind of excitement you felt when you were young. Be open to new experiences, let yourself feel a full range of emotions. Then we will see what is next."

"But you're asking me to unlearn everything that I've spent my life cultivating!"

"If you don't want to know what I have to teach, you have only to speak," Sangay said sharply and peered into Ben's eyes for a long time. Ben, his arms to his sides, remained silent.

"Good," Sangay said and rubbed the top of his closely-cut hair. "I'm fairly sure we'll be doing our lessons in person from now on. This astral projection business takes a lot out of me." Sangay stepped back, raised his hand in a gesture of peace and began to fade until there was just a spot of orange.

"Wait," Ben said. "Sangay, when will I see you again?"

Sangay reappeared and said, "In Zion. And isn't there another question you've been wanting to ask me, but haven't?"

Ben blushed. "And can you read my mind, too?"

"Yes, and you can read mine if you work at it."

Ben cleared his throat, looked down at the ground and took in a deep breath. "Okay, well, here goes nothing. What do you know of Maitreya?"

"Maitreya is the Bodhisattva of the future. He will come at the end of time. But don't you really want to ask me about Jesus?

Ben nodded sheepishly.

"I know what every man and woman knows who reaches a certain level of mindfulness," Sangay continued, "that He is the Christ, the ruler of this world. I serve Him, through my tradition."

Ben whistled. He never expected to hear that answer from Sangay. "Thank you for being my teacher," Ben said humbly.

Sangay bowed and faded into the dark earthy background.

So Ben tried out a beginner's mind as he walked back to the house. He smelled the air, watched two birds circle and land on the lawn, felt the warmth of the sun on his face. He decided he would hang out with Craig and Adam, both babies, hoping he might pick up a few pointers from them.

Early on a cloudy, blustery Saturday in late January, the dogs began barking down on the road leading to Santa Rosa. Soon more set up a din. The focus of their excitement was an old station wagon bouncing along toward the Martinez house. It was Elders Dawahoya and Stewart, along with Peter Butler.

Peter was almost out of the car before it stopped. Bundled in a sheepskin coat and cowboy hat, he loped across the lawn to the Reynolds' house in just a few strides. He pounded on the door. In a matter of seconds, Jody answered, and Peter's face lit up. "Hey there, Jody! Where's your old man?"

"Hi, Peter." Jody flashed him a big smile. "Down at the hay barn fixing something. Why?"

"Got news for him. Back later."

He found Jed draped over a tractor engine. "Goodday, mate!"

Jed dropped a 3/4" wrench and hollered. "Pete, old boy!"

"Hey, how ya doin', you old dog you?"

The two slapped each other on the back. "I'm fine. I thought you'd gone down under by now."

"Just the opposite. I'm headed home, out east." Peter's eyes twinkled mischievously.

"Gees, I'm glad you came back to say goodbye. How's the solar engine holding up?"

"It needs some fine tuning, but overall it's been steady going for a couple of thousand miles now."

Jed turned to put away his tools. Peter, who hadn't gotten the response he wanted, blurted out, "Hey, dummy, don't you get it? I said I'm headed home. We're all headed home!"

Jed's jaw dropped. He stood, frozen, for several long beats before he managed to stutter, "To...to...Zion? You mean NOW?"

"Nope, but soon. The apostles have invited you and me to travel with them to get the thing started. Then we'll be back for everybody.

"Everybody? Mormon and non-Mormon?"

"Everybody who wants to walk the walk and talk the talk, mate!"

"Well, that's me!" Jed crowed, pointing a finger to his chest. Then he suddenly grew somber. "We're leaving the women and children behind?"

"Can't be helped. We've got to go first and be witnesses while they dedicate the place. After that, we'll come back to get all of our friends and family. And then, Jeddy, my lad, we'll take them home to Zion and get down to the business of settin' up the Lord's Kingdom and preparin' it for the Ten Tribes and, of course, for His return." Peter paused, then his eyebrows rose and he crowed, "Mate, we'll be preparin' it for the whole bloomin' world!"

Jed let out a war whoop and shouted, "Praise the Lord," as he jigged and jagged over to the house to tell Jody the news with Peter just a few feet behind.

The apostles were at that moment conveying basically the

same news to the Martinez' household. They informed the group of the passing of President Sorenson. They had been directed by the new prophet, President Ueda, to go to Independence, Missouri to dedicate the land for the return of the Lord and the building up of His kingdom in the New Jerusalem. They invited five of the Melchizedek priesthood holders from El Puerto to join them—Jed, Peter, Nate, Neddy and Ben. But their instructions were to go only after the land had been cleansed, which, they were told, would take place at any time now.

It did not take long for the word spread to the rest of the LDS community in the village. The Saints, electrified, immediately began cleaning and deciding what to pack. But their euphoria was tempered by the knowledge that hundreds of thousands—even millions—of people would soon lose their lives in horrifying circumstances—in plagues, famines, natural disasters, and in history's most gruesomely waged wars. Like Ben and Peg, whose translating had provided them with a window into the terrible contours of the immediate future, the others were now beginning to catch glimpses of what lay in store for the world. They packed, prayed and sang hymns to keep up their spirits.

It was Grace who spent time counseling those Saints who were most distressed. She sat and talked with them over herbal tea, walked up and down the main road, her arm around them, explaining her vision and trying to get them to let go of their attachment to the idea that death was such a great tragedy. And it was Grace who knew hours in advance of the last of three quakes that would hit western Missouri—she knew and so did the animals who were skittish all that day. The dogs began howling, cows lowed, and horses neighed intermittently after dark.

It was the third day after the apostles arrived that Grace awoke at midnight, threw off the covers, grabbed her robe and padded down the hall to the Dubik's bedroom. Alex was still reading from the *Journal of Discourses*, a small bedside lamp illuminating his side of the bed. Moira was fast asleep on her side, facing Adam's crib. Alex jerked when Grace peeked around the door.

"You okay, Mom?" he asked anxiously.

"I'm fine, but the baby's about to be born."

"Whose baby?"

"The paradisiacal one–the Adamic baby is about to crown."

"Zion?" Alex's eyes flashed.

She nodded. He slipped out of bed, put on a red terry-cloth robe and slippers and followed her out into the kitchen. She made them both a cup of cocoa. They sat trying to make small talk while they waited. Then at 1:08 a.m. on January 27th, a quake measuring 9.0 cracked open the earth near Leavenworth, Kansas, a scant twenty miles or so from Kansas City–the largest earthquake ever recorded.

From the air, the area around Leavenworth looked like it had been hit by a meteor. Trees were flattened, buildings crushed and burning, rivers overflowing. The Kansas City gas mains erupted, sending walls of fire spewing out along newly-made tributaries of the Kansas and Missouri Rivers. Hills were now valleys; valleys had been thrust up into small mountains. High rises and freeways had collapsed under the intensity of the furious 30-second shaking. They were strewn over the area like huge discarded Lego pieces. There were almost no survivors in Leavenworth, while the Kansas City area lost over half a million people. Floods rushed into low-laying areas. Sleepy cows freed from the restraints of fences wandered over broken highways and into yards. Orange, sulfurous flames, straight from Hell, gamboled in the midnight sky. Although some dogs still roamed the city, not one yellow dog wagged its tail.

There were many valiant attempts to save the trapped and injured, yet people quickly realized they had to run or they themselves would die in the aftershocks, or be cut down by cholera or the plague. So they began to stream out into Kansas and south to Oklahoma. They were replaced by snakes and mice. So big was the mice population scurrying across Missouri that it was like the buffalo herds that had once roamed the plains, their brown backs dotting the plains as far as the eye could see. Only these creatures were tiny, deadly and inedible.

In Rosa's kitchen, lights flickered off and on, plates and pans rattled in the cupboard, but that was all that they felt as the quake hit. Many in El Puerto slept through it. In the morning the apostles called all the Saints to the Martinez' house to tell them of the tragedy and to explain that the apostles would wait until the Spirit prompted them to leave. They said they realized that they were asking a great deal of the men to go with them. They compared it to running back into a burning building or volunteering to climb into the jaws of a hungry lion. Elder Dawahoya offered a brief prayer. Then, to further reassure the men's families, he said, "The Lord is at this moment preparing a pathway for our journey. The angels are crowding around, anxious to help. They have waited for a long time for this time to occur. I assure you, we will travel with all the powers of heaven." A tender confirmation, an intimation of certainty and security, flowed from his words, speaking peace to the anxious hearts of the small group of Saints.

Later, at the apostles' request, Ben furtively dug up the plates and carried them back to the house. He laid the dirty garbage bag on the kitchen sink, and he and Peg carefully unwound the tie at the top. Peg peered, then reached in and pulled back the silk cloth. "Yes! No rust, no mildew," she said breathing a sigh of relief.

Ben carried the plates carefully to the bedroom, where he placed them in a small duffel bag he was packing. He tied the top of the silk cloth in a knot and put them in alongside the white shirt, pants, and temple bundle he had been asked to bring along. He packed his .22 and a box of ammunition. "Just in case," he told Peg. "I wonder what they're going to do with the plates there," he said somewhat wistfully.

"I don't know, but I'm sure we'll get another chance to work on them. Don't you?" Peg looked eagerly into Ben's face.

"If Sangay has anything to do with it, I think we will."

About five in the morning, two days later, a groggy Andrew Winder knocked on the Reynolds' door. Jed let him in. *He's the only one of the five kids who looks like Laurie*, he thought. *I surely hope he doesn't turn out like her.*

Andrew, struggling to keep his eyes open, reported, "My dad says it's time to go."

"Tell him I'll be right there," Jed said disappearing into the back of the house. He held Jody for a long time, kissed his sleeping son, patted his shoulder holster just to make sure the the handgun was still there, then walked out into the chilly dark morning. As he walked across the lawn to the Martinez', he could see the doors to the three cars standing open. People were milling around, carrying baggage to the cars. Peter was double checking the supplies and equipment in the back of the apostles' station wagon–inflatable rafts, tents, Coleman stove, dried foodstuffs.

Ben stood for a long moment hugging both Danny and Miriam in each arm. He tried not to sound as shaky as he felt. "This is so exciting. You guys are going to have to remember this day, okay?" They nodded sleepily. Miriam wanted him to take one of her favorite stuffed animals along for good luck, but Ben said they didn't need it, the Lord was going to protect them. She looked crestfallen, so he asked her to get something a lot smaller he could take in his pocket. She rushed to the bedroom get a small plastic horse she liked to use when she played house. Danny said he wanted his dad to take his compass so he wouldn't get lost.

Alex strode purposefully down the driveway in red robe, parka, slippers. Ben tried, but failed to read his face. He greeted a couple of people but was clearly headed for Ben and Peg. This gifted sculptor who had spent a lifetime craving and pursuing adventure would now be left behind, standing in his pajamas in a deserted driveway, while Ben and his friends launched out on one of the greatest adventures imaginable.

When Alex reached the family, he said to Ben, "I have a little gift I want you to take with you." He reached into his pocket and pulled out his red Swiss Army knife. "It's really handy," he said as he opened each of the blades, "even the cork screw." The three laughed. "Knowing you, Benjy, you'll find some way to use it."

Miriam rejoined them and gave Ben the small horse. "Now I'm ready to go," Ben said and reached down to kiss her on the cheek. Danny in bright yellow pajamas hadn't said much, but now he asked, "Uncle Alex, are you going to stay here and protect us while Daddy goes away?"

Alex knelt down and pulled both children to him. "I'm going to be the head guy who takes care of you and your mom from anybody who tries to hurt you. Okay?"

"Okay," Danny said, relieved. He went back and leaned under Peg's protective arm.

"I'm sorry you aren't coming," Ben said as Alex straightened up. But when he saw Alex's face begin to darken, Ben changed his tone and said lightly, "I always feel better when I'm out on a nature trip with you. You know me and my fear of bear bites."

"I'm sorry, too," Alex said in a low voice. "But," he brightened up, "I've got to heat up the Pecos a few degrees while you're gone." The corners of his mouth twitched as he tried to contain a smile. "If you think I'm going to get into that freezing water on some cold February day, you've got another thing coming."

"You...?" Ben stuttered.

"Yes, I want you to baptize me," Alex said slowly emphasizing each word.

Peg almost sang out, "Oh, how wonderful!"

The flood gates opened between the two old friends. Alex and Ben fell into each other arms, sobbed and laughed, then sobbed some more. Then Alex reached over and hugged Peg with one arm and said softly, "Thanks for your faith in me, Sis."

She kissed him on the cheek.

"Hey, what's happening over here," Nate said, in navy pea coat and knit cap.

"You tell him, Ben," Alex said, nudging Ben.

"Alex is going to be baptized when we get back."

Nate extended his hand to Alex. "That's the best news, next to this trip, I've heard in a very long time. Congratulations!"

"Does Moira know?" Peg asked.

"Not yet. I'm on my way to tell her now. I just wanted you to know before you left, Ben." The two embraced again. Then the group watched as Alex, his grey ponytail bobbing back and forth, disappeared out of the circle of light. Ben could hear him singing and whistling "When the Saints Go Marching In" as he headed back home.

Ben lingered with Peg and smelled her hair, then picked up the kids for a hug and kiss. Nate grabbed Missy lurking around the cars and said sternly, "No, no, you're not going to pull what you did in Nevada, young lady." She frowned but agreed to take Peg's hand and even waved as the men got into the solar-powered cars.

Elder Dawahoya turned on the headlights of the first car, and he and Elder Stewart waved to Brother and Sister Martinez and the small gathering. Nate, Ben and Neddy followed in the Toyota, and Jed and Peter brought up the rear. The sun was just rising over the eastern mesa as the small caravan bounced down the rutted road headed for Santa Rosa, then on to Texas and Oklahoma via Highway 24.

They met very little traffic or signs of the earthquake in their drive through Texas to Guymon, Oklahoma five hours later. They were, though, the only cars traveling such a distance. All cross country transportation had been disrupted. People who had gas-driven cars had to conserve what remained in their tanks. Those with battery-driven cars knew they could go only so many miles before there would be a run at the stores on electric car batteries, assuming they could be found.

It was at a lunch counter in Guymon that they heard about the tornadoes and hailstorms that had been generated by the earthquake. The locals at the Cherokee Grill told of roofs blown off, golf ball-sized hail pelting the area, and they had heard that Oklahoma City had been torn up by nearly twenty deadly tornadoes, while Houston had sunk several feet, causing massive destruction.

The seven men from Puerto de Luna, hearts in their throats, decided to push on to Wichita to spend the night. As they drew closer, they could see that the Arkansas River had flooded portions of highway leading into the city. They began to encounter distraught people walking along the highway, pushing or carrying a few personal belongings, headed west. Many of them were women with young children. The scene reminded Nate of television images from war-torn areas that had become so commonplace in other parts of the world.

On the outskirts of the city, Jed tuned into a ham radio transmission for Elder Stewart, which informed him that the chapel where the group was going to stay had sustained heavy structural damage, and the group was to be diverted to a stake president's house in the nearby suburbs.

"This reminds me of pictures of World War II movies after the Nazis had taken a city," Jed said to Nate as they drove through the vacant streets. Houses stood empty, doors ajar.

"Yeah, me too. And we're still a day's journey from Jackson County," Nate said, turning to pat his eldest son's arm. Neddy, who looked very much the seventh in a line of dark curly-haired pioneers, had not said much the entire journey. "What are you thinking, son?"

"Oh, nothing."

"Must be something going on in your head."

"I was just wishing I was back at school in Ukiah with my friends playing basketball. That seems a hundred years ago."

Just then the apostles' car turned into a cul-de-sac and stopped at a large two-story, white frame house. Nate pulled up behind him with Peter and Jed in the rear. "This must be the place," Ben said, trying to sound enthusiastic but very much wishing he were back in his warm bed with Peg and surrounded by his books.

That night was a strange one for every member of the party. When word leaked out that there were Mormon apostles in the area, people began showing up on the lawn, knocking at the door, begging them to help with their wounds, their dangerously ill children, or the severe cough that promised to develop into either cholera or the plague. Many of them were not Latter-day Saints. The medical facilities, which had been badly damaged, were overflowing with casualties and medical personnel just could not get to all the injured.

The seven men and the stake president formed teams of two to give blessings to person after person ushered into the house. The stake president's wife presided over the living room, dispensing hot drinks and warm blankets. Jed did double duty as nurse and priesthood healer. This parade of supplicants nearly lasted the night.

Ben and Jed were teamed up in the family room, which was dominated by trophies and photos of athletic events. The first person they blessed was a middle-aged man with a bandaged hand and a limp. Donald Mayes didn't want help for himself but for his young daughter, whom he carried.

Jed gently laid the little girl down on the couch and asked her father, "Are you a Mormon?"

The man shook his head. "You will help us anyway, won't you? I heard that the Mormons were healing people over here," he asked worriedly.

"We'll see what we can do to help, but it's really in the Lord's hands," Jed said sympathetically. The little girl looked about ten, Missy's and Danny's age.

"Do you believe in God?" Ben asked the grieving man.

"Yes."

"And do you believe He can help your daughter?"

"Honestly?"

Jed and Ben both nodded.

"I hope so, but it's hard to imagine."

"What happened here?" Ben asked the disheveled man in overalls.

"House fell down around us. She's been unconscious ever since."

"What's her full name?"

"Susanna Royal Mayes."

Ben took out his vial of oil, parted the girl's damp dark hair and placed a drop on her head. Then he and Jed lightly rested their hands on her cold head. He began the blessing with, "Susanna Royal Mayes, your Heavenly Father loves you."

Ben looked down at the sweet, pasty-white face and prayed silently that the Lord would produce a miracle like He had with Moira. Then in a voice that was both stern and yet tender, Ben proclaimed, "In the name of Jesus Christ and by the power of the Holy Melchizedek Priesthood, I bless you that you will be made whole."

Mr. Mayes began to sob, for when Ben and Jed lifted their hands off her head, Susanna's eyelids fluttered, then she opened her brown eyes. She took a deep breath and sat up.

All three men gasped. Her father cried out, "How can this be?" He took her into his arms, forgetting his bloody, bandaged hand.

Susanna looked up lovingly at the two men. "Thank you for bringing me back to my daddy," she said. Ben and Jed assured her that it wasn't their doing, but the Lord's. When the Mayes' walked out, Jed shut the door and said exuberantly, "Can you believe that?"

"This is the second time I've experienced a healing," Ben responded in a low, reverential voice, "and I've become a believer."

Jed shook his head not so much in incredulity now as in shock. All his life he had heard of the priesthood's powers, but until now he had not really had the chance to use his. He loved the miraculous stories, like the one about Joseph Smith blessing a handkerchief and others using it to heal Saints who had fallen ill. But now! Jed reached for the door handle and ushered in an African-American woman and her mother who had been blinded in one eye by a falling beam.

The group worked throughout the night, calling on the powers of the priesthood to heal and console, and when they were finished they lay down on beds and couches throughout the house and tried to rest. Nate and Neddy lay next to each other on twin beds in a guest bedroom. Neddy couldn't sleep. He was exuberant, with the day's events. He had to tell his exhausted father over and over about the paralyzed woman who, after receiving the blessing he and the stake president gave, got up and walked out of the house. Nate did not mind. This was the closest he had ever felt to his introverted son.

In the early morning, with little or no sleep, they left for Topeka. As they passed through the toll gate, they saw the bodies of two handsome young men, toll takers, still staring up, their mouths twisted in anguish, where they had been crushed by collapsing concrete. More and more refugees walked along the side of the road. Many shouted and waved their arms at the cars, trying to get them to turn around.

It was bright, sunny and a frigid twenty-five degrees. The highway was in good shape–a crack here or there but nothing they couldn't negotiate. Up ahead near Topeka they saw what looked like a large two-story silver golf tee, tilted at a 45° angle.

"What's that?" Neddy asked and leaned forward.

"Don't know," Nate said, "but it's the second one I've seen." It turned out to be a deserted rest stop with a restaurant and garage, both now in shambles. They drove on.

Broken-down farm houses and red barns, black cows with white faces wandering across the freeway, large black crows cawing loudly as they picked at carcasses along the road–it all seemed like a pastoral postcard gone mad. In this rather flat and denuded landscape, the sky seemed to take hold of one's imagination, to give it more power. Ben found himself looking out at the changing cloud formations overhead, if only to avoid peering into the shocked faces of the bewildered mobile population.

East of Topeka, in the hilly country near Lawrence, they came up over a rise and slammed on their brakes. A utility pole with four live lines had fallen over the highway. The apostles got out and walked back to Jed and Peter's car. They conferred briefly and decided there was nothing they could do to remove it. So Jed and Peter broke through a fence on the right side of the road, and they bumped over a field, forded a small stream, and reached the highway at the bottom of the hill.

That was the first time they actually saw the mice—mice carrying PDS who began infesting the East Coast, then spread to the South, decimating first the population of the very young and elderly, then other household members. The mosquitoes that accompanied them aggressively burrowed into human flesh and delivered a virus changeling that eluded UWEN researchers in their frantic attempt to stop the world-wide killer. Scurrying in the barren fields, these mice glimmered like corn silk in the chilly afternoon. The men involuntarily reached for car windows to see that they were sealed shut.

Down into Lawrence, they began to see the devastation up close. Any house visible from the freeway had been flattened. Yawning, gaping cracks in the highway menaced passersby. A huge smokestack off to the left in the distance leaned crazily like the Tower of Pisa. Dark, bare trees were mere pickup sticks, twisted from the ground by their roots. A hundred empty rigs, stored in a yard near the freeway, looked like a giant had tossed them down in heaps, tired of playing cars.

Crossing the Kansas River was a dangerous challenge, for the river had spread out for a mile in each direction. The cars bumped and slithered over fields, their tires spinning in mud up to the hubcaps until the drivers found a place where the river was dammed. There they managed to get across.

The toll gate at this end of the Kansas Tollway was also unmanned. Normally one would pay $7.50 on the drive from Wichita. They somehow felt a little guilty as they drove slowly past the booth without paying. A broken sign advertising the Agricultural Hall of Fame lay across the highway, and Ben wondered aloud if Ezra Taft Benson had made it into the museum. About five miles past the toll booth they mounted a rise and saw for the first time the outline of greater Kansas City. Fires and smoke still stained the air, four days after the quake. It would be impossible to get into the city proper—the overpasses had crashed down into a sea of muddy water that had once been the Missouri River.

Elder Dawahoya eased the car he was driving off the freeway onto a knob of a hill that looked freshly made. There was no foliage of any kind, just dirt. The others followed. As they got out and stretched, Peter pulled out the four large inflatable rafts along with foot pumps. He and Jed worked away for a half hour filling them with air. Then the men unloaded their gear onto the rafts and locked the cars. After a brief prayer that the cars would be unharmed when they returned, they pushed off. At first they paddled past the railroad yards. Nate looked down five or six feet to the tangle of trains below. It was nearly noon, but it was cold. The wind had begun to blow down from the north. Elder Stewart stopped to pull up the hood on his brown parka, then returned to paddle on the right side of the raft he occupied with Elder Dawahoya. Neddy and Nate shared a raft, as did Ben and Jed. Peter brought up the rear.

Ben who was working up a sweat, said to Jed, "I hope someday I can make sense of all this."

"It's definitely surreal, man," Jed said. He ducked down as they floated under a fallen section of the I-70 overpass. "It's like a scene out of a Japanese movie—Godzilla does Kansas City or something."

One, then another, bloated corpse bumped up against their raft. The men recoiled. Jed pushed the gray-faced woman away from the raft. The other, probably a man, floated face down. To the men's left and a thousand yards upstream, a fire wall eight feet high burned right out in the middle of the river, fed by a gas main somewhere. Other than the hissing and spitting of flame hitting water, it was quiet and cold, like a tomb stretching from horizon to horizon.

They paddled on for several miles, then up ahead on the right they drifted past the Kansas City Royals stadium, now reduced to a heap of rubble lying among tall pillars that looked like melted swizzle sticks. On the other side of the highway the Blue Ridge Bank-and-Trust's 10-story office building had been shaved down to four stories, three of which were under water.

"It's a good thing Elder Stewart was a regional representative in this area," Ben said. "Otherwise we'd probably never find the temple hill." He was warmer now, more relaxed, having established a stroking rhythm with Jed. A few more miles and the signs they could make out said they were in Harry Truman country."The water is receding or the hills are getting taller," Ben said hopefully. "I can't really tell."

"Yeah, I think you're right," Jed said. "It looks like we're about to scrape bottom." They had reached the old part of Independence.

"Watch for snakes, and mice, for that matter," Peter hollered as they tied up the boats at the courthouse. Independence had been hard hit, but the courthouse seemed intact, although it had been moved inches off its foundation. As they came to dock in the downtown area, Peter put down his oars, sat up on his knees and pointed out to his companions which buildings looked like they could be repaired. It seemed eerie to see no one in the area, but trusting the Lord, they left the rafts and supplies, took just their temple clothes and began to walk to the temple site.

This vitally important party of seven said nothing as they hurriedly climbed up Walnut Street. The RLDS temple with its distinctive spiral top, which had dominated the skyline, was now nowhere to be seen. Nor was the spacious auditorium across the parking lot. When they crossed Pleasant Street and got closer to the top of the hill, they discovered why. The auditorium had imploded and fallen in on itself, while the spiral-topped temple had snapped off at the base and crashed into the parking lot. It looked like an ice cream swirl that had fallen out of the cone.

Chapter Twenty-Seven

And it shall be called the New Jerusalem,
A land of peace, a city of refuge, a place of safety
For the Saints of the Most High God.
Doctrine and Covenants 45:66–67

Even though the men who were walking rapidly toward the stake center, up to the temple hill site, should have been exhausted, they weren't. They had spent the entire night in Wichita trying to help the casualties of the earthquake, and today they had rowed many miles and eaten very little. Yet they felt exhilarated despite the emotional and physical wreckage that had assaulted their senses since they had left the little haven of Puerto de Luna.

Now they hurried their pace to the temple site, occasionally talking in muted tones. Peter and Jed wondered aloud about the lack of looters or dead bodies. It was as though the scene had been swept clean, ready for the events that would soon come to pass there. Each man was filled with a certainty that in a short time he would be witness to that which was written in Revelations, that which Isaiah saw and Joseph Smith wrote so yearningly about. Even for Elder Dawahoya and Elder Stewart, it seemed almost too much to grasp.

As they turned up Walnut Street, another scene of devastation greeted them. Most of the stake center lay in rubble. They registered the horror on half-numbed senses. Elder Dawahoya left them to walk inside. The rest stood apart from one another, lost in their own thoughts. After a couple of anxious minutes the apostle emerged and said they were to continue on up the hill. The only sound to be heard was the tapping of their shoes on the cracked sidewalk.

The Visitor's Center had also sustained heavy damage. Windows were blown out, rubble covered the lobby, but the back area on the first floor, where films had been shown, was intact. The local church authorities had prepared a room warmed by a kerosene heater.

The apostles were greeted by a dozen men who were already dressed in their white temple clothes. Their wives, also in white temple dresses, stood behind a long table laid out with salads and casseroles filled with emergency food rations they had cooked over Dutch ovens all afternoon. The men from El Puerto shook hands with the assembled group of couples, then filled their plates. The atmosphere was so supercharged, Ben half-expected to see blue zigzags of electricity materialize out of thin air.

The group stood around the heater for a time, then only nibbled at the food. None of them, not even Neddy, found they could eat much. They were so taken up with what they were about to witness, they were hardly aware of their bodies.

When Elder Stewart could see the men had finished, he indicated they should get dressed in their temple whites. Ben tried to tie his white tie, but his hands were shaking too much, so he whispered to Nate, "Do you think you could help me with this?"

Nate walked over and said with a smile, "Only if you'll help me. I'm sort of shell shocked myself—to tell you the truth." They tied each other's ties in silence, then stood awkwardly waiting for the next set of instructions.

Looking around the room at the other people who had arrived before them, Ben whispered somberly, "I just wonder how they managed to survive."

"That's a good question. I don't know." Nate said and fell silent.

After a few minutes Elder Dawahoya signaled for everyone to gather round the stove. "Brethren, I want you to know what we plan to do. We're going to walk up the hill out there to the southeast end of the grassy area. There, those of you who have been asked to participate in the ceremony will form a prayer circle. The rest of you witnesses will form an outside circle but will not be involved in the actual prayer circle."

Ben nodded to Nate to indicate he understood they fell into the latter category.

"After that, we will move over to the cornerstone and form a square," Elder Dawahoya said, now addressing those who had been asked to be involved in the ceremony. Although he had a military bearing, he acted more like a kindly grandfather helping to organize a family gathering than a retired Air Force Colonel. "At that point Elder Stewart and I will be at the head and we'd like you to stand in this order. To the right of Elder Stewart, President Suifua, president of the Independence Stake, then Bishop Nguyen of the Riverview Ward, Elder LeRoy M. Washington, Bishop David S. Knox, Brother Raul Delgado...."

Nate leaned over to Ben and whispered, "Knox is a convert who comes from five generations of RLDS stock. Really great guy. Delgado was a Jesuit priest. He's from Panama. I'll introduce you to them afterward."

"Anyone need me to repeat it?" Elder Dawahoya asked. "No? Okay, then, the rest of you brothers and sisters will act as witnesses. Please stand wherever you want and the spirit moves you."

The group laughed nervously.

"We will be joined by another general authority who will lead us in prayer. I shouldn't think we'll be frozen by then," the apostle said to the excited and nervous group. Ben shot a quick glance at Nate, trying to guess who the church authority might be. Nate just shrugged.

As they began to leave the building, Ben pulled Elder Stewart aside and said, "The plates. They're in my duffel bag. Do you think they're safe here?"

"Oh, I'd forgotten about them, Ben. Let me think. Yes, leave them here. I don't think anyone is going to steal them, but let's put them under the counter in the foyer just in case. We have plans for them after the ceremony."

Ben shook his head and thought to himself, *Three thousand-year-old plates, the most significant archaeological discovery in two hundred years, casually stowed behind a dusty old counter! And yet Elder Stewart is right. Compared with what is about to happen, even these plates with their fabulous mysteries, are next to nothing,* he concluded.

Neddy fell in step with Ben as they walked out onto the cracked sidewalk. Ben reached out and tapped the scared boy affectionately on the shoulder, then returned to his musing as they began the walk uphill.

The wind had died down and the sun shone brightly as the group walked the two hundred yards to the crest of the hill. On the north side of the two and a half acre site were the littered remains of a white wooden building. Just the northwest section still stood.

As the group walked up onto the lawn, they could hear voices emanating from the building. Nate leaned over to Ben and explained, "That's the headquarters for the Church of Christ, Temple Lot—a small breakaway group from the original church. They own the property we want to dedicate."

"Really? I thought the RLDS Church owned it."

Nate shook his head.

Now the conversation from the building became heated. Ben could pick out part of the conversation. "I am saving this for the Lord's return and nobody but him is going to get me to give it up!" An older man's voice trembled with anger.

The other voice was low and soothing. "...I am authorized by the Lord...time is at hand...." Ben missed most of what the other man said.

Everyone gathered around a stone set into the ground that had been cracked in the quake. It read "S.E. Corner of Temple." From his position, Ben could see the two men as they emerged from the Church of Christ's building. The younger man shook the older man's hand, who had a King Lear look about him—white tangled hair and confused eyes. The first man said politely, "Thank you, Mr. Merriweather, you have been a great help to the Lord." Merriweather, his face wrinkled with astonishment, staggered slightly as he headed toward River Street and down to the city center.

Now, that same young man walked toward the group. He too was dressed in white. His face radiated pure delight. Ben could not take his eyes of this ebullient figure as he approached the group. He had never seen anyone so attractive, no, so compelling. Ben guessed he was 25 to 30. His dark eyes, almost luminescent, seemed to Ben to send out rays of rapture.

And, although it was noon, Ben was sure he could see a golden glow around the young man's body. *How can that be?* Ben puzzled. He looked around at all the other members of the dedication group, but no one else appeared to be glowing except this enigmatic general authority.

The man took each of the apostle's hands in his two hands and shook them warmly. Then he said to the waiting group, "Good day, brothers and sisters, I am John. The Lord has asked me to come today to represent Him at this most auspicious moment in world history."

The group gasped and Ben's legs nearly gave out from under him. He grabbed Peter for support. His first impulse was to drop to his knees in adoration, but he steadied himself. *Is this what the 22nd plate is talking about? A translated being?*

He turned to Peter and mouthed, "John?" Peter's face had gone completely white.

"John," he whispered and nodded reverently. Rarely was Peter overcome with emotion; now he stood riveted by John's pronouncement.

In a melodic voice, John began the ceremony with, "Beloved brothers and sisters, let us form a circle in order to pray in the fashion our Lord has taught us both in these times and in the times when I followed Him in his mortal ministry."

The men and women participating in the ceremony solemnly formed a circle and John took his place at the head. He knelt down on a white cloth and raised his arm. As he began to speak, everything that Ben had done in the temple suddenly made sense.

Ben, standing in the outer witness circle, could scarcely keep his head down and eyes closed. *To think that John, the translated apostle, the emissary sent to the ten tribes, is here, just an arm's span away, conducting a prayer circle. And John's spiritual state—what did that plate say? A state of divine incorruptibility! Here stands a man who lived 2,000 years ago—a divinely appointed servant of the Lord Jesus Christ! Here is a man who lived such a saintly life that the Lord, on the cross, asked him to care for his mother. And here is a man who chose to live a translated life, rather than go directly to the spirit world, to help draw humanity on to its evolutionary conclusion.* Ben put his hands to his mouth and shook his head. "This is just too much," he murmured.

When the authorities finished the prayer circle, John asked them, along with their wives, to move a couple of yards south, there to form a square around a beige stone which sat next to a large hole. Three shovels lay on the ground. The apostle offered a prayer of astonishing beauty and simplicity for the dedication of the temple. And Ben could have sworn he saw Sangay for just a second, or at least his orange robe.

Then, as John Taylor had seen in a vision, the twelve men dressed in their temple robes stood in a square with their hands raised. John informed them they represented the twelve gates of Zion. They consecrated the grounds and laid the cornerstone of the new Jerusalem—John the apostle, Elder Dawahoya, then Elder Stewart shoveled loose soil into the hole. Then four other white-robed men moved foreword, lowered the cornerstone of the temple into the hole, and covered it with dirt.

President Taylor said he saw "myriads of heavenly angels hovering over them. I heard the most beautiful music and singing that I ever listened to and these were the words they repeated: 'Now is established the Kingdom of our God and His Christ which shall no more be thrown down or given to another people.'"

The mortal people on temple hill only felt a dazzling rush of fiery energy; it was the Spirit, as on the day of Pentecost, coursing through their bodies. And for one exquisite moment each person looked like a saint from a medieval painting—all swept in gold, beatific, poised on the fulcrum of perfection. Couples embraced, then walked arm in arm back down from the consecrated hill.

As they were leaving, Elder Stewart and John made their way through the knot of people to Ben. He tried to turn away, but Elder Stewart called out, "Brother Taylor, please join us." Ben, his mouth dry and legs rubbery, steeled himself, then bowed his head and walked across the dry lawn.

Standing next to the translated apostle, Ben noticed a sweet odor, like a fine incense, emanating from John's body.

"Ben, I've told our guest that you come from the tribe of Judah," Elder Stewart said.

"Well, sir, my mother is Jewish." Ben blushed and looked down.

"So is mine," John said and smiled. He was a slight man with dark hair and a small beard. "Ben, I'm very glad you were here today." John's eyes rested on Ben, who thought he would be pulled right into the dark pools of transcendent love. Then John tapped Ben on the arm. His touch was warm, and real. He laughed, and his laugh was melodic. "I understand you are the translator of Sangay Tulku's plates."

"I'm trying." Ben felt like a kindergartner, reduced to two-word responses.

"Good. We'll have to talk later." Just then the two general authorities were joined by Elder Dawahoya, and the three headed back toward the Visitor's Center.

Ben watched John until he was out of sight. Then he dropped to his knees and prayed, "Lord, thank you for this privilege. If I never had another miraculous moment in my life, I should be content with this day. But I have to confess to one more secret desire." He began to cry. "I need to see your face and be in your presence again." Tears spilled down his face and onto his shirt. He heard nothing in return, but gradually, as on that day in the Catholic church in Eugene, it seemed to Ben that he was being drawn up into His Savior's waiting arms. And in that moment Ben felt more hopeful, more in love with the Lord and his church than he had ever imagined possible.

After the apostles made their way back down to the Visitor's

Center, John set apart the missionary couples' office to speak with several individuals. Ben was one of them. He sat outside the room, next in line, still in his white clothes, his duffel bag resting in his lap. He fiddled with the strap, straining to imagine what the Lord's emissary might ask him. Guilt gnawed at him. *I shouldn't have looked at those secret ceremonies,* Ben moaned. *I know he'll know that I have.*

Just then the door opened and Elder Stewart stepped out. "Please, won't you come in, Brother Taylor?" he asked warmly.

Once inside the small office, John greeted him, pointed to a chair on the other side of the desk and extended his hand. Ben took it, shook his smooth warm hand, then sat down. He remembered in the *Doctrine and Covenants* that Joseph had laid out a formula for determining whether a person was an angel or a resurrected being. It had to do with shaking or not shaking hands, but the details eluded him at that moment. After exchanging a few pleasantries, John then said, "Ben Taylor, translator of ancient plates, please relax." His smile was disarming. Ben thought his slight accent sounded a lot like a modern-day Israeli's. "The Lord is pleased with the work you've been doing, Ben," he continued. "But because of the difficulties up ahead, we'd like to take the plates and care for them, until you and your family can get settled."

A hint of disappointment flashed across Ben's face. He'd hoped that John would say he could continue working with them. John read his thoughts and said, "Oh, you'll get them back and more, I assure you."

Ben blushed. He was suddenly very glad he'd remembered to remove the handgun before handing over the faded blue, grass-stained bag. Seconds went by. Finally John broke the silence before Ben could pull himself forward in the chair to leave. "It seems you have another question of me," John said. It felt to Ben that John's eyes bore a hole clear to the back of his head. "Well, sir, ah...it's really not any of my business, but...."

"You were wondering what process the body goes through to become translated."

"Yes, sir. That's right, sir. I've been reading the plates and they mentioned that a man could reach a state of incorruptibility...."

"Suffice it to say, Ben, that the process is under the direction of the priesthood. When the time comes, you will be able to experience being translated, as I am, or resurrected, whichever the Lord deems necessary and appropriate."

"I see. If I could be so bold, sir, what does it feel like?" Ben asked, then thought, *What am I doing? Somebody is going to slap me up side the head any minute.*

John chuckled as he read Ben's thought. "No, Brother Taylor, nothing bad is going to happen to you for asking such questions."

Ben turned a significant shade of crimson.

In his melodic voice, John explained, "Translation feels like having your body become highly charged with an ambrosia as sweet as mother's milk–an intense feeling of supernal love. You don't have to sleep or eat. You can travel from one place to another with just a thought." John paused to see if Ben was following him. "You might be familiar with the concept of superconductivity," he said looking to Ben for confirmation.

Ben shook his head. "Peter Butler tried to explain it to me, but I'm really dense about such matters."

"Well, let me try anyway," John said and laughed lightly. "The body is primarily clay. In the translation process, the clay is transformed in such a manner that the outer shell now operates as an encasing, so that energy, once introduced into the body, never stops."

"I see. I guess. And does it hurt?"

"No, it's exhilarating."

Ben fell silent. He looked down at his hands and worked up the courage to ask his final question, "Are you able to see the Lord Jesus whenever you want?" he asked without looking up.

"One may see him, of course," John gently replied, "but such meetings must be arranged much the way you do with the prophet in this realm," John said and smiled.

"I see." Ben looked up and then down again trying to hide his disappointment.

"Ben Taylor, you needn't worry. You'll be able to see the Lord whenever you need to—and soon, I promise."

Tears filled Ben's eyes. "Thank you very much, sir. You've helped me understand as best I can." He stood up and numbly repeated, "Thank you very much. Is that all?"

John nodded, indicating it was. The translated apostle then made his way around the table that separated them, reached out and embraced Ben. At that moment Ben was sure his bones were going to totally dissolve. "We'll see much more of each other in the months ahead," the apostle said warmly as Ben turned to leave the room.

Ben didn't get any farther than the chair he had been sitting in outside the office. He fell heavily into it, put his head back against the cracked wall, closed his eyes and remained very still. Jed started to come across the room to speak to him, but Nate held him back. As the afternoon wore on, Ben was completely unaware of the conversations in the foyer as couples came in and out, preparing dinner. He felt he had ascended to another plane of reality, and he wanted to linger there as long as possible. Although the beloved apostle had said little, he had opened Ben's mind to many more truths that Ben could not put words to, but that he felt in his body.

Ben felt grateful to Sangay for preparing him for this moment. Maybe this was what Sangay meant by a beginner's mind. "Except ye become as little children," the Lord had said, and now Ben pictured himself as a boy of three or four, his head resting on Jesus' knee as the Lord stroked the boy's flaxen hair. Never again would the disembodied, embittered voice of his agnostic uncle be able to undermine Ben's spirit with whispering doubt. What this Jewish convert had experienced was literal and real.

Ben sat in that ecstasy until Nate came to whisper in his ear that everyone had eaten dinner. Would he like some? He said he was absolutely unable to have food pass through his lips. But he did agree to move into the room warmed by the stove. There he changed his clothes in slow motion.

Slowly pulling himself out of his trance, Ben looked around and could not figure out why everyone was still in the Visitor's Center. Dark had fallen. Kerosene lamps formed pools of light around the scene of destruction. Then, a little after eight, the group began to bundle up to walk back to the temple hill. A puzzled Ben asked Nate if he knew what was going on. "I don't know," Nate said. "All I know is that Elder Dawahoya has asked all of us to remain. You have been so caught up in whatever it was you were experiencing that I'm not surprised you didn't hear him."

The night was cloudy, no moon to be seen as the group made their way silently back up to the grassy knoll. Ben could see his breath; instinctively he drew his down coat more tightly around his body. As they walked across the lawn of the temple site, Ben reached into his pocket and pulled out the compass Danny had given him. He pressed the light button so he could see its face. To his surprise the pointer spun around and around, so he hit it several times with the palm of his hand, but it did not point north. He decided it must be broken and put it back, alongside Miriam's purple plastic horse.

John, who was waiting for them, gestured expansively as he greeted them. "Brothers and sisters, I have called you here tonight to show you the power and majesty of the Lord. I know some of you have wondered how Zion could become a sanctuary for the good in heart, especially in times of nuclear war, natural disasters and all the other horrors on this telestial plane." Several of them murmured that they had. Like a conductor leading some great stellar orchestra, John looked up to the sky. He raised his arm, and then commanded, in a loud voice, that the clouds part. And so they did—in a slow, breath-taking movement—like dark velvet curtains being drawn back at the beginning of a ballet performance.

There, burning above them, like fire in the sky, were undulating sheets of light—purple, green, red—shimmering and dancing as in an astral choreography. It was the aurora borealis.

"The northern lights!" Everyone gasped, then fell silent. After a long moment, Peter asked, "What has happened here? Are we seeing the northern lights? Or has the pole shifted?" He could barely ask the last question, thinking it so absurd.

"Which is it, my dear young man of science?"

Peter stared quizzically for a few seconds at John, who smiled broadly. Then Peter's expression shifted from puzzlement to astonishment. "The pole...it's shifted? We're standing directly under the magnetic north pole?"

John nodded and held up his arms toward the scintillating light show. "This beautiful solar storm was created on the sun and borne on solar winds." John projected his voice over the crowd like a Greek poet in an Athenian amphitheater. "It was drawn down by the earth's magnetic field to provide us with this bonfire of the firmament." He lowered his voice almost to a whisper. "Just as our spirits rush, beloved brothers and sisters, towards the love of Christ. And just as that love protects us from the fiery darts of the Evil One, so this energy field over Jackson County will shield Zion from anything that man can throw against it."

The small group of Saints joyfully embraced each other and looked up in throes of admiration. Finally Peter could not wait any longer to ask, "Well, then, is there a southern magnetic pole?"

"There is," John replied, "but not another Zion, because that pole is in the Indian Ocean."

"I see," Peter said, his face glowing with wonder.

Suddenly the configuration of lights shifted, and the rippling sheets were replaced by a giant pale-green spiral which turned slowly in the velvet sky.

"Velikovsky was right," Peter said aloud to himself.

"Who's Velikovsky?" Ben asked.

"A scientist who wrote in the 80s and 90s about polar shifts, meteors destroying the earth, things like that. He theorized that there had been polar shifts in the past because of radical changes on the earth. I guess the combination of nuclear blasts in the Arctic and massive earthquakes caused this to happen."

"That's right," John concurred. "And it will provide an endless source of energy for the people of Zion." John turned to the assembled Saints. "We will work with Brother Butler and several other scientists, showing them how to use this tremendous source of energy for the protection and benefit of Zion."

"And that's why Danny's compass didn't work," Ben said softly. Suddenly he felt a great ache around his heart. He wanted Peg and the children to be standing beside him. Next his thoughts went to the rafts and the cars they had left on the other side of Kansas City. *We're going to need those solar-powered cars if we're going to return to El Puerto and gather everyone to bring them back to Zion. To Zion!* Ben could not take in the magnitude of what he was saying. *We're about to embark on building the Lord's Zion temple right here, on this hill.*

Finally Ben returned from his reverie to hear Jed ask John, "Is the pole star going to shift too?"

The three men looked up into the star-filled sky.

"There will be a lot of shifting in the heavens," John said.

Ben was reminded of a line from Virgil, "As long as rivers shall run down to the sea, or shadows touch the mountain slopes...so long shall your honor, your name, your praises endure." A lone cricket, then a chorus of chirruping, filled the night air, as the group followed John back down the hill–each man and woman filled with the knowledge that Zion, even now, was becoming a sanctuary for the world in the tumultuous times ahead.

Afterword

A Man's life of any worth is a continual allegory
And very few eyes can see the Mystery of his life
A life like the scriptures, figurative...
John Keats

Joseph Smith has been called a spiritual giant by many people. The celebrated non-Mormon literary critic, Harold Bloom, wrote in his *The American Religion*, "Smith was an authentic religious genius, unique in our national history." Joseph's history is one marked by remarkable spiritual experiences, beginning in 1820, when he had an open vision of God and Jesus Christ.

In the next few years, Joseph began having a series of visits from the angel Moroni, a general who lived about 400 A.D. in southern Mexico or Central America. He told the young man where he had hidden records of his people in a hill in upstate New York. Joseph uncovered these plates and, through the help of divine inspiration translated them into the *Book of Mormon*, which chronicles over 1000 years of history of an ancient American civilization that began when a group of messianic Jews left Jerusalem around 600 B.C. In several chapters of the book, we read prophecies about the American continent in the last days.

In the *Doctrine and Covenants*, another scriptural text of pronouncements and revelations, Joseph Smith becomes quite specific about the pattern of the last days. For instance, in Section 57 Joseph received a revelation that the city of Zion, a sanctuary for all people who seek a non-violent life, will be built on the American continent with the administrative and spiritual center in Independence, Missouri.

The litmus test for any prophet is whether something he foretold, in detail, actually came to pass. Joseph told many individuals about their future lives, and he was correct. In one of his more famous prophecies given 25 December 1832 regarding the Civil War (nearly 29 years before its occurrence!), he said, "The wars that will shortly come to pass, beginning at the rebellion of South Carolina, will eventually terminate in the death and misery of many souls....(S)laves shall rise up against their masters."

In 1844, Joseph was murdered by an angry mob in a Carthage, Illinois jail. Two days before he died, he dreamed of his death and told a companion, W.W. Phelps, of his arrival at a city, "whose gold and silver steeples and towers were more beautiful than any I had ever seen or heard of on earth." There was "the greeting of old friends, the music from a thousand towers, and the light of God himself at the return of three of his sons." (Hyrum, his brother, was also killed at the same time. His younger brother, Samuel, weakened by the stress of bringing his brothers' bodies back to Nauvoo, contracted a fever and died a month later.)

About The Millennial Series

In Print:

Ephraim's Seed, the first in a series of millennial stories which chronicles the spiritual experiences and adventures of a group of friends, who as a large extended family, gather first in southern Utah at the beginning of world war, plagues, earthquakes and societal breakdown, and follows them on to the dedication of the land Zion for the return of the Saints.

Jacob's Cauldron, book two, follows the same group of friends as they assist in the building of Zion into a social-political reality under Peter, James and John's tutelage. They help with the building of the temple at Independence, they witness the return of the Ten Tribes, and they assist that part of the world population who are fleeing to Zion for sanctuary. Finally the temple is completed and the Lord appears in its sanctuary to the faithful.

Under Construction:

Michael's Fire, book three, chronicles the last three and a half years of the earth's telestial existence. We follow the same extended family in their romances and dangerous assignments. The final council at Adam-ondi-Ahman is convened; the 144,000 are sent out to teach the gospel to the world for the last time. The story follows two LDS prophets who preach in Jerusalem, where the temple is finally built. Armageddon explodes. Finally comes the return of the Lord to the whole world.

Enoch's Compass, book four, covers the first one hundred years of the Millennial era. Several members of the series' extended family are among those who remain on the earth. We follow them as they struggle to build a new world, one frequented by resurrected beings. Temples scatter the land; the Lord is seen by many. Social and political struggles ensue with non-members. The first visits to other telestial planets occur.